Margery (Gred)
A Tale Of Old Nuremberg — Complete

by

Georg Ebers

Double 9
BOOKS

Margery (Gred)
A Tale Of Old Nuremberg — Complete
by Georg Ebers

ISBN: 978-93-63051-22-5

Published by

DOUBLE 9 BOOKS
2/13-B, Ansari Road
Daryaganj, New Delhi – 110002
info@double9books.com
www.double9books.com
Tel. 011-40042856

ABOUT THE AUTHOR

Georg Moritz Ebers was a German Egyptologist and author who was born in Berlin on March 1, 1837, and died in Tutzing, Bavaria, on August 7, 1898. He bought the Ebers Papyrus, which is one of the oldest medical records from Egypt and is what made him famous. Georg Ebers was born in Berlin. He was the fifth child in a wealthy family of bankers and someone who made ceramics. After their father killed himself soon after Ebers was born, the children were raised by their mother alone. Smart people like Georg Wilhelm Friedrich Hegel, the Grimm Brothers, and Alexander von Humboldt liked going to the club that his mother ran. Ebers studied law in Gottingen and Oriental languages and history in Berlin. Egyptology was something he studied in depth, so in 1865 he was made Dozent in Egyptian language and antiquities at Jena. In 1868 he was made professor. In 1870, he was hired as a professor at Leipzig to teach these topics. He went to Egypt twice for research reasons. His first important work, Ägypten und die Bücher Mosco, came out in 1867 and 1868. In 1874, he edited the famous medical tablet called tablet Ebers, which he had found in Thebes (H. Joachim, 1890).

CONTENTS

INTRODUCTION

"PIETRO GIUSTINIANI, merchant, of Venice." This was the signature affixed to his receipt by the little antiquary in the city of St. Mark, from whom I purchased a few stitched sheets of manuscript. What a name and title!

As I remarked on the splendor of his ancestry he slapped his pocket, and exclaimed, half in pride and half in lamentation:

"Yes, they had plenty of money; but what has become of it?"

"And have you no record of their deeds?" I asked the little man, who himself wore a moustache with stiff military points to it.

"Their deeds!" he echoed scornfully. "I wish they had been less zealous in their pursuit of fame and had managed their money matters better!— Poor child!"

And he pointed to little Marietta who was playing among the old books, and with whom I had already struck up a friendship. She this day displayed some strange appendage in the lobes of her ears, which on closer examination I found to be a twist of thread.

The child's pretty dark head was lying confidentially against my arm and as, with my fingers, I felt this singular ornament, I heard, from behind the little desk at the end of the counter, her mother's shrill voice in complaining accents: "Aye, Sir, it is a shame in a family which has given three saints to the Church—Saint Nicholas, Saint Anna, and Saint Eufemia, all three Giustinianis as you know—in a family whose sons have more than once worn a cardinal's hat—that a mother, Sir, should be compelled to let her own child—But you are fond of the little one, Sir, as every one is hereabout. Heh, Marietta! What would you say if the gentleman were to give you a pair of ear-rings, now; real gold ear-rings I mean? Thread for ear-rings, Sir, in the ears of a Giustiniani! It is absurd, preposterous, monstrous; and a right-thinking gentleman like you, Sir, will never deny that."

How could I neglect such a hint; and when I had gratified the antiquary's wife, I could reflect with some pride that I might esteem myself a benefactor to a family which boasted of its descent from the Emperor Justinian, which had been called the 'Fabia gens' of Venice, and, in its day had given to the Republic great generals, far-seeing statesmen, and admirable scholars.

When, at length, I had to quit the city and took leave of the curiosity-dealer, he pressed my hand with heartfelt regret; and though the Signora Giustiniani, as she pocketed a tolerably thick bundle of paper money, looked at me with that kindly pity which a good woman is always ready to bestow on the inexperienced, especially when they are young, that, no doubt, was because the manuscript I had acquired bore such a dilapidated appearance. The margins of the thick old Nuremberg paper were eaten into by mice and insects, in many places black patches like tinder dropped away from the yellow pages; indeed, many passages of the once clear writing had so utterly faded that I scarcely hoped to see them made legible again by the chemist's art. However, the contents of the document were so interesting and remarkable, so unique in relation to the time when it was written, that they irresistibly riveted my attention, and in studying them I turned half the night into day. There were nine separate parts. All, except the very last one, were in the same hand, and they seemed to have formed a single book before they were torn asunder. The cover and title-page were lost, but at the head of the first page these words were written in large letters: "The Book of my Life." Then followed a long passage in crude verse, very much to this effect.

> "What we behold with waking Eye
> Can, to our judgment, never lie,
> And what through Sense and Sight we gain.
> Becometh part of Soul and Brain.
> Look round the World in which you dwell
> Nor, Snail-like, live within your Shell;
> And if you see His World aright
> The Lord shall grant you double Sight.
> For, though your Mind and Soul be small,
> If you but open them to all
> The great wide World, they will expand
> Those glorious Things to understand.
> When Heart and Brain are great with Love
> Man is most like the Lord above.
> Look up to Him with patient Eye

Not on your own Infirmity.
In pious Trust yourself forget
For others only toil and fret,
Since all we do for fellow Men
With right good Will, shall be our Gain.
What if the Folk should call you Fool
Care not, but act by Virtue's Rule,
Contempt and Curses let them fling,
God's Blessing shields you from their Sting.
Grey is my Head but young my Heart;
In Nuremberg, ere I depart,
Children and Grandchildren, for you
I write this Book, and it is true."
MARGERY SCHOPPER.

Below the verses the text of the narrative began with these words: "In the yere of our Lord M/CCCC/lx/VI dyd I begynne to wrtre in thys lytel Boke thys storie of my lyf, as I haue lyued it."

It was in her sixty-second year that the writer had first begun to note down her reminiscences. This becomes clear as we go on, but it may be gathered from the first lines on the second page which begins thus:

"I, Margery Schopper, was borne in the yere of our Lord M/
CCCC/IV on a Twesday after 'Palmarum' Sonday, at foure
houris after mydnyght. Myn uncle Kristan Pfinzing was god sib
to me in my chrystening. My fader, God assoyle his soul, was
Franz Schopper, iclyped the Singer. He dyed on a Monday after
'Laetare' —[The fourth Sunday in Lent.]— Sonday M/CCCC/IV.
And he hadde to wyf Kristine Peheym whyche was my moder.
Also she bare to hym my brethren Herdegen and Kunz Schopper.
My moder dyed in the vigil of Seint Kateryn M/CCCC/V. Thus
was I refte of my moder whyle yet a babe; also the Lord broughte
sorwe upon me in that of hys grace He callyd my fader out of
thys worlde before that ever I sawe the lyght of dai."

These few lines, which I read in the little antiquary's shop, betrayed me to my ruin; for, in my delight at finding the daily journal of a German housewife of the beginning of the fifteenth century my heart overflowed; forgetting all prudence I laughed aloud, exclaiming "splendid," "wonderful," "what a treasure!" But it would have been beyond all human power to stand speechless, for, as I read on, I found things which far exceeded my fondest expectations. The writer of these pages had not been content, like the other chroniclers of her time and of her native town-such as Ulman Stromer, Andres Tucher and their fellows—to register notable facts without any connection, the family affairs, items of expenditure and mercantile measures of her day; she had plainly and candidly recorded everything that had happened to her from her childhood to the close of her life. This Margery had inherited some of her father's artistic gifts; he is mentioned in Ulman Stromer's famous chronicle, where he is spoken of as "the Singer." It was to her mother, however, that she owed her bold spirit, for she was a Behaim, cousin to the famous traveller Behaim of Schwarzbach, whose mother is known to have been one of the Schopper family, daughter to Herdegen Schopper.

In the course of a week I had not merely read the manuscript, but had copied a great deal of what seemed to me best worth preservation, including the verses. I subsequently had good reason to be glad that I had taken so much pains, though travelling about at the time; for a cruel disaster befel the trunk in which the manuscript was packed, with other books and a few treasures, and which I had sent home by sea. The ship conveying them was stranded at the mouth of the Elbe and my precious manuscript perished miserably in the wreck.

The nine stitched sheets, of which the last was written by the hand of Margery Schopper's younger brother, had found their way to Venice — as was recorded on the last page—in the possession of Margery's great-grandson, who represented the great mercantile house of Im Hoff on the Fondaco, and who ultimately died in the City of St. Mark. When that famous firm was broken up the papers were separated from their cover and had finally fallen into the hands of the curiosity dealer of whom I bought them. And after surviving travels on land, risk of fire, the ravages of worms and the ruthlessness of man for four centuries, they finally fell a prey to the destructive fury of the waves; but my memory served me well as to the contents, and at my bidding was at once ready to aid me in restoring the narrative I had read. The copied portions were a valuable aid, and imagination was able to fill the gaps; and though it failed, no doubt, to reproduce Margery Schopper's memoirs phrase for phrase and word for word, I have on the whole succeeded in transcribing with considerable exactitude all that she herself had thought worthy to be rescued from oblivion. Moreover I have avoided the repetition of the mode of talk in the fifteenth century, when German was barely commencing to be used as a written language, since scholars, writers, and men of letters always chose the Latin tongue for any great or elegant intellectual work. The narrator's expressions would only be intelligible to a select few, and, I should have done my Margery injustice, had I left the ideas and descriptions, whose meaning I thoroughly understood, in the clumsy form she had given them. The language of her day is a mirror whose uneven surface might easily reflect the fairest picture in blurred or distorted out lines to modern eyes. Much, indeed which most attracted me in her descriptions will have lost its peculiar charm in mine; as to whether I have always supplemented her correctly, that must remain an open question.

I have endeavored to throw myself into the mind and spirit of my Margery and repeat her tale with occasional amplification, in a familiar style, yet with such a choice of words as seems suitable to the date of her narrative. Thus I have perpetuated all that she strove to record for her descendants out of her warm heart and eager brain; though often in mere outline and broken sentences, still, in the language of her time and of her native province.

BOOK 1

CHAPTER I

I, MARGERY SCHOPPER, was born in the year of our Lord 1404, on the Tuesday after Palm Sunday. My uncle Christan Pfinzing of the Burg, a widower whose wife had been a Schopper, held me at the font. My father, God have his soul, was Franz Schopper, known as Franz the Singer. He died in the night of the Monday after Laetare Sunday in 1404, and his wife my mother, God rest her, whose name was Christine, was born a Behaim; she had brought him my two brothers Herdegen and Kunz, and she died on the eve of Saint Catharine's day 1404; so that I lost my mother while I was but a babe, and God dealt hardly with me also in taking my father to Himself in His mercy, before I ever saw the light.

Instead of a loving father, such as other children have, I had only a grave in the churchyard, and the good report of him given by such as had known him; and by their account he must have been a right merry and lovable soul, and a good man of business both in his own affairs and in those pertaining to the city. He was called "the Singer" because, even when he was a member of the town-council, he could sing sweetly and worthily to the lute. This art he learned in Lombardy, where he had been living at Padua to study the law there; and they say that among those outlandish folk his music brought him a rich reward in the love of the Italian ladies and damsels. He was a well-favored man, of goodly stature and pleasing to look upon, as my brother Herdegen his oldest son bears witness, since it is commonly said that he is the living image of his blessed father; and I, who am now an old woman, may freely confess that I have seldom seen a man whose blue eyes shone more brightly beneath his brow, or whose golden hair curled thicker over his neck and shoulders than my brother's in the high day of his happy youth.

He was born at Eastertide, and the Almighty blessed him with a happy temper such as he bestows only on a Sunday-child. He, too, was skilled in the art of singing, and as my other brother, my playmate Kunz, had also a liking for music and song, there was ever a piping and playing in our orphaned and motherless house, as if it were a nest of mirthful grasshoppers, and more childlike gladness and happy merriment reigned there than in many another house that rejoices in the presence of father and mother. And I have ever been truly thankful to the Almighty that it was so; for as I have often seen, the life of children who lack a mother's love is like a day when the sun is hidden by storm-clouds. But the merciful God, who laid his hand on our mother's heart, filled that of another woman with a treasure of love towards me and my brothers.

Our cousin Maud, a childless widow, took upon herself to care for us. As a maid, and before she had married her departed husband, she had been in love with my father, and then had looked up to my mother as a saint from Heaven, so she could have no greater joy than to tell us tales about our parents; and when she did so her eyes would be full of tears, and as every word came straight from her heart it found its way straight to ours; and as we three sat round, listening to her, besides her own two eyes there were soon six more wet enough to need a handkerchief.

Her gait was heavy and awkward, and her face seemed as though it had been hewn out of coarse wood, so that it was a proper face to frighten children; even when she was young they said that her appearance was too like a man and devoid of charms, and for that reason my father never heeded her love for him; but her eyes were like open windows, and out of them looked everything that was good and kind and loving and true, like angels within. For the sake of those eyes you forgot all else; all that was rough in her, and her wide nose with the deep dent just in the middle, and such hair on her lip as many a young stripling might envy her.

And Sebald Kresz knew very well what he was about when he took to wife Maud Im Hoff when he was between sixty and seventy years of age; and she had nothing to look forward to in life as she stood at the altar with him, but to play the part of nurse to a sickly perverse old man. But to Maud it seemed as fair a lot to take care of a fellow-creature as it is to many another to be nursed and cherished; and it was the reward of her faithful care that she could keep the old man from the clutch of Death for full ten years longer. After his decease she was left a well-to-do widow; but instead of taking thought for herself she at once entered on a life of fresh care, for she undertook the duty of filling the place of mother to us three orphans.

As I grew up she would often instruct me in her kind voice, which was as deep as the bass pipe of an organ, that she had set three aims before her in bringing us up, namely: to make us good and Godfearing; to teach us to agree among ourselves so that each should be ready to give everything up to the others; and to make our young days as happy as possible. How far she succeeded in the first I leave to others to judge; but a more united family than we ever were I should like any man to show me, and because it was evident from a hundred small tokens how closely we clung together folks used to speak of us as "the three links," especially as the arms borne by the Schoppers display three rings linked to form a chain.

As for myself, I was the youngest and smallest of the three links, and yet I was the middle one; for if ever it fell that Herdegen and Kunz had done one thing or another which led them to disagree and avoid or defy each other, they always came together again by seeking me and through my means. But though I thus sometimes acted as peacemaker it is no credit to me, since I did not bring them together out of any virtue or praiseworthy intent, but simply because I could not bear to stand alone, or with only one ring linked to me.

Alas! how far behind me lies the bright, happy youth of which I now write! I have reached the top of life's hill, nay, I have long since overstepped the ridge; and, as I look back and think of all I have seen and known, it is not to the end that I may get wisdom for myself whereby to do better as I live longer. My old bones are stiff and set; it would be vain now to try to bend them. No, I write this little book for my own pleasure, and to be of use and comfort to my children and grandchildren. May they avoid the rocks on which I have bruised my feet, and where I have walked firmly on may they take example by an old woman's brave spirit, though I have learned in a thousand ways that no man gains profit by any experience other than his own.

So I will begin at the beginning.

I could find much to tell of my happy childhood, for then everything seems new; but it profits not to tell of what every one has known in his own life, and what more can a Nuremberg child have to say of her early growth and school life than ever another. The blades in one field and the trees in one wood share the same lot without any favour. It is true that in many ways I was unlike other children; for my cousin Maud would often say that I would not abide rule as beseems a maid, and Herdegen's lament that I was not born a boy still sounds in my ears when I call to mind our wild games. Any one who knows the window on the first floor, at the back of our house, from which I would jump into the courtyard to do as my brothers did, would be fairly frightened, and think it a wonder that I came out of it with whole bones; but yet I was not always minded to riot with the boys, and from my tenderest years I was a very thoughtful little maid. But there were things; in my young life very apt to sharpen my wits.

We Schoppers are nearly allied with every worshipful family in the town, or of a rank to sit in the council and bear a coat of arms; these being, in fact, in Nuremberg, the class answering to the families of the Signoria in Venice, whose names are enrolled in the Libro d'Oro. What the Barberighi, the Foscari, the Grimaldi, the Giustiniani and the like, are there, the families of Stromer, Behaim, Im Hoff, Tucher, Kresz, Baumgartner, Pfinzing, Pukheimer, Holzschuher, and so forth, are with us; and the Schoppers certainly do not rank lowest on the list. We who hold ourselves entitled to bear arms, to ride in tournaments, and take office in the Church, and who have a right to call ourselves nobles and patricians, are all more or less kith and kin. Wherever in Nuremberg there was a fine house we could find there an uncle and aunt, cousins and kinsmen, or at least godparents, and good friends of our deceased parents. Wherever one of them might chance to meet us, even if it were in the street, he would say: "Poor little orphans! God be good to the fatherless!" and tears would sparkle in the eyes of many a kindhearted woman. Even the gentlemen of the Council—for most of the elders of our friends were members of it—would stroke my fair hair and look at me as pitifully as though I were some poor sinner for whom there could be no mercy in the eyes of the judges of a court of justice.

Why was it that men deemed me so unfortunate when I knew no sorrow and my heart was as gay as a singing bird? I could not ask cousin Maud, for she was sorely troubled if I had but a finger-ache, and how could I tell her that I was such a miserable creature in the eyes of other folks? But I presently found out for myself why and wherefore they pitied me; for seven who called me fatherless, seventy would speak of me as motherless when they addressed me with pity. Our misfortune was that we had no mother. But was there not Cousin Maud, and was not she as good as any mother? To be sure she was only a cousin, and she must lack something of what a real mother feels.

And though I was but a heedless, foolish child I kept my eyes open and began to look about me. I took no one into the secret but my brothers, and though my elder brother chid me, and bid me only be thankful to our cousin for all her goodness, I nevertheless began to watch and learn.

There were a number of children at the Stromers' house—the Golden Rose was its name—and they were still happy in having their mother. She was a very cheerful young woman, as plump as a cherry, and pink and white like blood on snow; and she never fixed her gaze on me as others did, but would frolic with me or scold me sharply when I did any wrong. At the Muffels, on the contrary, the mistress was dead, and the master had not long after brought home another mother to his little ones, a stepmother, Susan, who was my maid, was wont to call her; and such a mother was no more a real mother than our good cousin—I knew that much from the fairy tales to which I was ever ready to hearken. But I saw this very stepmother wash and dress little Elsie, her husband's youngest babe and not her own, and lull her till she fell asleep; and she did it right tenderly, and quite as she ought. And then, when the child was asleep she kissed it, too, on its brow and cheeks.

And yet Mistress Stromer, of the Golden-Rose House, did differently; for when she took little Clare that was her own babe out of the water, and laid it on warm clouts on the swaddling board, she buried her face in the sweet, soft flesh, and kissed the whole of its little body all over, before and behind, from head to foot, as if it were all one sweet, rosy mouth; and they both laughed with hearty, loving merriment, as the mother pressed her lips against the babe's white, clean skin and trumpeted till the room rang, or clasped it, wrapped in napkins to her warm breast, as if she could hug it to death. And she broke into a loud, strange laugh, and cried as she fondled it: "My treasure, my darling, my God-sent jewel! My own, my own—I could eat thee!"

No, Mistress Muffel never behaved so to Elsie, her husband's babe. Notwithstanding I knew right well that Cousin Maud had been just as fond of me as Dame Stromer of her own babes, and so far our cousin was no way different from a real mother. And I said as much to myself, when I laid me down to sleep in my little white bed at night, and my cousin came and folded her hands as I folded mine and, after we had said the prayers for the Angelus together, as we did every evening, she laid her head by the side of mine, and pressed my baby face to her own big face. I liked this well enough, and I whispered in her ear: "Tell me, Cousin Maud, are you not my real, true mother?"

And she hastily replied, "In my heart I am, most truly; and you are a very lucky maid, my Margery, for instead of only one mother you have two: me, here below, to care for you and foster you, and the other up among the angels above, looking down on you and beseeching the all-gracious Virgin who is so nigh to her, to keep your little heart pure, and to preserve you from all ill; nay, perhaps she herself is wearing a glory and a heavenly crown. Look at her face." And Cousin Maud held up the lamp so that the light fell on a large picture. My eyes beheld the lovely portrait in front of me, and meseemed it looked at me with a deep gaze and stretched out loving arms to me. I sat up in my bed; the feelings which filled my little heart overflowed my lips, and I said in a whisper: "Oh, Cousin Maud! Surely my mammy might kiss me for once, and fondle me as Mistress Stromer does her little Clare."

Cousin Maud set the lamp on the table, and without a word she lifted me out of bed and held me up quite close to the face of the picture; and I understood. My lips softly touched the red lips on the canvas; and, as I was all the happier, I fancied that my mother in Heaven must be glad too.

Then my cousin sighed: "Well, well!" and murmured other words to herself; she laid me in the bed again, tucked the coverlet tightly round me as I loved to have it, gave me another kiss, waited till I had settled my head on the pillow, and whispered: "Now go to sleep and dream of your sainted mother."

She quitted the room; but she had left the lamp, and as soon as I was alone I looked once more at the picture, which showed me my mother in right goodly array. She had a rose on her breast, her golden fillet looked like the crown of the Queen of Heaven, and in her robe of rich, stiff brocade she was like some great Saint. But what seemed to me more heavenly than all the rest was her rose and white young face, and the sweet mouth which I had touched with my lips. Oh if I had but once had the happiness of kissing that mouth in life! A sudden feeling glowed in my heart, and an inward voice told me that a thousand kisses from Cousin Maud would never be worth one single kiss from that lovely young mother, and that I had indeed lost almost as much as my pitying friends had said. And I could not help sorrowing, weeping for a long time; I felt as though I had lost just what was best and dearest, and for the first time I saw that my good cousin was right ugly as other folks said, and my silly little head conceived that a real mother must be fair to look upon, and that however kind any one else might be she could never be so gracious and lovable.

And so I fell asleep; and in my dreams the picture came towards me out of the frame and took me in her arms as Madonna takes her Holy Child, and looked at me with a gaze as if all the love on earth had met in those eyes. I threw my arms round her neck and waited for her to fondle and play with me like Mistress Stromer with her little Clare; but she gently and sadly shook her head with the golden crownlet, and went up to Cousin Maud and set me in her lap.

"I have never forgot that dream, and often in my prayers have I lifted up my heart to my sainted mother, and cried to her as to the blessed Virgin and Saint Margaret, my name-saint; and how often she has heard me and rescued me in need and jeopardy! As to my cousin, she was ever dearer to me from that night; for had not my own mother given me to her, and when folks looked at me pitifully and bewailed my lot, I could laugh in my heart and think: 'If only you knew! Your children have only one mother, but we have two; and our own real mother is prettier than any one's, while the other, for all that she is so ugly, is the best.'"

It was the compassion of folks that first led me to such thoughts, and as I grew older I began to deem that their pity had done little good to my young soul. Friends are ever at hand to comfort every job; but few are they who come to share his heaviness, all the more so because all men take pleasure in comparing their own fair lot with the evil lot of others. Compassion—and I am the last to deny it—is a noble and right healing grace; but those who are so ready to extend it should be cautious how they do so, especially in the case of a child, for a child is like a sapling which needs light, and those who darken the sun that shines on it sin against it, and hinder its growth. Instead of bewailing it, make it glad; that is the comfort that befits it.

I felt I had discovered a great and important secret and I was eager to make our sainted mother known to my brothers; but they had found her already without any aid from their little sister. I told first one and then the other all that stirred within me, and when I spoke to Herdegen, the elder, I saw at once that it was nothing new to him. Kunz, the younger, I found in the swing; he flew so high that I thought he would fling himself out, and I cried to him to stop a minute; but, as he clutched the rope tighter and pulled himself together to stand firm on the board, he cried: "Leave me now, Margery; I want to go up, up; up to Heaven—up to where mother is!"

That was enough for me; and from that hour we often spoke together of our sainted mother, and Cousin Maud took care that we should likewise keep our father in mind. She had his portrait—as she had had my mother's—brought from the great dining-room, where it had hung, into the large children's room where she slept with me. And this picture, too, left its mark on my after-life; for when I had the measles, and Master Paul Rieter, the town physician and our doctor, came to see me, he stayed a long time, as though he could not bear to depart, standing in front of the portrait; and when he turned to me again, his face was quite red with sorrowful feeling— for he had been a favorite friend of my father, at Padua—and he exclaimed: "What a fortunate child art thou, little Margery!"

I must have looked at him puzzled enough, for no one had ever esteemed me fortunate, unless it were Cousin Maud or the Waldstromers in the forest;

and Master Paul must have observed my amazement, for he went on. "Yea, a happy child art thou; for so are all babes, maids or boys, who come into the world after their father's death." As I gazed into his face, no less astonished than before, he laid the gold knob of his cane against his nose and said: "Remember, little simpleton, the good God would not be what he is, would not be a man of honor—God forgive the words—if he did not take a babe whom He had robbed of its father before it had seen the light or had one proof of his love under His own special care. Mark what I say, child. Is it a small thing to be the ward of a guardian who is not only Almighty but true above all truth?" And those words have followed me through all my life till this very hour.

CHAPTER II

Thus passed our childhood, as I have already said, in very great happiness; and by the time that my brothers had left the leading strings far behind them, and were studying their 'Donatus', Cousin Maud was teaching me to read and write, and that with much mirth and the most frolicsome ways. For instance, she would stamp four copies of each letter out of sweet honey-cakes, and when I knew them well she gave me these tiny little A. B. C. cakes, and one I ate myself, and gave the others to my brothers, or Susan, or my cousin. Often I put them in my satchel to carry them into the woods with me, and give them to my Cousin Gotz's favorite hound or his cross-beak; for he himself did not care for sweets. I shall have many things to tell of him and the forest; even when I was very small it was my greatest joy to be told that we were going to the woods, for there dwelt the dearest and most faithful of all our kinsmen: my uncle Waldstromer and his family. The stately hunting-lodge in which he dwelt as head forester of the Lorenzerwald in the service of the Emperor and of our town, had greater joys for me than any other, since not only were there the woods with all their delights and wonders, but also, besides many hounds, a number of strange beasts, and other pastimes such as a town child knows little of.

But what I most loved was the only son of my uncle and aunt Waldstromer, for whose dog I kept my cake letters; for though Cousin Gotz was older than I by eleven years, he nevertheless did not scorn me, but whenever I asked him to show me this or that, or teach me some light woodland craft, he would leave his elders to please me.

When I was six years old I went to the forest one day in a scarlet velvet hood, and after that he ever called me his little "Red riding-hood," and I liked to be called so; and of all the boys and lads I ever met among my brothers' friends or others I deemed none could compare with Gotz; my guileless heart was so wholly his that I always mentioned his name in my little prayers.

Till I was nine we had gone out into the forest three or four times in each year to pass some weeks; but after this I was sent to school, and as Cousin Maud took it much to heart, because she knew that my father had set great store by good learning, we paid such visits more rarely; and indeed, the strict mistress who ruled my teaching would never have allowed me to break through my learning for pastime's sake.

Sister Margaret, commonly called the Carthusian nun, was the name of the singular woman who was chosen to be my teacher. She was at once the most pious and learned soul living; she was Prioress of a Carthusian nunnery and had written ten large choirbooks, besides others. Though the rule of her order forbade discourse, she was permitted to teach.

Oh, how I trembled when Cousin Maud first took me to the convent.

As a rule my tongue was never still, unless it were when Herdegen sang to me, or thought aloud, telling me his dreams of what he would do when he had risen to be chancellor, or captain-in chief of the Imperial army, and had found a count's or a prince's daughter to carry home to his grand castle. Besides, the wild wood was a second home to me, and now I was shut up in a convent where the silence about me crushed me like a too tight bodice. The walls of the vast antechamber, where I was left to wait, were covered with various texts in Latin, and several times repeated were these words under a skull.

"Bitter as it is to live a Carthusian, it is right sweet to die one."

There was a crucifix in a shrine, and so much bright red blood flowed from the Crown of Thorns and the Wounds that the Sacred Body was half covered with it, and I was sore afraid at the sight—oh I can find no words for it! And all the while one nun after another glided through the chamber in silence, and with bowed head, her arms folded, and never so much as lifting an eye to look at me.

It was in May; the day was fine and pleasant, but I began to shiver, and I felt as if the Spring had bloomed and gone, and I had suddenly forgotten how to laugh and be glad. Presently a cat stole in, leapt on to the bench where I sat, and arched her back to rub up against me; but I drew away, albeit I commonly laved to play with animals; for it glared at me strangely with its green eyes, and I had a sudden fear that it would turn into a werewolf and do me a hurt.

At length the door opened, and a woman in nun's weeds came in with my cousin; she was the taller by a head. I had never seen so tall a woman, but the nun was very thin, too, and her shoulders scarce broader than my own. Ere long, indeed, she stooped a good deal, and as time went on I saw her ever with her back bent and her head bowed. They said she had some hurt of the back-bone, and that she had taken this bent shape from writing, which she always did at night.

At first I dared not look up in her face, for my cousin had told me that with her I must be very diligent, that idleness never escaped her keen eyes; and Gotz Waldstromer knew the meaning of the Latin motto with which she began all her writings: "Beware lest Satan find thee idle!" These words flashed through my mind at this moment; I felt her eye fixed upon me, and I started as she laid her cold, thin fingers on my brow and firmly, but not ungently, made me lift my drooping head. I raised my eyes, and how glad I was when in her pale, thin face I saw nothing but true, sweet good will.

She asked me in a low, clear voice, though hardly above a whisper, how old I was, what was my name, and what I had learnt already. She spoke in brief sentences, not a word too little or too many; and she ever set me my tasks in the same manner; for though, by a dispensation, she might speak, she ever bore in mind that at the Last Day we shall be called to account for every word we utter.

At last she spoke of my sainted parents, but she only said: "Thy father and mother behold thee ever; therefore be diligent in school that they may rejoice in thee.—To-morrow and every morning at seven." Then she kissed me gently on my head, bowed to my cousin without a word, and turned her back upon us. But afterwards, as I walked on in the open air glad to be moving, and saw the blue sky and the green meadows once more, and heard the birds sing and the children at play, I felt as it were a load lifted from my breast; but I likewise felt the tall, silent nun's kiss, and as if she had given me something which did me honor.

Next morning I went to school for the first time; and whereas it is commonly the part of a child's godparents only to send it parcels of sweetmeats when it goes to school, I had many from various kinsfolks and other of our friends, because they pitied me as a hapless orphan.

I thought more of my riches, and how to dispense them, than of school and tasks; and as my cousin would only put one parcel into my little satchel I stuffed another—quite a little one, sent me by rich mistress Grosz, with a better kind of sweeties—into the wallet which hung from my girdle.

On the way I looked about at the folks to see if they observed how I had got on, and my little heart beat fast as I met my cousin Gotz in front of Master Pernhart's brass-smithy. He had come from the forest to live in the town, that he might learn book-keeping under the tax-gatherers. We greeted each other merrily, and he pulled my plait of hair and went on his way, while I felt as if this meeting had brought me good luck indeed.

In school of course I had to forget such follies at once; for among Sister Margaret's sixteen scholars I was far below most of them, not, indeed in stature, for I was well-grown for my years, but in age and learning and this I was to discover before the first hour was past.

Fifteen of us were of the great city families, and this day, being the first day of the school-term, we were all neatly clad in fine woollen stuffs of Florence or of Flanders make, and colored knitted hose. We all had fine lace ruffs round the cuffs of our tight sleeves and the square cut fronts of our bodices; each little maid wore a silken ribbon to tie her plaits, and almost all had gold rings in her ears and a gold pin at her breast or in her girdle. Only one was in a simple garb, unlike the others, and she, notwithstanding her weed was clean and fitting, was arrayed in poor, grey home spun. As I looked on her I could not but mind me of Cinderella; and when I looked in her face, and then at her feet to see whether they were as neat and as little as in the tale, I saw that she had small ankles and sweet little shoes; and as for her face, I deemed I had never seen one so lovely and at the same time so strange to me. Yea, she seemed to have come from another world than this that I and the others lived in; for we were light or brown haired, with blue or grey eyes, and healthy red and white faces; while Cinderella had a low forehead and with big dark eyes strange, long, fine silky lashes; and heavy plaits of black hair hung down her back.

Ursula Tetzel was accounted by the lads the comeliest maiden of us all; and I knew full well that the flower she wore in her bodice had been given to her by my brother Herdegen early that morning, because he had chosen her for his "Lady," and said she was the fairest; but as I looked at her beside this stranger I deemed that she was of poorer stuff.

Moreover Cinderella was a stranger to me, and all the others I knew well, but I had to take patience for a whole hour ere I could ask who this fair Cinderella was, for Sister Margaret kept her eye on us, and so long as I was taught by her, no one at any time made so bold as to speak during lessons or venture on any pastime.

At last, in a few minutes for rest, I asked Ursula Tetzel, who had come to the convent school for a year past. She put out her red nether-lip with a look of scorn and said the new scholar had been thrust among us but did not belong to the like of us. Sister Margaret, though of a noble house herself, had forgot what was due to us and our families, and had taken in this grey hat out of pity. Her father was a simple clerk in the Chancery office and was accountant to the convent for some small wage. His name was Veit Spiesz, and she had heard her father say that the scribe was the son of a simple lute-player and could hardly earn enough to live. He had formerly served in a merchant's house at Venice. There he had wed an Italian woman, and all his children, which were many, had, like her, hair and eyes as black as the devil. For the sake of a "God repay thee!" this maid, named Ann, had been brought to mix with us daughters of noble houses. "But we will harry her out," said Ursula, "you will see!"

This shocked me sorely, and I said that would be cruel and I would have no part in such a matter; but Ursula laughed and said I was yet but a green thing, and turned away to the window-shelf where all the new-comers had laid out their sweetmeats at the behest of the eldest or first of the class; for, by old custom, all the sweetmeats brought by the novices on the first day were in common.

All the party crowded round the heap of sweetmeats, which waxed greater and greater, and I was standing among the others when I saw that the scribe's daughter Ann, Cinderella, was standing lonely and hanging her head by the tiled stove at the end of the room. I forthwith hastened to her, pressed the little packet which Mistress Grosz had given me into her hand—for I had it still hidden in my poke—and, whispered to her: "I had two of them, little Ann; make haste and pour them on the heap."

She gave me a questioning look with her great eyes, and when she saw that I meant it truly she nodded, and there was something in her tearful look which I never can forget; and I mind, too, that when I passed the little packet into her hand it seemed that I, and not she, had received the favor.

She gave the sweetmeats she had taken from me to the eldest, and spoke not a word, and did not seem to mark that they all mocked at the smallness of the packet. But soon enough their scorn was turned to glee and praises; for out of Cinderella's parcel such fine sweetmeats fell on to the heap as never another one had brought with her, and among them was a little phial of attar of roses from the Levant.

At first Ann had cast an anxious look at me, then she seemed as though she cared not; but when the oil of roses came to light she took it firmly in her hand to give to me. But Ursula cried out: "Nay. Whatsoever the new-comers bring is for all to share in common!" Notwithstanding, Ann laid her hand on mine, which already held the phial, and said boldly: "I give this to Margery, and I renounce all the rest."

And there was not one to say her nay, or hinder her; and when she refused to eat with them, each one strove to press upon her so much as fell to her share.

When Sister Margaret came back into the room she looked to find us in good order and holding our peace; and while we awaited her Ann whispered to me, as though to put herself right in my eyes: "I had a packet of sweetmeats; but there are four little ones at home."

Cousin Maud was waiting at the convent gate to take me home. As I was setting forth at good speed, hand in hand with my new friend, she looked at the little maid's plain garb from top to toe, and not kindly. And she made me leave hold, but yet as though it were by chance, for she came between us to put my hood straight. Then she busied herself with my neckkerchief and whispered in my ear: "Who is that?"

So I replied: "Little Ann;" and when she went on to ask who her father might be, I told her she was a scrivener's daughter, and was about to speak of her with hearty good will, when my cousin stopped me by saying to Ann: "God save you child; Margery and I must hurry." And she strove to get me on and away; but I struggled to be free from her, and cried out with the wilful pride which at that time I was wont to show when I thought folks would hinder that which seemed good and right in my eyes: "Little Ann shall come with us."

But the little maid had her pride likewise, and said firmly: "Be dutiful, Margery; I can go alone." At this Cousin Maud looked at her more closely, and thereupon her eyes had the soft light of good will which I loved so well, and she herself began to question Ann about her kinsfolk. The little maid answered readily but modestly, and when my Cousin understood that her father was a certain writer in the Chancery of whom she had heard a good report, she was softer and more gentle, so that when I took hold again of Ann's little hand she let it pass, and presently, at parting, kissed her on the brow and bid her carry a greeting to her worthy father.

Now, when I was alone with Cousin Maud and gave her to understand that I loved the scribe's little daughter and wished for no dearer friend, she answered gravely, "Little maids can hold no conversation with any but those whose mothers meet in each other's houses. Take patience till I can speak to Sister Margaret." So when my Cousin went out in the afternoon I tarried in the most anxious expectation; but she came home with famous good tidings, and thenceforward Ann was a friend to whom I clung almost as closely as to my brothers. And which of us was the chief gainer it would be hard to say, for whereas I found in her a trusted companion to whom I might impart every thing which was scarce worthy of my brothers' or my Cousin's ears, and foremost of all things my childish good-will for my Cousin Gotz and love of the Forest, to her the place in my heart and in our house were as a haven of peace when she craved rest after the heavy duties which, for all she was so young, she had already taken upon herself.

CHAPTER III

True it is that the class I learnt in at the convent was under the strictest rule, and that my teacher was a Carthusian nun; and yet I take pleasure in calling to mind the years when my spirit enjoyed the benefit of schooling with friendly companions and by the side of my best friend. Nay, even in the midst of the silent dwelling of the speechless Sisters, right merry laughter might be heard during the hours of rest, and in spite of the thick walls of the class-room it reached the nuns' ears. Albeit at first I was stricken with awe, and shy in their presence, I soon became familiar with their strange manner of life, and there was many an one whom I learnt truly to love: with some, too, we could talk and jest right merrily, for they, to be sure, had good ears, and we, were not slow in learning the language of their eyes and fingers.

As concerning the rule of silence no one, to my knowledge, ever broke it in the presence of us little ones, save only Sister Renata, and she was dismissed from the convent; yet, as I waxed older, I could see that the nuns were as fain to hear any tidings of the outer life that might find a way into the cloister as though there was nothing they held more dear than the world which they had withdrawn from by their own free choice.

For my part, I have ever been, and remain to the end, one of those least fitted for the Carthusian habit, notwithstanding that Sister Margaret would paint the beatitudes and the purifying power of her Order in fair and tempting colors. In the hours given up to sacred teaching, when she would shed out upon us the overflowing wealth and abundant grace of her loving spirit—insomuch that she won not less than four souls of our small number to the sisterhood—she was wont and glad to speak of this matter, and would say that there was a heavenly spirit living and moving in every human breast. That it told us, with the clear and holy voice of angels, what was divine and true, but that the noise of the world and our own vain imaginings sounded louder and would not suffer us to hear. But that they who took upon them the Carthusian rule and hearkened to it speechless, in a silent home, lending no ear to distant outer voices, but only to those within, would ere long learn to mark the heavenly voice with the inward ear and know its warning. That voice would declare to them the glory and the will of the Most High God, and reveal the things that are hidden in such wise as that even here below he should take part in the joys of paradise.

But, for all that I never was a Carthusian nun, and that my tongue was ever apt to run too freely, I conceive that I have found the Heavenly Spirit in the depths of my own soul and heard its voice; but in truth this has befallen me most clearly, and with most joy, when my heart has been most filled with that worldly love which the Carthusian Sisters shut out with a hundred doors. And again, when I have been moved by that love towards my neighbor which is called Charity, and wearied myself out for him, sparing nothing that was my own, I have felt those divine emotions plainly enough in my breast.

The Sister bid us to question her at all times without fear, and I was ever the foremost of us all to plague her with communings. Of a certainty she could not at all times satisfy my soul, which thirsted for knowledge, though she never failed to calm it; for I stood firm in the faith, and all she could tell me of God's revelation to man I accepted gladly, without doubt or cavil. She had taught us that faith and knowledge are things apart, and I felt that there could be no more peace for my soul if I suffered knowledge to meddle with faith.

Led by her, I saw the Saviour as love incarnate; and that the love which He brought into the world was still and ever a living thing working after His will, I strove to confess with my thinking mind. But I beheld even the Archbishops and Bishops go forth to battle, and shed the blood of their fellow men with vengeful rage; I saw Pope excommunicate Pope—for the great Schism only came to an end while I was yet at school; peaceful cities in their sore need bound themselves by treaties, under our eyes, for defence against Christian knights and lords. The robber bands of the great nobles plundered merchants on the Emperor's highway, though they were of the same creed, while the citizens strove to seize the strongholds of the knights. We heard of many more letters of defiance than of peacemaking and friendship. Even the burgesses of our good Christian town—could not the love taught by the Redeemer prevail even among them? And as with the great so with the simple; for was it love alone that reigned among us maidens in a Christian school? Nay, verily; for never shall I forget how that Ursula Tetzel, and in fellowship with her a good half of the others, pursued my sweet, sage Ann, the most diligent and best of us all, to drive her out of our midst; but in vain, thanks to Sister Margaret's upright justice. Nay, the shrewish plotters were fain at last to see the scrivener's daughter uplifted to be our head, and this compelled them to bend their pride before her.

All this and much more I would say to the good Sister; nay, and I made so bold as to ask her whether Christ's behest that we should love our enemy were not too high for attainment by the spirit of man. This made her grave and thoughtful; yet she found no lack of comforting words, and said that the Lord had only showed the way and the end. That men had turned sadly from both; but that many a stream wandered through divers windings from the path to its goal, the sea, before it reached it; and that mankind was wondrous like the stream, for, albeit they even now rend each other in bloody fights, the day will come when foe shall offer to foe the palm of peace, and when there shall be but one fold on earth and one Shepherd.

But my anxious questioning, albeit I was but a child, had without doubt troubled her pure and truthful spirit. It was in Passion week, of the fifth year of my school-life—and ever through those years she had become more bent and her voice had sunk lower, so that many a time we found it hard to hear her—that it fell that she could no longer quit her cell; and she sent me a bidding to go to her bedside, and with me only two of us all: to wit my Ann, and Elsa Ebner, a right good child and a diligent bee in her work.

And it befell that as Sister Margaret on her deathbed bid us farewell for ever, with many a God speed and much good council for the rest likewise, her heart waxed soft and she went on to speak of the love each Christian soul oweth to his neighbor and eke to his enemy. She fixed her eye in especial on me, and confessed with her pale lips that she herself had ofttimes found it hard to love evil-minded adversaries and those whose ways had been contrary to hers, as the law of the Saviour bid her. To those young ones among us who had made their minds up to take the veil she had, ere this, more especially shown what was needful; for their way lay plain before them, to walk as followers of Christ how bitter soever it might be to their human nature; but we were bound to live in the world, and she could but counsel us to flee from hate as the soul's worst foe and the most cunning of all the devils. But an if it should befall that our heart could not be subdued after a brave struggle to love such or such an one, then ought we to strive at least to respect all that was good and praiseworthy in him, inasmuch as we should ever find something worthy of honor even in the most froward and least pleasing to ourselves. And these words I have ever kept in mind, and many times have they given me pause, when the hot blood of the Schoppers has bid me stoop and pick up a stone to fling at my neighbor.

No longer than three days after she had thus bidden us to her side, Sister Margaret entered into her rest; she had been our strait but gentle teacher, and her learning was as far above that of most women of her time as the heavens are high; and as her mortal body lay, no longer bent, but at full length in the coffin, the saintly lady, who before she took the vows had been a Countess of Lupfen, belonged, meseemed, to a race taller than ours by a head. A calm, queenlike dignity was on her noble thin face; and, this corpse being the first, as it fell, that I had ever looked on, it so worked on my mind that death, of which I had heretofore been in terror, took the image in my young soul of a great Master to whom we must indeed bow, but who is not our foe.

I never could earn such praise as Ann, who was by good right at our head; notwithstanding I ever stood high. And the vouchers I carried home were enough to content Cousin Maud, for her great wish that her foster-children should out-do others was amply fulfilled by Herdegen, the eldest. He was indeed filled with sleeping learning, as it were, and I often conceived that he needed only fitting instruction and a fair start to wake it up. For even he did not attain his learning without pains, and they who deem that it flew into his mouth agape are sorely mistaken. Many a time have I sat by his side while he pored over his books, and I could see how he set to work in right earnest when once he had cast away sports and pastime. Thus with three mighty blows he would smite the nail home, which a weaker hand could not do with twenty. For whole weeks he might be idle and about divers matters which had no concern with schooling; and then, of a sudden, set to work; and it would so wholly possess his soul that he would not have seen a stone drop close at his feet.

My second brother, Kunz, was not at all on this wise. Not that he was soft-witted; far from it. His head was as clear as ever another's for all matters of daily life; but he found it hard to learn scholarship, and what Herdegen could master in one hour, it took him a whole livelong day to get. Notwithstanding he was not one of the duptences, for he strove hard with all diligence, and rather would he have lost a night's sleep than have left what he deemed a duty only half done. Thus there were sore half-hours for him in school-time; but he was not therefor to be pitied, for he had a right merry soul and was easily content, and loved many things. Good temper and a high spirit looked out of his great blue eyes; aye, and when he had played some prank which was like to bring him into trouble he had a look in his eyes—a look that might have melted a stone to pity, much more good Cousin Maud.

But this did not altogether profit him, for after that Herdegen had discovered one day how easily Kunz got off chastisement he would pray him to take upon himself many a misdeed which the elder had done; and Kunz, who was soft-hearted, was fain rather to suffer the penalty than to see it laid on his well-beloved brother. Add to this that Kunz was a well-favored, slender youth; but as compared with Herdegen's splendid looks and stalwart frame he looked no more than common. For this cause he had no ill-wishers while our eldest's uncommon beauty in all respects, and his hasty temper, ever ready to boil over for good or evil, brought upon him much ill-will and misliking.

When Cousin Maud beheld how little good Kunz got out of his learning, in spite of his zeal, she was minded to get him a private governor to teach him; and this she did by the advice of a learned doctor of Church-law, Albrecht Fleischmann, the vicar and provost of Saint Sebald's and member of the Imperial council, because we Schoppers were of the parish of Saint Sebald's, to which church Albrecht and Friedrich Schopper, God rest their souls, had attached a rich prebendary endowment.

His Reverence the prebendary Fleischmann, having attended the Council at Costnitz, whither he was sent by the town elders with divers errands to the Emperor Sigismund, who was engaged in a disputation with John Huss the Bohemian schismatic, brought to my cousin's knowledge a governor whose name was Peter Pihringer, a native of Nuremberg. He it was who brought the Greek tongue, which was not yet taught in the Latin schools of our city, not in our house alone, but likewise into others; he was not indeed at all like the high-souled men and heroes of whom his Plutarch wrote; nay, he was a right pitiable little man, who had learnt nothing of life, though all the more out of books. He had journeyed long in Italy, from one great humanistic doctor to another, and while he had sat at their feet, feeding his soul with learning, his money had melted away in his hands—all that he had inherited from his father, a worthy tavern-keeper and master baker. Much of his substance he had lent to false friends never to see it more, and it would scarce be believed how many times knavish rogues had beguiled this learned man of his goods. At length he came home to Nuremberg, a needy traveller, entering the city by the same gate as that by which Huss had that same day departed, having tarried in Nuremberg on his way to Costnitz and won over divers of our learned scholars to his doctrine. Now, after Magister Peter had written a very learned homily against the said Hans Huss, full of much Greek—of which, indeed, it was reported that it had brought a smile to the dauntless Bohemian's lips in the midst of his sorrow—he found a patron in Doctor Fleischmann, who was well pleased with this tractate, and he thenceforth made a living by teaching divers matters. But he sped but ill, dwelling alone, inasmuch as he would forget to eat and drink and mislay or lose his hardly won wage. Once the town watch had to see him home because, instead of a book, he was carrying a ham which a gossip had given him; and another day he was seen speeding down the streets with his nightcap on, to the great mirth of the lads and lasses.

Notwithstanding he showed himself no whit unworthy of the high praise wherewith his Reverence the Prebendary had commended him, inasmuch as he was not only a right learned, but likewise a faithful and longsuffering teacher. But his wisdom profited Herdegen and Ann and me rather than Kunz, though it was for his sake that he had come to us; and as, touching this strange man's person, my cousin told me later that when she saw him for the first time she took such a horror of his wretched looks that she was ready to bid him depart and desire the Reverend doctor to send us another governor. But out of pity she would nevertheless give him a trial, and considering that I should ere long be fully grown, and that a young maid's heart is a strange thing, she deemed that a younger teacher might lead it into peril.

At the time when Master Pihringer came to dwell with us, Herdegen was already high enough to pass into the upper school, for he was first in his 'ordo'; but our guardian, the old knight Hans Im Hoff, of whom I shall have much to tell, held that he was yet too young for the risks of a free scholar's life in a high school away from home, and he kept him two years more in Nuremberg at the school of the Brethren of the Holy Ghost, albeit the teaching there was not of the best. At any rate Master Pihringer avowed that in all matters of learning we were out of all measure behind the Italians; and how rough and barbarous was the Latin spoken by the reverend Fathers and taught by them in the schools, I myself had later the means of judging.

Their way of imparting that tongue was in truth a strange thing; for to fix the quantity of the syllables in the learners' mind, they were made to sing verses in chorus, while one of them, on whose head Father Hieronymus would set a paper cap to mark his office, beat the measure with a wooden sword; but what pranks of mischief the unruly rout would be playing all the time Kunz could describe better than I can.

The great and famous works of the Roman chroniclers and poets, which our Master had come to know well in Italy—having besides fine copies of them—were never heard of in the Fathers' school, by reason, that those writers had all been mere blind heathen; but, verily, the common school catechisms which were given to the lads for their instruction, contained such foolish and ill-conceived matters, that any sage heathen would have been ashamed of them. The highest exercise consisted of disputations on all manner of subtle and captious questions, and the Latin verses which the scholars hammered out under the rule of Father Jodocus were so vile as to rouse Magister Peter to great and righteous wrath. Each morning, before the day's tasks began, the fine old hymn Salve Regina was chanted, and this was much better done in the Brothers' school than in ever another, for those Monks gave especial heed to the practice of good music. My Herdegen profited much thereby, and he was the foremost of all the singing scholars. He likewise gladly and of his own free will took part in the exercises of the

Alumni, of whom twelve, called the Pueri, had to sing at holy mass, and at burials and festivals, as well as in the streets before the houses of the great city families and other worthy citizens. The money they thus earned served to help maintain the poorer scholars, and to be sure, my brother was ready to forego his share; nay, and a great part of his own pocket-money went to those twelve, for among them were comrades he truly loved.

There was something lordly in my elder brother, and his fellows were ever subject to his will. Even at the shooting matches in sport he was ever chosen captain, and the singing pueri soon would do his every behest. Cousin Maud would give them free commons on many a Sunday and holy-day, and when they had well filled their hungry young crops at our table for the coming week of lean fare, they went out with us into the garden, and it presently rang with mirthful songs, Herdegen beating the measure, while we young maids joined in with a will.

For the most part we three: Ann, Elsa Ebner, and I—were the only maids with the lads, but Ursula Tetzel was sometimes with us, for she was ever fain to be where Herdegen was. And he had been diligent enough in waiting upon her ere ever I went to school. There was a giving and taking of flowers and nosegays, for he had chosen her for his Lady, and she called him her knight; and if I saw him with a red knot on his cap I knew right well it was to wear her color; and I liked all this child's-play myself right well, inasmuch as I likewise had my chosen color: green, as pertaining to my cousin in the forest.

But when I went to the convent-school all this was at an end, and I had no choice but to forego my childish love matters, not only for my tasks' sake, but forasmuch as I discerned that Gotz had a graver love matter on hand, and that such an one as moved his parents to great sorrow.

The wench to whom he plighted his love was the daughter of a common craftsman, Pernhart the coppersmith, and when this came to my ears it angered me greatly; nay, and cost me bitter tears, as I told it to Ann. But ere long we were playing with our dollies again right happily.

I took this matter to heart nevertheless, more than many another of my years might have done; and when we went again to the Forest Lodge and I missed Gotz from his place, and once, as it fell, heard my aunt lamenting to Cousin Maud bitterly indeed of the sorrows brought upon her by her only son—for he was fully bent on taking the working wench to wife in holy wedlock—in my heart I took my aunt's part. And I deemed it a shameful and grievous thing that so fine a young gentleman could abase himself to bring heaviness on the best of parents for the sake of a lowborn maid.

After this, one Sunday, it fell by chance that I went to mass with Ann to the church of St. Laurence, instead of St. Sebald's to which we belonged. Having said my prayer, looking about me I beheld Gotz, and saw how, as he leaned against a pillar, he held his gaze fixed on one certain spot. My eyes followed his, and at once I saw whither they were drawn, for I saw a young maid of the citizen class in goodly, nay—in rich array, and she was herself of such rare and wonderful beauty that I myself could not take my eyes off her. And I remembered that I had met the wench erewhile on the feast-day of St. John, and that uncle Christian Pfinzing, my worshipful godfather, had pointed her out to Cousin Maud, and had said that she was the fairest maid in Nuremberg whom they called, and rightly, Fair Gertrude.

Now the longer I gazed at her the fairer I deemed her, and when Ann discovered to me, what I had at once divined, that this sweet maid was the daughter of Pernhart the coppersmith, my child's heart was glad, for if my cousin was without dispute the finest figure of a man in the whole assembly Fair Gertrude was the sweetest maid, I thought, in the whole wide world.

If it had been possible that she could be of yet greater beauty it would but have added to my joy. And henceforth I would go as often as I might to St. Laurence's, and past the coppersmith's house to behold Fair Gertrude; and my heart beat high with gladness when she one day saw me pass and graciously bowed to my silent greeting, and looked in my face with friendly inquiry.

After this when Gotz came to our house I welcomed him gladly as heretofore; and one day, when I made bold to whisper in his ear that I had seen his fair Gertrude, and for certain no saint in heaven could have a sweeter face than hers, he thanked me with a bright look and it was from the bottom of his soul that he said: "If you could but know her faithful heart of gold!"

For all this Gotz was dearer to me than of old, and it uplifted me in my own conceit that he should put such trust in a foolish young thing as I was. But in later days it made me sad to see his frank and noble face grow ever more sorrowful, nay, and full of gloom; and I knew full well what pained him, for a child can often see much more than its elders deem. Matters had come to a sharp quarrel betwixt the son and the parents, and I knew my cousin well, and his iron will which was a by-word with us. And my aunt in the Forest was of the same temper; albeit her body was sickly, she was one of those women who will not bear to be withstood, and my heart hung heavy with fear when I conceived of the outcome of this matter.

Hence it was a boon indeed to me that I had my Ann for a friend, and could pour out to her all that filled my young soul with fears. How our cheeks would burn when many a time we spoke of the love which was the bond between Gotz and his fair Gertrude. To us, indeed, it was as yet a mystery, but that it was sweet and full of joy we deemed a certainty. We would have been fain to cry out to the Emperor and the world to take arms against the ruthless parents who were minded to tread so holy a blossom in the dust; but since this was not in our power we had dreams of essaying to touch the heart of my forest aunt, for she had but that one son and no daughter to make her glad, and I had ever been her favorite.

Thus passed many weeks, and one morning, when I came forth from school, I found Gotz with Cousin Maud who had been speaking with him, and her eyes were wet with tears; and I heard him cry out:

"It is in my mother's power to drive me to misery and ruin; but no power in heaven or on earth can drive me to break the oath and forswear the faith I have sworn!"

And his cheeks were red, and I had never seen him look so great and tall.

Then, when he saw me, he held out both hands to me in his frank, loving way, and I took them with all my heart. At this he looked into my eyes which were full of tears, and he drew me hastily to him and kissed me on my brow for the first time in all his life, with strange passion; and without another word he ran out of the house-door into the street. My cousin gazed after him, shaking her head sadly and wiping her eyes; but when I asked her what was wrong with my cousin she would give me no tidings of the matter.

The next day we should have gone out to the forest, but we remained at home; Aunt Jacoba would see no one. Her son had turned his back on his parents' dwelling, and had gone out as a stranger among strangers. And this was the first sore grief sent by Heaven on my young heart.

CHAPTER IV

Many of the fairest memories of my childhood are linked with the house where Ann's parents dwelt. It was indeed but a simple home and not to be named with ours—the Schopperhof—for greatness or for riches; but it was a snug nest, and in divers ways so unlike ever another that it was full of pleasures for a child.

Master Spiesz, Ann's father, had been bidden from Venice, where he had been in the service of the Mendel's merchant house, to become head clerk in Nuremberg, first in the Chamber of Taxes, and then in the Chancery, a respectable post of much trust. His father was, as Ursula Tetzel had said in the school, a luteplayer; but he had long been held the head and chief of teachers of the noble art of music, and was so greatly respected by the clergy and laity that he was made master and leader of the church choir, and even in the houses of the city nobles his teaching of the lute and of singing was deemed the best. He was a right well-disposed and cheerful old man, of a rare good heart and temper, and of wondrous good devices. When the worshipful town council bid his son Veit Spiesz come back to Nuremberg, the old man must need fit up a proper house for him, since he himself was content with a small chamber, and the scribe was by this time married to the fair Giovanna, the daughter of one of the Sensali or brokers of the German Fondaco, and must have a home and hearth of his own.

> [Sensali—Agents who conducted all matters of business between
> the German and Venetian merchants. Not even the smallest
> affair was settled without their intervention, on account of the
> duties demanded by the Republic. The Fondaco was the name
> of the great exchange established by the Republic itself for the
> German trade.]

The musician, who had as a student dwelt in Venice, hit on the fancy that he would give his daughter-in-law a home in Nuremberg like her father's house, which stood on one of the canals in Venice; so he found a house with windows looking to the river, and which he therefore deemed fit to ease her homesickness. And verily the Venetian lady was pleased with the placing of her house, and yet more with the old man's loving care for her; although the house was over tall, and so narrow that there were but two windows on each floor. Thus there was no manner of going to and fro in the Spiesz's house, but only up and down. Notwithstanding, the Venetian lady loved it, and I have heard her say that there was no spot so sweet in all Nuremberg as the window seat on the second story of her house. There stood her spinning-wheel and sewing-box; and a bright Venice mirror, which, in jest, she would call "Dame Inquisitive," showed her all that passed on the river and the Fleisch-brucke, for her house was not far from those which stood facing the Franciscan Friars. There she ruled in peace and good order, in love and all sweetness, and her children throve even as the flowers did under her hand: roses, auriculas, pinks and pansies; and whosoever went past the house in a boat could hear mirth within and the voice of song. For the Spiesz children had a fine ear for music, both from their grandsire and their mother, and sweet, clear, bell-like voices. My Ann was the queen of them all, and her nightingale's throat drew even Herdegen to her with great power.

Only one of the scribe's children, little Mario, was shut out from the world of sound, for he was a deaf-mute born; and when Ann tarried under our roof, rarely indeed and for but a short while, her stay was brief for his sake; for she tended him with such care and love as though she had been his own mother. Albeit she thereby was put to much pains, these were as nothing to the heartfelt joys which the love and good speed of this child brought her; for notwithstanding he was thus born to sorrow, by his sister's faithful care he grew a happy and thankful creature. Ofttimes my Cousin Maud was witness to her teaching of her little brother, and all Ann did for the child seemed to her so pious and so wonderful, that it broke down the last bar that stood in the way of our close fellowship. And Ann's well-favored mother likewise won my cousin's good graces, albeit she was swift to mark that the Italian lady could fall in but ill with German ways, and in especial with those of Nuremberg, and was ever ready to let Ann bear the burthen of the household.

All our closest friends, and foremost of these my worshipful godfather Uncle Christian Pfinzing, ere long truly loved my little Ann; and of all our fellows I knew of only one who was ill-disposed towards her, and that was Ursula Tetzel, who marked, with ill-cloaked wrath, that my brother Herdegen cared less and less for her, and did Ann many a little courtesy wherewith he had formerly favored her. She could not dissemble her anger, and when my eldest brother waited on Ann on her name day with the 'pueri' to give her a 'serenata' on the water, whereas, a year agone, he had done Ursula the like honor, she fell upon my friend in our garden with such fierce and cruel words that my cousin had to come betwixt them, and then to temper my great wrath by saying that Ursula was a motherless child, whose hasty ways had never been bridled by a loving hand.

As I mind me now of those days I do so with heartfelt thankfulness and joy. To be sure it but ill-pleased our grand-uncle and guardian, the knight Im Hoff, that Cousin Maud should suffer me, the daughter of a noble house, to mix with the low born race of a simple scrivener; but in sooth Ann was more like by far to get harm in our house, among my brethren and their fellows, than I in the peaceful home by the river, where none but seemly speech was ever heard and sweet singing, nor ever seen but labor and good order and content.

Right glad was I to tarry there; but yet how good it was when Ann got leave to come to us for the whole of Sunday from noon till eventide; when we would first sit and chatter and play alone together, and talk over all we had done in school; thereafter we had my brothers with us, and would go out to take the air under the care of my cousin or of Magister Peter, or abide at home to sing or have merry pastime.

After the Ave Maria, the old organist, Adam Heyden, Ann's grand uncle, would come to seek her, and many sweet memories dwell in my mind of that worthy and gifted man, which I might set down were it not that I am Ann's debtor for so many things that made my childhood happy. It was she, for a certainty, who first taught me truly to play; for whereas my dolls, and men-at-arms and shop games, albeit they were small, were in all points like the true great ones, she had but a staff of wood wrapped round with a kerchief which she rocked in her arms for a babe; and when she played a shop game with the little ones, she marked stones and leaves to be their wares and their money, and so found far greater pastime than we when we played with figs and almonds and cloves out of little wooden chests and linen-cloth sacks, and weighed them with brass weights on little scales with a tongue and string. It was she who brought imagination to bear on my pastimes, and many a time has she borne my fancy far enough from the Pegnitz, over seas and rivers to groves of palm and golden fairy lands.

Our fellowship with my brethren was grateful to her as it was to me; but meseems it was a different thing in those early years from what it was in later days. While I write a certain summer day from that long past time comes back to my mind strangely clear. We had played long enough in our chamber, and we found it too hot in the loft under the roof, where we had climbed on to the beams, which were great, so we went down into the garden. Herdegen had quitted us in haste after noon, and we found none but Kunz, who was shaping arrows for his cross-bow. But he ere long threw away his knife and came to be with us, and as he was well-disposed to Ann as being my friend, he did his best to make himself pleasing, or at least noteworthy in her sight. He stood on his head and then climbed to the top of the tallest fruit-tree and flung down pears, but they smote her head so that she cried out; then he turned a wheel on his hands and feet, and a little more and his shoe would hit her in the face; and when he marked that he was but troubling us, he went away sorrowful, but only to hide behind a bush, and as we went past, to rush out on a sudden and put us in fear by wild shouting.

My eldest brother well-nigh affrighted us more when he presently joined us, for his hair was all unkempt and his looks wild. He was now of an age when men-children deem maids to be weak and unfit for true sport, but nevertheless strive their utmost to be marked and chosen by them. Hence Ursula's good graces, which she had shown right openly, had for a long while greatly pleased him, but by this time he was weary of her and began to conceive that good little Ann, with her nightingale's voice, was more to his liking.

After hastily greeting us, he forthwith made us privy to an evil matter. One of his fellowship, Laurence Abenberger, the son of an apothecary, who was diligent in school, and of a wondrous pious spirit, gave up all his spare time to all manner of magic arts, and albeit he was but seventeen years of age, he had already cast nativities for many folks and for us maids, and had told us of divers ill-omens for the future. This Abenberger, a little fellow of no note, had found in some ancient papers a recipe for discovering treasure, and had told the secret to Herdegen and some other few. To begin, they went at his bidding to the graveyard with him, and there, at the full moon, they poured hot lead into the left eye-hole of a skull and made it into arrow-heads. Yesternight they had journeyed forth as far as Sinterspuhel, and there, at midnight, had stood at the cross-roads and shot with these same arrow-heads to the four quarters, to the end that they might dig for treasure wheresoever the shafts might fall. But they found no treasure, but a newly-buried body, and on this had taken to their heels in all haste. Herdegen only had tarried behind with Abenberger, and when he saw that there were deep wounds on the head of the dead man his intent was to carry the tidings to the justices in council; nevertheless he would delay a while, because Abenberger had besought him to keep silence and not to bring him to an evil end. But as he had gone past the school of arms he had learnt that an apprentice was missing, and that it was feared lest he had been waylaid by pillagers, or had fallen into evil hands; so he now deemed it his plain duty to keep no longer silence concerning the finding of the body, and desired to be advised by me and Ann. While I, for my part, shortly and clearly declared that information must at once be laid before his worship the Mayor, a strange trembling fell on Ann, and notwithstanding she could not say me nay, she was in such fear that grave mischief might overtake Herdegen by reason of his thoughtless deed, that tears ran in streams down her cheeks, and it cost me great pains or ever I could comfort her, so brave and reasonable as she commonly was. But Herdegen was greatly pleased by her too great terrors; and albeit he laughed at her, he called her his faithful, fearful little hare, and stuck the pink he wore in his jerkin into her hair. At this she was soon herself again; she counselled him forthwith to do that it was his duty to do; and when thereafter the authorities had made inquisition, it came to light that our lads had in truth come upon the body of the slain apprentice. And though Herdegen did his best to keep silence as touching Abenberger's evildoings, they nevertheless came out through other ways, and the poor wight was dismissed from the school.

By the end of two years after this, matters had changed in our household.

The twelve 'pueri' had been our guests at dinner, and were in the garden singing merry rounds well known to us, and I joined in, with Ann and Ursula Tetzel. Now, while Herdegen beat the time, his ear was intent on Ann's singing, as though there were revelation on her lips; and his well-beloved companion, Heinrich Trardorf, who erewhile had, with due modesty, preferred me, Margery, seemed likewise well affected to her singing; and when we ceased he fell into eager talk with her, for he had bewailed to her that, albeit he loved me well, as being the son of simple folk he might never lift up his eyes so high.

Herdegen's eyes rested on the twain with some little wrath; then he hastily got up! He snatched the last of Cousin Maud's precious roses from her favorite bush and gave them to Ursula, and then waited on her as though she were the only maid there present. But ere long her father came to fetch her, and so soon as she had departed, beaming, with her roses, Herdegen hastily came to me and, without deeming Ann worthy to be looked at even, bid me good even. I held his hand and called to her to come to me, to help me hinder him from departing, inasmuch as one of the pueri was about to play the lute for the rest to dance. She came forward as an honest maid should, looked up at him with her great eyes, and besought him full sweetly to tarry with us.

He pointed with his hand to Trardorf and answered roughly: "I care not to go halves!" And he turned to go to the gate.

Ann took him by the hand, and without a word of his ways with Ursula, not in chiding but as in deep grief, she said: "If you depart, you do me a hurt. I have no pleasure but when you are by, and what do I care for Heinrich?"

This was all he needed; his eye again met hers with bright looks, and from that hour of our childhood she knew no will but his.

From that hour likewise Ann held off from all other lads, and when he was by it seemed as though she had no eyes nor ears save for him and me alone. To Kunz she paid little heed; yet he never failed to wait on her and watch to do her service, as though she were the daughter of some great lord, and he no more than her page.

Ann freely owned to me that she held Herdegen to be the noblest youth on earth, nor could I marvel, when I was myself of the same mind. What should I know, when I was still but fourteen and fifteen years old, of love and its dangers? I had felt such love for Gotz as Ann for my elder brother, and as I had then been glad that my dear Cousin had won the love of so fair a maid as Gertrude, I likewise believed that Ann would some day be glad if Herdegen should plight his troth to a fair damsel of high degree. Hence I did all that in me lay to bring them together whenever it might be, and in truth this befell often enough without my aid; for not music alone was a bond between them, nor yet that Herdegen and I taught her to ride on a horse, on the sandy way behind our horse-stalls—the Greek lessons for which Magister Peter had come into the household were a plea on which they passed many an hour together.

I was slow to learn that tongue; but Ann's head was not less apt than my brother's, and he was eager and diligent to keep her good speed at the like mark with his own, as she was so quick to apprehend. Thus both were at last forward enough to put Greek into German, and then Magister Peter was bidden to lend them his aid. Now, the change in the worthy man, after eating for four years at our table, was such that many an one would have said it was a miracle. At his first coming to us he himself said he weened he was a doomed son of ill-luck, and he scarce dared look man or woman in the face; and what a good figure he made now, notwithstanding the divers pranks played on his simplicity by my brothers and their fellows, nay, and some whiles by me.

Many an one before this has marked that the god Amor is the best schoolmaster; and when our Magister had learnt to stoop less, nay almost to hold himself straight, when as now, he wore his good new coat with wide hanging sleeves, tight-fitting hose, a well-stiffened, snow-white collar, and even a smart black feather in his beretta, when he not alone smoothed his hair but anointed it, all this, in its beginnings, was by reason of his great and true love for my Ann, while she was yet but a child.

My cautious Cousin Maud had, it is true, done the blind god of Love good service; for many a time she would, with her own hand, set some matter straight which the Magister had put on all askew, and on divers occasions would give him a piece of fine cloth, and with it the cost of the tailor's work, in bright new coin wrapped in colored paper. She brought him to order and to keep his hours, and when grave speech availed not she could laugh at him with friendly mockery, such as hurts no man, inasmuch as it is the outcome of a good heart. Thus it was, that, by the time when Herdegen was to go to the high school at Erfurt, Magister Peter was not strangely unlike other learned men of his standing; and when it fell that he had to discourse of the great masters of learning in Italy, or of the glorious Greek writers, I have seen his eye light up like that of a youth.

Our guardian kept watch over my brothers' speed in learning. The old knight Im Hoff was a somewhat stern man and shy of his kind, but scarce another had such great wealth, or was so highly respected in our town. He was our grand-uncle, as old Adam Heyden was Ann's, and two men less alike it would be hard to find.

When we were bid to pay our devoir to my guardian it was seldom done but with much complaining and churlishness; whereas it was ever a festival to be suffered to go with Ann to the organist's house. He dwelt in a fine lodging high up in the tower above the city, and he could look down from his windows, as God Almighty looks down on the earth from the bright heavens, over Nuremberg, and the fortress on the hill, the wide ring of forest which guards it on the north and east and south, the meadows and villages stretching between the woods, and the walls and turrets of our good city, and the windings of the river Pegnitz. He loved to boast that he was the first to bid the sun welcome and the last to bid it good-night; and perchance it was to the light, of which he had so goodly a share, that his spirit owed its ever gay good-cheer. He was ever ready with a jest and some little gift for us children; and, albeit these were of little money's worth, they brought us much joy. And indeed there was never another man in Nuremberg who had given away so many tokens and made so many glad hearts and faces thereby as Adam Heyden. True, indeed, after a short but blessed wedded life he had been left a widower and childless, and had no care to save for his heirs; and yet Gottfried Spiesz, Ann's grandfather, was in the right when he said that he had more children than ever another in Nuremberg, inasmuch as that he was like a father to every lad and maid in the town.

When he walked down the street all the little ones were as glad though they had met Christ the Lord or Saint Nicholas; and as they hung on to his long gown with the left hand, with the right they crammed their mouths with the apples or cakes whereof his pockets seemed never to be empty.

But Master Adam had his weak side, and there were many to blame him for that he was over fond of good liquor. Albeit he did his drinking after a manner of his own, in no unseemly wise. To wit, on certain year-days he would tarry alone in his tower, and his lamp might be seen gleaming till midnight. There he would sit alone, with his wine jar and cup, and he would drink the first and second and third in silence, to the good speed of Elsa, his late departed wife. After that he began to sing in a low voice, and before each fresh cup as he raised it he cried aloud "Prosit, Adam!" and when it was empty: "I Heartily thank you, Heyden!"

·Thus would he go on till he had drunk out divers jugs, and the tower seemed to be spinning round him. Then to his bed, where he would dream of his Elsa and the good old days, the folks he had loved, his youthful courtships, and all the fine and wondrous things which his lonely drinking bout had brought to his inward eye. Next morning he was faithfully at his duty. Common evenings, which were of no mark to him, he spent with the Spiesz folks in the little house by the river, or else in the Gentlemen's tavern in the Frohnwage; for albeit none met there but such as belonged to the noble families of the town, and learned men, and artists of mark, Adam Heyden the organist was held as their equal and a right welcome guest.

And now as touching our grand-uncle and guardian the Knight Sir Sebald Im Hoff.

Many an one will understand how that my fear of him grew greater after that I one evening by mishap chanced to go into his bed chamber, and there saw a black coffin wherein he was wont to sleep each night, as it were in a bed. It was easy to see in the man himself that some deep sorrow or heavy sin gnawed at his heart, and nevertheless he was one of the stateliest old gentlemen I have met in a long life. His face seemed as though cast in metal, and was of wondrous fine mould, but deadly and unchangefully pale. His snowy hair fell in long locks over his collar of sable fur, and his short beard, cut in a point, was likewise of a silver whiteness. When he stood up he was much taller than common, and he walked with princelike dignity. For many years he had ceased to go to other folks' houses, nevertheless many others sought him out. In every family of rank, excepting in his own, the Im Hoff family, wherever there was a manchild or a maid growing up they were brought to him; but of them all there were but two who dare come nigh him without fear. These were my brother Herdegen and Ursula Tetzel; and throughout my young days she was the one soul whom mine altogether shut out.

Notwithstanding I must for justice sake confess that she grew up to be a well-favored damsel. Besides this, she was the only offspring of a rich and noble house. She went from school a year before Ann and I did, and after that her father, a haughty and eke a surly man, who had long since lost his wife, her mother, prided himself on giving her such attires as might have beseemed the daughter of a Count or a Prince-Elector. And the brocades and fine furs and costly chains and clasps she wore graced her lofty, round shape exceeding well, and she lorded it so haughtily in them that the worshipful town-council were moved to put forth an order against over much splendor in women's weed.

She was, verily and indeed, the last damsel I could have wished to see brought home as mistress of the "Schopperhof," and nevertheless I knew full well, before my brother went away to the high school, that our grand uncle was counting on giving her and him to each other in marriage. Master Tetzel likewise would point to them when they stood side by side, so high and goodly, as though they were a pair; and this old man, whose face was as grey and cold and hueless as all about his daughter was bright and gay, would demean himself with utter humbleness and homage to the lad, who scarce showed the first down on his lip and chin, by reason that he looked upon him, who was his granduncle's heir, as his own son-in-law.

It was, to be sure, known to many that rich old Im Hoff was minded to leave great endowments to the Holy Church, and meseemed that it was praiseworthy and wise that he should do all that in him lay to gain the prayers of the Blessed Virgin and the dear Saints; for the evil deed which had turned him from a dashing knight into a lonely penitent might well weigh in torment on his poor soul. I will here shortly rehearse all I myself knew of that matter.

In his young days my grand uncle had carried his head high indeed, and deemed so greatly of his scutcheon and his knightly forbears that he scorned all civic dignities as but a small matter. Then, whereas in the middle of the past century all towns were forbid by imperial law to hold tournaments, he went to Court, and had been dubbed knight by the Emperor Charles, and won fame and honor by many a shrewd lance-thrust. His more than common manly beauty gained him favor with the ladies, and since he preferred what was noble and knightly to all other graces he would wed no daughter of Nuremberg but the penniless child of Baron von Frauentrift. But my grand-uncle had made an evil choice; his wife was high-tempered and filled full of conceits. When princes and great lords came into our city, they were ever ready to find lodging in the great and wealthy house of the Im Hoffs; but then she would suffer them to pay court to her, and grant them greater freedom than becomes the decent honor of a Nuremberg citizen's hearth. Once, then, when my lord the duke of Bavaria lay at their house with a numerous fellowship, a fine young count, who had courted my grand uncle's wife while she was yet a maid, fanned his jealousy to a flame; and, one evening, at a late hour, while his wife was yet not come home from seeing some friends, as it fell he heard a noise and whispering of voices, beneath their lodging, in the courtyard wherein all these folks' chests and bales were bestowed. He rushed forth, beside himself; and whereas he shouted out to the courtyard and got no reply, he thrust right and left at haphazard with his naked sword among the chests whence he had heard the voices, and a pitiful cry warned him that he had struck home. Then there came the wailing of a woman; and when the squires and yeomen came forth with torches and lanterns, he could see that he had slain Ludwig Tetzel, Ursula's uncle, a young unwedded man. He had stolen into the courtyard to hold a tryst with the fair daughter of the master-weigher in the Im Hoffs' house of trade, and the loving pair, in their fear of the master, had not answered his call, but had crept behind the baggage. Thus, by ill guidance, had my grand-uncle become a murderer, and the judges broke their staff over him; albeit, since he freely confessed the deed of death, and had done it with no evil intent, they were content to make him pay a fine in money. But some said that they likewise commanded the hangman to nail up a gallows-cord behind his house door; others, rather, that he had taken upon himself the penance of ever wearing such a cord about his neck day and night.

As touching the Tetzels themselves, they made no claim for blood; and for this he was so thankful to them, all his life through, that he gave them his word that he would name Ursula in his testament; whereas he ever hated the Im Hoffs to the end, after that they, on whom he had brought so much vexation by his wilful and haughty temper, took counsel after the judgment as to whether it behooved them not to strip him of their good old name and thrust him forth from their kinship. Four only, as against three, spoke in his favor, and this his haughty spirit could so ill endure that never an Im Hoff dared cross his threshold, though one and another often strove to win back his favor.

He had little comfort from his wife in his grief, for when he was found guilty of manslaughter she quitted him to return to the Emperor's court at Prague, and there she died after a wild hunt which she had followed in King Wenzel's train, while she was not yet past her youth.

CHAPTER V

Three years were past since Herdegen had first gone to the High School, and we had never seen him but for a few weeks at the end of the first year, when he was on his way from Erfurt to Padua. In the letters he wrote from thence there was ever a greeting for Mistress Anna, and often there would be a few words in Greek for her and me; yet, as he knew full well that she alone could crack such nuts, he bid me to the feast only as the fox bid the stork. While he was with us he ever demeaned himself both to me and to her as a true and loving brother, when he was not at the school of arms proving to the amazement of the knights and nobles his wondrous skill in the handling of the sword, which he had got in the High School. And during this same brief while be at divers times had speech of Ursula, but he showed plainly enough that he had lost all delight in her.

He had found but half of what he sought at Erfurt, but deemed that he was ripe to go to Padua; for there, alone, he thought—and Magister Peter said likewise—could he find the true grist for his mill. And when he told us of what he hoped to gain at that place we could but account his judgment good, and wish him good speed and that he might come home from that famous Italian school a luminary of learning. When, at his departing, I saw that Ann was in no better heart than I was, but looked right doleful, I thought it was by reason of the sickness which for some while past had now and again fallen on her good father. Kunz likewise had quitted school, and he could not complain that learning weighed too heavily on his light heart and merry spirit. He was now serving his apprenticeship in our grand uncle's business, and whereas the traffic was mainly with Venice he was to learn the Italian tongue with all diligence. Our Magister, who was well-skilled in it, taught him therein, and was, as heretofore, well content to be with us. Cousin Maud would never suffer him to depart, for it had grown to be a habit with her to care for him; albeit many an one can less easily suffer the presence of a man who needs help, than of one who is himself of use and service.

Master Peter himself, under pretence of exercising himself in the Italian tongue, would often wait upon Dame Giovanna. We on our part would remember the fable of the Sack and the Ass and laugh; while Ann slipped off to her garret chamber when the Magister was coming; and she could never fail to know of it, for no son of man ever smote so feebly as he with the knocker on the door plate.

Thus the years in which we grew from children into maidens ran past in sheer peace and gladness. Cousin Maud allowed us to have every pastime and delight; and if at times her face was less content, it was only by reason that I craved to wear a longer kirtle than she deemed fitting for my tender years, or that I proved myself over-rash in riding in the riding school or the open country.

My close friendship with Ann brought me to mark and enjoy many other and better things; and in this I differed from the maidens of some noble families, who, to this day, sit in stalls of their own in church, apart from such as have no scutcheon of arms. But indeed Ann was an honored guest in many a lordly house wherein our school and playmates dwelt.

In summer days we would sometimes go forth to the farm belonging to us Schoppers outside the town, or else to Jorg Stromer our worthy cousin at the mill where paper is made; and at holy Whitsuntide we would ride forth to the farm at Laub, which his sister Dame Anna Borchtlin had by inheritance of her father. Nevertheless, and for all that there was to see and learn at the paper-mill, and much as I relished the good fresh butter and the black home-bread and the lard cakes with which Dame Borchtlin made cheer for us, my heart best loved the green forest where dwelt our uncle Conrad Waldstromer, father to my cousin Gotz, who still was far abroad.

Now, since I shall have much to tell of this well-beloved kinsman and of his kith and kin, I will here take leave to make mention that all the Stromers were descended from a certain knight, Conrad von Reichenbach, who erewhile had come from his castle of Kammerstein, hard by Schwabach, as far forth as Nuremberg. There had he married a daughter of the Waldstromers, and the children and grandchildren, issue of this marriage, were all named Stromer or Waldstromer. And the style Wald—or wood— Stromer is to be set down to the fact that this branch had, from a long past time, heretofore held the dignity of Rangers of the great forest which is the pride of Nuremberg to this very day. But at the end of the last century the municipality had bought the offices and dignities which were theirs by inheritance, both from Waldstromer and eke from Koler the second ranger; albeit the worshipful council entrusted none others than a Waldstromer or a Koler with the care of its woods; and in my young days our Uncle Conrad Waldstromer was chief Forester, and a right bold hunter.

Whensoever he crossed our threshold meseemed as though the fresh and wholesome breath of pine-woods was in the air; and when he gave me his hand it hurt mine, so firm and strong and loving withal was his grip, and that his heart was the same all men might see. His thick, red-gold hair and beard, streaked with snowy white, his light, flax-blue eyes and his green forester's garb, with high tan boots and a cap of otter fur garnished with the feather of some bird he had slain—all this gave him a strange, gladsome, and gaudy look. And as the stalwart man stepped forth with his hanger and hunting-knife at his girdle, followed by his hounds and badger-dogs, other children might have been affrighted, but to me, betimes, there was no dearer sight than this of the terrible-looking forester, who was besides Cousin Gotz's father.

Well, on the second Sunday after Whitsunday, when the apple blossoms were all shed, my uncle came in to town to bid me and Cousin Maud to the forest lodge once more; for he ever dwelt there from one Springtide till the next, albeit he was under a bond to the Council to keep a house in the city. I was nigh upon seventeen years old; Ann was past seventeen already, and I would have expressed my joy as freely as heretofore but that somewhat lay at my heart, and that was concerning my Ann. She was not as she was wont to be; she was apt to suffer pains in her head, and the blood had fled from her fresh cheeks. Nay, at her worst she was all pale, and the sight of her thus cut me to the heart, so I gladly agreed when Cousin Maud said that the little house by the river was doing her a mischief, and the grievous care of her deaf-mute brother and the other little ones, and that she lacked fresh air. And indeed her own parents did not fail to mark it; but they lacked the means to obey the leech's orders and to give Ann the good chance of a change to fresh forest air.

When my uncle had given his bidding, I made so bold as to beseech him with coaxing words that he would bid her go with me. And if any should deem that it was but a light matter to ask of a good-hearted old man that he should harbor a fair young maid for a while, in a large and wealthy house, he will be mistaken, inasmuch as my uncle was wont, at all times and in all places, to have regard first to his wife's goodwill and pleasure.

This lady was a Behaim, of the same noble race as my mother, whom God keep; and what great pride she set on her ancient and noble blood she had plainly proven in the matter of her son's love-match. This matter had in truth no less heavily stricken his father's soul, but he had held his peace, inasmuch as he could never bring himself to play the lord over his wife; albeit he was in other matters a strict and thorough man; nay a right stern master, who ruled the host of foresters and hewers, warders and beaters, bee-keepers and woodmen who were under him with prudence and straitness. And yet my aunt Jacoba was a feeble, sickly woman, who rarely went forth to drink in God's fresh air in the lordly forest, having lost the use of her feet, so that she must be borne from her couch to her bed.

My uncle knew her full well, and he knew that she had a good and pitiful heart and was minded to do good to her kind; nevertheless he said his power over her would not stretch to the point of making her take a scrivener's child into her noble house, and entertaining her as an equal. Thus he withstood my fondest prayers, till he granted so much as that Ann should come and speak for herself or ever he should leave the house.

When she had hastily greeted my cousin and me, and Cousin Maud had told her who my uncle was, she went up to him in her decent way, made him a curtsey, and held out her hand, no whit abashed, while her great eyes looked up at him lovingly, inasmuch as she had heard all that was good of him from me.

Thereupon I saw in the old forester's face that he was "on the scent" of my Ann—to use his own words—so I took heart again and said: "Well, little uncle?"

"Well," said he slowly and doubtingly. But he presently uplifted Ann's chin, gazed her in the face, and said: "To be sure, to be sure! Peaches get they red cheeks better where we dwell than here among stone walls." And he pulled down his belt and went on quickly, as though he weened that he might have to rue his hasty words: "Margery is to be our welcome guest out in the forest; and if she should bring thee with her, child, thou'lt be welcome."

Nor need I here set down how gladly the bidding was received; and Ann's parents were more than content to let her go. Thenceforth had Cousin Maud, and our house maids, and Beata the tailor-wife, enough on their hands; for they deemed it a pleasure to take care to outfit Ann as well as me, since there were many noble guests at the forest lodge, especially about St. Hubert's day, when there was ever a grand hunt.

Dame Giovanna, Ann's mother, was in truth at all times choicely clad, and she ever kept Ann in more seemly and richer habit than others of her standing; yet she was greatly content with the summer holiday raiment which Cousin Maud had made for us. Likewise, for each of us, a green riding habit, fit for the forest, was made of good Florence cloth; and if ever two young maids rode out with glad and thankful hearts into the fair, sunny world, we were those maids when, on Saint Margaret's day in the morning—[The 13th July, old style.]—we bid adieu and, mounted on our saddles, followed Balzer, the old forester, whom my uncle had sent with four men at arms on horseback to attend us, and two beasts of burthen to carry Susan and the "woman's gear."

As we rode forth at this early hour, across the fields, and saw the lark mount singing, we likewise lifted up our voices, and did not stop singing till we entered the wood. Then in the dewy silence our minds were turned to devotion and a Sabbath mood, and we spoke not of what was in our minds; only once—and it seems as I could hear her now—these simple words rose from Ann's heart to her lips: "I am so thankful!"

And I was thankful at that hour, with my whole heart; and as the great hills of the Alps cover their heads with pure snow as they get nearer to heaven, so should every good man or woman, when in some happy hour he feels God's mercy nigh him, deck his heart with pure and joyful thanksgiving.

At last we drew up on a plot shut in by tall trees, in front of a bee-keeper's hut, and while we were there, refreshing on some new milk and the store Cousin Maud had put into our saddle bags, we heard the barking of hounds and a noise of hoofs, and ere long Uncle Conrad was giving us a welcome.

He was right glad to let us wait upon him and fell to with a will; but he made us set forth again sooner than was our pleasure, and as we fared farther the old forest rang with many a merry jest and much laughter. To Ann it seemed that my uncle was but now opening her eyes and ears to the mystery of the forest, which Gotz had shown me long years ago. How many a bird's pipe did he teach her to know which till now she had never marked! And each had its special significance, for my uncle named them all by their names and described them; whereas his son could copy them so as to deceive the ear, twittering, singing, whistling and calling, each after his kind. To the end that Ann and my uncle should learn to come together closely I put no word into his teaching.

Not till we came to the skirts of the clearing, where the forest lodge came in sight against the screen of trees, was my uncle silent; then, while he lifted me from the saddle, he asked me in a low tone if I had already warned Ann of my aunt's strange demeanor. This I could tell him I had indeed done; nevertheless I saw by his face that he was not easy till he could lead Ann to his wife, and had learnt that the maid had found such favor in her eyes as, in truth, nor he nor I were so bold as to hope. But with what sweet dignity did the clerk's daughter kiss the somewhat stern lady's hand—as I had bidden her, and how modestly, though with due self-respect, did she go through Dame Jacoba's inquisition. For my part I should have lost patience all too soon, if I had thus been questioned touching matters concerning myself alone; but Ann kept calm till the end, and at the same time she spoke as openly as though the inquisitor had been her own mother. This, in truth, somewhat moved me to fear; for, albeit I likewise cling to the truth, meseemed it showed it a lack of prudence and foresight to discover so freely and frankly all that was poor or lacking in her home; inasmuch as there was much, even there, which could not be better or more seemly in the richest man's dwelling. In truth, to my knowledge there was not the smallest thing in the little house by the river of which a virtuous damsel need feel ashamed. But at night, in our bed-chamber, Ann confessed to me that she had taken it as a favor of fortune that she should be allowed, at once, to lay bare to the great lady who had been so unwilling to open her doors to her, exactly what she was and to whom she belonged.

"To be deemed unworthy of heed by my lady hostess," said she, "would have been hard to bear; but whereas she truly cared to question me, a simple maid, and I have nothing hid, all is clear and plain betwixt us."

My aunt doubtless thought in like manner; for she was a truthful woman, and Ann's honest, firm, and withal gentle way had won her heart. And yet, since she was strait in her opinions, and must deem it unseemly in me and my kinsfolk to receive a maid of lower birth as one of ourselves, she stoutly avowed that Ann's worthy father, as being chief clerk in the Chancery, might claim to be accounted one of the Council. Never, as she said to my uncle, would she have suffered a workingman's daughter to cross her threshold, whereas she had a large place, not alone at her table but in her heart, for this gentle daughter of a worthy member of the worshipful Council.

And such speech was good to my ears and to my uncle Conrad's; but the best of all was that already, by the end of a week or two, Ann seemed likely to supplant me wholly in the love my aunt had erewhile shown to me; Ann thenceforth was diligent in waiting on the sick lady, and such loving duty won her more and more of my uncle's love, who found his weakly, suffering wife much on his hands, and that in the plainest sense of the words, since, whenever he might be at home, she would allow no other creature to lift her from one spot to another.

Now, whereas Uncle Conrad had taught Ann to mark the divers voices of the forest, so did she open my eyes to the many virtues of my aunt, which, heretofore, I had been wont to veil from my own sight out of wrath at her hardness to my cousin Gotz.

Ann, in her compassion and thankfulness, had truly learnt to love her, and she now led me to perceive that she was in many ways a right wise and good woman. Her low, sheltered couch in the peaceful chimney-corner was, as it were, the centre of a wide net, and she herself the spider-wife who had spun it, for in truth her good counsel stretched forth over the whole range of forest, and over all her husband's rough henchmen. She knew the name of every child in the furthest warders' huts, and never did she suffer one of the forest folks to die unholpen. She was, indeed, forced to see with other eyes and give with other hands than her own, and notwithstanding this she ever gave help where it was most needed, since she chose her messengers well and lent an ear to all who sought her.

She soon found work for us, making us do many a Samaritan-task; and many a time have we marvelled to mark the skill with which she wove her web, and the wisdom coupled with her open-handed bounty.

No one else could have found a place in the great books which she filled with her records; but to her they were so clear that the craft of the most cunning was put to shame when she looked into them. Never a soul, whether master or man, said her nay in the lightest thing, to my knowledge, and this was a plea for the one fault which had hitherto set me against her.

Everything here was new to Ann; and what could be more delightful, what could give me greater joy than to be able to show all that was noteworthy and pleasant, and to me well-known, to a well-beloved friend, and to tell her the use and end of each thing. In this two men were ever ready to help me: Uncle Conrad and the young Baron von Kalenbach, a Swabian who had come to be my uncle's disciple and to learn forestry.

This same young Baron was a slender stripling, well-grown and not ill-favored; but it seemed as though his lips were locked, and if a man was fain to hear the sound of his voice and get from him a "yea" or "nay" there was no way but by asking him a plain question. His eye, on the other hand, was full of speech, and by the time I had been no more than three weeks at the Lodge it told me, as often as it might, that he was deeply in love with me, nay, he told the reverend chaplain in so many words that his first desire was that he might take me home as his wife to Swabia, where he had rich estates.

Never would I have said him yea, albeit I liked him well; nor did I hide it from him; nay indeed, now and again I may have lent him courage, though truly with no evil intent, since I was not ill pleased with the tale his eyes told me. And I was but a young thing then, and wist not as yet that a maid who gives hope to a suitor though she has no mind to hear him, is guilty of a sin grievous enough to bring forth much sorrow and heart-ache. It was not till I had had a lesson which came upon me all too soon, that I took heed in such matters; and the time was at hand when men folks thought more about me than I deemed convenient.

As I have gone so far as to put this down on paper, I, an old woman now, will put aside bashfulness and freely confess that both Ann and I were at that time well-favored and good to look upon.

I was of the greater height and stouter build, while she was more slender and supple; and for gentle sweetness I have never seen her like. I was rose and white, and my golden hair was no whit less fine than Ursula Tetzel's; but whoso would care to know what we were to look upon in our youth, let him gaze on our portraits, before which each one of you has stood many a time. But I will leave speaking of such foolish things and come now to the point.

Though for most days common wear was good enough at the Forest Lodge, we sometimes had occasion to wear our bravery, for now and again we went forth to hunt with my uncle or with the Junker, on foot or on horseback, or hawking with a falcon on the wrist. There was no lack of these noble birds, and the bravest of them all, a falcon from Iceland beyond seas, had been brought thence by Seyfried Kubbeling of Brunswick. That same strange man, who was my right good friend, had ere now taught me to handle a falcon, and I could help my uncle to teach my friend the art.

I went out shooting but seldom, by reason that Ann loved it not ever after she had hit one of the best hounds in the pack with her arrow; and my uncle must have been well affected to her to forgive such a shot, inasmuch as the dogs were only less near his heart than his closest kin. They had to make up to him for much that he lacked, and when he stood in their midst he saw round him, yelping and barking on four legs, well nigh all that he had thought most noteworthy from his childhood up. They bore names, indeed, of no more than one or two syllables, but each had its sense. They were for the most part the beginning of some word which reminded him of a thing he cared to remember. First he had, in sport, named some of them after the metrical feet of Latin verse, which had been but ill friends of his in his school days, and in his kennel there was a Troch, Iamb, Spond and Dact, whose full names were Trochee, Iambus, Spondee and Dactyl. Now Spond was the greatest and heaviest of the wolfhounds; Anap, rightly Anapaest, was a slender and swift greyhound; and whereas he found this pastime of names good sport he carried it further. Thus it came to pass that the witless creatures who shared his loneliness were reminders of many pleasant things. One of a pair of fleet bloodhounds which were ever leashed together was named Nich, and the other Syn, in memory that he had been betrothed on the festival of Saint Nicodemus and wedded on Saint Synesius' day. A noble hound called Salve, or as we should say Welcome, spoke to him of the birth of his first born, and every dog in like manner had a name of some signification; thus Ann took it not at all amiss that he should call a fine young setter after her name. There had long been a Gred, short for Margaret.

Nevertheless we spent much more time in seeing the sick to whom my aunt sent us on her errands, than we did in shooting or heron-hawking.

She ever packed the little basket we were to carry with her own hands, and there was never a physic which she did not mingle, nor a garment she had not made choice of, nor a victual she had not judged fit for each one it was sent to.

Thus many a time our souls ached to see want and pain lying in darksome chambers on wretched straw, though we earned thanks and true joy when we saw that healing and ease followed in our steps. And whatever seemed to me the most praiseworthy grace in my Aunt Jacoba, was, that albeit she could never hear the hearty thanksgiving of those she had comforted and healed, she nevertheless, to the end of her days, ceased not from caring for the poor folks in the forest like a very mother.

My Ann was never made for such work, inasmuch as she could never endure to see blood or wounds; yet was it in this tending of the sick that I had reason to mark and understand how strong was the spirit of this frail, slender flower.

Since a certain army surgeon, by name Haberlein, had departed this life, there was no leech at the Forest lodge, but my aunt and the chaplain, a man of few words but well trained in good works and a right pious servant of the Lord, were disciples of Galen, and the leech from Nuremberg came forth once a week, on each Tuesday; and since the death of Doctor Paul Rieter, of whom I have made mention, it was his successor Master Ulsenius. His duty it was to attend on the sick mistress, and on any other sick folks if they needed it; and then it was our part to wait on the leech, and my aunt would diligently instruct us in the right way to use healing drugs, or bandages.

The first time we were bidden to a woman who gathered berries, who had been stung in the toe by an adder; and when I set to work to wash the wound, as my aunt had taught me, Ann turned as white as a linen cloth. And whereas I saw that she was nigh swooning I would not have her help; but she gave her help nevertheless, though she held her breath and half turned away her face. And thus she ever did with sores; but she ever paid the penalty of the violence she did herself. As it fell Master Ulsenius came to the Forest one day when my aunt's waiting-woman had fared forth on a pilgrimage to Vierzelmheiligen, and my uncle likewise being out of the way, the leech called us to him to lend him a helping hand. Then I came to know that a fall unawares with her horse had been the beginning of my aunt's long sickness. She had at that time done her backbone a mischief, and some few months later a wound had broken forth which was part of her hurt.

Now when all was made ready Aunt Jacoba begged of Ann that she should hold the sore closed while Master Ulsenius made the linen bands wet. I remembered my friend's weakness and came close to her, to take her place unmarked; but she whispered: "Nay, leave me," in a commanding voice, so that I saw full well she meant it in earnest, and withdrew without a word. And then I beheld a noble sight; for though she was pale she did as she was bidden, nor did she turn her eyes off the wound. But her bosom rose and fell fast, as if some danger threatened her, and her nostrils quivered, and I was minded to hold out my arms to save her from falling. But she stood firm till all was done, and none but I was aware of her having defied the base foe with such true valor.

Thenceforth she ever did me good service without shrinking; and whensoever thereafter I had some hateful duty to do which meseemed I might never bring myself to fulfil, I would remember Ann holding my aunt's wound. And out of all this grew the good saying, "They who will, can"—which the children are wont to call my motto.

CHAPTER VI

Summer wore away; the oats in the forest were garnered and the vintage had begun in the vine-lands. It was a right glorious sunny day; and if you ask me at which time of the year forest life is the sweeter, whether in Springtide or in Autumn, I could scarce say.

Aye, it is fair indeed in the woods when Spring comes gaily in. Spring is the very Saviour, as it were, of all the numberless folk, great and small, which grow green and blossom there, wherefore the forest holds festival for his birthday and cradle feast as is but fitting! The fir-tree lights up brighter tips to its boughs, as children do with tapers at Christmastide. Then comes the largesse. It lasts much more than one evening, and the gifts bestowed on all are without number, and bright and various indeed to behold. As a father's tinkling bell brings the children together, so the snowdrop bells call forth all the other flowers. First and foremost comes the primrose, and cowslips—Heaven's keys as we call them—open the gates to all the other children of the Spring. "Come forth, come forth!" the returning birds shout from out the bushes, and silver-grey catkins sprout on every twig. Beech leaves burst off their sharp, brown sheaths and open to the light, as soft as taffety and as green as emeralds.

The other trees follow the example, and so teach their boughs to make a leafy shade against the sun as it mounts higher. Every creature that loves its kind finds a voice under the blossoming May, and the dumb forest is full of the call and answer of thankful and gladsome loving things which have met together, and of sweet tunefulness and songs of bridal joy.

Round nests have come into being in a thousand secret places—in the tree-tops, in the thick greenwood of the bushes, in the reeds of the marsh; ere long young living things are twittering there, the father and mother-birds call each other, singing to be of good cheer, and taking joy in caring for their young. At that season of love, of growth, of unfolding life, meseems, as I walk through the woods, that the loving-kindness of the Most High is more than ever nigh unto me; for the forest is as a church, a glorious cathedral at highest festival, all filled with light and song, and decked in every nook and corner with gay fresh flowers and leafy garlands.

Then all is suddenly hushed. It is summer.

But in Autumn the forest is a banqueting-hall where men must say farewell, but with good cheer, in hope of a happy meeting. All that has lived is hasting to the grave. Nevertheless on some fair days everything wears as it were the face of a friend who holds forth a hand at parting. The wide vaults of the woods are finely bedecked with red and yellow splendor, and albeit the voices of birds are few, albeit the cry of the jay, and the song of the nightingale, and the pipe of the bull-finch must be mute, the greenwood is not more dumb than in the Spring; the hunter's horn rings through the trees and away far over their tops, with the baying of the hounds, the clapping of the drivers, and the huntsmen shouting the view halloo. Every bright, strong, healthful child of man, then feels himself lord of all that creeps or flies, and his soul is ready to soar from his breast. How pure is the air, how spicy is the scent from the fallen leaves on such an autumn day! In Spring, truly, white and rose-red, blue and yellow chequer the green turf; but now gold and crimson are bright in the tree tops, and on the service trees. The distance is clearer than before, and fine silver threads wave in the air as if to catch us, and keep us in the woods whose beauty is so fast fading.

The sunny autumn air was right full of these threads when on St. Maurice's day—[September 22nd]—Ann and I went forth to our duty of fetching in the birds which had been caught in the springes set for them.

When birds are early to flock and flee
Hard and cold will winter be,

saith the woodman's saw; and they had gathered early this year—thrushes and field-fares; many a time the take was so plentiful that our little wallets could scarce hold them, and among them it was a pity to see many a merry, tuneful red-breast.

The springes were set at short spaces apart on either side of two forest paths. I went down one and Ann down the other. They met again nigh to the road leading to the town. Balzer set the snares, and we prided ourselves on which should carry home the greater booty; and when we had done our task as we sat on a grassy seat which the Junker had made for me, we told the tale of birds and thought it right good sport. Nor did we need a squire, inasmuch as Spond, the great hound, would ever follow us.

This day I was certain I had the greater number of birds in my wallet, and I walked in good heart toward the end of the path.

Methought already I had heard the noise of hoofs on the highway, and now the hound sniffed the air, so, being inquisitive, I moved my feet somewhat faster till I caught sight of a horseman, who sprang from his saddle, and leaving his steed, hurried toward the clearing whither Ann must presently come from her side. Thereupon I forced my way through the underwood which hindered me from seeing, and when I presently saw Ann coming and had opened my lips to call, something, meseemed, took me by the throat, and I was fain to stand still as though I had taken root there, and could only lend eye and ear, gasping for breath, to what was doing yonder by the highroad. And verily I knew not whether to rejoice from the bottom of my heart, or to lament and be wroth, and fly forth to put an end to it all.

Nevertheless I stirred not a limb, and my tongue was spell-bound. The heart in my bosom and the veins in my head beat as though hammers were smiting within; mine eyes were dazed, albeit they could see as well as ever they did, and I espied first, on one side of the clearing, the horseman, who was none other than Herdegen, my well-beloved elder brother, and on the other side thereof Ann carrying her wallet in her hand, and numbering the birds she had taken from the snares, with a contented smile.

But ere I had time to hail the returned traveller a voice rang through the wood—it was my brother's voice, and yet, meseemed it was not; it spoke but one word "Ann!" And in the long drawn cry there was a ring of heart's delight and lovesick longing such as I had never heard save from the nightingale lover when in the still May nights he courts his beloved. This cry pierced to my heart, even mine; and it brought the color to Ann's face, which had long ceased to be pale. Like a doe which comes forth from a thicket and finds her young grazing in the glade, she lifted her head and looked with brightest eyes away to the high road whence the call had come. Then, though they were yet far asunder, his eyes met hers, and hers met his, and they uplifted their arms, as though some invisible power had moved them both, and flew to meet each other. There was no doubt nor pause; and I plainly perceived that they were borne along as flowers are in a raging torrent; albeit she, or ever she reached him; was overcome by maiden shamefacedness, and her arms fell and her head was bent. But the little bird had ventured too far into the springe, and the fowler was not the man to let it escape; before Ann could foresee such a deed he had both his arms round her, and she did not hinder him, nay, for she could not. So she clung to him and let him lift up her head and kiss her eyes and then her mouth, and that not once, no, but many a time and again, and so long that I, a sixteen-year-old maid, was in truth affrighted.

There stood I; my knees quaked, and I weened that this which was doing was a thing that beseemed not a pious maid, and that must ill-please the heart of a virtuous daughter's mother; yea, it was a grief to me that it should have been done, and that I knew that of my Ann which she would fain hide from the light. Nevertheless I could not but find a joy in it, and meseemed it was a cruel act to fetch her away so soon from such sweet bliss.

When presently their lips were free, and at last he spoke a few words to her, methought it was now time for me to greet my brother. I called up all my strength and while I walked toward them my spirit's sense came back to me, for indeed it had altogether left me, and a voice within asked: "What shall come of this?"

He put forth his arm to hold her to him again, and forasmuch as I was abashed to think of coming in to their secret, before I stepped forth, from the thicket, I hailed Herdegen by name. And soon I was in his arms; but although that he kissed me lovingly, meseemed that something strange was on his lips which pleased me not, and I yet remember that I put my kerchief to my mouth to wipe that from it.

And then we walked homeward. Herdegen led his horse by the bridle, and Ann went between him and me and gazed up into his face with shining eyes, for in these two years he had grown in stature and in manhood. She listened wide-eared to all his tidings, but once, when his horse grew restive, so that he turned away from us women-kind she kissed my cheek, but in great haste, as though she would not have him see it. We were gladly welcomed at the forest lodge. How truly my uncle and aunt rejoiced at my brother's home-coming could be seen in their eyes, though the mother, who had banished her own son, was cut to the heart by the sight of such another well-grown youth.

The evening before guests had come to the lodge his excellency the Lord Justice Wigelois von Wolfstein, and Master Besserer of Ulm. Now we had to make ready in all haste for dinner, and never had Ann made such careful and diligent use of our little mirror. As it fell, we could be alone together for a few minutes only, and had no chance of speaking to each other privily. This was likewise the case at table, and then, as my uncle had prepared for a hunt in the afternoon, in honor of his guests, and as the supper afterwards lasted until midnight, the not over-strong thread of my good patience was not seldom in danger of giving way. But many things were going forward which gave me matter for thought, and increased the distress I already felt. Ann threw herself into the sport with all her heart, and on the way back fell behind with Herdegen in such wise that they did not reach home till long after the door closed on the last of us.

At supper she nodded to me many times with much contentment; except for that I might have been buried for aught she noted, for she hearkened only to Herdegen's tales as though they were a revelation from above. For his part, he now and again stole a hasty, fiery glance at her; otherwise he of set purpose made a show of having little to do with her. He often lay back as though he were weary; and yet, when their Excellencies questioned him of any matter, he was ever ready with a swift and discreet answer. He had lost nothing of his wonderfully clear and shrewd wit; nevertheless, I was not so much at my ease with him as of old time. When my uncle said in jest that the wise owl from Padua seemed to wear a motley of gay feathers, his intent was plain as soon as one looked at my brother; and in the fine clothes he had chosen to wear at supper the noble lad was less to my mind than in the hunting weed which he had journeyed in, inasmuch as the too great length of the sleeves of his mantle was in his way when eating, and the over-long points to his shoes hindered him in walking.

When, presently, my Aunt Jacoba left the hall that the men might the better enjoy the heady wine and freer speech, we maidens were bound to follow her duteously; but Herdegen signed to me to come apart with him, and now I hoped he would open his heart to me and treat me as he had been wont, as my true and dear brother, whose heart had ever been on the tip of his tongue. Far from it; he spoke nought but flattery, as "how fair I had grown," and then desired news of Cousin Maud, and Kunz, and our grand-uncle, and at last of Ursula Tetzel, which made me wroth.

I answered him shortly, and asked him whether he had no more than that to say to me. He gazed down at the ground and said to himself: "To be sure, to be sure." But in a minute he went back to his first manner, and when I bid him good-night in anger he put his arm round me and turned me about as if to dance.

I got myself free and went away, up to our chamber, hanging my head. There I found my old Sue, taking off Ann's fine gown; and whereas Ann nodded to me right sweetly and, as I thought, with a secret air, I guessed that it was the waiting-woman who stayed her speech and I sent my nurse away.

Now I should sooner have looked for the skies to fall than for Ann, my heart's closest friend, to keep the secret of what had befallen that very morning; and yet she kept silence.

We were commonly wont to chirp like a pair of crickets while we braided our hair and got into our beds; but this night there was not a sound in the chamber. Commonly we laid us down with a simple "Good night, Margery," "Sleep well, Ann," after we had said our prayers before the image of the Blessed Virgin; but this night my friend held me close in her arms, and as I was about to get into bed she ran to me again and kissed me with much warmth. Whether I was so loving to her I cannot, at this day, tell; but I remember well that I remained dumb, and my heart seemed to ache with sorrow and pain. I thought myself defrauded, and my true love scorned. Was it possible? Did my Ann trust me no longer, or had she never trusted me?

Nay more. Was she at all such as I had believed, if she could carry on an underhand and forbidden love-making with Herdegen behind my back; and this, Merciful Virgin, peradventure, for years past!

The taper had burnt out. We lay side by side striving to sleep, while distress of mind and a wounded heart brought the tears into my eyes.

Then I heard a strange noise from her bed, and was aware that Ann likewise was weeping, more bitterly and deeply every minute. This pierced the very depths of my soul. Yet I tried to harden my heart till I heard her voice saying: "Margery!"

That was an end of our silence, and I answered: "Ann."

Then she sobbed out: "As we came home from the hunt he made me promise never to reveal it, but it is bursting my heart. Oh! Margery, Margery, I ought to hide and bury it in my soul; so he bid me, and nevertheless...."

I sat up on the pillow as if new life had come to me, and cried: "Oh Ann, you can tell me nothing that I know not already, for I saw him dismount and how he embraced you."

And then, before I was aware of her, she leaped up and was kneeling on her knees by the head of my bed, and her lips were kissing mine, and her cheeks were against my face and her tears running down my cheeks and neck and bosom while she confessed all. In our peaceful little chamber there was a wild outpouring of vows of love and words of fear, of plans for the future, and long tales of how it all had come to pass.

I had with mine own eyes seen it in the bud and, unwittingly indeed, had fostered its growth. How then could I be dismayed when now I beheld the flower?

Their meeting this morning had been as the striking of flint and steel, and if sparks had come of it how could they help it? And I took Ann's word when she said that she would have flown into the arms of her beloved, if father and mother and a hundred more had been standing round to warn her.

All she said that night was full of perfect and joyful assurance, and it took hold of my young soul; and albeit I could not blind myself, but saw that great and sore hindrances stood in the way of my brother's choice, I vowed to myself that I would smooth their path so far as in me lay.

All was now forgotten that I had taken amiss that evening in the returned wanderer; and when I gave Ann a last kiss that night how well I loved her again!

CHAPTER VII

The cocks had already crowed before I fell asleep, and when I awoke Ann was sitting in front of the mirror, plaiting her hair. I knew full well what had led her to quit her bed so early, and, as she met her lover at breakfast, her form and face meseemed had gained in beauty, so that I could not take my eyes off from her. My aunt and his Excellency marked the wonderful change which had taken effect in her that night, and the gentleman thenceforth waited closely on Ann and sued for her favor like a young man, in spite of his grey hair, while worthy Master Besserer followed his ensample.

At the first favorable chance I drew Herdegen apart. Ann had already told him that I had been witness to their first meeting again; this indeed pleased him ill, and when I asked him as to how he purposed to demean himself henceforth towards his betrothed, he answered that matters had not gone so far with them; and that until he had taken his Doctor's hood we must keep the secret I had by chance discovered closely hidden from all the good people of Nuremberg; that much water would flow into the sea or ere he could bid me wag my tongue, if our grand-uncle should continue to bear the weight of his years so bravely. For the present he was one of the happiest of men on earth, and if I loved him I must help him to enjoy his heart's desire, and often see the lovely violet which had bloomed so sweetly for him here in the deep heart of the forest.

His bright young spirit smiled upon my soul once more as it had done long ago. Only his unloving mention of our grand-uncle, who had been as a second father to him, struck to my heart, and this I said to him; adding likewise, that it must be a point of honor with him to give and take rings with Ann, even though it should be in secret.

This he was ready and glad to do; I gave him the gold ring, with a hearty good will, which Cousin Maud had given me for my confirmation, and he put it on his sweetheart's finger that very day, albeit her silver ring was too small for his little finger. So he bid her wear it, and solemnly promised to keep his troth, even without a ring, till the next home-coming; and Ann put her trust in her lover as surely as in rock and iron.

Many were the guests who came to the forest that fair autumn tide; there was no end of hunting and sport of all kinds, and Ann was ever ready and well content to share her lover's fearless delight in the chase; when she came home from the forest the joy of her heart shone more clearly than ever in her eyes; and seeing her then and thus, no man could doubt that she was at the crown and top of human happiness. Albeit, up on that height meseemed a keen wind was blowing, which she did battle with so hardly that through many a still night I could hear her sighs. Withal she showed a strange selfishness such as I had never before marked in her, which, however, only concerned her lover, with constant unrest when apart from others whom she loved; and all this grieved me, though indeed I could not remedy it.

Strangest of all, as it seemed to me, was it that these twain who erewhile had never spent an hour together without singing, would now pass day after day without a song. But then I remembered how that the maiden nightingale likewise pipes her sweetest only so long as her bosom is full of pining love; but so soon as she has given her heart wholly to her mate, her song grows shorter and less tender.

Not that this pair had as yet gone so far as this; and once, when I gave them warning that they should not forget how to sing, they marvelled at their own neglect, and as thereupon they began to sing it sounded sweeter and stronger than in former days.

Among the youths who at that time enjoyed the hospitality of the Waldstromers, Herdegen's friend, Franz von Welemisl, held the foremost place. He was the son of a Bohemian baron, and his mother, who was dead, had been of one of the noblest families of Hungary. And whereas his name was somewhat hard to the German tongue, we one and all called him simply Ritter Franz or Sir Franz. He was a well made and well favored youth in face and limb, who had found such pleasure in my brother's company at Erfurt that he had gone with him to Padua. His father's sudden death had taken him home from college sooner than Herdegen, and he was now in mourning weed. He ever held his head a little bowed, and whereas Herdegen, with his brave, splendid manners and his long golden locks, put some folks in mind of the sun, a poet might have likened his friend to the moon, inasmuch as he had the same gentle mien and pale countenance, which seemed all the more colorless for his thick, sheeny black hair which framed it, with out a wave or a curl. His voice had a sorrowful note, and it went to my heart to see how loving was his devotion to my brother. He, for his part, was well pleased to find in the young knight the companionship he had erewhile had in the pueri.

After the young Bohemian's father had departed this life, the Emperor himself had dubbed his sorrowing son Knight, and nevertheless he was devoid alike of pride and scornfulness. When, with his sad black eyes, he looked into mine, humbly and as though craving comfort, I might easily have lulled my soul with the glad thought that I likewise had opened the door to Love; but then I cared not if I saw him, and I thought of him but coldly, and this gave the lie to such hopes; what I felt was no more than the compassion due to a young man who was alone in the world, without parents or brethren or near kin.

One morning I went to seek Herdegen in the armory and there found him stripped of his jerkin, with sleeves turned up; and with him was the Bohemian, striving with an iron file to remove from my brother's arm a gold bracelet which was not merely fastened but soldered round his arm. So soon as he saw that I had at once descried the band, though he attempted to hide it with his sleeve, he sought to put off my questioning, at first with a jest and then with wrathful impatience flung on his jerkin and turned his back on me. Forthwith I examined Ritter Franz, and he was led to confess to me that a fair Italian Marchesa had prevailed on Herdegen to have this armlet riveted on to his arm in token of his ever true service.

On learning this I was moved to great dread both for my brother's sake and for Ann's; and when I presently upbraided him for his breach of faith he threw his arms round me with his wonted outrageous humor and boisterous spirit, and said: What more would I have, since that I had seen with my own eyes that he was trying to be quit of that bond? To get at the Marchesa he would need to cross a score of rivers and streams; and even in our virtuous town of Nuremberg it was the rule that a man might be on with a new love when he had left the third bridge behind him.

I liked not this fashion of speech, and when he saw that I was ill-pleased and grieved, instead of falling in with his merry mood, he took up a more earnest vein and said: "Never mind, Margery. Only one tall tree of love grows in my breast, and the name of it is Ann; the little flowers that may have come up round it when I was far away have but a short and starved life, and in no case can they do the great tree a mischief."

Then with all my heart I besought him that, as he had now bound up the life and happiness of the sweetest and most loving maid on earth with his own, he would ever keep his faith and be to her a true man. Seeing, however, that he was but little moved by this counsel, the hot blood of the Schoppers mounted to my head and thereupon I railed at his sayings and doings as sinful and cruel, and he likewise flared out and bid me beware how I spoke ill of my own father; for that like as he, Herdegen, had carried the image of Ann in his heart, so had father carried that of our dear mother beyond the Alps, and nevertheless at Padua he had played the lute under the balcony of many a blackeyed dame, and won the name of "the Singer" there. A living fire, quoth he, waxed not the colder because more than one warmed herself thereat; all the matter was only to keep the place of honor for the right owner, and of that Ann was ever certain.

Sir Franz was witness to these words, and when presently Herdegen had quitted the room, he strove to appease and to comfort me, saying that his greatly gifted friend, who was full of every great and good quality, had but this one weakness: namely, that he could not make a manful stand against the temptations that came of his beauty and his gifts. He, Franz himself was of different mould.

And he went on to confess that he loved me, and that, if I would but consent to be his, he would ever cherish and serve me, with more humility and faithfulness even than his well-beloved Lord and King, who had dubbed him knight while he was yet so young.

And his speech sounded so warm and true, so full of deep and tender desires, that at any other time I might have yielded. But at that hour I was minded to trust no man; for, if Herdegen's love were not the truth, whereas it had grown up with him and was given to one above me in so many ways, what man's mind could I dare to build on? Yea, and I was too full of care for the happiness of my brother and of my friend to be ready to think of my own; so I could only speak him fair, but say him nay. Hardly had I said the words when a strange change came over him; his calm, sad face suddenly put on a furious aspect, and in his eyes, which hitherto had ever been gentle, there was a fire which affrighted me. Nay and even his voice, as he spoke, had a sharp ring in it, as though the bells had cracked which erewhile had tolled so sweet a peal. And all he had to say was a furious charge against me who had, said he, led him on by eye and speech, only to play a cruel trick upon him, with words of dreadful purpose against the silent knave who had come between him and me to defraud him; and by this he meant the Swabian, Junker von Kalenbach.

I was about to upbraid him for his rude and discourteous manners when we heard, outside, a loud outcry, and Ann ran in to fetch me. All in the Lodge who had legs came running together; all the hounds barked and howled as though the Wild Huntsman were riding by, and mingling therewith lo! a strange, outlandish piping and drumming.

A bear-leader, such as I had before now seen at the town-fair, had made his way to the Lodge, and the swarthy master, with his two companions, as it might be his brothers, were like all the men of their tribe. A thick growth of hair covered the mouth below an eaglenose, and on their shaggy heads they wore soft red bonnets. One was followed by a tall camel, slowly marching along with an ape perched on his hump; the other led a brown bear with a muzzle on his snout.

The master's wife, and a dark-faced young wench, were walking by the side of a little wagon having two wheels, to which an over-worked mule was harnessed. A youth, of may-be twelve years of age, blew upon a pipe for the bear to dance, and inasmuch as he had no clothes but a ragged little coat, and a sharp east wind was blowing, he quaked with cold and shivered as he piped. Notwithstanding he was a fine lad, well-grown, and with a countenance of outlandish but well nigh perfect beauty. He had come, for certain, from some distant land; yet was he not of the same race as the others.

When we had seen enough of the show, my uncle commanded that meat should be brought for the wanderers; and when pease-pottage and other messes had been given them, they fetched, from under the wagon-tilt, a swarthy babe, which, meseemed was a sweet little maid albeit she was so dark-colored.

Ann and I gazed at these folks while they ate, and it seemed strange to us to see that the well-favored lad put away from him with horror the bacon which the old bear-leader set before him; and for this the man dealt him a rude blow.

After their meal the master went on his way; and when we likewise had eaten our dinner, my dear godfather and uncle, Christian Pfinzing, came from the town, bringing a troop of mercenaries to the camp where they were to be trained that they might fight against the Hussites. He, like the other guests, made friends with the strangers, and in his merry fashion he bid the older bear leader tell our fortunes by our hands, while the young ones should dance.

The man then read the future for each of us; my fortune was sheer folly, whereof no single word ever came true. He promised my brother a Count's coronet and a wife from a race of princes; and when Ann heard it, and held up her finger at Herdegen for shame, he whispered in her ear that she was of the race of the Sovereign Queen of all queens—of Venus, ruler of the universe. All this she heard gladly; yet could no one persuade her to let her hand be read.

At last it was the woman's turn to dance; before she began she had smoothed her hair and tied it with small gold pieces; and indeed she was a well grown maid and slender, well-favored in face and shape, with a right devilish flame in her black eyes. It was a strange but truly a pleasing thing to see her; first she laid a dozen of eggs in a circle on the grass, and then she beat her tambourine to the piping of the lad and the drumming of one of the men who had remained with her, and rattled it over her head with wanton lightness till the bells in the hoop rang out, while she turned and bent her supple body in a mad, swift whirl, bowing and rising again. Her falcon eyes never gazed at the ground, but were ever fixed upwards or on the bystanders, and nevertheless her slender bare feet never went nigh the eggs in the wildest spinning of her dance.

The gentlemen, and we likewise, clapped our hands; then, while she stayed to take breath, she snatched Herdegen's hat from his head — and she had long had her eye on him — and gathered all the eggs into it with much bowing and bending to the measure of the music. When she had put all the eggs into the hat she offered it to my brother kneeling on one knee, and she touched the rim of her tambourine with her lips. The froward fellow put his fingers to his lips, as the little children do to blow a kiss, and when his eyes fell on that wench's, meseemed that this was not the first time they had met.

It was now a warm and windless autumn day, and after dinner my aunt was carried out into the courtyard. When the dancing was at an end, she, as was her wont, questioned the men and the elder woman as to all she desired to know; and, learning from them that the men were likewise tinkers, she bid Ann hie to the kitchen and command that the house-keeper should bring together all broken pots and pans. But now, near by the wagon, was a noise heard of furious barking, and the pitiful cry of a child.

The Junker, who had set forth early in the day to scour the woods, had but now come home; the hounds with him had scented strangers, and had rushed on the brown babe, which was playing in the sand behind the wagon, making cakes and pasties. The dogs were indeed called off in all haste, but one of them, a spiteful badger-hound, had bitten deep into the little one's shoulder.

I ran forthwith to the spot, and picked up the babe in my arms, seeing its red blood flow; but the elder woman rushed at me, beside her wits with rage, to snatch it from me; and whereas she was doubtless its mother or grand-dame, I might have yielded up the child, but that Ritter Franz came to me in haste to bid me, from my Aunt Jacoba, carry it to her.

Who better than she knew the whole art and secret of healing the wounds of a hound's making? And so I told the old dame, to comfort her, albeit she struggled furiously to get the babe from me. Nay and she might have done so if the little thing had not clung round my neck with its right arm that had no hurt, as lovingly as though it had been mine own and no kin to the shrieking old woman.

But ere long a clear and strange light was cast on the matter; for when we had loosened the child's little shirt, and my aunt had duly washed the blood from the wounds, under the dark hue of its skin behold it was tender white, and so it was plain that here was a stolen child, needing to be rescued.

Then the house-stewardess, the widow of a forester whose husband had been slain by poachers, and who labored bravely to bring up her five orphan children, with my aunt's help—this woman, I say, now remembered that when she had made her pilgrimage, but lately, to Vierzehnheiligen, the Knight von Hirschhorn, treasurer to the Lord Bishop of Bamberg at Schesslitz, not far from the place of pilgrimage, had lost a babe, stolen away by vagabond knaves. Then Aunt Jacoba bethought herself that restitution and benevolence might be made one; and, quoth she, this matter might greatly profit the housekeeper and her little ones, inasmuch as that the sorrowing father had promised a ransom of thirty Hungarian ducats to him who should bring back his little daughter living; and forthwith the whole tribe of the bear-leaders were to be bound. The old beldame gave our men a hard job, for she tried to make off to the forest, and called aloud: "Hind—Hind!" which was the young wench's name, with outlandish words which doubtless were to warn her to flee; but the serving men gained their end and made the wild hag fast.

Ann was pale and in pain with her head aching, but she helped my aunt to tend the child; and I was glad, inasmuch as I conceived that I knew where to find Herdegen and the young dancing wench, and I cared only to save his poor betrayed sweetheart from shame and sorrow. I crept away, unmarked, through the garden of herbs behind the lodge, to a moss but which my banished cousin had built up for me, in a covert spot between two mighty beech-trees, while I was yet but a school maid.

Verily my imagination was not belied, for whereas I passed round the pine-grove I heard my brother cry out: "Ah—wild cat!" and the hussy's loathsome laugh. And thereupon they both came forth, only in the doorway he held her back to kiss her. At this she showed her white teeth, and meseemed she would fain bite him; she thrust him away and laughed as she said: "To-night; not too much at once." Howbeit he snatched her to him, and thereupon I called him by name and went forward.

He let her go soon enough then, but he stamped with his foot for sheer rage. This, indeed, moved me not; with a calm demeanor I bid the wench follow me, and to that faithless knave I cried: "Fie!" in a tone of scorn which must have made his ears burn a good while. Before we entered the garden I bid him go round about the house and come upon the others from the right hand; she was to come with me and round by the left side.

I now saw that there were shreds of moss and dry leaves in the young woman's hair and bid her brush them out. This she did with a mocking smile, and said in scorn: "Your lover?"

"Nay," said I, "far from it. But yet one whom I would fain shield from evil." She shrugged her shoulders; I only said: "Come on."

As we went round to the front of the house the elder woman was being led away with her hands bound, and no sooner did the young one descry her than she picked up her skirts and with one wild rush tried to be off and away. I called Spond, my trusty guard, and bid him stay her; and the noble hound dogged her steps till the men could catch her and lead her to my aunt. The lady questioned her closely, deeming that so young and comely a creature might be less stubborn that the old hag who had grown grey in sins; but Hind stood dumb and made as though she knew not our language. As to Herdegen, he meanwhile had greeted Ann with great courtesy; nevertheless he had kept close to the dancing wench, and took upon himself to tie her bonds and lead her to the dungeon cell. He sped well, inasmuch as he got away with her alone, as he desired; for Sir Franz delayed me again, and such a suit as he now pleaded can but seldom have found a match, for I was bent only on following my brother, to rescue him from the vagabond woman's snares; and while the knight held me fast by the hand, and swore he loved me, I was only striving to be free, and gazing after Herdegen and Hind, heeding him not. At length he hurt my hand, which I could not get away from him; and whereas he was beginning to look wildly and to seem crazed, I besought him to leave me free henceforth and try his fortune elsewhere. But still he would never have set me free so hastily if an evil star had not brought the Swabian Junker to the spot.

Sir Franz, without a word of greeting or warning, went up to him and upbraided him for having caused a mischief to a helpless babe through his heedless conduct. But if Sir Franz knew not already that he, to whom he spoke as roughly as though he were a froward serving man, was in truth son and heir of a right noble house, he learnt it now. His last words were: "And for the future have your savage hounds in better governance!" Whereupon the other coolly answered: "And you, your tongue."

On this the other shrugged his shoulders and replied in scorn that to be sure his tongue was for use and not for silence like some folks'. And I marvelled where the Swabian, who was so slow of speech, found the words for retort and answer, till at length it was too much for him and he laid his hand on his hanger as a second and a sharper tongue.

CHAPTER VIII

The dancing-wench was locked into the cell with the rest of the wanderers, and as I looked in through the window at the fine young creature, squatting in a corner, I had pity on her, and for my part I would fain have sent her forth and away never to see her more.

I could nowhere find Herdegen; I had no mind for Uncle Christian's jests; and when, at last, I betook me to my own chamber, meseemed that some horrible doom was in the air, from which there was no escape. And matters were no better when Ann, who of late had been free from her bad headache, came up to bed, to hide her increasing pain among the pillows. So I sat dumb and thoughtful by her side, till Aunt Jacoba sent for me to lay cold water on the arm of the little kidnapped maid. The child had been well washed, and lay clean and fresh between the sheets, and the swarthy dirty little changeling was now a sweet, fair-haired darling. I tended it gladly; all the more when I thought of the joy it would bring to its father and mother; notwithstanding the evil nightmare would not be cast off, not even when the clatter of wine cups and Uncle Christian's big laugh fell on my ear.

Seldom had I so keenly missed Herdegen's mirthful voice. The housekeeper told me that he had gone on horseback into the town at about the hour of Ave Maria. My grand-uncle had bidden him to go to him. The vagabond knaves had already been put to the torture in my brother's presence, but they had confessed nothing of their guilt; inasmuch, indeed, as in our dungeon there were none other instruments of torture than the rack, the thumbscrew, and scourges needful for the Bamberg torture, and a Pomeranian cap, made to crush the head somewhat; but in Nuremberg there was a store, less mild and of more active effect.

The air was hot and heavy, the sun had set behind black clouds, yellow and dim, like a blind eye. A strange languor came over me, though I was wont to be so brisk, and with it a long train of dismal and hideous images. First I saw the Junker and Sir Franz, who had fallen out about me, a foolish maid; then it was my Ann, pining with grief, paler than ever with a nun's veil on her; or standing by the Pegnitz, on the very spot where, erewhile, in the sweet Springtide, a forsaken maid had cast herself in.

The first lightning rent the sky and the storm came up in haste, bursting above our heads, and as the thunder roared closer and closer after the flash I was more and more frightened. Moreover the sick child wept piteously and waxed restless with fever and pain. By this time all was still in the dining-hall; but when my aunt bid me let the housekeeper take my place by the little one's bed and go to my rest, I would not; for indeed I could in no wise have slept.

They let me have my way, and soon after midnight, seized with fresh dread anent Herdegen, I was at the open window to let the rough wind fan my hot head, when suddenly the hounds set up a furious barking, as though the Forest lodge were beset on all sides by robbers. And at the same time I saw, by the glare of the lightning, that the old lime-tree in the midst of my aunt's herb garden was lying on the earth. This cut me to the heart, inasmuch as this tree was dear to my uncle, having been planted by his grandfather; and there was never a spot where his ailing wife was so fain to be in the hot summer days as under its shadow. Aye, and all my young life's happiness, meseemed, was like that tree-torn up by the roots, and I gazed spellbound at the blasted lime-tree till I was affrighted by a new horror; on the furthest rim of the sky, on the side where the town lay, I beheld a line of light which waxed broader and brighter till it was rose and blood-red.

A wild uproar came up from the kennels and foresters' huts, and I heard a medley of many voices; and whereas the distant flare began to soar more brightly heavenward I believed those who were saying below that all Nuremberg was in flames.

Even Aunt Jacoba had quitted her bed, and every soul under that roof looked forth at the fire and gave an opinion as to whether it were waxing or waning. And, thanks be to the Blessed Virgin, the latter were in the right; some few granaries, or stores of goods it might be, had been burnt out, and I, among other fainting hearts, was beginning to breathe more easily, when the watchman's cry was heard once more and what next befell showed that my fears had not been groundless.

It was the vigil of Saint Simon and Saint Jude's day—[October 28th]—in the year of our Lord 1420, and never shall I forget it. The great things which befell that night are they not written in the Chronicles of the town, and still fresh in many minds? but peradventure in none are they more deeply printed than in mine; and while I move my pen I can, as it were, see the great hall of the hunting lodge with my very eyes. Many folks are astir, and all in scant attire and full of eager thirst for tidings. The alarm of fire has brought them from their pillows in all haste, and they press close and gaze through the door, which stands wide open, at the light spot in the sky. Not one dares go forth in the wild wind, and many a one draws his garment or cloak or coverlet closer round him; the gale sweeps in with such fury that the pitch torches against the wall are well nigh blown out, and the red and yellow glare casts a weird light in the hall.

Then the watchman's call is silent, and the growling and wailing of the forest folk comes nigher and nigher.

Presently a man totters across the threshold, upheld with sore difficulty by the gate-keeper Endres inasmuch as his own knees quake; and he who comes home thus, as he might be drunken or grievously hurt, is none other than my brother Herdegen. The torchlight falls on his face, and whereas my eyes descry him I cry aloud, and my soul has no thought of him but sheer pity and true love.

I haste to take Endres' place while Eppelein, his faithful serving-man, whom he had not taken with him as is his wont, holds him up on the other hand.

But touch him where we may he feels a hurt; and while Uncle Conrad and the rest press him with questions, he can only point to his head and lips, which are too weak for thinking or speaking.

Alas! that poor fellow, meseems, bears but little likeness to my noble Herdegen, on whose arm the Italian Marchesa riveted her golden fetter. His face is swollen and bloodshot in one part, and cruelly torn in others. Where are the lovelocks that graced him so well? His left arm is helpless, his rich attire hangs about him in rags. He might be a battered, wretched beggar picked up in the high-road, and I rejoice truly to think that Ann is within the shelter of her bed and escapes the sight.

My aunt, who had long ere this been carried down to the hall, felt all his limbs and joints, and found that no bones were broken, while my uncle questioned him; and he told us in broken words that his horse had taken fright in the forest at a flash of lightning, had thrown him, and then dragged him through the brushwood; it was his man's nag which, as it fell, he had taken out that evening, and it was roaming now about the woods.

He had scarce ended his tale, when one of the warders of the dungeon and the gate-keeper rushed in with the tidings that one of the prisoners, and that the young wench, had escaped, although the door of the keep was locked and the window barred. She was clearly a witch, and only one thing was possible; namely that she had flown through the barred window, after the manner of witches on a broomstick, or in the shape of a bird, a bat, or an owl; nay, this was as good as certain, inasmuch as that the watchman had seen a wraith in the woods at about the hour of midnight, and the same face had appeared to the kennel-keeper. Both swore they had crossed themselves thereat, and said many paternosters. The other captives bore witness to the same, declaring that the wench had never been one of them, but had joined herself unawares to their company last midsummer eve, without saying whence, or whither she would go. She had flown off some hours since in the form of a monstrous vampire, but had fallen upon them first with tooth and nail; and albeit they were an evil-disposed crew their tale seemed truthful, whereas they were covered with many scratches which were not caused by the torture.

At these tidings my brother lost all heart, and fell back in the armchair as pale as ashes. I was presently left alone with him; but he answered nothing to my questions, and meseemed he slept. As day dawned I was chilled with the cold, so, inasmuch I could do nothing to help him, I went down stairs. There I found our gentlemen taking leave, for one was off to the city to make inquisition as to the fire, and the other would fain seek his warm bed.

Hot elecampane wine had been served to give them comfort, when again we heard horses' hoofs and the watchman's call. Everybody came out in haste, only Uncle Christian Pfinzing did not move, for, so long as the wine jug was not empty, it would have needed more than this to stir him. He was a mighty fat man, with a short brick-red neck, cropped grey hair, and a round, well-favored countenance, with shrewd little eyes which stood out from his head.

We young Schoppers loved this jolly, warm-hearted uncle, who was childless, with all our hearts; but I clung to him most of all, since he was my dear godfather; likewise had he for many years chown an especial and truly fatherly care for Ann.

Well, Uncle Christian had peacefully gone on drinking the fiery liquor, waiting for the others; but when they came to tell him what tidings the horseman had brought, the cup fell from his hand, clattering down on the paved floor and spilling the wine; and at the same time his kind, faithful head dropped to one side, and for a few minutes his senses had left him. Albeit we were able ere long to bring him back to life again, I found, to my great distress, that his tongue seemed to have waxed heavy. Howbeit, by the help of the Blessed Virgin, he afterwards was so far recovered that when he sat over his cups his loud voice and deep laugh could be heard ringing through the room.

The tidings delivered by the messenger and which brought on this sickness—of which the leech Ulsenius had ere this warned him—might have shaken the heart of a sterner man; for my Uncle Christian lodged in the Imperial Fort as its warder, and his duty it was to guard it. Near it, likewise, on the same hill-crag, stood the old castle belonging to the High Constable, or Burgrave Friedrich. Now the Burgrave had come to high words with Duke Ludwig the Bearded, of Bayern-Ingolstadt, so that the Duke's High Steward, the noble Christoph von Laymingen, who dwelt at Lauf, had made so bold, with his lord at his back, as to break the peace with Friedrich, although he had lately become a powerful prince as Elector of the Mark of Brandenburg.

The said Christoph von Laymingen, so the horsemen told us, had ridden forth to Nuremberg this dark night and had seized the castle—not indeed the Imperial castle, which stood unharmed, but the stronghold of the old Zollern family which had stood by its side—and bad burnt it to the ground. This, indeed, was no mighty offence in the eyes of the town-council, inasmuch as it bore no great friendship to his Lordship the Constable and Elector, and had had many quarrels with him-nay, long after this the council was able to gain possession of the land and ruins by purchases—till, uncle Christian bitterly rued having sent his men-at-arms, whose duty it was to defend the castle, out into the country, though it were for so good a purpose as fighting against the Hussites.

It might have brought him into bad favor with the Elector; however, it did him no further mischief. One thing was certainly proven beyond doubt: that knavish treason had been at work in this matter; at Nuremberg, under the torture, it came out that the bear-master had been a spy and tell-tale bribed by Laymingen to discover whither Pfinzing and his men had removed.

And lest any one should conceive that here was an end to the woes that had fallen on the forest lodge in that short time from midnight to daybreak, I must record one more; for the new day, which dawned with no hue of rose, grey and dismal over the tawny woods, brought us fresh sorrow and evil.

Behind the moss-hut, wherein I had found my Herdegen with the dancing hussy, the Swabian Junker and Ritter Franz had fought, without any heed of the law and order of such combat—fought for life or death, and for my sake. And as though in this cruel time I were doomed to go through all that should worst wound my poor heart, I must need go forth to see the stricken limetree at that very moment when the Junker had dealt his enemy a deadly stroke and came rushing away with his hair all abroad like a mad man. It was indeed a merciful chance that my Uncle Conrad and the chaplain likewise had come forth to the garden, so that I might go with them to see the wounded knight.

The youth was lying on the wet grass, now much paler than ever, and his lips trembling with pain. A faded leaf had fallen on his brow and was strange to behold against his ashen skin; but I bent me down and took it off. By him was lying the uprooted limetree, from which that leaf had fallen, and whereas the rain was dropping from it fast, meseemed it was weeping.

And my heart was knit as it never had been before, to this young knight who had shed his blood in my behalf; but while I gazed down right lovingly into his face the Swabian came close up to him with ruthful eyes, and from those of the wounded man there shot at me a glance so full of hate and malice that I shuddered before it. This was an end, then, to all pity and tenderness. And yet, as I looked on his cold, set face, as pale and white as dull chalk, I could not forbear tears; for it is ever pitiful to see when death overtakes one who is not ripe for dying, as we bewail the green corn which is smitten by the hail, and hold festival when the reaper cuts the golden ears.

Thus were there three sick and wounded in the forest-lodge, besides my aunt; for Uncle Christian must have some few days of rest and nursing. Howbeit there was no lack of us to tend them; Ann was recovered to-day and Cousin Maud had come in all haste so soon as she knew of what had befallen Herdegen; for, of us all, he held the largest room in her heart; and even when he was at school, albeit he had money and to spare of his own, she had given him so freely of hers that he was no whit behind the sons of wealthy Counts.

Biding the time till my cousin should come—and she could not until the evening—it was my part to stay with my brother; but whereas Ann would fain have helped me, this Aunt Jacoba conceived to be in no way fitting for a young maid; much less then would she grant my earnest desire that I might devote me to the care of Sir Franz; though she had it less in mind to consider its fitness, than to conceive that it would be of small benefit to the wounded man, at the height of his fever, to know that the maid for whose love he had vainly sued was at his side.

Thus I was forbidden to see Ann in my brother's chamber; nevertheless I had much on my heart and I could guess that she likewise was eager to speak with me; but when at last I was alone with her in our bed chamber, she had matter for speech of which I had not dreamed. When I asked her what message she might desire me to give Herdegen from her, she besought me as I loved her not to name her at all in his presence. This, indeed, amazed me not a little, inasmuch as I weened not that she knew of all the grief I had suffered yestereve. But this was not so; I learnt now that she had marked everything, and had heard the men's light talk about the dashing youth whom the dark-eyed hussy had been so swift to choose from among them all. I, indeed, tried to make the best of the matter, but she gave me to understand that, if her lover had not done himself a mischief, it had been her intent to question him that very day as to whether he was in earnest with his love-pledges, or would rather that she should give him back his ring and his word. All this she spoke without a tear or a sigh, with steadfast purpose; and already I began, for my part, to doubt of the truth of her love; and I told her this plainly. Thereupon she clasped me to her, and while the tears gathered and sparkled in her great eyes, expounded to me all the matter; and in truth it was all I should myself have said in her place. She, of simple birth, would enter the circle of her betters on sufferance, and her new friends would, of a certainty, not do her more honor than her own husband. On his manner of treating her therefore would depend what measure of respect she might look for as his wife. And so long as their promise to marry was a secret, she would have him show, whether to her alone or before all the world, that he held her consent as of no less worth than that of the wealthiest and highest born heiress.

All this she spoke in hot haste while her cheeks glowed red. I saw the blue veins swell on her pure brow, and can never forget the image of her as she raised her tearful eyes to Heaven and pressing her hands on her panting bosom cried: "To go forth with him to want or death is as nothing! But never will I be led into shame, not even by him."

When presently I left her, after speaking many loving words to her, and holding her long in my arms, she was ready to forgive him; but she held to this: "Not a word, not a glance, not a kiss, until Herdegen had vowed that yesterday's offence should be the first and last she should ever suffer."

How clearly she had apprehended the matter!

Albeit she little knew how deeply her beloved had sinned against the truth he owed her. They say that Love is blind, and so he may be at first. But when once his trust is shaken the bandage falls, and the purblind boy is turned into a many-eyed, sharp-sighted Argus.

CHAPTER IX

Every one was ready to nurse the little maid who called herself "little Katie." But as to Herdegen, I was compelled for the time to say nothing to him of what Ann required of him, for he lay sick of a fever. He was faithfully tended by Eppelein, the son of a good servant of our father's who had lost his life in waiting on his master when stricken with the plague. Eppelein had indeed grown up in our household, among the horses; even as a lad he had by turns helped Herdegen in his sports, and rendered him good service, and had ever shown him a warmer love than that of a hireling.

It fell out one day that my brother's best horse came to harm by this youth's fault, and when Herdegen, for many days, would vouchsafe no word to him the lad took it so bitterly to heart that he stole away from the house, and whereas no one could find him, we feared for a long time that he had done himself a mischief. Nevertheless he was alive and of good heart. He had passed the months in a various life; first as a crier to a wandering quack, and afterwards, inasmuch as he was a nimble and likely lad, he had waited on the guests at one of the best frequented inns at Wurzberg. It came then to pass that his eminence Cardinal Branda, Nuncio from his Holiness the Pope, took up his quarters there, and he carried the lad away with him as his body-servant to Italy, and treated him well till the restless wight suddenly fell into a languor of home-sickness, and ran away from this good master, as erewhile he had run away from our house. Perchance some love-matter drove him to fly. Certain it is that in his wandering among strangers he had come to be a mighty handy, wide-awake fellow, with much that was good in him, inasmuch as with all his subtlety he had kept his true Nuremberger's heart.

When he had journeyed safely home again he one day stole unmarked into our courtyard, where his old mother lived in an out-building on the charity of the Schoppers; he went up to her and stood before her, albeit she knew him not, and laid the gold pieces he had saved one by one on the work-table before her. The little old woman scarce knew where she was for sheer amazement, nor wist she who he was till he broke out into his old loud laugh at the sight of her dismay. Verily, as she afterwards said, that laugh brought more gladness to her heart and had rung sweeter in her ears than the gold pieces.

Then Susan had called us down to the courtyard, and when a smart young stripling came forth to meet us, clad in half Italian and half German guise, none knew who he might be till he looked Herdegen straight in the face, and my brother cried out: "It is our Eppelein!" Then the tears flowed fast down his cheeks, but Herdegen clasped him to him and kissed him right heartily on both cheeks.

All this did I bring to mind as I saw this said Eppelein carefully and sorrowfully laying a wet cloth, at my aunt's bidding, on his master's head where it was so sorely cut; and methought how well it would have been if Herdegen were still so ready to follow the prompting of his heart.

Understanding anon that I was not needed by this bed, where Eppelein kept faithful watch and ward, and that Sir Franz's chamber was closed to me, I went down stairs again, for I had heard a rumor that the swarthy lad— who had yesterday played on the pipe—was to be put to the torture. This I would fain have hindered, whereas by many tokens I was certain that the said comely youth was not one of the vagabond crew, but, like little Katie, might well be a child knavishly kidnapped from some noble house. Whereas I reached the hall, Balzer, the keeper, was about bringing the lad in. Outside indeed it was dim and wet, but within it was no less comfortable, for a mighty fire was blazing in the wide chimney-place. My aunt was warming her thereat, and Ann likewise was of the company, with Uncle Conrad, Jost Tetzel, my godfather Christian Pfinzing, and the several guests.

I joined myself to them and in an under tone told them what I had noted, saying that, more by token the youth must have a good conscience; for, whereas he had not been cast into the cell but had been locked into a stable to take charge of the camels and the ape, he had nevertheless not tried to escape, although it would have been easy.

To this opinion some inclined; and seeing that the boy spoke but a few words of German, but knew more of Italian, I addressed him in that tongue; and then it came to light that he was verily and indeed a stolen child. The vagabonds had bartered for him in Italy, giving a fair girl whom they had with them in exchange; likewise he said he was of princely birth, but had fallen into slavery some two years since, when a fine galley governed by his father, an Emir or prince of Egypt, had fought with another coming from Genoa in Italy.

When I had presently interpreted these words to the others, Jost Tetzel, Ursula's father, declared them to be sheer lies and knavery; even Uncle Conrad deemed them of little worth; and for this reason: that if the lad had indeed been the son of some grand Emir of Egypt the bear-leader would for certain have made profit of him by requiring his ransom.

But when I told the lad of this he fixed his great eyes very modestly on me, and in truth there was no small dignity in his mien and voice as he asked me:

"Could I then bring poverty on my parents, who were ever good to me, to bestow wealth on that evil brood? Never should those knavish rogues have learnt from me what I have gladly revealed to thee who are full of goodness and beauty!"

This speech went to my heart; and if it were not truth then is there no truth in all the world! But when again I had interpreted his words, and Tetzel still would but shrug his shoulders, this vexed me so greatly that it was as much as I could do to refrain myself, and hold my peace.

I had seen from the first, in Uncle Christian's eyes, that he was of the same mind with me; yet could I not guess what purpose he had in his head, although to judge by her face it was something passing strange, when he muttered some behest to Ann with his poor fettered tongue. Then, when she told me what my godfather required of me, I was not in any haste to obey, for, indeed, maidenly bashfulness and pity hindered me. Yet, whereas the brave old man nodded to spur me on, with his heavy head, still covered with a cold wet cloth, I called up all my daring, and before the lad was aware I dealt him a slap on the cheek.

It was not a hard blow, but the lad seemed as much amazed as though the earth had opened at his feet. His dark face turned ashen-grey and his great eyes looked at me in tearful enquiry, but so grievously that I already rued my unseemly deed.

Soon, however, I had cause to be glad; the youth's demeanor won his cause. Uncle Christian had only desired to prove him. He knew men well, and he knew that youths of various birth take a blow in the face in various ways; now, the Emir's son had demeaned him as one of his rank, and had stood the ordeal! So my aunt Jacoba told him, for she had at once seen through Uncle Christian's purpose, and presently Jost Tetzel himself, though ill-pleased and sullen, confessed his error. Then, when they had promised the youth that he should be spared all further ill-usage, he opened the lining of his garment and showed us a gem which his mother had privily hung about his neck, and which was a lump or tablet of precious sky-blue turkis-stone, as large as a great plum, whereon was some charm inscribed in strange, outlandish signs which the Jewish Rabbi Hillel, when he saw it, declared to be Arabic letters.

The bear-leader had called the lad Beppo; but his real name was a long one and hard to utter, out of which my forest uncle picked up two syllables for a name he could speak with ease, calling him Akusch.

With Cousin Maud's assent the black youth was attached to my service as Squire, inasmuch as it was I who at first had "dubbed him knight;" and when I gave him to understand this he could not contain himself for joy, and from that hour he ever proved my most ready servant, ever alert and thankful; and the little benevolence it was in my power to shew the poor lad bore fruit more than a thousand fold in after times, to me and mine.

After noon that same day Ann confessed to me that she had it in her mind to quit the lodge that very evening, journeying home with Master Ulsenius; and when she withstood all my entreaties she told Cousin Maud likewise that she had indeed already left her own kin too long without her succor.

Aunt Jacoba was in her chimney corner, and how she took this sudden purpose on Ann's part, may be imagined.

It was so gloomy a day that there was scarce a change when dusk fell. Grey wreaths of cloud hung over the tree-tops, and fine rain dripped with a soft, steady patter, as though it would never cease; nor was there another sound, inasmuch as neither horn, nor watchman's cry, nor bell might break the silence, for the sake of the wounded men; nay, even the hounds, meseemed, understood that the daily course of life was out of gear.

Ann had gone to pack her little baggage with Susan's help, but she had bid me remain with the child. It was going on finely; it would play with the doll my Aunt had given it in happy pastime, and now I did the little one's bidding and was right glad to be her play fellow for a while. Time slipped on as I sat there making merry with little Katie, doing the dolly's leather breeches and jerkin off and on, blowing on the child's little shoulder when it smarted or giving her a sweetmeat to comfort her, and still Ann came not, albeit she had promised to join me so soon as her baggage was ready.

Hereupon a sudden fear seized me, and as soon as the housekeeper came up I went to seek Ann in our chamber. There stood all her chattel, so neat as only she could make them; and I learnt from Susan that Ann had gone down, some time since, into Aunt Jacoba's chamber.

I was minded to seek her there, and went by the ante-chamber where the sick lady's writing-table and books stood, and which led to the sitting chamber. I trod lightly by reason that the knight's chamber was beneath; thus no one heard me; but I could see beyond the dark ante-chamber into the further one, where wax lights were burning in a double candlestick, and lo! Ann was on her knees by the sick lady's couch, like to the linden-tree which the storm had overthrown yesternight; and she hid her face in my aunt's lap and sobbed so violently that her slender body shook as though in a fever. And Aunt Jacoba had laid her two hands on Ann's head, as it were in blessing. And I saw first one large tear, and then many more, run down the face of this very woman who had cast out her own fair son. Often had I marked on her little finger a certain ring in which a little white thing was set; yet was this no splinter of the bone of a Saint, but the first tooth her banished son had shed. And, when she deemed that no man saw her, she would press her hand to her lips and kiss the little tooth with fervent love. And now, whereas love had waked up again in her heart, that son had his part and share in it; for albeit none dared make mention of him in her presence she ever loved him as the apple of her eye.

I was no listener, yet could I not shut mine ears; I heard how the frail old lady exhorted the love-sick maid, and bid her trust in God, and in Herdegen's faithfulness. Also I heard her speak well indeed of my brother's spirit and will as noble and upright; and she promised Ann to uphold her to the best of her power.

She bid her favorite farewell with a fond kiss, and many comforting words; and as she did so I minded me of a wondrously fair maiden, the daughter of Pernhart the coppersmith, known to young and old in the town as fair Gertrude, who, each time I had beheld her of late, meseemed had grown even sadder and paler, and whom I now knew that I should never see more, inasmuch as that only yestereve Uncle Christian had told us, with tears in his eyes, that this sweet maid had died of pining, and had been buried only a day or two since with much pomp. Now my aunt had heard these tidings, and she had shaken her head in silence and folded her hands, as it were in prayer, fixing her eyes on the ground.

Cousin Gotz and Herdegen—fair Gertrude and my Ann; what made them so unlike that my aunt should bring herself to mete their bonds of love with so various a measure?

I quitted the room when Ann came forth, and outside the door I clasped her in my arms; and in the last hour we spent together at the forest lodge she bid me greet her heart's beloved from her, and gave me for him the last October rose-bud, which my uncle had plucked for her at parting. Yet she held to her demands.

She left us after supper, escorted by Master Ulsemus. She had come hither one sunny morn with the song of the larks, and now she departed in darkness and gloom.

CHAPTER X

"By Saint Bacchus—if there be such a saint in the calendar, there is stuff in the lad, my boy!" cried burly Uncle Christian Pfinzing, and he thumped the table with his fists so that all the vessels rang. His tongue was still somewhat heavy, but he had mended much in the three weeks since Ann had departed, and it was hard enough by this time to get him away from the wine-jug.

It was in the refectory of the forest lodge that he had thus delivered himself to my Uncle Conrad and Jost Tetzel, Ursula's father; and it was of my brother Herdegen that he spoke.

Herdegen was healed of his bruises and his light limbs had never been more nimble than now; still he bore his left arm in a sling, for there it was, said he, that the horse's hoof had hit him. Whither the horse had fled none had ever heard; nor did any man enquire, inasmuch as it was only Eppelein's nag, and my granduncle had given him a better one.

My silly brain, from the first, had been puzzled to think wherefor my brother should have taken that nag to ride to see his guardian, who thought more than other men of a good horse. And in truth I was not far from guessing rightly, so I will forthwith set down whither indeed my dear brother's horse had vanished, and by what chance and hap he had fallen into so evil a plight.

He had aforetime met the young wench on his way from Padua to Nuremberg, not far from Dachau and had then and there begun his tricks with her, giving her to wit that she might find him again at the forest lodge in the Lorenzer wall. Now when matters took so ill a turn, he pledged himself to get her safe away from the dungeon cell. To this end he feigned that he would ride into the town, after possessing himself of the key of the black hole and after stowing a suit of his man's apparel and a loaf of bread into his saddle-poke. Then he wandered about the wood for some time, and as soon as it fell dark he stole back to the house again on foot. He had made a bold and well-devised plan, and yet he might have come to a foul end; for, albeit the hounds, who knew him well, let him pass into the cell, within he was so fiercely set upon that it needed all his strength and swiftness to withstand it. The froward wretches had plotted to fall upon him and to escape with the wench from their prison, even if it were over his dead body.

One of the bear-leaders had made shift to strip the cords from his hands, and when my brother entered into the dark place where the prisoners lay, they flew at him to fell him. But even on the threshold Herdegen saw through their purpose, and had no sooner shut the door than he drew his hunting knife. Then the old beldame gripped him by the throat and clawed him tooth and nail; one of the ruffians beat him with a stave torn from the bedstead till he weened he had broken or bruised all his limbs, while the other, whose hands were yet bound, pressed between him and the door. In truth he would have come to a bad end, but that the younger woman saved him at the risk of her own life. The man who had rid himself of his bonds had raised the heavy earthen pitcher to break Herdegen's head withal, when the brave wench clutched the wretch by the arm and hung on to him till Herdegen stuck him with his knife. Thus the ringleader fell, and my brother pulled up his deliverer and dragged her to the door. As he opened it the old woman and the other prisoner put forth their last strength to force their way out, but with his strong arm he thrust them back and locked the door upon them.

Thus he led the young woman, who had come off better than he had feared in the fray, forth to freedom, to keep his word to her.

Out in the wood, in spite of thunder and lightning, he made her to put on Eppelein's weed and mount the nag. Thereafter he led her horse to the brook, which floweth through the woods down to the meadow-land, and bid her ride along in the water so far as she might, to put the hounds off the scent. The bread in the saddle-bag would feed her for a few days, and now it lay with her to escape pursuit. And this good deed of my brother's had smitten the lost creature to the heart; when he was about to help her to mount he dropped down on the wet ground from loss of blood, but as he opened his eyes again, behold, his head was resting on her lap and she kissed his brow. Despite her own peril she had not left him in such evil plight, but had done all she could to bring him to his senses; nay, she had gathered leaves by the glare of the lightning to staunch the blood which flowed freely from the worst of his wounds. Nor was she to be moved to go on her way till he showed her that in truth he could walk.

Thus it befel that I long after thought of her with kindness; and indeed, she was not wholly vile; and every human soul hath in it somewhat good which spurs forth to love, inasmuch as it is love which can cast light on all, and that full brightly; and what is bright is good; and that light dieth not till the last spark is dead.

As to Herdegen, verily I have never understood how he could find it in his heart to peril his life for the sake of keeping his word to a vagabond hussy while, at the same time, he was breaking troth with the fairest and sweetest maid on earth. Yet I count it to him chiefly for good that he could risk life and honor to hinder those who fell upon him so foully from escaping the arm of justice; and it is this upholding of the law which truly does more to lift men above us women-folk than any other thing.

Well, by that evening when Uncle Christian thus pledged my brother, Herdegen was quite himself again in mind and body. At first it had seemed as though a wall had been raised up between us; but after that I had told him that I had concealed from Ann all that I had seen by ill-hap at the moss-hut, he was as kind and trusting as of old, and he showed himself more ready to give Ann the pledge she required than I had looked to find him, stiff-necked as he ever was. And he hearkened unmoved when I told him what Ann had said: "That she was ready to follow him to death, but not to shame."

"That," quoth he, "she need never fear from any true man, and with all his wildness he might yet call himself that." Then he stretched himself at full length on his chair, and threw his arms in the air, and cried:

"Oh, Margery. If you could but slip for one half-hour into your mad brother's skin. In your own, which is so purely white, you can never, till the day of doom, understand what I am. If ever I have seemed weary it is but to keep up a mannerly appearance; verily I could break forth ten times a day and shoot skywards like a rocket for sheer joy in life. When that mood comes over me there is no holding me, and I should dare swear that the whole fair earth had been made and created for my sole and free use, with all that therein is—and above all other creatures the dear, sweet daughters of Eve!—and I can tell you, Margery, the women agree with me. I have only to open my arms and they flutter into them, and not to close them tight—that, Margery, is too much to look for; yet is there but one true bliss, and but one Ann, and the best of all joys is to clasp her to my heart and kiss her lips. I will keep faith with her; I will have nought to say to the rest. But how shall I keep them away from me? Can I wish that those rascals had put my eyes out, had crippled my limbs, had thrashed me to a scare-crow, to the end that the maids should turn their backs on me? Nay, and even no rain-torrent could cool the hot blood of the Schoppers; no oak staff nor stone pitcher could kill the wild cravings within. There is nothing for it but to cast my body among thorns like Saint Francis. But what would even that profit me? You see yourself how well this skin heals of the worst wounds!"

Hereupon I earnestly admonished him of his devoir to that lady who was so truly his, and with whom he had exchanged rings. But he cried: "Do you believe that I did not tell myself, every hour of the day, that she was a thousand-fold more worth than all the rest put together? Never could I deem any maid so sweet as she has been ever since we were children together; nay, and if I lost her I should utterly perish, for it is from her that I, a half-ruined wretch, get all that yet is best in me!"

And many a time did I hear him utter the like; and when I saw his large blue eyes flash as he spoke, while he pushed the golden curls back from his brow, verily he was so goodly a youth to look upon that it was easy to view that the daughters of Eve might be ready to cast themselves into his arms.

This evening, as it fell, Aunt Jacoba was not with her guests, but unwillingly, inasmuch as we were to depart homewards next morning, and the gentlemen sat late over their farewell cups. It had become Cousin Maud's care to hinder Uncle Christian from drinking more freely than he ought; but this evening he had made the task a hard one; nay, when she steadfastly forbade him a third cup he got it by craft and in spite of her, nor could she persuade him to forego the dangerous joy. When he had cried, as has been told, that "there was stuff" in my brother, it was by reason of his having perceived that Herdegen had already filled his cup for the fourteenth time, and when the youth had drunk it off the old man sang out in high glee:

"Der Eppela Gaila von Dramaus
Reit' allezeit zu vierzeht aus!"
[An old popular rhyme in Nuremberg. "Eppela (Apollonius)
Gaila of Dramaus—or Drameysr—could always go as far
as fourteen cups." Apollonius von Gailingen was a brigand
chief who brought much damage and vexation on the town.
Drameysel, in popular form Dramaus, was his stronghold near
Muggendorf in Swiss Franconia.]

"Now, if the boy can drink three times the mystic seven, he will do what I could do at his age."

And presently Herdegen did indeed drink his one and twenty cups, and when at last he paced the whole length of the great dining hall on one seam of the flooring the old man was greatly pleased, and rewarded him with the gift of a noble tankard which he himself had won of yore at a drinking bout. All this made good sport for us, save only for Jost Tetzel, who was himself a right moderate man; indeed, in aftertimes, when at Venice I saw how that wealthy and noble gentlemen drank but sparingly of the juice of the grape, I marvelled wherefor we Germans are ever proud of a man who is able to drink deep, and apt to look askance at such as fear to see the bottom of the cup. And if I had an answer ready, that likewise I owed to my uncle Christian; inasmuch as that very eve, when I would fain have warned Herdegen against the good liquor, my uncle put in his word and said it was every man's duty to follow in the ways of Saint George the dragon-killer, and to quell and kill every fiend; be it what it might. "Now in the wine cup, quoth he, there lurks a dragon named drunkenness, and it beseemeth German valor and strength not merely to vanquish it, but even to make it do good service: The fiend of the grape, like the serpent killed by the saint, has two wide pinions, and the true German drinker must make use of them to soar up to the seventh heaven."

And as concerns my Herdegen, I must confess that when he had well drunk his spirits were higher, his mind clearer, and his song more glad; and this is not so save in those dragon-slayers who have been blessed with a fine temper and a strong brain inherited from their parents.

Every evening had there been the like mirthful doings over their wine; but Sir Franz had been ever absent. He was even now forced to remain in his chamber, albeit Master Ulsenius had declared that his life was out of danger. The damage done to his lungs he must to be sure carry to his grave, nor could he be able to follow us for some weeks yet. He was not to think of making the journey to his own home in Bohemia during this winter season, and at this farewell drinking bout we held council as to whose roof he might find lodging under. He, for his part, would soonest have found shelter with us; but Cousin Maud refused it, and with good reason, inasmuch as I had freely told her that never in this world would I hearken to his suit.

At last it seemed plain that it was Jost Tetzel's part to offer him a home in his great house; nor did he refuse, by reason that Sir Franz von Welemisl was a man of birth and wealth, and his Bohemian and Hungarian kin stood high at the Imperial court.

Next morning, as we drank the stirrup cup, my eyes filled with tears, and it was with a sad heart that I bid farewell to the woods, to my uncle, and to Aunt Jacoba, whom I had during my sojourn learnt to love as was her due. I, like Ann, rode home in a more sober mood than I had come in; for I was no more a child and an end must ever come to wild mirth.

My new squire Akusch rode behind me, and thus, on a fine November day, we made our way back to Nuremberg, in good health and spirits. The camels, the bear, and the monkeys, which had been taken from the vagabonds, were safely cared for in the Hallergarden, and the rogues themselves had been hanged God have mercy on their souls!

Ann had had tidings of our home-coming, yet I found her not at our house, and when I had waited for her till evening, and in vain, I sought her in her own dwelling. But no sooner had I crossed the threshold of the Venice house than I was aware that all was not well; inasmuch as that here, where there were ever half a dozen pairs of little feet hopping up and down, and no end of music and singing from morning till night, all was strangely silent. I stood to hearken, and I now perceived that the metal plate whereon the knocker fell was wrapped in felt.

This foreboded evil, and a vision rose before me of two biers; on one lay Ann, pale and dumb, and on the other my Cousin Gotz's sweetheart, fair Gertrude, the copper-smith's daughter. Then I heard steps on the stair and the vision faded; and I breathed once more, for Ann's grandfather, the old lute-player Gottlieb Spiesz, came towards me, with deep lines of sorrow on his kind face and a finger on his lips; and he told me that his son was lying sick of a violent brain fever, and that Master Ulsenius had feared the worst since yestereve.

His voice broke with sheer grief; nevertheless his serving lad was carrying his lute after him, and as he gave me his hand to bid me good-day he told me that Ann was above tending her father. "And I," quoth he, and his voice was weary but not bitter, "I must go to work—there is so much needed here, and food drops into no man's lap! First to the Tetzels to teach the young ones a madrigal to sing for Master Jost's fiftieth birthday. And they count on your help and your brother's, sweet Mistress.—Well, children, be happy while it is yet time!"

He passed his hand across his eyes, and glanced up at the top room where his son lay with aching head, and so went forth to teach light hearted young creatures to sing festal rounds and catches.

In a minute I had Ann in my arms; yea, and she was as sweet and bright as ever. The stern duty she had had to do had been healthful, albeit she had good cause to fear for the future; for, with her father, the household would lose the bread-winner.

It was an unspeakable joy to me to be able to assure her of Herdegen's faithful love, and to repeat to her the many kind words he had spoken concerning her. And she was right glad to hear them; and whereas true love is a flower which, when it droops, needs but a little drop of dew to uplift it again, hers had already raised its head somewhat after my last letter.

And at this, the time of the worst sorrow she had known, another great comfort had been vouchsafed to her: Master Ulsenius and his good wife, having had her to lodge with them the night of her return from the forest, had taken much fancy to her, and the goodhearted leech, a man of great learning, had been fain to admit her to the use of his fine library. Thus I found Ann of brave cheer notwithstanding her woe; and if heartfelt prayers for a sick man might have availed him, it was no blame to me when her father made a sad and painful end on the fifth day after my home-coming. When I heard the tidings meseemed that a cold hand had been laid on my glad faith; for it was hard indeed for a poor, short-sighted human soul to see to what end and purpose this man should have been snatched away in the prime of age and strength.

To keep his large family, to free the little house from debt, and to lay aside a small sum, he had undertaken, besides the duties of his place, the stewardship of certain private properties; thus he had many a time turned night into day, and finally, albeit a stalwart man, he had fallen ill of the brain fever which had carried him off. It seemed, then, that honest toil and brave diligence had but earned the heaviest dole that could befall a man in his state of life; namely: to depart from those he loved or ever he could provide for their future living.

We all followed him to the grave, and it was by the bier of her worthy father that Ann for the first time met my brother once more. There was a great throng present, and he could do no more than press her hand with silent ardor; yet, at the same time he met her eye with such a truthful gaze that it was as a promise, a solemn pledge of faithfulness.

The prebendary of Saint Laurence, Master von Hellfeld, spoke the funeral sermon, and that in a right edifying manner; and whereas he took occasion to say that our Lord and Redeemer would bid all to be his guests and hold Himself their debtor who should show true Christian love towards these who henceforth had no father, Herdegen privily clasped my hand tightly.

Kunz likewise was present, and standing by the body of the man who had ever loved him best of us three, he wept as sorely as though he had lost his own father.

The gentlemen of the council were all assembled to do the last honors to one whose office had brought them closely together, and I marked that more than one nudged his neighbor to note Ann's more than common beauty, who in her black weed stood among her young brethren and sisters as a consoling angel, who weepeth with them that weep and comforteth the sorrowing. And so it came about that I heard many a father of fair daughters confess that this maid had not her like for beauty in all Nuremberg. And this came to Herdegen's ears, and I could see that it uplifted his spirit and confirmed him in good purpose.

It soon befell that he might show by deed of what mind he was. Master Holzschuher, the notary, who was near of kin and a right good friend of Cousin Maud's, had been named guardian of his children by the deceased Master Spiesz, and he it was who, in our house one day, said that the widow and orphans were in better care than he had looked for, and could keep their little house over their heads if wealthy neighbors could be moved to open their purses and pay off a debt that was upon it. Then my brother sprang up and declared that the family of an upright and faithful servant of the State, and of a friend of the Schoppers, should have some better and more honorable means of living than beggars' pence. He was not yet of full age, but it was his intent to demand forthwith of our guardian Im Hoff so much of that which would be his, as might be needed to release the house from the burden of debt; and albeit Master Holzschuher shook his head thereat, and this was no light thing that Herdegen had undertaken, he departed at once to seek his granduncle.

From him indeed he met with rougher treatment than he had looked for; for the old man made the diligent stewardship of these trust-moneys a point of honor, to the end that when he should give an account of them before the city council it might be seen, by the greatness of the sum, how wise and well advised he had been in getting increase. What my brother called "beggars' pence," he said, was a well-earned guerdon which did the dead clerk's family an honor and was no disgrace; he was indeed minded to pay one-third of the whole sum at his own charges. As to the moneys left to us three by our parents, not a penny thereof would he ever part with. Moreover, Ann's rare charm had touched even my grand-uncle's heart, and he must have been dull-witted indeed if he had not hit on Herdegen's true reasons; and these in his eyes would be the worst of the matter, forasmuch as he was firmly bent on bringing Ursula Tetzel and Herdegen together so soon as my brother should have won his doctor's hood.

Thus it came to pass that, for the first time, our grand-uncle parted from his favorite nephew in wrath, and when Herdegen came home with crimson cheeks and almost beside himself, he confessed to me that for the present he had not yet been so bold as to tell the old man how deeply he was pledged to Ann, but in all else had told him the plain truth.

At supper Herdegen scarce ate a morsel, for he could not bring himself to endure that his betrothed should sink so low as to receive an alms. He rose from table sullen and grieved, and whereas Cousin Maud could not endure to see her favorite go to rest in so much distress of mind, she led him aside, and inasmuch as she had already guessed how matters stood betwixt him and Ann, not without some fears, she spoke to him kindly, and declared herself ready to free the Spiesz household from debt without any help of strangers. To see him and her dear Ann happy she would gladly make far greater sacrifices, for indeed she did not at all times know what she might do with her own money.

No later than next morning the matter was privily settled by our notary; and albeit Master Holzschuher did so dispose things as though the deceased had left money to pay the debt withal, Ann saw through this, whereas her beautiful mother did but thoughtlessly rejoice over such good fortune.

Henceforth it was Ann's little hand which ruled the fatherless household with steadfast thrift, while Mistress Giovanna, as had ever been her wont, lived only to take care of the children's garments, that they should be neat and clean, of the flowers in the window and the beautiful needlework, and to fondle the little ones, so soon as she had got through her light toil in the kitchen.

It was granted to her and hers that they should dwell henceforth forever in the house by the Pegnitz, humbly indeed, but honorably and without the aid of strangers. One alms to be sure was bestowed on them soon after the first day of each month, and that right privily; for at that time without fail a little packet in which were two Hungarian ducats was found on the threshold of the hall. And who was the giver of this kind token would have remained secret till doomsday had not Susan by chance, and to his great vexation, betrayed my brother Kunz. My grand-uncle had granted him three ducats a month since he had left school, and of these he ever privily gave two to help the household ruled over by Ann. Our old Susan it was who aided him in the matter, so, when he was by any means hindered from laying the little packet on the threshold, she had to find an excuse for going to the little house by the river.

The worshipful council and many friends whose good-will the deceased scribe had won, got the orphans into the best schools in the town, and what Ann had learned as head of the school at the Carthusian convent she now handed down to her younger sisters by diligent teaching; and, as of yore, she gave her most loving care to her little deaf and dumb brother.

CHAPTER XI

Herdegen was to be back in Padua before Passion week, and I shall remember with thankfulness to the day of my death the few months after worthy Veit Spiesz's burial and before my brother's departure. Not a day passed without our meeting; and after my heart had moved me to tell Cousin Maud all that had happened, and Herdegen had given his consent, we were rid once for all of the mystery which had at first weighed on our souls.

Verily the worthy lady found it no light matter to look kindly on this early and ill-matched betrothal; yet had she not the heart, nor the power, to make any resistance. When two young folks who are dear to her are brimfull of high happiness, the woman who would turn them out of that Garden of Eden and spoil their present bliss with warnings of future woe must be of another heart and mind than Cousin Maud. She indeed foresaw grief to come in many an hour of mistrust by day and many a sleepless night, more especially by reason of her awe and dread of my grand-uncle; and indeed, she herself was not bereft of the old pride of race which dwells in every Nuremberger who is born under a knight's coat of arms. That Ann was poor she held of no account; but that she was not of noble birth was indeed a grief and filled her with doubts. But then, when her best-beloved Herdegen's eyes shone so brightly, and she saw Ann cling to him with maidenly rapture, vexation and care were no more.

If I had sung a loud hymn of praise in the woods over their spring and autumn beauty—and verily it had welled up from my heart—I was ready to think winter in the town no less gladsome, in especial under the shelter of a home so warm and well built as our old Schopper-hof.

In the last century, when, at the time of the Emperor Carolus—[Charles IV., 1348]—coming to the throne, the guilds, under the leadership of the Gaisbarts and Pfauentritts, had risen against the noble families and the worshipful council, they accused the elders of keeping house not as beseemed plain citizens but after the manner of princes; and they were not far wrong, for indeed I have heard tell that when certain merchants from Scandinavia came to our city, they said that the dwelling of a Nuremberg noble was a match in every way for their king's palace.

[Gaisbart (goat's beard) and Pfauentritt (peacock-strut), were

nicknames given to the leaders of the guilds who rebelled against
the patrician families in Nuremberg, from whom alone the
aldermen or
town-council could be elected. This patrician class originated in
1198 under the Emperor Henry IV., who ennobled 38 families of
the
citizens. They were in some sort comparable with the families
belonging to the Signoria at Venice, from whom, in the same way,
the
great council was chosen.]

As touching our house, it was four stories high, and with seven windows in every story; with well devised oriels at the corners, and pointed turrets on the roof. The gables were on the street, in three steps; over the great house door there was our coat of arms, the three links of the Schopppes and the fool's head with cap and bells as a crest on the top of the casque. The middle windows of the first and second stories were of noble size, and there glittered therein bright and beautiful panes of Venice glass, whereas the other windows were of small roundels set in lead.

And while from outside it was a fine, fair house to look upon, I never hope to behold a warmer or more snug and comfortable dwelling than the living-rooms within which was our home the winter through; albeit I found the saloons and chambers in the palaces of the Signori at Venice loftier and more airy, and greater and grander. Whenever I have been homesick under the sunny blue sky of Italy, it was for the most part that I longed after the rich, fresh green foliage and flowing streams of my own land; but, next to them, after our pleasant chamber in the Schopper-house, with its warm, green-tiled stove, with the figures of the Apostles, and the corner window where I had spun so many a hank of fine yarn, and which was so especially mine own—although I was ever ready and glad to yield my right to it, when Herdegen required it to sit in and make love to his sweetheart.

The walls of this fine chamber were hung with Flanders tapestry, and I can to this day see the pictures which were so skilfully woven into it. That I loved best, from the time when I was but a small thing, was the Birth of the Saviour, wherein might be seen the Mother and Child, oxen and asses, the three Holy Kings from the East—the goodliest of them all a blackamoor with a great yellow beard flowing down over his robes. On the other hangings a tournament might be seen; and I mind me to this day how that, when I was a young child, I would gaze up at the herald who was blowing the trumpet in fear lest his cheeks should burst, inasmuch as they were so greatly puffed out and he never ceased blowing so hard. Between the top of these hangings and the ceiling was a light wood cornice of oak-timber, on which my father, God rest him, had caused various posies to be carved of his own devising. You might here read:

"*Like a face our life may be*
To which love lendeth eyes to see."

Or again,

"*The Lord Almighty hides his glorious face*
That so we may not cease to seek his grace."

Or else,

"*The Lord shall rule my life while I sit still,*
And rule it rightly by his righteous will."

And whereas my father had loved mirthful song he had written in another place:

"*If life be likened to a thorny place*
Song is the flowery spray that lends it grace."

Some of these rhymes had been carved there by my grandfather, for example these lines:

"*By horse and wain I've journeyed up and down,*
Yet found no match for this my native town."

And under our coat of arms was this posy.

"*While the chain on the scutcheon holds firm and fast*
The fool on the crest will be game to the last."

Of the goodly carved seats, and the cushions covered with motley woven stuffs from the Levant, right pleasant to behold, of all the fine treasures on the walls, the Venice mirrors, and the metal cage with a grey parrot therein, which Jordan Kubbelmg, the falconer from Brunswick, had given to my dear mother, I will say no more; but I would have it understood that all was clean and bright, well ordered and of good choice, and above all snug and warm. Nay, and if it had all been far less costly and good to look at, there was, as it were, a breath of home which must have gladdened any man's heart: inasmuch as all these goodly things were not of yesterday nor of to-day, but had long been a joy to many an one dear to us; so that our welfare in that dwelling was but the continuing of the good living which our parents and grandparents had known before us.

Howbeit, those who will read this writing know what a patrician's house in Nuremberg is wont to be; and he who hath lived through a like childhood himself needs not to be told how well hide and seek may be played in a great hall, or what various and merry pastime can be devised in the twilight, in a dining hall where the lights hang from the huge beams of the ceiling; and we for certain knew every game that was worthy to be named.

But by this time all this was past and gone; only the love of song would never die out in the dwelling of the man who had been well-pleased to hear himself called by his fellows "Schopper the Singer." Ah! how marvellous well did their voices sound, Ann's and my brother's, when they sang German songs to the lute or the mandoline, or perchance Italian airs, as they might choose. But there was one which I could never weary of hearing and which, meseemed, must work on Herdegen's wayward heart as a cordial. The words were those of Master Walther von der Vogelweirde, and were as follows:

> *"True love is neither man nor maid,*
> *No body hath nor yet a soul,*
> *Nor any semblance here below,*
> *Its name we hear, itself unknown.*
> *Yet without love no man may win*
> *The grace and favor of the Lord.*
> *Put then thy trust in those who love;*
> *In no false heart may Love abide."*

And when they came to the last lines Kunz would ofttimes join in, taking the bass part or continuo to the melody. Otherwise he kept modestly in the background, for since he had come to know that Herdegen and Ann were of one mind he waited on her as a true and duteous squire, while he was now more silent than in past time, and in his elder brother's presence almost dumb. Yet at this I marvelled not, inasmuch as I many a time marked that brethren are not wont to say much to each other, and even between friends the one is ready enough to be silent if the other takes the word. Moreover at Easter Kunz was likewise to quit home, and go to Venice at my granduncle's behest. Herdegen's love for his brother had, of a certainty, suffered no breach; but, like many another disciple of Minerva, he was disposed to look down on the votaries of Mercury.

Nevertheless the links of the Schopper chain, to which Ann had now been joined as a fourth, held together right bravely, and when we sang not, but met for friendly talk, our discourse was but seldom of worthless, vain matters, forasmuch as Herdegen was one of those who are ready and free of speech to impart what he had himself learned, and it was Ann's especial gift to listen keenly and question discreetly.

And what was there that my brother had not learned from the great Guarino, and the not less great Humanist, his disciple Vittorino da Feltre, at that time Magistri at Padua? And how he had found the time, in a right gay and busy life, to study not merely the science of law but also Greek, and that so diligently that his master was ever ready to laud him, was to me a matter for wonder. And how gladly we hearkened while he told us of the great Plato, and gave us to know wherefore and on what grounds his doctrine seemed to him, Herdegen, sounder and loftier than that of Aristotle, concerning whom he had learned much erewhile in Nuremberg. And whereas I was moved to fear lest these works of the heathen should tempt him to stray from the true faith, my soul found comfort when he proved to us that so glorious a lamp of the Church as Saint Augustine had followed them on many points. Also Herdegen had written out many verses of Homer's great song from a precious written book, and had learned to master them well from the teaching of the doctor of Feltre. They were that portion in which a great hero in the fight, or ever he goes forth to battle, takes leave of his wife and little son; and to me and Ann it seemed so fine and withal so touching, that we could well understand how it should be that Petrarca wrote that no more than to behold a book of Homer made him glad, and that he longed above all things to clasp that great man in his arms.

Indeed, the poems and writings of Petrarca yielded us greater delights than all the Greek and Roman heathen. Master Ulsenius had before now lent them to Ann, and she like a bee from a flower would daily suck a drop of honey from their store. Yet was there one testimony of Petrarca's—who was, for sure, of all lovers the truest—which she loved above all else. In the dreadful time of the Black Death which came as a scourge on all the world, and chiefly on Italy, in the past century, the lady to whom he had vowed the deepest and purest devotion, appeared to him in a dream one fair spring morning as an angel of Heaven. And whereas he inquired of her whether she were in life, she answered him in these words: "See that thou know me; for I am she who led thee out of the path of common men, inasmuch as thy young heart clung to me." And lo! on that very sixth of April, which brought him that vision, one and twenty years after that he had first beheld her, Laura had made a pious end.

With beseeching eyes Ann would repeat to her best beloved, as they sat together in the oriel bay, how that Laura had led her Petrarca from the ways of common men; and it went to my heart to hear her entreat him, with timid and yet fond and heartfelt prayer, to grant to her to be his Laura and to guide him far from the beaten path, forasmuch as it was narrow and low for his winged spirit. And while she thus spoke her great eyes had a marvellous clear and glorious light, and when I looked in her face wrapped in the veil of her mourning for her father, my spirit grew solemn, as though I were in church. Herdegen must have felt this likewise, methinks, for he would bend the knee before her and hide his face in her lap, and kiss her hands again and again.

But these solemn hours were few.

First and last it was a happy fellowship, free and gay, though mingled with earnest, that held us together; and when Ann's father had been some few weeks dead our old gleefulness came back to us again, and then, after gazing at her for a while, Herdegen would suddenly strike the lute and sing the old merry round:

"Come, sweetheart, come to me.
Ah how I pine for thee!
Ah, how I pine for thee
Come, sweetheart, come to me.
Sweet rosy lips to kiss,
Come then and bring me bliss,
Come then and bring me bliss,
Sweet rosy lips to kiss!"

And we would all join in, even Cousin Maud; nay and she would look another way or quit the chamber, stealing away behind Kunz and holding up a warning finger, when she perceived how his Ann's "sweet, rosy lips" tempted Herdegen's to kiss them. But there were other many songs, and ofttimes, when we were in a more than common merry mood, we strange young things would sing the saddest tales and tunes we knew, such as that called "Two Waters," and yet were we only the more gay.

Herdegen could not be excused from his duty of paying his respects from time to time to the many friends of our honorable family, yet would he ever keep away from dances and feastings, and when he was compelled to attend I was ever at his side, and it was a joy to me to see how courteous, and withal how cold, was his demeanor to all other ladies.

The master's fiftieth birthday was honored in due course at the Tetzels' house, and to please my granduncle, Herdegen could not refuse to do his part in song and in the dance, and likewise to lead out Ursula, the daughter of the house, in the dances. Nor did he lose his gay but careless mien, although she would not quit his side and chose him to dance with her in "The Sulkers," a dance wherein the man and maid first turn their backs on each other and then make it up and kiss. But when it came to this, maiden shame sent the blood into my cheeks; for at the sound of the music, in the face of all the company she fell into his arms, as it were by mishap; and it served her right when he would not kiss her lips, which she was ready enough to offer, but only touched her brow with his.

Forasmuch as she had danced with him the Dance of Honor or first dance, it was his part to beg her hand for the last dance—the "grandfather's dance;"—[Still a well-known country dance in Germany.]—but she would fain punish him for the vexation he had caused her and turned her back upon him. He, however, would have none of this; he grasped her hand ere she was aware of him, and dragged her after him. It was vain to struggle, and soon his strong will was a pleasure to her, and her countenance beamed again full brightly, when as this dance requires, he had led the way with her, the rest all following, through chamber and hall, kitchen and courtyard, doors and windows, nay, and even the stables. In the course of this dance each one seized some utensil or house-gear, as we do to this day; only never a broom, which would bring ill-luck. Ursula had snatched up a spoon, and when the mad sport was ended and he had let go her hand, she rapped him with it smartly on the arm and cried: "You are still what you ever were, in the dance at least!"

But my brother only said: "Then will I try to become not the same, even in that."

Round the Christmas tree and at the sharing of gifts which Cousin Maud made ready for Christmas eve, we were all friendly and glad at heart, and Ann found her way to join us after that she had put the little ones to bed.

Herdegen said she herself was the dearest gift for which he could thank the Christ-child, and he had provided for her as a costly token the great Petrarca's heroic poem of Africa, in which he sings the deeds of the noble Scipio, and likewise his smaller poems, all written in a fair hand. They made three neat books, and on the leathern cover, the binder, by Herdegen's orders, had stamped the words, "ANNA-LAURA," in a wreath of full-blown roses. Nor was she slow to understand their intent, and her heart was uplifted with such glad and hopeful joy that the Christ-child for a certainty found no more blissful or thankful creature in all Nuremberg that Christmas eve.

The manifold duties which filled up all her days left her but scant time wherein to work for him she loved; nevertheless she had wrought with her needle a letter pouch, whereon the Schoppers' arms were embroidered in many colored silks, and the words 'Agape' and 'Pistis'—which are in Greek Love and Faithfulness in Greek letters with gold thread. Cousin Maud had dipped deep into her purse and likewise into her linen-press, and on the table under the Christmas-tree lay many a thing fit for the bride-chest of a maid of good birth; and albeit Ann could not but rejoice over these gifts for their own sake, she did so all the more gladly, inasmuch as she guessed that Cousin Maud was well-disposed to speed her marriage.

We were all, indeed, glad and thankful; all save the Magister, whose face was ill-content and sour by reason that he had culled many verses and maxims concerning love, for the most part from the Greek and Latin poets, and yet all his attempts to repeat them before Ann came to nothing, inasmuch as she was again and again taken up with Herdegen and with me, after she had once shaken hands with him and given him her greetings.

At supper he was as dumb as the carp which were served, and it befell that for the first time Herdegen took his seat between him and his heart's beloved; and verily I was grieved for him when, after supper, he withdrew downcast to his own chamber. The rest of us went forth to Saint Sebald's church, where that night there would be midnight matins, as there was every year, and a mass called the Christ mass. Cousin Maud and Kunz were with us, as in the old happy days when we were children and when we never missed; and in the streets as we went, we met all manner of folks singing gladly:

> *Puer natus in Bethlehem,*
> *Sing, rejoice, Jerusalem!*

or the carol:

> *Congaudeat turba fadelium!*
> *Natus est rex, Salvator omnium*
> *In Bethlehem.*

and we joined in; and at last all went together to see Ann to her home.

Next evening there were more costly gifts, but albeit Puer natus was still to be heard in the streets, we no longer were moved to join in.

CHAPTER XII

Every Christmas all my grand-uncle's kith and kin, or so many of them as were on good terms with him, assembled in the great house of the Im Hoffs. Everything in that dwelling spoke of ease and wealth, and no banqueting-hall could be more brightly lighted or more richly decked than that where the old man welcomed us on the threshold; and yet, how well soever the hearth was piled or the stove heated, a chill breath seemed to blow there.

While great and small were rejoicing over the grand old knight's bounty he himself would ever stand apart, and his calm, hueless countenance expressed no change. Meseemed he cared but little for the pleasure he gave us all; yet was he not idle in the matter, nor left it to others; for there was no single gift which he had not himself chosen as befitting him to whom it should be given.

The trade of his great house was for the most part with Venice, and it would have been easy to fancy oneself in some fine palazzo on the grand canal as one marked the carpets, the mirrors, the brocade, and the vessels in his house; and not a few of his tokens had likewise been brought from thence.

Before this largesse in his own house he was wont to bestow another, and a very noble one, on the old men and women of the poor folks in the town; and when this was over he went with them to the church of Saint Aegidius, and washed the feet of about a score of them, which act of penitential humility he was wont to repeat in Passion week.

Then when he had welcomed his kin, each one to his house, he would say to such as thanked him, if it were a child, very soberly: "Be a good child." But for elder folks he had no more than "It is well," or an almost churlish: "That is enough."

This evening he had given me a gown of costly brocade of Cyprus; to Kunz everything that a Junker might need on his travels; and to Herdegen the same sword which he himself had in past time worn at court; the hilt was set with gems and ended in the lion rampant, couped, of the Im Hoffs.

Ursula Tetzel, like me, had had a gown-piece which was lying near by the sword.

Herdegen, holding the jewelled weapon in his hand, thanked his grand-uncle, who muttered as was his wont "'Tis well, 'tis well," when Jost Tetzel put in his word, saying that the gift of a sword was supposed to part friends, but that this ill-effect might be hindered if he who received it made a return-offering to the giver, and so the token was made into a purchase.

At this Herdegen hastened to take out a gold pin set with sapphire stones, which Cousin Maud had given him, from his neck-kerchief, to offer it to his uncle; but the elder would have nothing to say to such foolishness, and pushed the pin away. But then when my brother did not cease, but besought him to accept it, inasmuch as he cared so greatly for his uncle's fatherly kindness, the old knight cried that he wanted no such sparkling finery, but that the day might come when he should require some payment and that Herdegen was then to remember that he was in his debt.

At this minute they were hindered from further speech by the servants, who came in to bid us to supper, and there stood ready wild fowl and fish, fruits and pastry, with the rarest wines and the richest vessels; the great middle table and the side buffet alike made such a show as though Pomona, Ceres, Bacchus, and Plutus had heaped it with prodigal hand. Yet was there no provision for merry-making. My grand-uncle loved to be quit of his guests at an early hour; hence no table was laid for them to sit down to meat, and each one held his plate in one hand.

Presently, as I strove to get free of young Master Vorchtel who had served me—and by the same token made love to me—I found my cousin in speech with my grand-uncle, and the last words of his urgent discourse, spoken as I came up with them, were that a woman of sound understanding, as she commonly seemed, should no longer suffer such a state of things.

Then Cousin Maud answered him, saying: "But you, my noble and worshipful Cousin Im Hoff, know how that a Schopper is ever ready to run his head against a wall. If we strive to thwart this hot-headed boy, he will of a certainty defy us; but if we leave him for a while to go his own way, the waters will not be dammed up, but will run to waste in the sand."

This was evil hearing, and much as it vexed me Ursula chafed me even more, whereas she made a feint of caring for none of the company present excepting only Sir Franz—who was yet her housemate—and being still pale and weak needed a friendly woman's hand for many little services, inasmuch as even now he could scarce use his right arm. Nay, and he seemed to like Ursula well enough as his helper; albeit he owed all her sweet care and loving glances to Herdegen, for she never bestowed them but when he chanced to look that way.

When we all took leave my grand-uncle bid Herdegen stay, and Kunz waited on us; but notwithstanding all his merry quips as we went home, not once could we be moved to laughter. My heart was indeed right heavy; a bitter drop had fallen into it by reason of Cousin Maud. I had ever deemed her incapable of anything but what was truest and best, and she had proved herself a double-dealer; and young as I was, and rejoicing in life, I said, nevertheless, in my soul's dejection, that if life was such that every poor human soul must be ever armed with doubt, saying, "Whom shall I trust or doubt?" then it was indeed a hard and painful journey to win through.

I slept in my cousin's room, and albeit Cousin Maud wist not that I had overheard her counsel given to my grand-uncle, she kept out of my way that night, and we neither of us spoke till we said good-night. Then could I no longer refrain myself, and asked whether it were verily and indeed her intent to part Herdegen from Ann.

And her ill-favored countenance grew strangely puckered and her bosom heaved till suddenly she cried beside herself: "Cruel! Unhappy! Oh! It will eat my heart out!" And she sobbed aloud, while I did the same, crying:

"But you love them both?"

"That I do, and that is the very matter," she broke in sadly enough. "Herdegen, and Ann! Why, I know not which I hold the dearer. But find me a wiser man in all Nuremberg than your grand-uncle. But verily, merciful Virgin, I know not what I would be at—I know not...!"

On this I forgot the respect due to her and put in: "You know not?" And whereas she made no reply, I railed at her, saying: "And yet you gave her the linen, and half the matters for her house-gear as a Christmas gift, as though they were known for a bride and groom to all the town. As old as you are and as wise, can you take pleasure in a love-match and even speed it forward as you have done, and yet purpose in your soul to hinder it at last? And is this the truth and honesty whereof early and late you have ever taught me? Is this being upright and faithful, or not rather speaking with two tongues?"

My fiery blood had again played me an evil trick, and I repented me when I perceived what great grief my violent speech had wrought in the dear soul. Never had I beheld her so feeble and doubting, and in a minute I was in her arms and a third person might have marvelled to hear us each craving pardon, she for her faint-hearted fears, and I for my unseemly outbreak. But in that hour I became her friend, and ceased to be no more than her child and fondling.

Herdegen was to be ready to set forth before Passion week; but ere he quitted home he made all the city ring with his praises, for, whereas he had hitherto won fame in the school of arms only, by the strength and skill of his arm, he now outdid every other in the procession of masks. Albeit this custom is still kept up to this very day, yet many an one may have forgotten how it first had its rise, although in my young days it was well known to most folks.

This then is to record, that in the days when the guilds were in revolt against the city council, the cutlers and the fleshers alone remained true to the noble families, and whereas they refused to take any guerdon for their faithfulness, which must have been paid them at the cost of the rest, they craved no more than the right of a making a goodly show in a dance and procession at the Carnival; and they were by the same token privileged at that time to wear apparel of velvet and silk, like gentle folks of noble and knightly degree.

Now this dance and its appurtenances were known at the masked show, and inasmuch as the aid of the governing class was needed to keep the streets clear for the throng of craftsmen, and as likewise the yearly outlay was beyond their means, the sons of the great houses took a pride in paying goodly sums for the right of taking a place in the procession. And as for our high-spirited young lord, skilled as he was with his weapon, he had seen and taken part in many such gay carnival doings among the Italians, and it was a delight to him to join in the like sport at home, and many were fain to gaze at him rather than at the guilds.

They assembled under the walls in two bands, and marched past the town hall and from thence to a dance of both guilds. Each had a dance of its own. The Fleshers' was such a dance as in England is called a country dance and they held leather-straps twisted to look like sausages; the cutlers' dance was less clumsy, and they carried naked swords.

But the show which most delighted the bystanders was the procession of masks, wherein, indeed, there were many things pleasant and fair to behold.

A party of men in coarse raiment called the men of the woods, carrying sheaves of oak boughs with acorns, and a number of mummers in fools' garb, wielding wooden bats, cleared the way for the procession; first then came minstrels, with drums and pipes and trumpets and bag-pipes, and merry bells ringing out withal. Next came one on horseback with nuts, which he flung down among the children, whereat there was merry scuffling and screaming on the ground. From the windows likewise and balconies there was no end of the laughter and cries; the young squires gave the maids and ladies who sat there no peace for the flowers and sweetmeats they cast up at them, and eggs filled with rose-water.

This year, whereof I write, many folks in the procession wore garments of the same color and shape; but among them there were some who loved a jest, and were clothed as wild men and women, or as black-amoors, ogres that eat children, ostrich-birds, and the like. Last of all came the chief glory of the show, various great buildings and devices drawn by horses: a Ship of Fools, and behind that a wind-mill, and a fowler's decoy wherein Fools, men and women both, were caught, and other such pastimes.

My Herdegen had mingled with this wondrous fellowship arrayed as a knight crusader leading three captive Saracen princes; namely, the two young Masters Loffelholz and Schlebitzer, who had stirred him to dress in the fencing-school, mounted on horses, and between them my squire Akusch on the bear-leader's camel, all in white as a Son of the Desert; and the three of them fettered with chains made of wood.

My grand-uncle had lent Herdegen the suit of mail he himself had worn in his youth at a tournament.

Cousin Maud had provided his white cloak with a red cross, and as he rode forth on a noble black steed in mail-harness with scarlet housings—the finest and stoutest horse in the Im Hoffs' stables-and his golden hair shining in the sun, many a maid could not take her eyes off from him.

Kunz, in the garb of a fool, hither and thither, nay, and everywhere at once, doubtless had the better sport; but Herdegen's heart beat the higher, for he could hear a thousand voices proclaiming him the most comely and his troop the most princely of all; from many a window a flower was shed on him, or a ribband, or a knot. At last, when the dance was all over, the guilds with the town-pipers betook them to the head constable's quarters, where they were served with drink and ate the Shrove-Tuesday meal of fish which was given in their honor. When the procession was past and gone my grand-uncle bid Herdegen go to him, and that which the old man then said and did to move him to give up his love was shrewdly planned and not without effect on his mind. After looking at him from head to foot, saying nothing but with no small contentment, he clapped him kindly on the shoulder and led him, as though by chance, up to the Venice mirror in the dining-hall. Then pointing to the image before him: "A Tancred!" he cried, "a Godfrey! Richard of the Lion-heart! And the bride a miserable scrivener's wench!—a noble bride!" Thereupon Herdegen fired up and began to speak in praise of Ann's rare and choice beauty; but his guardian stopped him short, laid his arm round his shoulders, and muttered in his ear that in his young days likewise youths of noble birth had to be sure made love to the fair daughters of the common citizens, but the man who could have thought of courting one of them in good faith....

Here he broke off with a sharp laugh, and drawing the boy closer to him, cried:

"No harm is meant my Tancred! And you may keep the black horse in remembrance of this hour."

It was old Berthold, my uncle's body-servant who told me all this; Herdegen when he came home answered none of my questions. He would not grant my prayer that he should show himself to Ann in his knight's harness, and said somewhat roughly that she loved not such mummery. Thus it was not hard to guess what was in his mind; but how came it to pass that this old man, whose princely wife had wrought ruin to his peace and happiness, could so diligently labor to lead him he best loved on earth into the like evil course? And among many matters of which I lacked understanding there was yet this one: Wherefore should Eppelein, who so devoutly loved his master, and who knew right well how to value a young maid's beauty—and why should my good Susan and the greater part of our servitors have turned so spitefully against Ann, to whom in past days they were ever courteous and serviceable, since they had scented a betrothal between her and my eldest brother?

From the first I had been but ill-pleased to see Herdegen so diligent over this idle sport and spending so many hours away from his sweetheart, when he was so soon to quit us all. Nevertheless I had not the heart to admonish him, all the more as in many a dull hour he was apt to believe that, for the sake of his love, he must need deny himself sundry pleasures which our father had been free to enjoy; and I weened that I knew whence arose this faint-heartedness which was so little akin to his wonted high spirit.

Looking backward, a little before this time, I note first that Ann had not been able to keep her love-matters a secret from her mother. Albeit the still young and comely widow had solemnly pledged herself to utter no word of the matter, like most Italian women—and may be many a Nuremberger—

she could not refrain herself from telling that of which her heart and brain were full, deeming it great good fortune for her child and her whole family; and she had shared the secret with all her nearest friends. Eight days before Shrove Tuesday Cousin Maud and we three Schoppers had been bidden to spend the evening in the house by the river, and Dame Giovanna, kind-hearted as ever, but not far-seeing, had likewise bidden her father-in-law, the lute-player, and Adam Heyden from the tower, and Ann's one and only aunt, the widow of Rudel Hennelein.

This Hennelein had been the town bee-master, the chief of the bee-keepers, who, then as now, had their business out in the Lorenzer-Wald. His duties had been to hold an assize for the bee-keepers three times in the year at a village called Feucht, and to lend an ear to their complaints; and albeit he had fulfilled his office without blame, he had dwelt in strife with his wife, and being given to rioting, he was wont rather to go to the tavern than sit at table with his cross-grained wife.

When he presently died there was but small leaving, and the widow in the little house in the milk market had need to look twice at every farthing, although she had not chick nor child. And whereas full half of the offerings sent by the bee-keepers to help out their master's widow were in honey, she strove to turn this to the best account, and to this end she would by no means sell it to the dealers who would offer to take it, but carried it herself in neat little crocks, one at a time, to the houses of the rich folks, whereby her gains were much the greater.

Whereas her husband had been a member of the worshipful class of magistrates, she deemed that such trading ill-beseemed her dignity; and she at all times wore a great fur hat as large round as a cart-wheel of fair size, and all the other array of a well-to-do housewife, though in truth somewhat threadbare. Then she would offer her honey as a gift to the mothers of children for their dear little ones; nor could she ever be moved to name a price for her gift, inasmuch as it was not fitting that a bee-master's widow should do so, while it was all to her honor when a little bounty was offered as civil return.

Her honey was good enough, and the children were ever glad to see her: all the more so for that they had their sport of her behind her back, inasmuch as that she was a laughable little body, who had a trick of repeating the last word of every sentence she spoke. Thus she would say not: "Ah! here comes Kunz," but, "Here comes Kunz Kunz." Moreover, she ever held her head between her two hands, tightly, as though with that great fur cap her thin neck were in danger of breaking.

In this way she had dealings with most of our noble families; and the young ones would call her not Hennelein, as her name was, but Henneleinlein, in jest at her foolish trick of repeating her last word.

So long as I could remember, Mistress Henneleinlein had been wont to bring honey to our house, and had received from Cousin Maud, besides many a bright coin, likewise sundry worn but serviceable garments as "remembrances." And Herdegen foremost of us all had been ready to make sport of her; but it had come to his knowledge that she was ever benign to lovers, and had helped many a couple to come together.

The glad tidings that her niece was chosen by fate to rule over the house of the Schoppers had filled her above all others with pride and contentment, and Dame Giovanna having told her this secret and then bidden her to meet us, she stuck so closely to Herdegen that Ann was filled with vexation and fears. I could not but mark that my brother was sorely ill-pleased when Dame Henneleinlein patted his arm; and when she kissed his sweetheart on the lips he shrank as though someone had laid afoul hand on his light-hued velvet doublet. He had always felt a warm friendship for the worthy lute-player, who was a master in his own art; yea, and many a time had he right gladly mounted the tower-stairs to see the old organist; but now, to be treated as a youngster of their own kith by these two good men filled him with loathing; for it may well be that many an one whom we are well pleased to seek and truly value in his own home and amid his own company, seems another man when he makes claim to live with us as one of ourselves.

Cousin Maud had not chosen to accept Dame Giovanna's bidding, perchance for my grand-uncle's sake; she thus escaped the vexation of seeing Herdegen, on this first night spent with his future kindred, so silent and moody that he was scarce like himself. He turned pale and bit his nether lip, as he never did but when he was mastering his temper with great pains, when Mistress Henneleinlein who had hitherto known him only as a roystering young blade and now interpreted his reserve and silence after her own fashion noted mysteriously that the Junker would have to take a large family with his young bride—though, indeed, there was a hope that the burden might ere long be lighter. For she went on to say, with a leer at Mistress Giovanna, that so comely a step-mother would have suitors in plenty, and she herself had one in her eye, if he were but brought to the point, who would provide abundantly not only for the mother but for all the brood of little ones.

This and much more did he himself repeat to me as we walked home, speaking with deep ire and in tones of wrath; and what else Dame Henneleinlein had poured into his ear was to me not so much unpleasing as a cause of well-grounded fears, inasmuch as the old body had told him that the man who was fain to pay his court to Mistress Giovanna was none other than the coppersmith, Ulman Pernhart, the father of the fair maid for whose sake Aunt Jacoba had banished her only son.

In vain did I in all honesty speak the praises of the coppersmith; Herdegen turned a deaf ear, even as my uncle and aunt had done. The thought that his wife should ever be required to honor this handicraftsman, if only as a step-father, and that he should hear himself addressed by him as "Son," was too shrewd a thrust.

The next morning the Junkers had carried him off to the school of arms and then to the gentlemen's tavern to take his part in the masquerade; and when, at a later hour, after the throng had scattered, Ann came to our house, her lover was not at home: he had gone off again to the revels at the tavern where he would meet such workingmen as his sweetheart's future step-father.

At the same time, as it fell, Brother Ignatius, of the order of Grey Friars, had come many times to hold forth at our house, by desire of my grand-uncle whose almoner he was, and when Herdegen announced to us on Ash Wednesday that the holy man had craved to be allowed to travel in his company as far as Ingolstadt, I foresaw no good issue; for albeit the Father was a right reverend priest, whose lively talk had many a time given me pleasure, it must for certain be his intent to speed my uncle's wishes.

In spite of all, Herdegen was in such deep grief at departing that I put away all doubts and fears.

Ann, who felt in all matters as he felt and put her whole trust in him, was wise enough to know that he could have no bond with her kith and kin; nay, that it must be hard on him to have to call such a woman as Mistress Henneleinlein his aunt. Also he and she had agreed that hereafter he should dwell no more at Nuremberg, but seek some office and duty in the Imperial service; and Sir Franz had been diligent in asking his uncle's good word, he being one of those highest in power at the Emperor's court.

Now, when a short time before his departing they were alone with me, Ann, bearing in mind this pact they had made, cried out: "You promise me we shall build our nest in some place far from hence; and be it where it may, wherever we may be left to ourselves and have but each other, a happy life must await us."

At this his eyes flashed, and he cried with a lad's bold spirit:

"With a doctor's hood, at the Emperor's court, I shall ere long be councillor, and at last, God willing, Chancellor of the Realm!"

After this they spoke yet many loving and touching words, and when he was already in the saddle and waved her a last farewell, tears flowed from his eyes—

I saw them for certain.—And at that moment I besought the Lord that He would rather chastise and try me with pain and grief, but bring these two together and let their marriage be crowned by the highest bliss ever vouchsafed to human hearts.

CHAPTER XIII

Spring was past, and again the summer led me and Ann back into the green wood. Aunt Jacoba's sickness was no whit amended, and the banishment of her only and comely son gnawed at her heart; but the more she needed tending and cheering the more Ann could do for her and the dearer she became to the heart of the sick woman.

Kunz was ever in Venice. Herdegen wrote right loving letters at first from Padua, but then they came less often, and the last Ann ever had to show me was a mere feint which pleased me ill indeed, inasmuch as, albeit it was full of big words, it was empty of tidings of his life or of his heart's desire. What all this must mean Ann, with her clear sense and true love, could not fail to see; nevertheless she ceased not from building on her lover's truth; or, if she did not, she hid that from all the world, even from me.

We came from the forest earlier than we were wont, on Saint Maurice's day, forasmuch as that Ann could not be longer spared and, now more than ever, I could not bear to leave her alone.

Uncle Christian rode to the town with us, and if he had before loved her well, in this last long time of our all being together he had taken her yet more into his heart. And now, whereas he had given her the right to warn him against taking too much wine, he was fain to call her his little watchman, by reason that it is the watchman's part to give warning of the enemy's onset.

But while Ann was so truly beloved at the Forest lodge, on her return home she found no pleasant welcome. In her absence the coppersmith Pernhart had wooed her mother in good earnest, and the eldest daughter not being on the spot, had sped so well that the widow had yielded. Ann once made bold to beseech her mother with due reverence to give up her purpose, but she fell on her child's neck, as though Ann were the mother, entreating her, with many tears, to let her have her will. Ann of a certainty would not now be long under her roof to cherish the younger children, and it was not in her power as their mother to guide them in the way in which their father would have them to walk. For this Ulman Pernhart was the fittest man. Her dead husband had been a schoolmate of her suitor's, and of his brother the very reverend lord Bishop, and he had thought highly of

Master Ulman. This it was gave her strength to follow the prompting of her heart. In this way did the mother try to move her child to look with favor on the desire of her fiery Italian heart, now shame-faced and coaxing, and anon with tears in her eyes; and albeit the widow was past five and thirty and her suitor nigh upon fifty, yet no man seeing the pair together would have made sport of their love. The Venice lady had lost so little of her youthful beauty and charms that it was in truth a marvel; and as to Master Pernhart, he was not a man to be overlooked, even among many.

As he was at this time he might be taken for the very pattern of a stalwart and upright German mastercraftsman; nay, nor would a knight's harness of mail have ill-beseemed him. Or ever he had thought of paying court to Mistress Giovanna I had heard the prebendary Master von Hellfeld speak of Pernhart as a right good fellow, of whom the city might be proud; and he then spoke likewise of Master Ulman's brother, who had become a servant of the Holy Church, and while yet a young man had been raised to the dignity of a bishop.

When the great schism had come to a happy ending, and one Head, instead of three, ruled the Church, Pope Martin V. had chosen him to sit in his council and kept him at Rome, where he was one of the powers of the Curia.

Albeit his good German name of Pernhart was now changed to Bernardi, he had not ceased to love his native town and his own kin, and had so largely added to the wealth and ease of his own mother and his only brother that the coppersmith had been able to build himself a dwelling little behind those of the noble citizens. He had been forlorn in his great house of late, but no such cause as that was needed to move him to cast his eye on the fair widow of his very reverend brother's best friend.

While Ann was away in the forest Mistress Giovanna had let Pernhart into the secret of her daughter's betrothal to Herdegen, and so soon as the young maid was at home again he had spoken to her of the matter, telling her, in few but hearty words, that she would be ever welcome to his house and there fill the place of his lost Gertrude; but that if she was fain to wed an honest man, he would make it his business to provide her outfit.

These things, and much more, inclined me in his favor, little as I desired that he should wed the widow, for Herdegen's sake; and when I met him for the first time as betrothed to Ann's mother, and the grandlooking man shook my hand with hearty kindness, and then thanked me with warmth and simplicity for whatsoever I had done for her who henceforth would be his dearest and most precious treasure, I returned the warm grasp of his hand with all honesty, and it was from the bottom of my heart that I answered him, saying that I gladly hailed him as a new friend, albeit I could not hope for the same from my brother.

He heard this with a strange smile, half mournful, but, meseemed, half proud; then he held forth his horny, hard-worked hand, and said that to be sure it was an ill-matched pair when such a hand as that should clasp a soft and white one such as might come out of a velvet sleeve; that whereas, in order to win the woman he loved, he had taken her tribe of children into the bargain, and fully purposed to have much joy of them and be a true father to them, my lord brother, if his love were no less true, must make the best of his father-in-law, whose honor, though he was but of simple birth, was as clean as ever another man's in the eyes of God.

And as we talked I found there was more and nobler matter in his brain and heart than I had ever weened I might find in a craftsman. We met often and learned to know each other well, and one day it fell that I asked him whether he had in truth forgiven the Junker through whom he had lost the one he loved best.

He forthwith replied that I was not to lay the blame on one whom he would ever remember as a brave and true-hearted youth, inasmuch as it was not my cousin, but he himself who had put an end to the love-making between Gotz and Gertrude. It was after the breach between Gotz and his parents that it had been most hard to turn a deaf ear to the prayers of the devoted lover and of his own child. But, through all, he had borne in mind the doctrine by which his father had ever ruled his going, namely, not to bring on our neighbor such grief as would make our own heart sore. Therefore he examined himself as to what he would feel towards one who should make his child to wed against his will with a suitor he liked not; and whereas his own dignity as a man and his care for his daughter's welfare forbade that he should give her in marriage to a youth whose kinsfolks would receive her with scorn and ill-feeling, rather than with love and kindness, he had at last set his heart hard against young Waldstromer, whom he had loved as his own son, and forced him to go far away from his sweetheart. I, in my heart, was strangely wroth with my cousin in that he had not staked his all to win so fair a maid; nay, and I made so bold as to confess that in Gertrude's place I should have gone after my lover whithersoever he would, even against my father's will.

And again that proud smile came upon Ulman Pernhart's bearded lips, and his eye flashed fire as he said: "My life moves in a narrow round, but all that dwell therein bend to my will as the copper bends under my hammer. If you think that the Junker gave in without a struggle you are greatly mistaken; after I had forbidden him the house, he had tempted Gertrude to turn against me and was ready to carry her off; nay, and would you believe it, my own mother sided with the young ones. The priest even was in readiness to marry them privily, and they would have won the day in spite of me. But the eyes of jealousy are ever the sharpest; my head apprentice, who was madly in love with the maid, betrayed the plot, and then, Mistress Margery, were things said and done—things concerning which I had best hold my peace. And if you crave to know them, you may ask my mother. You will see some day, if you do not scorn to enter my house and if you gain her friendship—and I doubt not that you will, albeit it is not granted to every one—she will be glad enough to complain of my dealings in this matter—mine, her own son's, although on other points she is wont to praise my virtues over-loudly."

This discourse raised my cousin once more to his old place in my opinion, and I knew now that the honest glance of his blue eyes, which doubtless had won fair Gertrude's heart, was trustworthy and true.

Master Ulman Pernhart was married in a right sober fashion to fair Mistress Giovanna, and I remember to this day seeing them wed in Saint Laurence's Church. It was a few months before this that I was taken for the first time to a dance at the town hall. There, as soon as I had forgotten my first little fears, I took my pleasure right gladly to the sound of the music, and I verily delighted in the dance. But albeit I found no lack of young ladies my friends, and still less of youths who would fain win my favor, I nevertheless lost not the feeling that I had left part of my very being at home; nay, that I scarce had a right to these joys, since my brothers were in a distant land and Ann could not share them with me, and while I was taking my pleasure she had the heart-ache.

Then was there a second dance, and a third and fourth; and at home there came a whole troop of young men in their best apparel to ask of Cousin Maud, each after his own fashion, to be allowed to pay court to me; but albeit they were all of good family, and to many a one I felt no dislike, I felt nothing at all like love as I imagined it, and I would have nothing to say to any one of them. And all this I took with a light heart, for which Cousin Maud many a time,—and most rightly—reproved me.

But at that time, and yet more as the months went on, I hardly knew my own mind; another fate than my own weighed most on my soul; and I thought so little of my own value that meseemed it could add to no man's happiness to call me his. All else in life passed before my eyes like a shadow; a time came when all joy was gone from me, and my suitors sought me in vain in the dancing-hall, for a great and heavy grief befell me.

All was at an end—even now I scarce can bear to write the words— between Ann and Herdegen; and by no fault of hers, but only and wholly by reason of his great and unpardonable sin.

But I will write down in order how it came about. So early as at Martinmas I heard from Cousin Maud—and my grand-uncle had told her—that Herdegen had quitted Padua and that it was his intent to take the degree of doctor at Paris whither the famous Gerson's great genius was drawing the studious youth of all lands; and his reason for this was that a bloody fray had made the soil of Italy too hot for his feet. "These tidings boded evil; all the more as neither we nor Ann had a word from Herdegen in his own hand to tell us that he had quitted the country and his school. Then, in my fear and grief, I could not help going to my grand-uncle, but he would have nothing to say to me or to Cousin Maud, or else he put us off with impatient answers, or empty words that meant nothing. Thus we lived in dread and sorrow, till at last, a few days before Pernhart was married, a letter came to me from Eppelein, and I have it before me now, among other papers all gone yellow.

"From your most duteous and obedient servant Eppelein Gockel to the lady Margery Schopper," was the superscription. And he went on to excuse himself in that he knew not the art of writing, and had requested the service of the Magister of the young Count von Solms.

"And inasmuch as I erewhile pledged my word as a man to the illustrious and worshipful Mistress Margery, in her sisterly care, that I would write to her if we at any time needed the favor of her counsel and help, I would ere now have craved for the Magister's aid if the all-merciful Virgin had not succored us in due season.

"Nevertheless my heart was moved to write to you, gracious and worshipful Mistress Margery, inasmuch as I wist you would be in sorrow, and longing for tidings of my gracious master; for it is by this time long since I gave his last letter for the Schopperhof in charge to the German post-runner; and meseems that my gracious master has liked to give his precious time to study and to other pastimes rather than to those who, being his next of kin, are ever ready and willing to be patient with him; as indeed they could if they pleased enquire of my lord the knight Sebald Im Hoff as to his well-being. My gracious master gave him to know by long letters how matters were speeding with him, and of a certainty told him how that the old Marchese and his nephews, malicious knaves, came to blows with us at Padua by reason of the old Marchese's young and fair lady, who held my gracious master so dear that all Padua talked thereof.

"Nevertheless it was an evil business, inasmuch as three of them fell on us in the darkness of night; and if the merciful Saints had not protected us with their special grace nobler and more honorable blood should have been shed than those rogues. Also we came to Paris in good heart; and safe and sound in body; and this is a city wherein life is far more ravishing than in Nuremberg.

"Whereas I have known full well that you, most illustrious Mistress Margery, have ever vouchsafed your gracious friendship to Mistress Ann Spiesz—and indeed I myself hold her in the highest respect, as a lady rich in all virtue—I would beseech her to put away from her heart all thought of my gracious master as soon as may be, and to strive no more to keep his troth, forasmuch as it can do no good: Better had she look for some other suitor who is more honest in his intent, that so she may not wholly waste her maiden days—which sweet Saint Katharine forbid! Yet, most worshipful Mistress Margery, I entreat you with due submission not to take this amiss in your beloved brother, nor to withdraw from him any share of your precious love, whereas my gracious master may rightly look higher for his future wife. And as touching his doings now in his unmarried state, of us the saying is true: Like master, like man. And whereas I, who am but a poor and simple serving man, have never been fain to set my heart on one only maid, no less is to be looked for in my gracious master, who is rich and of noble birth."

This epistle would of a certainty have moved me to laughter at any other time but, as things stood, the matter and manner of the low varlet's letter in daring to write thus of Ann, roused me to fury. And yet he was a brave fellow, and of rare faithfulness to his master; for when the Marchese's nephew had fallen upon Herdegen, he had wrenched the sword out of the young nobleman's hand at the peril of his own life and had thereafter modestly held his peace as to that brave deed. It was, in truth, hard not to betray the coming of this letter, even by a look; yet did I hide it; but when another letter was brought, not long after, all care and secrecy were vain.

Oh! that dreadful letter. I could not hide the matter of it; but I let pass her mother's wedding before I confessed to Ann what my brother had written to me.

That cruel letter lies before me now. It is longer than any he had written me heretofore, and I will here write it fair, for indeed I could not, an I would, copy the writing, so wild and reckless as it is.

"All must be at an end, Margery, betwixt Ann and me"—and those first words stung me like a whip-lash. "There. 'Tis written, and now you know it. I was never worthy of her, for I have sold my heart's love for money, as Judas sold the Lord.

"Not that my love or longing are dead. Even while I write I feel dragged to her; a thousand voices cry to me that there is but one Ann, and when a few weeks ago the young Sieur de Blonay made so bold as to vaunt of his lady and her rose-red as above all other ladies and colors, my sword compelled him to yield the place of honor to blue—for whose sake you know well.

"And nevertheless I must give her up. Although I fled from temptation, it pursued me, and when it fell upon me, after a short battle I was brought low. The craving for those joys of the world which she tried to teach me to scorn, is strong within me. I was born to sin; and now as matters stand they must remain. A wight such as I am, who shoots through life like a wild hawk, cannot pause nor think until a shaft has broken his wings. The bitter fate which bids me part from Ann has stricken me thus, and now I can only look back and into my own soul; and the fairer, the sweeter, the loftier is she whom I have lost, the darker and more vile, meseemeth, is all I discover in myself.

"Yet, or ever I cast behind me all that was pure and noble, righteous and truly blissful, I hold up the mirror to my own sinful face, and will bring, myself to show to you, my Margery, the hideous countenance I behold therein.

"I will not cloke nor spare myself in anything; and yet, at this hour, which finds me sober and at home, having quitted my fellows betimes this night, I verily believe that I might have done well, and not ill, and what was pleasing in the sight of God, and in yours, my Margery, and in the eyes of Ann and of all righteous folk, if only some other hand had had the steering of my life's bark.

"Margery, we are orphans; and there is nothing a man needs so much, in the years while he is still unripe and unsure of himself, as a master whom he must revere in fear or in love. And we—I—Margery, what was my grand-uncle to me?

"You and I again are of one blood and so near in age that, albeit one may counsel the other, it is scarce to be hoped that I should take your judgment, or you mine, without cavil.

"Then Cousin Maud! With all the mother's love she has ever shown us, all I did was right in her eyes; and herein doubtless lies the difference between a true mother, who brought us with travail into the world, and a loving foster-mother, who fears to turn our hearts from her by harshness; but the true mother punishes her children wherein she deems it good, inasmuch as she is sure of their love. My cousin's love was great indeed, but her strictness towards me was too small. Out of sheer love, when I went to the High School she kept my purse filled; then, as I grew older, our uncle did likewise, though for other reasons; and now that I have redenied Ann, to do his pleasure, I loathe myself. Nay, more and more since I am raised to such fortune as thousands may envy me; inasmuch as my granduncle purposes to make me his heir by form of law. Last night, when I came home with great gains from play in my pocket, I was nigh to put an end to the woes of this life....

"But have no fear, Margery. A light heart soon will bring to the top again what ruth, at this hour, is bearing to the deeps. Of what use is waiting? Am I then the first Junker who has made love to a sweet maid of low birth, only to forget her for a new lady love?

"Sooth to say, Margery, my confessor, to whom—albeit with bitter pains—I am laying open every fold of my heart—yes, Margery, if Ann's cradle had been graced with a coat of arms matters would be otherwise. But to call a copper-smith father-in-law, and little Henneleinlein Madame Aunt! In church, to nod from the old seats of the Schoppers to all those common folk as my nearest kin, to meet the lute-player among my own people, teaching the lads and maids their music, and to greet him as dear grandfather, to see my brethren and sisters-in-law busy in the clerks' chambers or work-shops—all this I say is bitter to the taste; and yet more when the tempter on the other side shows the gaudy young gentleman the very joys dearest to his courtly spirit. And with what eloquence and good cheer has Father Ignatius set all this before mine eyes here in Paris, doubtless with honest intent; and he spoke to my heart soberly and to edification, setting forth all that the precepts of the Lord, and my old and noble family required of me.

"Much less than all this would have overruled so feeble a wight as I am. I promised Father Ignatius to give up Ann, and, on my home-coming, to submit in all things to my uncle and to agree with him as to what each should yield up and renounce to the other—as though it were a matter of merchandise in spices from the Levant, or silk kerchiefs from Florence; and thereupon the holy Friar gave me his benediction, as though my salvation were henceforth sure in this world and the next.

"I rode forth with him even to the gate, firm in the belief that I had thrown the winning number in life's game; but scarce had I turned my horse homeward when I wist that I had cast from me all the peace and joy of my soul.

"It is done. I have denied Ann—given her up forever—and whereas she must one day hear it, be it done at once. You, my poor Margery, I make my messenger. I have tried, in truth, to write to Ann, but it would not do. One thing you must say, and that is that, even when I have sinned most against her, I have never forgotten her; nay, that the memory of that happy time when she was fain to call herself my Laura moved me to ride forth to Treviso, where, in the chapel of the Franciscan Brethren, there may be seen a head of the true Laura done by the limner Simone di Martino, the friend of Petrarca, a right worthy work of art. Methought she drew me to her with voice and becks. And yet, and yet—woe, woe is me!

"My pen has had a long rest, for meseemed I saw first Petrarca's lady with her fair braids, and then Ann with her black hair, which shone with such lustrous, soft waves, and lay so nobly on the snow-white brow. Her eyes and mien are verily those of Laura; both alike pure and lofty. But here my full heart over-flows; it cannot forget how far Ann exceeds Laura in sweet woman's grace.

"Day is breaking, and I can but sigh forth to the morning: 'Lost, lost! I have lost the fairest and the best!'

"Then I sat long, sunk in thought, looking out of window, across the bare tree-tops in the garden, at the grey mist which seems as though it ended only at the edge of the world. It drips from the leafless boughs, and mine eyes—I need not hide it—will not be kept dry. It is as though the leaves from the tree of my life had all dropped on the ground—nay, as though my own guilty hand had torn them from the stem."

"I have but now come home from a right merry company! It is of a truth a merciful fashion which turns night into day. Yes, Margery, for one whose first desire is to forget many matters, this Paris is a place of delight. I have drunk deep of the wine-cup, but I would call any man villain who should say that I am drunk. Can I not write as well as ever another—and this I know, that if I sold myself it was not cheap. It has cost me my love, and whereas it was great the void is great to fill. Wherefore I say: 'Bring hither all that giveth joy, wine and love-making, torches and the giddy dame in velvet and silk, dice and gaming, and mad rides, the fresh greenwood and bloody frays!' Is this nothing? Is it even a trivial thing?

"How, when all is said and done, shall we answer the question as to which is the better lot: heavenly love, soaring on white swan's wings far above all that is common dust, as Ann was wont to sing of it, or earthly joys, bold and free, which we can know only with both feet on the clod?

"I have made choice and can never turn back. Long life to every pleasure, call it by what name you will! You have a gleeful, rich, and magnificent brother, little Margery; and albeit the simple lad of old, who chose to wife the daughter of a poor clerk, may have been dearer to you—as he was to my own heart—yet love him still! Of his love you are ever sure; remember him in your prayers; and as for that you have to say to Ann, say it in such wise that she shall not take it over much to heart. Show her how unworthy of her is this brother of yours, though in your secret soul you shall know that my guardian saint never had, nor ever shall have, any other face than hers.

"Now will I hasten to seal this letter and wake Eppelein that he may give it to the post-rider. I am weary of tearing up many sheets of paper, but if I were to read through in all soberness that I have written half drunk, this letter would of a certainty go the way of many others written by me to you, and to my beloved, faithful, only love, my lost Ann."

CHAPTER XIV

Master Pernhart was wed on Tuesday after Palm Sunday. Ann was wont to come to our house early on Wednesday morning, and this was ever a happy meeting to which we gave the name of "the Italian spinning-hour," by reason that one of us would turn her wheel and draw out the yarn, while the other read aloud from the works of the great Italian poets.

Nor did Ann fail to come on this Wednesday after the wedding; but I had thrust Herdegen's letter into the bosom of my bodice and awaited her with a quaking heart.

Her spirit was heavy; I could see in her eyes that they had shed tears, and at my first question they filled again. Had she not seen her mother this morn beaming with happiness, and then remembered, with new pangs of heartache, the father she had lost scarce a year ago and whose image seemed to have faded out of the mind of the wife he had so truly loved.

When I said to her that I well understood her sorrow, but that I had other matter to lay before her which might bring her yet more cruel grief, she knew that it must be as touching Herdegen; and whereas before I spoke I could only clasp her to me and could not bring out a single word, she thrust me from her and cried: "Herdegen? Speak! Some ill has come upon him! Margery—Merciful Virgin! How you are sobbing!—Dead—is he dead?"

As she said these words her cheeks turned pale and, when I shook my head, she seized my hand and asked sadly: "Worse? Then he has broken faith once more?"

Meseemed I could never speak again; and yet I might not keep silence, and the words broke from my bursting heart: "Ah, worse and far worse; more strange, more terrible! I have it here, in his hand.—Henceforth—my uncle, his rich inheritance.... All is over, Ann, betwixt him and you. And I— oh, that he should have left it to me to tell it!"

She stood in front of me as if rooted to the ground, and it was some time before she could find a word. Then she said in a dull voice: "Where is the letter?"

I snatched it out of the bosom of my dress and was about to rend it as I went towards the hearth, but she stood in my way, snatched the letter violently from me, and cried: "Then if all is at an end, I will at any rate be clear about it. No false comfort, no cloaking of the truth!"

And she strove to wrench Herdegen's letter from me. But my strength was greater than hers, indeed full great for a maid; yet my heart told me that in her case my will would have been the same, so I made no more resistance but yielded up the letter. Then and there she read it; and although she was pale as death and I marked how her lips trembled and every nerve in her body, her eyes were dry, and when she presently folded the letter and held it forth to me, she said with light scorn which cut in—to the heart: "This then is what matters have come to! He has sold his love and his sweetheart! Only her face, it would seem, is not in the bargain by reason that he keeps that to rob his saint of her holiness! Well, he is free, and the wild joys of life in every form are to make up for love; and yet—and yet, Margery, pray that he may not end miserably!"

Gentle pity had sounded in these last words, and I took her hand and besought her right earnestly: "And you, Ann. Do you pray with me." But she shook her head and replied: "Nay, Margery; all is at an end between him and me, even thoughts and yearning. I know him no more—and now let me go." With this she put on her little cloak, and was by the door already when Cousin Maud came in with some sweetmeats, as she was ever wont to do when we thus sat spinning; and as soon as she had set down that which she was carrying she opened her arms to the outcast maid, to clasp her to her bosom and comfort her with good words; but Ann only took her hand, pressed it to her lips, and vanished down the stairs.

At dinner that morning the dishes would have been carried out as full as they were brought in, if Master Peter had not done his best to hinder it; and as soon as the meal was over I could no longer bear myself in the house, but went off straight to the Pernharts'.

There the air seemed warmer and lighter, and Mistress Giovanna welcomed me to her new home right gladly; but she would not suffer me to go to Ann's chamber, forasmuch as that she had a terrible headache and had prayed to see no one, not even me. Yet I felt strongly drawn to her, and as the new-made wife knew that she and I were as one she did not forbid me from going upstairs, where Pernhart had made dead Gertrude's room all clean and fresh for Ann. Now whereas I knew that when her head ached every noise gave her pain, I mounted the steps with great care and opened the door softly without knocking. Also she was not aware of my coming. I would fain have crept away unseen; or even rather would have fallen on my knees by her side to crave her forgiveness for the bitter wrong my brother had done her. She was lying on the bed, her face hidden in the pillows, and her slender body shook as in an ague fit, while she sobbed low but right bitterly. Nor did she mark my presence there till I fell on my knees by the bed and cast my arms about her. Then she suddenly raised herself from the pillows, passed her hand across her wet eyes, and entreated me to leave her. Yet I did not as she bade me; and when she saw how deeply I took her griefs to heart, she rose from her couch, on which she had lain down with all her clothes on, and only prayed me that this should be the last time I would ever speak with her of Herdegen.

Then she led me to her table and showed me things which she had laid out thereon; poor little gifts which my brother had brought her; every one, except only the Petrarca with the names in gold: Anna-Laura. And she desired that I would take them all and send them back to Herdegen at some fitting time.

As I nodded sadly enough, she must have seen in my face that I missed the little volumes and, ere I was aware, she had taken them out of her chest and thrown them in with the rest.

Then she cried in a changed voice: "That likewise—Ah, no, not that! It is the best gift he ever made me, and he was so good and kind then—You do not know, you do not know!—How I long to keep the books! But away, away with them!"

Then she put everything into a silken kerchief, tied it up with hard knots, pushed the bundle into my hand, and besought me to go home.

I went home, sick at heart, with the bundle in my cold hand, and when the door was opened by Akusch, who, poor wight, bore our bitter winters but ill, I heard from above-stairs loud and right merry laughter and glee; and I knew it for the voice of Cousin Maud who seemed overpowered by sheer mirth. My wrath flared up, for our house this day was of a certainty the last where such merriment was fitting.

My cheeks were red from the snow-storm, yet rage made them even hotter as I hastened up-stairs. But before I could speak a single word Cousin Maud, with whom were the Magister and old Pirkheimer the member of council, cried out as soon as she saw me: "Only imagine, Margery, what rare tidings his Excellency has brought us." And she went on to tell me, with great joy, while his worship added facts now and then, that the Magister had since yestereve become a rich man, inasmuch as his godmother, old Dame Oelhaf, had died, leaving him no small wealth.

This was verily marvellous and joyful hearing, for many had imagined the deceased to be a needy woman who had carried on the business left her by her husband, albeit she had no service but that of an ill-paid shop-lad, who was like one of the lean ears of Pharaoh's dream and moreover blind of one eye. Nevertheless I remembered well that her little shop, which was no greater than a fair-sized closet, had ever been filled with buyers when we had stolen in, against all commands, to buy a few dried figs. I can see the little crippled mistress now as she limped across the shop or along the street, and the boys would call after her: "Hip hop! Lame duck!" and all Nuremberg knew her better by the nickname of the Lame Duck than by her husband's.

That the poor little woman had departed this life we had all heard yestereve; but even the Magister had fully believed that her leavings would scarce be worth the pains of a walk to the town hall. But now the learned advocate told him that by her will, drawn up and attested according to law, she had devised to him all she had to leave as being the only child she had ever been thought worthy to hold at the font.

Then, due inquisition being made in her little place, a goodly number of worn stockings were found in the straw of her bed and other hiding places, and in them, instead of her lean little legs, many a gulden and Hungarian ducat of good gold. Moreover she had a house at Nordlingen and a mill at Schwabach, and thus the inheritance that had come to Magister Peter was altogether no small matter.

The simple man had never hoped for such fortune, and it was in truth laughable to see how he forgot his dignity, and leaped first on one foot and then the other, crying: "No, no! It cannot be true! Then poor Irus is become rich Croesus!"

And thus he went on till he left us with Master Perkheimer. Then I laughed with my cousin; and when I was once more alone I marvelled at the mercy of a benevolent Providence, by whose ruling a small joy makes us to forget our heavy griefs, though it were but for a moment.

At night, to be sure, I could not help thinking with fresh sorrow of that which had come upon us; but then, on the morrow, I saw the Magister again, and would fain have rejoiced in his gladness; but lo, he was now silent and dull, and at the first opening he led ne aside and said, right humbly and with downcast eyes: "Think no evil of me, Mistress Margery, in that yestereve my joy in earthly possessions was over much for my wits; believe me, it was not the glitter of mammon, but far other matters that turned my brain." And he confessed to me that he had ever borne Ann in his heart, even when she was but a young maid at school, and had made the winning of her the goal of his life. To this end, and whereas without some means of living he could not hope, he had laid by every penny he had earned by teaching at our house and in the Latin classes, and had foregone the buying of many a fine and learned book, or even of a jar of wine to drink in the company of his fellows. Thus had he saved a goodly sum of money; nay, he had thought himself within reach of his high aim when he had discovered, that Christmas eve before Herdegen's departing, that the Junker had robbed him of his one ewe lamb. There was nought left for him to do but to hold his peace, albeit in bitter sorrow, till within the last few days Heaven had showered its mercies on him. The powerful Junker—for so it was that he ever spoke and thought of my elder brother—had it seemed, released the lamb, and he himself was now in a state of life in which he might right well set up housekeeping. Then he went on to beseech me with all humbleness to speak a word for him to the lady of his choice, and I found it not in my heart to give the death-blow forthwith to his fond and faithful hopes, albeit I wist full surely that they were all in vain. Thus I bid him to have patience at least till Christmas, inasmuch as he should give Ann time to put away the memory of Herdegen; and he consented with simple kindness, although he had changed much and for the better in these late years, and could boast of good respect among the learned men of our city; and thus, albeit not a wealthy man, and in spite of his mature years, he would be welcomed as a son-in-law by many a mother of daughters.

Thus the Magister, who had waited so long, held back even yet awhile. One week followed another, the third Sunday in Advent went by, and the holy tide was at hand when the delay should end which the patient suitor had allowed.

I had seen Ann less often than in past times. In the coppersmith's great household she commonly had her hands full, and I felt indeed that her face was changed towards me. A kind of fear, which I had not marked in her of old, had come over her of late; meseemed she lived ever in dread of some new insult and hurt; also she had courteously but steadfastly refused to join in the festivities to which she was bidden by Elsa Ebner or others of the upper class, and even said nay to uncle Christian's bidding to a dance, to be given this very day, being his name-day, at his lodgings in the Castle. I likewise was bidden and had accepted my godfather's kindness; but my timid endeavor to move Ann to do his will, as her best and dearest old friend, brought forth the sorrowful answer that I myself must judge how little she was fit for any merry-makings of the kind. My friendship with her, which had once been my highest joy, had thus lost all its lightheartedness, albeit it had not lost all its joys, nor was she therefore the less dear to me though I dealt with her now as with a well-beloved child for whose hurt we are not wholly blameless.

Now it fell that on this day, the 20th December, being my godfather's name-day, I found her not with the rest, but in her own chamber in violent distress. Her cheeks were on fire, and she was in such turmoil as though she had escaped some terrible persecution. Thereupon I questioned her in haste and fear, and she answered me with reserve, till, on a sudden, she cried:

"It is killing me! I will bear it no more!" and hid her face in her hands, I clasped her in my arms, and to soothe her spoke in praise of her stepfather, Master Pernhart, and his high spirit and good heart; then she sobbed aloud and said: "Oh, for that matter! If that were all!"

And suddenly, or even I was aware, she had cast her arms about me and kissed my lips and cheeks with great warmth. Then she cried out: "Oh, Margery! You cannot turn from me! I indeed tried to turn from you; and I could have done it, even if it had cost me my heart's blood! But now and here I ask you: Is it just that I should lay myself on the rack because he has so cruelly hurt me? No, no. And I need your true soul to help me to shake off the burden which is crushing me to the earth and choking me. Help me to bear it, or I shall come to a bad end—I shall follow her who died here in this very chamber."

My soul had ever stood open to her and so I told her right heartily, and her face became once more as it had been of old; and albeit those things she had to tell me were not indeed comforting, still I could in all honesty bid her to be of good heart; and I presently felt that to unburden herself of all that had weighed upon her these last few weeks, did her as much good as a bath. For it still was a pain to her to see her mother cooing like a pigeon round her new mate. She herself was full of his praises, albeit this man, well brought up and trained to good manners, would ever abide by the old customs of the old craftsmen, and his venerable mother likewise held fast by them, so that his wife had striven in vain to change the ways of the house. Thus master and mistress, son and daughter, foreman and apprentice, sewing man and maid all ate, as they had ever done, at the same table. And whereas the daughters, by old custom, sat in order on the mother's side, the youngest next to her and the oldest at the end, it thus fell that Ann was placed next to the foreman, who was that very one who had betrayed Gotz Waldstromer to his master because he had himself cast an eye on Gertrude. The young fellow had ere long set his light heart on Ann; and being a fine lad, and the sole son of a well-to-do master in Augsburg, he was likewise a famous wooer and breaker of maiden hearts, and could boast of many a triumphant love affair among the daughters of the simpler class. He was, in his own rank of life, cock of the walk, as such folks say; and I remembered well having seen him at an apprentices' dance at the May merrymakings, whither he had come apparelled in a rose-colored jerkin and light-hued hose, bedecked with flowers and greenery in his cap and belt; he had fooled with the daughters of the master of his guild like the coxcomb he was, and whirled them off to dance as though he did them high honor by paying court to them. It might, to be sure, have given him a lesson to find that his master's fair daughter scorned his suit; yet that sank not deep, inasmuch as it was for the sake of a Junker of high degree. With Ann he might hope for better luck; for although from the first she gave him to wit that he pleased her not, he did not therefore leave her in peace, and this very morning, finding her alone in the hall, he had made so bold as to put forth his hand to clasp her. Albeit she had forthwith set him in his place, and right sharply, it seemed that to protect herself against his advances there was no remedy but a complaint to his master, which would disturb the peace of the household. She was indeed able enough to take care of herself and to ward off any unseemly boldness on his part; but she felt her noble purity soiled by contact with that taint of commonness of which she was conscious in this young fellow's ways, and in many other daily experiences.

Every meal, with the great dish into which the apprentice dipped his spoon next to hers, was a misery to her; and when the master's old mother marked this, and noted also how uneasily she submitted to her new place and part in life, seeing likewise Ann's tear-stained eyes and sorrowful countenance, she conceived that all this was by reason that Ann's pride could hardly bend to endure life in a craftsman's dwelling. And her heart was turned from her son's step-daughter, whom at first she had welcomed right kindly; she overlooked her as a rule, or if she spoke to her, it was in harsh and ungracious tones. This, as Ann saw its purpose, hurt her all the more, as she saw more clearly that the new grandmother was a warm-hearted and worthy and right-minded woman, from whose lips fell many a wise word, while she was as kind to the younger children as though they had been her own grandchildren. Nay, one had but to look at her to see that she was made of sound stuff, and had head and heart both in the right place.

A few hours since Ann had opened her heart to her Father confessor, the reverend prebendary von Hellfeld; and he had counselled her to take the veil and win heavenly bliss in a convent as the bride of Christ. And whereas all she craved was peace, and a refuge from the world wherein she had suffered so much, and Cousin Maud and I likewise deemed it the better course for her, she would gladly have followed this good counsel, but that her late dear father had ever been strongly averse to the life of the cloister. Self-seeking, he would say, is at the root of all evil, and he who becomes an alien from this world and its duties to seek happiness in a convent—inasmuch as that beatitude for which monks and nuns strive is nothing else than a higher form of happiness, extending beyond the grave to the very end of all things—may indeed intend to pursue the highest aim, and yet it is but self-seeking, although of the loftiest and noblest kind. Also, but a few days ere he died, he had admonished Ann, in whom he had long discerned the true teacher of his younger children, to warn them above all things against self-seeking, inasmuch as now that the hand of death was already on him, he found his chiefest comfort in the assurance of having labored faithfully, trusting in his Redeemer's grace, to do all that in him lay for his own kith and kin, and for other folks' orphans, whether rich or poor.

This discourse had sunk deep into Ann's soul, and had been in her mind when she spoke such brave words to Herdegen, exhorting him to higher aims. Now, again, coming forth from the good priest's door, she had met her grand-uncle the organist, and asking him what he would say if a hapless and forlorn maid should seek the peace she had lost in the silence of the cloister, the simple man looked her full in the eyes and murmured sadly to himself: "Alack! And has it come to this!" Then he went close up to her, raised her drooping head, and cried in a cheering voice:

"In a cloister? You, in a cloister! You, our Ann, who have already learnt to be so good a mother in the Sisters's school? No child, and again and again I say No. Pay heed rather to the saying which your old grand-uncle once heard from the lips of a wise and good man, when in the sorest hour of his life he was about to knock at the gate of a Cistercian convent.—His words were: 'Though thou lose all thou deemest thy happiness, if thou canst but make the happiness of others, thou shalt find it again in thine own heart.'"

And at a later day old Heyden himself told me that he, who while yet but a youth had been the prefectus of the town-pipers, had been nigh to madness when his wife, his Elslein, had been snatched from him after scarce a year and a half of married life. After he had recovered his wits, he had conceived that any balance or peace of mind was only to be found in a convent, near to God; and it was at that time that the wise and excellent Ulman Stromer had spoken the words which had been thenceforth the light and guiding line of his life. He had remained in the world; but he had renounced the more honorable post of prefect of the town-musicians, and taken on him the humble one of organist, in which it had been granted to him to offer up his great gift of music as it were a sacrifice to Heaven. This maxim, which had spared the virtuous old man to the world, made its mark on Ann likewise; and whereas I saw how gladly she had received the doctrine that happiness should be found in making others happy, I prayed her to join me in taking it henceforth as the guiding lamp of our lives. At this she was well pleased;

and she went on to point wherein and how we should henceforth strive to forget ourselves for our neighbor's sake, with that soaring flight of soul in which I could scarce follow her but as a child lags after a butterfly or a bird.

Then, when I presently saw that she was in better heart, I took courage, but in jest, being sure of her refusal, to plead the Magister's suit. This, however, was as I was departing; I had already stayed and delayed her over-long, inasmuch as I had yet to array myself for the feast at Uncle Christian's. But, as I was about to speak; a serving man came in with a letter written by the kind old man to Ann herself, his "dear watchman" in which, for the third time, he besought her, with pressing warmth, not to refuse to go to him on his name day and pledge him in the loving cup to his health and happiness.

With the help of this tender appeal I made her say she would go; yet she spoke the words in haste and great agitation.

My uncle's messenger had hindered my suing, so while we hastily looked through Ann's store of holiday raiment, I brought my pleading for Master Peter to an end; and what I looked for came, in truth, to pass: without seeming one whit surprised she steadfastly rejected his suit, saying that he was the poor, good, faithful Magister, and worthy to win a wife whose heart was all his own.

At my uncle's house that night, with the exception of certain learned and reverend gentlemen, Ann alone was not of gentle birth. Yet was she in no wise the least, neither in demeanor nor in attire; and when I beheld her in the ante-chamber, all lighted up with wax tapers, in her sky-blue gown, thanking the master of the house and his sister—who kept house for him—for their condescension, as she upraised her great eyes with loving respect, I could have clasped her in my arms in the face of all the world, and I marvelled how my brother Herdegen could have sinfully cast such a jewel from him.

Then, when we went on together into the guest chamber, it fell that the town-pipers at that minute ceased to play and there was silence on all, as though a flourish of trumpets had warned of the approach of a prince; and yet it was only in honor of Ann and her wondrous beauty. Each and all of the young men there would, meseemed, gladly have stepped into Herdegen's place, and she was so fully taken up with dancing that she could scarce mark how diligently all the mothers and maidens overlooked her. Howbeit, Ursula Tetzel was not content with that, but went up to her and with a sneer enquired whether Junker Schopper at Paris were well.

Ann drew herself up with pride and hastily answered that if any one craved news of him he had best apply to Mistress Ursula Tetzel, inasmuch as she was ever wont to have a keen eye on her dear cousin.

At this Ursula cried out: "How well our old schoolmate remembers the lessons she learnt; even the fable of the Fox and the Grapes!" then, turning to me she added: "Nor has she lost her skill in learning; she has not long been in her stepfather's dwelling and she has already mastered the art of hitting blows as the coppersmiths do." And she turned her back on us both.

And presently, when it came to her turn to join the chain in which Ann was taking part, I marked well that she urged the youth she danced with to stand away from the craftsman's daughter. Howbeit I at once brought her plot to naught and the young gentleman to shame. Not that she needed any such defence, for her beauty led every man to seek her above all others. And when, at supper, Uncle Christian called her to his side and made it fully manifest to all present how dear she was to his faithful heart, I hoped that indeed the day was won for her, and that henceforth our friendship would be regarded as a matter apart from any concern with her step-father the coppersmith. What need she care about those discourteous women, who made it, to be sure, plain enough at their departing, that they took her presence there amiss.

On our way home methought she was in a meditative mood, and as we parted she bid me go to see her early next morning. This I should have done in any case, inasmuch as I knew no greater pleasure, after a feast or dance at which we had been together, than to talk with her of any matter we might each have marked, but there was something more than this in her mind.

Next day, indeed, when I had greeted her, she had lost her cheerful mien of the day before; it was plain to see that she had not slept, and I presently learned that she had been thinking through the night what her life must be, and how she could best fulfill the vow we had both made. The more diligently she had considered of the matter, the more worthy had she deemed our purpose; and the dance at my Uncle Christian's had clearly proven to her that among our class there were few to whom her presence could be welcome, and none to whom it could bring any real pleasure.

In this she was doubtless right; yet was I startled when, with the steadfast will which she ever showed, she said that, after duly weighing the matter, she had made up her mind to accept the Magister.

When she perceived how greatly I was amazed, she besought me, with the same eager haste as I had marvelled at the day before, that I would not contend against a conclusion she had fully weighed; inasmuch as that the

Magister was a worthy man whom she could make truly happy. Moreover, his newly-acquired wealth would enable her to help many indigent persons in their need and misery. I enquired of her earnestly how about any love for him, and she broke out with much vehemence, saying that I must know for certain that for her all love and the joys of love were numbered with the dead. She would tell this to Master Peter with all honesty, and she was sure that he would be content with her friendship and warm goodwill.

But all this she poured out as though she could not endure to hear her own words. An inward voice at the same time warned me that she had made up her mind to this step, in order that Herdegen might fully understand that to him she was lost for ever, albeit I had not given up all hope that they might some day come together, and that Ann's noble love of what was best in my brother might thus rescue him from utter ruin. Hence her ill-starred resolve filled me with rage, to such a degree that I railed at it as a mad and sinful deed against her own peace of mind, and indeed against him whom she had once held as dear as her own life.

But Ann cut me short, and bade me sharply to mind my promise, and never speak of Herdegen again. My hot blood rose at this and I made for the door; nay, I had the handle of the latch in my hand when she flew after me, held me back by force, and entreated me with prayers that I would let her do her will, for that she had no choice. She purposed in solemn earnest henceforth at all times to devote herself to the happiness of others, and whereas that demanded heavy sacrifice, she was now ready to make it. If indeed I still refused to carry her answer to the Magister, then would she send it through her step-father or Dame Henneleinlein, who was apt at such errands, and bid her suitor come to see her.

Then I perceived that there was but small hope; with a heavy heart, and, indeed, a secret intent behind, I took the task upon me, for I saw plainly that my refusal would ruin all. All the same, meseemed it was a happy ordering that the Magister should have set forth early that morning to spend a few days at Nordlingen, to take possession of the house he had fallen heir to; for, when a great misfortune lies ahead, a hopeful soul clings to delay as the harbinger of deliverance.

I made my way home full of forebodings, and in front of our door I saw my Forest uncle's horses in waiting. He was above stairs with cousin Maud, and I soon was informed that he had come to bid me and Ann to the great hunt which was to take place at the New Year. His Highness Duke Albrecht of Bavaria, with divers other knights and gentlemen, had promised to take part in it, and he needed our help for his sick and suffering wife; also, said he, he loved to see "a few smart young maids" at his board. Already he and cousin Maud had discussed at length whether it would be seemly to bring the coppersmith's stepdaughter into the company of such illustrious guests; and the balance in her favor had been struck in his mind by his opinion that a fair young maid must ever be pleasing in the hunter's eyes out in the forest, whatever her rank might be.

He had now but one care, and that was that neither he nor any other man had hitherto dared to utter the name of Master Ulman Pernhart to my aunt Jacoba, and that she therefore knew not of his marriage with her dear Ann's mother. Yet must the lady be informed thereof; so, finding that my cousin Maud made no secret of her will to speed the Magister's wooing, while I weened, with good reason, that my aunt would gladly support me in hindering it, I then and there made up my mind to go back with my uncle, and hold council with his shrewd-witted wife.

CHAPTER XV

We reached the forest lodge that evening with red faces and half-frozen hands and feet. The ride through the deep snow and the bitter December wind had been a hard one; but the woods in their glittering winter shroud, the sharp, refreshing breath of the pure air, and a thousand trifling matters— from the white hats that crowned every stock and stone to the tiny crystals of snow that fell on the green velvet of my fur-lined bodice—were a joy to me, albeit my heart was heavy with care. The evening star had risen or ever we reached the house; and out here, under God's open heavens, among the giants of the forest and its sturdy, weather-beaten folk, it scarce seemed that it could be true that I should see my bright, young Ann sharing the sorry life of the Magister, an alien from all this world's joys. Those who dwelt out here in these wilds must, methought, feel this as I felt it; and so in truth it proved. After I had taken my place at the hearth by my aunt's side, and she had mingled some spiced wine for us with her own feeble hands, she bid me speak. When she heard what it was that had brought me forth to the forest so late before Christmas, which we ever spent with our grand-uncle Im Huff she at first did but laugh at our Magister's suit; but as soon as I told her that it was Ann's earnest purpose to wed with him, she swore that she would never suffer such a deed of mad folly.

Master Peter had many times been her guest at the lodge; and she, though so small and feeble herself, loved to see tall and stalwart men, so that she had given him the name of "the little dry Bookworm," hardly accounting him a man at all. When she heard of his newly-gained wealth, she said: "If instead of being the richer by these thousands he could but be the same number of years younger, lift a hundredweight more, and see a hundred miles further out into the world, I would not mind his seeking his happiness with that lovely child!"

As for my uncle, he did but hum a burly bass to the tune of the "Little wee wife." But, being called away, he turned to me before closing the door behind him, and asked me very keenly, as though he had been restraining his impatience for some space: "And how about your brother? How is it that this matter has come about? Was not Herdegen pledged to marry Ann?"

Thereupon I told my aunt all I knew, and gave her Herdegen's letter to read, which I had taken care to bring with me; and even as she read it her countenance grew dark and fearful to look upon; she set her teeth like a raging hound, and hit her little hand on the table that stood by her couch so that the cups and phials standing thereon danced and clattered. Nay, she forgot her weakness, and made as though she would spring up, but the pain was more than she could bear and she fell back on her pillows with a groan.

She had never loved my grand-uncle Im Hoff, and, as soon as she had recovered herself, she vowed she would bring his craft to nought and likewise would let her nephew, now in Paris, know her opinion of his knavish unfaith to a sacred pledge.

I then went on to tell her how hard and altogether insufferable Ann's life had become, and at length took courage to inform her who the man was whom she now called step-father. To this she at first said not a word, but cast down her eyes as though somewhat confused; but presently she asked wherefore and how it was that she had not heard of this marriage long since, and when I told her that folks for the most part had feared to speak the name of Master Ulman Pernhart in her presence, she again suddenly started up and cried in my face that in truth she forbade any mention of that villain and caitiff who had taken foul advantage of her son's youth and innocence to turn his heart from his parents and bring him to destruction.

And this led me, for the first time in my life, to break through the reverence I owed to the venerable lady, who so well deserved to be in all ways respected and spared; for I made so bold as to point out to her her cruel injustice, and to plead Master Ulman's cause with earnest zeal. For some time she was speechless with wrath and amazement, inasmuch as she was not wont to be thus reproved; but then she paid me back in the like coin; one word struck forth the next, and my rising wrath hastened me on so that at last I told her plainly, that Master Pernhart had turned her son Gotz out of doors to hinder him from a breach of that obedience he owed to his parents. Furthermore I informed her of all that the coppersmith's mother had told me of the attempt to carry away Gertrude, and what the end of that had been. Indeed, so soon as the foreman had betrayed the lovers' plot, Master Ulman had locked his daughter into her chamber; and when her lover, after waiting for her in vain at the altar with the hireling priest, came at last to seek her, her father told him that unless he—Gotz—ceased his suit, he should exert his authority as her father to compel Gertrude to marry the foreman and go with him to Augsburg, or give her the choice of taking the veil. And this he confirmed by a solemn oath; and when Gotz, like one in a frenzy, strove to make good his claim to see his sweetheart, and hear from her own lips whether she were minded to yield to her father's yoke, they came to blows, even on the stairs leading to Gertrude's chamber, and there was a fierce battle, which might have had a bloody end but that old dame Magdalen herself came between them to part them. And then Master Ulman had sworn to Gotz that he would keep his daughter locked up as a captive unless the youth pledged himself to cease from seeing Gertrude till he had won his parents' consent. Thereupon Gotz went forth into a strange land; but he did not forget his well-beloved, and from time to time a letter would reach her assuring her of his faithfulness.

At the end of three years after his departing he at last wrote to the coppersmith that he had found a post which would allow of his marrying and setting up house and he straightly besought Master Ulman no longer to keep apart two who could never be sundered. Nor did Pernhart delay to answer him, hard as he found it to use the pen, inasmuch as there was no more to say than that Gertrude was sleeping under the sod with her lover's ring on her finger and the last violets he had ever given her under her head, as she had desired.

Thus ended the tale of poor Gertrude; but before I had half told it my wrath had cooled. For my aunt sat in silence, listening to me with devout attention. Nor were my eyes dry, nor even those of that strong-willed dame, and when, at the end, I said: "Well, Aunt?" she woke, as it were, from a dream, and cried out: "And yet those craftsmen folk robbed me of my son, my only child!"

And she sobbed aloud and hid her face in her hands, while I knelt by her side, and threw my arms about her, and kissed her thin fingers which covered her eyes, and said softly, as if by inspiration: "But the craftsman loved his child; yea, and she was a sweet and lovely maid, the fairest in all the town, and her father's pride. And what was it that snatched her so early away but that she pined for your son? Gotz may soon be recalled to his mother's arms; but the coppersmith may never see his child—fair Gertrude, the folks called her—never see her more. And he might have been rejoiced in her presence to this day if..."

She broke in with words and gestures of warning, and when I nevertheless would not cease from entreating her no longer to harden her heart, but to bid her son come home to her, who was her most precious treasure, she commanded me to quit her chamber. Such a command I must obey, whether I would or no; nay, while I stood a moment at the door she signed to me to go; but, as I turned away, she cried after me: "Go and leave me, Margery. But you are a good child, I will tell you that!"

At supper, which I alone shared with my uncle and the chaplain, I told my uncle that I had spoken to his wife of Master Pernhart, and when he heard that I had even spoken a good word for him, he looked at me as though I had done a right bold deed; yet I could see that he was highly pleased thereat, and the priest, who had sat silent—as he ever did, gave me a glance of heartfelt thanks and added a few words of praise. It was long after supper, and my uncle had had his night-draught of wine when my aunt sent the house-keeper to fetch me to her. Kindly and sweetly, as though she set down my past wrath to a good intent, she bid me sit down by her and then desired that I would repeat to her once more, in every detail, all I could tell her as touching Gotz and Gertrude. While I did her bidding to the best of my powers she spoke never a word; but when I ended she raised her head and said, as it were in a dream: "But Gotz! Did he not forsake father and mother to follow after a fair face?"

Then again I prayed her right earnestly to yield to the emotions of her mother's heart. But seeing her fixed gaze into the empty air, and the set pout of her nether lip, I could not doubt that she would never speak the word that would bid him home.

I felt a chill down my back, and was about to rise and leave, but she held me back and once more spoke of Herdegen and that matter. When she had heard all the tale, she looked troubled: "I know my Ann," quoth she. "When she has once given her promise to the Bookworm all the twelve Apostles would not make her break it, and then she will be doomed to misery, and her fate and your brother's are both sealed."

She then went on to ask when the Magister was to return home, and as I told her he was expected on the morrow great trouble came upon her.

It was past midnight or ever I left her, and as it fell I slept but ill and late, insomuch that I was compelled to make good haste, and as it fell that I went to the window I saw the snow whirling in the wind, and behold, in the shed, a great wood-sleigh was being made ready, doubtless for some sick man to be carried to the convent.

I found my aunt in the hall, whither she scarce ever was carried down before noon-day; and instead of her every-day garb—a loose morning-gown—-she was apparelled in strange and shapeless raiment, so muffled in kerchiefs and cloaks as to seem no whit like any living woman, much less herself, insomuch that her small thin person was like nothing else than a huge, shapeless, many-coated onion. Her little face peeped out of the veils and kerchiefs that wrapped her head, like a half-moon out of thick clouds; but her bright eyes shone kindly on me as she cried: "Come, haste to your breakfast, lie-a-bed! I thought to find you fitted and ready, and you are keeping the men waiting as though it were an every-day matter that we should travel together."

"Aye, aye! She is bent on the journey," my uncle said with a groan, as he cast a loving glance at his frail wife and raised his folded hands to Heaven. "Well, chaplain, miracles happen even in our days!" And his Reverence, silent as he was, this time had an answer ready, saying with hearty feeling: "The loving heart of a brave woman has at all times been able to work miracles."

"Amen," said my uncle, pressing his lips on the top of his wife's muffled head.

Howbeit I remembered our talk yesternight, and the sleigh I had seen being harnessed; indeed, the look alone which the unwonted traveller cast on me was enough to tell me what my sickly aunt purposed to do for the sake of Ann. Then something came upon me, I know not what; with a passion all unlike that of yesterdayeve, I fell on my knees and kissed her as a child whose mother has made it a Christmas gift of what it most loves and wishes to have, while my lips were pressed to her eyes, brow, and cheeks, wherever the wrappings covered them not, and she cried out:

"Leave me, leave me, crazy child! You are choking me. What great matter is it after all? One woman will ride through the snow to Nuremberg for the sake of a chat with another, and who turns his head to look at her? Now, foolish wench, let me be. What a to-do for nothing at all!"

How I ate my porridge in the winking of an eye, and then sprang into the sleigh, I scarce could tell, and in truth I marked little of our departing; mine eyes were over full of tears. Packed right close to my aunt, whereas she filled three-fourths of the seat, I flew with her over the snow; nor did we need any great following on horseback to bear us company, inasmuch as my uncle rode on in front, and the Buchenauers and Steinbachers and other highway robbers who made the roads unsafe about Nuremberg, all lived in peace with uncle Waldstromer for the sake of the shooting.

When we got into the town, and I bid the rider take us to the Schopperhof, my aunt said: "No, to Ulman Pernhart's house, the coppersmith."

At this the faithful old serving-man, who had heard many rumors of his banished young master's dealings with the craftsman's fair daughter, and who was devoted to Gotz, muttered the name of his protecting saint and looked about him as though some giant cutthroat were ready to rush out of the brush wood and fall upon the sleigh; nor, indeed, could I altogether refrain my wonder. Howbeit, I recovered myself at once, and pointed out to her that it scarce beseemed her to enter a stranger's house for the first time in such attire. Moreover, Akusch had been sent in front to announce her coming to cousin Maud. I could send for Ann; as, indeed, it beseemed her, the younger, to wait upon my aunt.

But she held to her will to go to Master Ulman's dwelling; yet, whereas the kerchiefs and wraps were a discomfort to her, she agreed to lay them aside at our house first.

Cousin Maud pressed her almost by force to take rest and meat and drink; but she refused everything; though all was in readiness and steaming hot; till, as fate would have it, as she was being carried down and out again, the Magister came in from his journey to Nordlingen. In his high fur boots and the heavy wrapping he had cast about his head to screen him from the wintry blast, he had not to be sure, the appearance of a suitor for a fair young maiden; and the glance cast at him by my aunt, half in mockery and half in wrath, eyeing him from head to foot, would have said plainly enough to other men than Master Peter—who, for his part made her a right humble and well-turned speech—"Wait awhile, young fellow! I am here now! And if you find a flea in your ear, you have me to thank for it!"

Apparelled now as befitted a lady of her degree, in a furred cloak and hood, she was borne off in Cousin Maud's well-curtained litter. I had sent Akusch to Ann with a note, but he had not found her within, and awaited me in the street; thus it fell that no one at the Pernharts was aware of what was coming upon them.

When presently the bearers set down the litter, Aunt Jacoba looked at the fine house before which we stood, and enquired what this might mean, whereas it was seven years since she had been in the city, and the master's new dwelling was not at that time built. Also she was greatly amazed to find a craftsman in so great a house. But better things were to come: as I was about to knock at the door it opened, and five gentlemen of the Council, all men of the first rank among the Elders of the city, appeared on the threshold, and Master Pernhart in their midst. They shook hands with him as with one of themselves, and he towered above them all; nay, if he had not stood there as he had come from the forge, in his leathern apron, with his smith's cap in his hand, any one might have conceived him to be the chief of them all.

Now these gentlemen had come to Master Pernhart to announce to him that he had been chosen one of the eight wardens of the guilds who at that time formed part of the worshipful town council of forty-two. Veit Gundling, the old master-brewer, had lately departed this life, and the electors had been of one mind in choosing the coppersmith to fill his place, and he was likewise approved by the guilds. They had come to him forthwith, albeit their choice would not be declared till Saint Walpurgis day, inasmuch as it was deemed well to have the matter settled before the close of the old year.

Thus it came to pass that my aunt was witness while they took leave, and he returned thanks in a few heartfelt words. These, to be sure, were cut short by her coming, by reason that she was well-known to these five noble gentlemen, who all, as in duty bound, assured her of their surprise and pleasure in greeting her once more, here in the town.

That the feeble and suffering lady had come to Pernhart's dwelling not merely to order a copper-lid or a preserving pan was easy to be understood, but she cut short all inquisition, and the litter was forthwith carried in through the widely-opened door.

The master received her in the hall.

He had till now never seen her but from a distance, yet had he heard enough about her to form a clear image of her. With her it was the same. She saw this man, to whom she owed such bitter grudge, for the first time here, under his own roof, and it was right strange to behold the two eyeing each other so keenly; he with a slight bow, almost timidly, and cap in hand; she unabashed, but with an expression as though she well knew that nothing pleasant lay before her.

The master spoke first, bidding her welcome to his dwelling, in accents of truth but with all due respect, and never speaking of it, as is the wont of his class, as "humble" or "poor," and as he was about to help her out of the litter I could see her face brighten, and this assured me that she would let bygones be bygones, as they say, and declare to Master Pernhart in plain words to what intent and purpose she had knocked at his door. By the time she was in the best chamber, the last sour curl had disappeared from her mouth; and indeed all was snug and seemly therein; Dame Giovanna being well-skilled in giving things a neat appearance, well pleasing to the eye.

Pernhart meanwhile had said but little, and his face was still dark, almost solemn of aspect. The master's mother again, to whom Gertrude had been all-in-all, and who had done what she could to speed her marriage, could read the other woman's heart, and understood how great had been the sacrifice she had taken upon herself. There was no trace of the old grudge in her speech, and it sounded not ill when, as she put my aunt's cushions straight, she said she could not envy her, forasmuch as she the elder was thus permitted to be of service to the younger. When Pernhart presently quitted the chamber, perchance to don more seemly attire the two old women sat in eager talk; and if the lady were thin and sickly and the craftsman's mother stout and sturdy, yet were there many points of resemblance between them. Both, for certain, loved to rule, and as I watched them, seeing each shoot out her nether lip if the other spoke a word to cross her, I found it right good sport; but at the same time I was amazed to hear how truly old Dame Pernhart understood and spoke of Ann. I had indeed hitherto seen many a thing in my friend with other eyes, and yet I could not accuse the good woman of injustice, or deny that the coppersmith's step-daughter, from knowing me and from keeping company with us, had grown up with manners and desires unlike those of ever another clerk's or even a craftsman's daughter.

Albeit she strove to hide her deep discomfort, the old woman said, she could by no means succeed. A household was a body, and any member of it who could not be content with its ways was ill at ease with the rest, and made it hard for them to do it such service and pleasure as they would fain do. Ann fulfilled her every duty, down to the very least of them, by reason that she had a steadfast spirit and great dominion over herself; but she got small thanks, and by her own fault, inasmuch as she did it joylessly. To look for bright cheer from her was to seek grapes on a birch-tree; and whereas the grandmother had till lately hoped to find in this gentle maid one who might fill the place of her who was no more, she could now only wish that she might find some other home.

To all this my aunt agreed, and presently, when Pernhart came in, clad in his holiday garb—a goodly man and well fitted for his new dignity, Aunt Jacoba bid me go look out for Ann. I saw that she desired my absence that she might deal alone with the mother and son, so I hastily departed and stayed in the upper chambers with the children till I caught sight of Ann and her mother coming towards the house. I ran down to meet them and behold! as we all three went into the guest chamber, Pernhart was in the act of bending over my aunt's hand to press it to his lips, and tears were sparkling in his eyes as well as in those of the women; nay, they were so greatly moved that no one heard the door open, and the old woman believed herself to be alone with her son as she cried to my aunt: "Oh wherefor did not Heaven vouchsafe to guide you to us some years since!"

My aunt only nodded her head in silence, and Dame Magdalen doubtless took this for assent; but I read more than this in her face, and something as follows: "We have hurt each other deeply, and I am thankful that all is past and forgiven; yet, much as I may now esteem you, in the matter you had so set your heart on I would no more have yielded to-day than I did at that time."

CHAPTER XVI

Ann looked right sweetly as she told my aunt that she felt put to shame by the great loving-kindness which had brought the feeble lady out through the forest in the bitter winter weather for her sake, and she kissed the thin, small hand with deep feeling; and even the elder woman unbent and freely gave vent before her favorite to the full warmth of her heart, which she was not wont to display. She had told the Pernharts what were the fears which had brought her into the town, so the chamber was presently cleared, and the master called away Mistress Giovanna after that my aunt had expressed her admiration of her rare charms.

As I too was now preparing to retire, which methought but seemly Aunt Jacoba beckoned me to stay. Ann likewise understood what had brought her sickly friend to her, and she whispered to me that albeit she was deeply thankful for the abundant goodness my aunt had ever shown her, yet could she never swerve from her well-considered purpose. To this I was only able to reply that on one point at least she must change her mind, for that I knew for certain that old grand-dame Pernhart loved her truly. At this she cried out gladly and thankfully: "Oh, Margery! if only that were true!"

So soon as we three were left together, my aunt went to the heart of the matter at once, saying frankly to what end she had come hither, that she knew all that Ann had suffered through Herdegen, and how well she had taken it, and that she had now set her mind on wedding with the Magister.

And whereas Ann here broke in with a resolute "And that I will!" my aunt put it to her that she must be off with one or ever she took on the other lover. Herdegen had come before Master Peter, and the first question therefor was as to how matters stood with him.

At this Ann humbly besought her to ask nothing concerning him; if my aunt loved her she would forbear from touching on the scarce-healed wound. So much as this she said, though with pain and grief; but her friend was not to be moved, but cried: "And do I not thank Master Ulsenius when he thrusts his probe to the heart of my evil, when he cuts or burns it? Have you not gladly approved his saying that the leech should never despair so long as the sick man's heart still throbs? Well then, your trouble with Herdegen is sick and sore and lies right deep...."

But Ann broke in again, crying: "No, no, noble lady, the heart of that matter has ceased to beat. It is dead and gone for ever!"

"Is it so?" said my aunt coolly. "Still, look it close in the face. Old Im Hoff—I have read the letter-commands your lover to give you up and do his bidding. Yet, child, does he take good care not to write this to you. Finding it over hard to say it himself, he leaves the task to Margery. And as for that letter; a Lenten jest I called it yestereve; and so it is verily! Read it once more. Why, it is as dripping with love as a garment drips when it is fished out of a pool! While he is trying to shut the door on you he clasps you to his heart. Peradventure his love never glowed so hotly, and he was never so strongly drawn to you as when he wrote this paltry stuff to burst the sacred bands which bind you together. Are you so dull as not to feel this?"

"Nay, I see it right well," cried Ann eagerly, "I knew it when I first read the letter. But that is the very point! Must not a lover who can barter away his love for filthy lucre be base indeed? If when he ceased to be true he had likewise ceased to love, if the fickle Fortunatus had wearied of his sweetheart—then I could far more easily forgive."

"And do you tell me that your heart ever throbbed with true love for him?" asked her friend in amazement, and looking keenly into her eyes as though she expected her to say No. And when Ann cried: "How can you even ask such a question?" My aunt went on: "Then you did love him? And Margery tells me that you and she have made some strange compact to make other folks happy. Two young maids who dare to think they can play at being God Almighty! And the Magister, I conceive, was to be the first to whom you proposed to be a willing sacrifice, let it cost you what it may? That is how matters stand?"

Ann was not now so ready to nod assent, and my aunt murmured something I could not hear, as she was wont to do when something rubbed her against the grain; then she said with emphasis: "But child, my poor child, love, and wounded pride, and heart-ache have turned your heart and good sense. I am an old woman, and I thank God can see more clearly. It is real, true love, pleasing to the Father, Son, and Holy Ghost, aye and to the merciful Virgin and all the saints who protect you, which has bound you and Herdegen together from your infancy. He, though faithless and a sinner, still bears his love in his heart and you have not been able to root yours up and cast it out. He has done his worst, and in doing it—remember his letter—in doing it, I say, has poisoned his own young life already. In that Babel called Paris he does but reel from one pleasure to another. But how long can that last? Do you not see, as I see, that the day must come when, sickened and loathing all this folly he will deem himself the most wretched soul on earth, and look about him for the firm shore as a sailor does who is tossed about in a leaking ship at sea? Then will he call to mind the past, his childhood and youth, his pure love and yours. Then you yourself, you, Ann, will be the island haven for which he will long. Then—aye, child, it is so, you will be the only creature that may help him; and if you really crave to create happiness—if your love is as true as—not so long ago—you declared it to be, on your knees before me and with scalding tears, he, and not Master Peter must be the first on whom you should carry out your day-dreams— for I know not what other name to give to such vain imaginings."

At this Ann sobbed aloud and wrung her hands, crying: "But he cast me off, sold me for gold and silver. Can I, whom he has flung into the dust, seek to go after him? Would it beseem an honest and shamefaced maid if I called him back to me? He is happy—and he will still be happy for many long, long years amid his reckless companions; if the time should ever come of which you speak, most worshipful lady, even then he will care no more for Ann, bloomless and faded, than for the threadbare bravery in which he once arrayed himself. As for me and my love, warmly as it will ever glow in my breast, so long as I live and breathe, he will never need it in the life of pleasure in which he suns himself. It is no vain imagining that I have made my goal, and if I am to bring joy to the wretched I must seek others than he."

"Right well," said my aunt, "if so be that your love is no worthier nor better than his."

And from the unhappy maid's bosom the words were gasped out: "It is verily and indeed true and worthy and deep; never was truer love..."

"Never?" replied my aunt, looking at her enquiringly. "Have you not read of the love of which the Scripture speaketh? Love which is able and ready to endure all things."

And the words of the Apostle came into my mind which the Carthusian sister had graven on our memories, burning them in, as it were, as being those which above all others should live in every Christian woman's heart; and whereas I had hitherto held back as beseemed me, I now came forward and said them with all the devout fervor of my young heart, as follows: "Charity suffereth long and is kind; Charity envieth not; Charity vaunteth not itself, is not puffed up; seeketh not her own, is not easily provoked, thinketh no evil; beareth all things, believeth all things, hopeth all things, endureth all things."

While I spoke Ann, panting for breath, fixed her eyes on the ground, but my aunt rehearsed the words after me in a clear voice: "beareth all things, believeth all things, hopeth and endureth all things." And she added right earnestly; "therefore do thou believe and hope and endure yet longer, my poor child, and tell me in all truth: Does it seem to you a lesser deed to lead back the sinner into the way of righteousness and bliss in this world and the next, than to give alms to the beggar?"

Ann shook her head, and my aunt went on: "And if there is any one— let me repeat it—who by faithful love may ever rescue Herdegen, albeit he is half lost, it is you. Come, come," and she signed to her, and Ann did her bidding and fell on her knees by her, as she had done erewhile in the forest-lodge. The elder lady kissed her hair and eyes, and said further: "Cling fast to your love, my darling. You have nothing else than love, and without it life is shallow indeed, is sheer emptiness. You will never find it in the Magister's arms, and that your heart is of a certainty, not set on marrying a well-to-do man at any cost...."

But she did not end her speech, inasmuch as Ann imploringly raised her great eyes in mild reproach, as though to defend herself from some hurt. So my aunt comforted her with a few kind words, and then went on to admonish her as follows: "Verily it is not love you lack, but patient trust. I have heard from Margery here what bitter disappointments you have suffered. And it is hard indeed to the stricken heart to look for a new spring for the withered harvest of joy. But look you at my good husband. He ceases not from sowing acorns, albeit he knows that it will never be vouchsafed to him to see them grown to fine trees, or to earn any profit from them. Do you likewise learn to possess your soul in patience; and do not forget that, if Herdegen is lost, the question will be put to you: 'Did you hold out a hand to him while it was yet time to save him, or did you withdraw from him your love and favor in faint-hearted impatience at the very first blow?'"

The last words fell in solemn earnest from my aunt's lips, and struck Ann to the heart; she confessed that she had many times said the same things to her self, but then maiden pride had swelled up in her and had forbidden her to lend an ear to the warning voice; and nevertheless none had spoken so often or so loudly in her soul, so that her heart's deepest yearning responded to what her friend had said.

"Then do its bidding," said my aunt eagerly, and I said the same; and Ann, being not merely overruled but likewise convinced, yielded and confessed that, even as Master Peter's wife, she could never have slain the old love, and declared herself ready to renounce her pride and wrath.

Thus had my aunt's faithful love preserved her from sin, and gladly did I consent to her brave spirit when she said to Ann: "You must save yourself for that skittle-witted wight in Paris, child; for none other than he can make you rightly happy, nor can he be happy with any other woman than my true and faithful darling!"

Ann covered my aunt's hands with kisses, and the words flowed heartily and gaily from her lips as she cried: "Yes, yes, yes! It is so! And if he beat me and scorned me, if he fell so deep that no man would leap in after him, I, I, would never let him sink."

And then Ann threw herself on my neck and said: "Oh, how light is my heart once more. Ah, Margery! now, when I long to pray, I know well enough what for."

My aunt's dim eyes had rarely shone so brightly as at this hour, and her voice sounded clearer and firmer than it was wont when she once more addressed us and said: "And now the old woman will finish up by telling you a little tale for your guidance. You knew Riklein, the spinster, whom folks called the night-spinster; and was not she a right loving and cheerful soul? Yet had she known no small meed of sorrows. She died but lately on Saint Damasius' day last past, and the tale I have to tell concerns her. They called her the night-spinster, by reason that she ofttimes would sit at her wheel till late into the night to earn money which she was paid at the rate of three farthings the spool. But it was not out of greed that the old body was so keen to get money.

"In her youth she had been one of the neatest maids far and wide, and had set her heart on a charcoal burner who was a sorry knave indeed, a sheep-stealer and a rogue, who came to a bad end on the rack. But for all that Riklein never ceased to love him truly and, albeit he was dead and gone, she did not give over toiling diligently while she lived yet for him. The priest had told her that, inasmuch as her lover had taken the Sacrament of the Lord's Supper on the scaffold, the Kingdom of Heaven was not closed to him, yet would it need many a prayer and many a mass to deliver him from the fires of purgatory. So Riklein, span and span, day and night, and stored up all she earned, and when she lay on her death-bed, not long ago, and the priest gave her the Holy Sacrament, she took out her hoard from beneath her mattress and showed it to him, asking whether that might be enough to pay to open the way for Andres to the joys of Heaven? And when the chaplain said that it would be, she turned away her face and fell asleep. So do you spin your yarn, child, and let the flax on your distaff be glad assurance; and, if ever your heart sinks within you, remember old Riklein!"

"And the Farmer's daughter in 'Poor Heinrich,'" I said, "who gladly gave her young blood to save her plighted lord from leprosy."

Thus had my aunt gained her end; but when she strove to carry Ann away from her home and kindred, and keep her in the forest as her own child—to which Master Pernhart and his mother gave their consent—she failed in the attempt. Ann was steadfast in her desire to remain with her mother and the children, and more especially with her deaf and dumb brother, Mario. If my aunt should at any time need her she had but to command her, and she would gladly go to her, this very day if she desired it; howbeit duly to work out her spinning—and by this she meant that she bore Riklein in mind—she must ever do her part for her own folk, with a clear conscience.

Thus it was fixed that Ann should go to the Forest lodge to stay till Christmas and the New Year were past, only she craved a few hours delay that she might remove all doubt from the Magister's mind. I offered to take upon myself this painful task; but she altogether rejected this, and how rightly she judged was presently proved by her cast-off suitor's demeanor; inasmuch as he was ever after her faithful servant and called her his gracious work-fellow. When she had told him of her decision he swore, well-nigh with violence, to become a monk, and to make over his inheritance to a convent, but Ann, with much eloquence, besought him to do no such thing, and laid before him the grace of living to make others happy; she won him over to join our little league and whereas he confessed that he was in no wise fit for the life, she promised that she would seek out the poor and needy and claim the aid only of his learning and his purse. And some time after she made him a gift of an alms-bag on which she had wrought the words, "Ann, to her worthy work-fellow."

Here I am bound to tell that, not to my aunt alone, but to me likewise did the good work which the old organist had pointed out to my friend, seem a vain imagining when it had led her to accept a lover whom she loved not. But when it became a part of her life, stripped of all bigotry or overmuch zeal, and when the old musician had led us to know many poor folks, it worked right well and we were able to help many an one, not alone with money and food, but likewise with good counsel and nursing in sore need. Whenever we might apply to the Magister, his door and purse alike were open to us, and peradventure he went more often to visit and succor the needy than he might otherwise have done, inasmuch as he thereby found the chance of speech with his gracious "work-fellow," of winning her praises and kissing her hand, which Ann was ever fain to grant when he had shown special zeal.

We were doubtless a strange fellowship of four: Ann and I, the organist and Master Peter, and, albeit we were not much experienced in the ways of the world, I dare boldly say that we did more good and dried more tears than many a wealthy Abbey.

At the New Year I followed Ann to the forest, and helped to grace the hunter's board "with smart wenches;" and when she and I came home together after Twelfth day, she found that the forward apprentice had quitted her step-father's house. Not only had my aunt told old Dame Magdalen of his ill-behaving, but his father at Augsburg was dead, and so Pemhart could send him home to the dwelling he had inherited without disgracing him. Yet, after this, he made so bold as to sue for Ann in a right fairly written letter, to which she said him nay in a reply no less fairly written.

CHAPTER XVII

A thoughtful brain could never cease to marvel at the wonders which happen at every step and turn, were it not that due reflection proves that strange events are no less necessary and frequent links in the mingled chain of our life's experience than commonplace and every-day things; wherefor sheer wonder at matters new to our experience we leave for the most part to children and fools. And nevertheless the question many a time arose in my mind: how a woman whose heart was so truly in the right place as my aunt's could cast off her only son for the cause of an ill-match, and notwithstanding strive with might and main to remove all hindrances in the way of another such ill-match.

This indeed brought to my mind other, no less miracles. Thus, after Ann's home-coming, when I would go to see her at Pernhart's house, I often found her sitting with the old dame, who would tell her many things, and those right secret matters. Once, when I found Ann with the old woman from whom she had formerly been so alien, they were sitting together in the window-bay with their arms about each other, and looking in each other's face with loving but tearful eyes. My entrance disturbed them; Dame Magdalen had been telling her new favorite many matters concerning her son's youthful days, and it was plain to see that she rejoiced in these memories of the best days of her life, when her two fine lads had ever been at the head of their school. Her eldest, indeed, had done so well that the Lord Bishop of Bamberg, in his own person, had pressingly desired her late departed husband to make him a priest. Then the father had apprenticed Ulman to himself, and dedicated the elder, who else should have inherited the dwelling-house and smithy, to the service of the Church, whereupon he had ere long risen to great dignity.

None, to be sure, listened so well as Ann, open-eared to all these tales, and it did old Dame Magdalen good to see the maid bestir herself contentedly about the house-keeping; but her changed mind proceeded from yet another cause. My aunt had done a noble deed of pure human kindness, of real and true Christian charity, and the bright beam of that love which could drag her feeble body out into the winter's cold and to her foe's dwelling, cast its light on both these miracles at once. This it was which had led the high-born dame to cast aside all the vanities and foolishness in which she had grown up, to the end that she might protect a young and oppressed creature whom she truly cared for from an ill fate. Yea, and that sunbeam had cast its light far and wide in the coppersmith's home, and illumined Ann likewise, so that she now saw the old mother of the household in a new light.

When the very noblest and most worshipful deems it worthy to make a great sacrifice out of pure love for a fellow-creature, that one is, as it were, ennobled by it; it opens ways which before were closed; and such a way was that to old Dame Magdalen's heart, who now, on a sudden, bethought her that she found in Ann all she had lost in her well-beloved grandchild Gertrude.

Never had Ann and I been closer friends than we were that winter, and to many matters which bound us, another was now added—a sweet secret, concerning me this time, which, strange to tell, drew us even more near together.

The weeks before Lent presently came upon us; Ann, however, would take part in no pleasures, albeit she was now a welcome guest, since her step-father was a member of the worshipful council. Only once did she yield to my beseeching and go with me to a dance at a noble house; but whereas I perceived that it disturbed her cheerful peace of mind, although she was treated with hearty respect, I troubled her no more, and for her sake withdrew myself in some measure from such merry-makings.

After Easter, when the spring-tide was already blossoming, my soul likewise went forth to seek joy and gladness, and now will I tell of the new marvel which found fulfilment in my heart.

A grand dance was to be given in honor of certain ambassadors from the Emperor Sigismund, who had come to treat with his Highness the Elector and the Town Council as to the Assembly of the States to be held in the summer at Ratisbon, at the desire of Theodoric, Archbishop of Cologne. The illustrious chief of this Embassy, Duke Rumpold of Glogau in Silesia, had been received as guest in a house whither, that very spring, the eldest son had come home from Padua and Paris, where he had taken the dignity of Doctor of Ecclesiastical and Civil Laws with great honors, and he it was who first moved my young heart to true love.

As a child I had paid small heed to Hans Haller, as a lad so much older that he overlooked little Margery, and by no means took her fancy like Cousin Gotz; thus he came upon me as one new and strange.

He had dwelt five years in other lands and the first time ever I looked into his truthful eyes methought that the maid he should choose to wife was born in a lucky hour.

But every mother and daughter of patrician rank doubtless thought the same; and that he should ever uplift me, giddy, hasty Margery, to his side, was more than I dared look for. Yet, covertly, I could not but hope; inasmuch as at our first meeting again he had seemed well-pleased and amazed at my being so well-favored, and a few days later, when many young folks were gathered together at the Hallers' house, he spoke a great while and right kindly with me in especial. Nor was it as though I were some unripe child, such as these young gentlemen are wont to esteem us maids under twenty—nay, but as though I were his equal.

And thus he had brought to light all that lay hid in my soul. I had answered him on all points freely and gladly; yet, meanwhile, I had been on my guard not to let slip any heedless speech, deeming it a precious favor to stand well in the opinion of so noble and learned a gentleman.

And presently, when it was time for departing, he held my hand and pressed it; and, as he wrapped me in my cloak, he said in a low voice that, whereas he had thought it hard to make himself at home once more in our little native town, now, if I would, I might make Nuremberg as dear—nay, dearer to him than ever it had been of yore; and the hot blood boiled in my veins as I looked up at him beseechingly and bid him never mock me thus.

But he answered with all his heart that it was sacred earnest and that, if I would make home sweet to him and himself one of the happiest of mankind, I must be his, inasmuch as in all the lands of the earth he had seen nought so dear to him as the child whom he had found grown to be so sweet a maid, and, quoth he, if I loved him never so little, would I not give him some little token.

I looked into his eyes, and my heart was so full that no word could I say but his Christian name "Hans," whereas hitherto I had ever called him Master Hailer. And meseemed that all the bells in the town together were ringing a merry peal; and he understood at once the intent of my brief answer, and murmured right loving words in mine ear. Then did he walk home with me and Cousin Maud; and meseemed the honored mothers among our friends, who were wont so to bewail my loneliness as a motherless maid, had never looked upon me with so little kindness as that evening which love had made so blessed.

By next morning the tidings were in every mouth that a new couple had plighted their troth, and that the Hallers' three chevronells were to be quartered with the three links of the Schoppers.

Ann was the first to be told of my happiness, and whereas she had hitherto been steadfastly set on eschewing the great dances of the upper class so long as she was unwed, this time she did our will, for that she had no mind to spoil my pleasure by her absence.

Thus had Love taken up his abode with me likewise; and meseemed it was like a fair, still, blooming morning in the Forest. A pure, perfect, and peaceful gladness had opened in my soul, a way of seeing which lent sweetness and glory to all things far and wide, and joyful thanksgiving for that all things were so good.

As I looked back on that morning when Ann had flown to Herdegen's breast, and as I called to mind the turmoil of passion of which I had read in many a poem and love-tale, I weened that I had dreamed of somewhat else as the first blossoming of love in my heart, that I had looked to feel a fierce and glowing flame, a burning anguish, a wild and stormy fever. And yet, as it had come upon me, methought it was better; albeit the sun of my love had not risen in scarlet fire, it was not therefore small nor cool; the image of my dear mother was ever-present with me; and methought that the love I felt was as pure and fair as though it had come upon me from her heavenly home.

And how loving and hearty was the welcome given me by my lover's parents, when they received me in their noble dwelling, and called me their dear daughter, and showed me all the treasures contained in the home of the Hallers'. In this fine house, with its broad fair gardens—a truly lordly dwelling, for which many a prince would have been fain to exchange his castle and hunting demesne—I was to rule as wife and mistress at the right hand of my Hans' mother, whose kind and dignified countenance pleased me well indeed, and by whose friendly lips I, an orphan, was so glad to be called "Child" and daughter. Nor were his worshipful father and his younger brethren one whit less dear to me. I was to become a member— nay, as the eldest son's wife, the female head—of one of the highest families in the town, of one whose sons would have a hand in its government so long as there should be a town-council in Nuremberg.

My lover had indeed been elected to sit in the minor council soon after his homecoming, being no longer a boy, but near on thirty years of age. And his manners befitted his years; dignified and modest, albeit cheerful and full of a young man's open-minded ardor for everything that was above the vulgar. With him, for certain, if with any man, might I grow to be all I desired to become; and could I but learn to rule my fiery temper, I might hope to follow in the ways of his mother, whom he held above all other women. The great dance, of which I have already made mention, and whither Ann had agreed to come with us, was the first I should go to with my well-beloved Hans. The worshipful Council had taken care to display all their best bravery in honor of the Emperor's envoys; they had indeed allied themselves with the constable of the Castle, the Prince Elector, to do all in their power to have the Assembly held at Nuremberg, rather than at Ratisbon, and to that end it was needful to win the good graces of the Ambassadors.

All the patricians and youth of the good city were gathered at the town-hall, and the beginning of the feast was pure enjoyment. The guests were indeed amazed at the richness of our great hall and civic treasure, as likewise at the brave apparel and great show of jewels worn by the gentlemen and ladies.

There were six envoys, and at their head was Duke Rumpold of Glogau; but among the knights in attendance on him I need only name that very Baron Franz von Welemisl who had been so sorely hurt out in the forest garden for my sake, and a Junker of Altmark, by name Henning von Beust, son of one of the rebellious houses who strove against the customs, laws, and rights over the marches, as claimed by our Lord Constable the Elector.

Baron Franz was now become chamberlain to the emperor and, albeit cured indeed of his wounds, was plagued by a bad cough. Still he could boast of the same noble and knightly presence as of old, and his pale face, paler than ever I had known it, under his straight black hair, with the feeble tones of his soft voice, went right to many a maiden's heart; also his rich black dress, sparkling with fine gems, beseemed him well.

Presently, when he saw that Hans and I were plighted lovers, he feigned as though his heart were stricken to death; but I soon perceived that he could take comfort, and that he had bestowed the love he had once professed for me, with compound increase on Ursula Tetzel. She was ready enough to let him make love to her, and I wished the swarthy courtier all good speed with the damsel.

A dancing-hall is in all lands a stew full of fish, as it were, for gentlemen from court, and Junker Henning von Beust had no sooner come in than he began to angle; and whereas Sir Franz's bait was melancholy and mourning, the Junker strove to win hearts by sheer mirth and bold manners.

My lover himself had commended him to my favor by reason that the gentleman was lodging under his parents' roof; and he and I and Ann had found much pleasure these two days past in his light and openhearted friendliness. Nought more merry indeed might be seen than this red-haired young nobleman, in parti-colored attire, with pointed scallops round the neck and arm-holes, which fluttered as he moved and many little bells twinkling merrily. Light and life beamed forth out of this gladsome youth's blue eyes. He had never sat at a school-desk; while our boys had been poring over their books, he had been riding with his father at a hunt or a fray, or had lurked in ambush by the highway for the laden wagons of those very "pepper sacks"—[A nickname for grocery merchants]—whose good wine and fair daughters he was so far from scorning in their own town-hall.

He had already fallen in love with Ann at the Hallerhof, and never quit her side although, after I had overheard certain sharp words by which Ursula Tetzel strove to lower the maid in his opinion, I told him plainly of what rank and birth she was.

For this he cared not one whit; nay, it increased his pleasure in making much of her and trying to spoil her shrewish foe's sport. It seemed as though he could never have enough of dancing with Ann, and so soon as the town pipers struck up, with cornets, trumpets, horns, and haut-boys, fiddles, sack-buts and rebecks, the rattle of drums and the groaning of bagpipes, while the Swiss fifes squeaked shrilly above the clatter of the kettle-drums, methought the music itself flung him in the air and brought him low again. With his free and mirthful ways he carried all before him, and when presently it was plain to all that he could outdo our nimblest dancers, and was a master of each kind of dance which was held in favor at every court, whether of Brandenburg, of Saxony, of Bohemia, or at our own Emperor Sigismund's Hungarian court, he was ere long entreated to show us some new figures of the dance; nor was he loth to do so.

Nay, he presently went to such lengths that our Franconian and Nuremberg nobles could but turn away their faces, inasmuch as he began so wild and unseemly a dance as was overmuch even for me, despite my youth and sheer delight in the quick measure.

My Hans, the young councillor, took pleasure in leading me forth in the Polish dance, or with due dignity in the Swabian figure, but he held back, as was fitting, from the mad whirl of the gipsy dance and of the "Dove dance;" and he, and I likewise, courteously withstood his bidding to join in the Dance of the Dead as it was in use in Brandenburg, Hungary, and Schleswig: one has to be for dead, and as he lieth another shall come to wake him with a kiss. On this Junker von Beust, who was, as the march—men say, the dance-corpse, entrapped Ann in a strange adventure. Ann kissed not his cheek, but in the air near by it, and the bold knave, who had no mind to forego so sweet a boon, declared to her after the dance was over that she was his debtor, and that he would give her no peace till she should pay him his due.

Ann courteously prayed him that he would be a merciful creditor and remit the payment of that she had indeed omitted, though truly out of no ill-will. And whereas he would by no means consent, the dispute was taken up by others present and Jorg Loffelholz devised the fancy of holding a Court of Love to decide the case.

This met with noisy approval, and albeit I and my dear Hans, and some others with us, made protest, the damsels were presently seated in a circle and Jorg Loffelholz, who was chosen to preside, asked of each to pronounce sentence. Thus it came to the turn of Ursula Tetzel and she, looking round on Junker Henning or ever she spoke, said, with a proud curl of her red lips, that she could give no opinion, inasmuch as she only knew what beseemed young maids of noble birth.

On this the Junker answered with such high and grave dignity as I should not have looked for in so scatter-brained a wight: "The best patent of nobility, fair lady, is that of the maid to whom God Almighty has vouchsafed the gentlest soul and sweetest grace; and in all this assembly I have found none more richly endowed with both than the damsel against whom I in jest have made complaint. Wherefor I pray the presiding judge of this Court of Love to ask you once more for your verdict."

Ursula found this ill to brook; nevertheless her high spirit was ready to meet it. She laughed loudly, and with seeming lightness, as she hastily answered him: "Then you haughty lords of the marches allow not that it is in the Emperor's power to grant letters of nobility, but ascribe it to Heaven alone! A bold opinion. Howbeit, I care not for politics, and will pronounce my sentence. If it had been Margery Schopper, who had refused the kiss, or Elsa Ebner, or any one of us whose ancestors bore arms by grace of the Emperor, and not of the God of the Brandenburgers, I would have condemned her to give you, in lieu of one kiss, two, in the presence of witnesses; but inasmuch as it is Mistress Ann Spiesz who has dared to withhold from a noble gentleman, a guest of the town, what we highborn damsels would readily have paid I grant her of our mercy, grace and leave to kiss the hand of Junker Henning von Beust, in token of penitence." The words were spoken clearly and steadfastly; all were silent, and I will confess that as Ursula gave her answer to the Junker with beaming eyes and quivering lips, never had I seen her more fair. It could plainly be seen by her heaving bosom how gladly she gave free vent to her old cherished grudge; and that she had in truth wounded the maid she hated to the very soul, Ann showed by her deathly paleness. Yet found she not a word in reply; and while Ursula was speaking, meseemed in the fullness of my wrath and grief as though a cloud were rising before my eyes. But so soon as she ceased and my eyes met the triumphant look in hers, my mind suddenly grew clear again, and never heeding the multitude that stood about us, I went a step forward, and cried: "We all thank you, Junker; you have taken the worthier part; the only part, Ursula," and I looked her sternly in the face, "the only part which I would have a friend of mine take, or any true heart."

The Junker bowed, and with a reproachful glance at Ursula he said: "Would to God I might never have a harder choice to make!" Whereupon he turned his back on her and went up to Ann; but Ursula again laughed loudly and called after him in defiance: "Oh! may heaven ever keep your wits clear when you have to choose, and especially when you have to discern on the high-road betwixt what is your own and what belongs to other folks."

The blood mounted to the Junker's face, and, as with a hasty gesture he smoothed back the fierce hair on his lip, methought he might seem the same as when he rose in his saddle to rush down on our merchants' wains; for indeed it was the Beusts, with the Alvenslebens, their near kinsfolks, who had fallen upon the train of waggons belonging to the Muffels and the Tetzels, near Juterbock, not a year ago.

But, hotly as his blood boiled, the Junker refrained himself, inasmuch as knightly courtesy forbade him to repay Ursula in the like coin; and as it fell Cousin Maud was enabled to aid him in this praiseworthy selfrule. She came forward with long strides, and her eyes flashed wrathful threats, till meseemed they were more fiery than the jewels in the tall plumes she wore on her head. She thrust aside the young men and maid who made up the Court of Love as a swift ship cuts through the small fry in the water. Without let or pause she pushed on, and as soon as she caught sight of Ann she seized her by the arm, stroked her hair and cheeks, and flung a few sharp words at Ursula:

"I will talk to you presently!" Then she bid me remain behind with Hans and withdrew, carrying Ann with her, while Junker Henning followed praying to be forgiven for all the discomfort she had suffered by reason of him. This Ann gladly granted, and besought us and him alike to come with her no further.

When he came back to us Ursula, who was aggrieved by the looks of displeasure she met on all sides, cried out: "Back already, Sir Junker? If you had so lightly yielded your rights to kiss of mine, you may be certain that I would have appealed to any one who would do my behest to call you to account for such scorn!"

She eyed the young nobleman with a bold gaze, never weening that this challenge was all he waited for. He tossed his curly head, and cried with sparkling eyes: "Then, mistress, I would have you to know that I would take no kiss from you, even if you were to offer it. I have spoken—now call forth your champions."

He was silent a moment, and then, glancing round at the bystanders with defiant looks, he went on: "If any gentleman here present sets a higher price than I, the high-born Henning Beust, heir and Lord of Busta and Schadstett, on a kiss from the lips which have wronged my fair lady with spiteful speech, let him now stoop and pick up my glove. There it lies!"

And he flung it on the ground, while Ursula turned pale. Her eyes turned from one to another of the young gentlemen who paid her court and they were many—and the longer silence reigned the faster came her breath and the hotter waxed her ire. But on a sudden she was calm; her eyes had lighted on Sir Franz von Welemisl, and all might read what she demanded of him. The Bohemian understood her; he picked up the glove and muttered to the Junker with a shrug: "Mistress Ursula commands me!"

A look of pain passed over the brave youth's merry face, for that heretofore the young knight and he had been in good fellowship, and he hastily answered: "Nay, Sir Knight; I would have crossed swords with you readily enough or ever you had felt the prick of Swabian steel; but now you are not yet fully yourself again, and to fight with a friend who is sick is against the rule of my country."

The words were spoken from a kind and honest heart, and I saw in Sir Franz's face that he knew their intent was true; but as he put forth his hand to grasp the Junker's, Ursula tossed her head in high disdain. Sir Franz hastily changed his mien, and cried: "Then you will do well to act against the rule of your country, and fight the champion of the lady you have offended."

Here the dispute had an end, forasmuch as that my lord the duke, leader of the embassy, hearing the Brandenburger's fierce voice, came in haste from the supper-board to restore peace; and as he led away the Junker it was plain to all that he was taking him sharply to task. It was, in truth, a criminal misdeed in one of the Imperial envoy to cast down his glove at a dance, where he was the guest of a peaceful city; and that the duke imposed no severe penance for it the Junker might thank the worshipful members of the council who were present; they were indeed disposed to let well alone, inasmuch as they had it at heart to send the whole party home again well-pleased with Nuremberg.

The music was soon sounding merrily again in the solemn town-hall, and of all the young folks who danced so gleefully, and laughed and chattered Ursula was the last to let it be seen how this grand revel had been troubled by her fault. Her eyes were bright with glad contentment, and she was so free with Sir Franz that it might have seemed that they would quit the town hall a plighted couple.

The festival was drawing to an end, and when I had danced the last dance, and was looking about me, I beheld to my amazement Ursula Tetzel in eager speech with Junker Henning. On our way home the young gentleman informed me that she had given him to understand that, during the meeting of the Imperial Assembly, he might look to be waited on by a noble youth who would pick up his glove in duty to her, and prove to him that there were other than sick champions glad to draw the sword for her.

The Brandenburger would fain have known with whom he would have to deal; but I held my peace, albeit I felt certain that Ursula had set her hopes on none other than my brother Herdegen.

On the morrow the whole of the Ambassadors' fellowship rode away, back to the emperor's court; I, for my part made my way to the Pernharts, where I found Ann amazed rather than wroth or distressed by Ursula's base attack. Also she was to have some amends; my dear godfather, Uncle Christian, with certain other gentlemen of the council, had notified old Tetzel that he was required to crave pardon of Ann and her stepfather for his daughter's haughty and reckless speech.

The proud and surly old man would have to submit to this penance without cavil, by reason that Pernhart had, since Saint Walpurgis' day, been a member of the council, and he and his family had part and share in the patrician festival. For, albeit craftsmen and petty merchants were excluded, the worshipful councillors chosen by the guilds enjoyed the same rights as those born to that high rank.

It was by mishap only that the coppersmith had not been at the town-hall yestereve, and on a later day, when he and his wife appeared there, they were among the finest of the elder couples. Ann did not, indeed, go with them; but it was neither vexation nor sorrow that kept her at home. My great gladness as it were warmed her likewise, and we were looking for Herdegen's speedy home-coming.

She looked forward to this with such firm hope as filled me with fears, when I minded me of my brother's letters, in which he never had aught to tell of but vain pleasures and pastimes.

My betrothal to Hans Haller was after his own heart; he wrote of him as of a man whose gifts and birth were worthy of me; and went on to say that he would follow his example, and, whereas he had renounced love in seeking a bride, he would take counsel of his head, and not of his heart, and quarter our ancient coat of arms with one no less noble.

CHAPTER XVIII

Though Ann's hopeful mood distressed me, these same hopes in my world-wise Aunt Jacoba raised my spirit; but again, when I heard my grand-uncle speak of Herdegen as his duteous son, it fell as low as before. The old man had shown much contentment at my plighting to Hans, and had given me a precious set of rubies as a wedding gift; yet could I scarce take pleasure in them, inasmuch as he told me then and there that he had the like in store for the noble damsel whom Herdegen should wed.

Cousin Maud was in great wrath, when she knew that we had it in our minds even yet to bring Ann and Herdegen together; howbeit this did not hinder her from being as kind to Ann as she was ever wont to be, and giving her pleasure with gifts great and small whenever she might. She had her own thoughts touching my brother's faithlessness. She deemed it a triumph of noble blood over the yearnings of his heart; and the more she loved to think well of her darling the more comfort she found in this interpretation.

Among those few who had known of his betrothal to Ann was the bee-master's widow, Dame Henneleinlein; and she had cradled herself so gladly in the hope of being ere long kin to a noble family, that its wrecking filled her heart with bitter rage, and in all the houses whither she carried her honey she never failed to speak slander of Herdegen.

All this would never have troubled me, if only I might have rejoiced in the presence of my dear love; but alas! no more than three weeks after our betrothal he was sent, as squire to Master Erhart Schurstab, away to court, where they were to lay before the Emperor Sigismund in the name of Nuremberg the various hindrances in the way of our trafficking with Venice, whereas since the late war his Majesty had been mightily ill-disposed towards that great and famous city.

There was no remedy but patience; my lover wrote to me often, and his loving letters would have filled me with joy, if it had not been that in each one there was ever some sad tidings of Junker Henning, whom I yet held in high esteem. This young lord, who was in attendance on his Majesty— who never held his court for more than a few days at the same place—or ever he left Vienna to go to Ratisbon, had made a close friendship with my plighted master, and had been serviceable to him in all things wherein he might; and Hans had said of him that he was one in whom there was no guile, with the open heart and bright temper of a child. Such an one, indeed, was his; yet, in the midst of the gayest mirth, his grief of heart would so mightily come upon him that he fell into a sudden gloom; and out of the fulness of his sorrow he confessed to Hans that he could never cease to think of Ann. Whereupon my dear love conceived that it must be his woeful duty to tell his friend that the lady of his choice had no free heart to give him. Yet to the Junker's question whether she were plighted to another, and whether he were minded to wed her, Hans was forced in truth to say nay. This gave the lovesick youth new courage, and at length he went so far as that Hans enquired of me whether Ann might not after all be willing to give up Herdegen, who well deserved it at her hands, and to take pity on so brave and true-hearted a lover as the Junker.

To this I could make no answer other than: "Never—never;" inasmuch as, having shown Ann this letter, and, moreover, loudly sung the praise of her suitor, she asked me right sadly whether I was weary of confirming her in her love for my brother; and when I eagerly denied this, she cried: "And you know me well! And you must know that nothing on earth—nor you, nor Mistress Jacoba, nor all Nuremberg, could turn my heart from my love!"

This did I forthwith write to Hans; but that letter never reached him, and thus was he delivered from the grievous duty of robbing the Junker of his last hope.

Alas, my Hans! How sorely I did long for thee every hour! And yet shall I ever remember the month of June in that year with thankfulness.

Day after day did we maidens sit in the Hallers' garden, for Hans' worthy mother had soon taken Ann into her heart, and it became a fear to me ere long lest her rare beauty should turn the head of his younger brother Paulus, a likely lad of nineteen. As the summer waxed hot we went into the forest at the bidding of my uncle and aunt, who took great joy in seeing their favorite in right good heart and wondrous beauty, Mistress Giovanna having provided her with seemly and brave apparel. Nor was there any lack of good fellowship; many young noblemen bore us company, and whereas the town was full of illustrious guests, many of them found their way out to the forest.

This was by reason that the Prince Electors and the other rulers of the Empire, and foremost of them all our High Constable, had, indeed, declared that the great Assembly should be held at Nuremberg and not at Ratisbon; and when they were all gathered in our good town, the Emperor Sigismund, after he had waited for five days at Ratisbon, was fain at last, whether or no, to follow them hither. Then had his Chamberlains been sent before him, and among them again came Duke Rumpold von Glogau and Junker Henning von Beust, while his Majesty kept my Hans still about his person. Now, when the Emperor's forerunners had fulfilled their duties, they likewise were bidden to the forest-lodge; and with them came the lord of Eberstein, and an Italian Conte, Fazio di Puppi, both well skilled in song and the lute. Yet was my brother Herdegen still absent, albeit we had looked for him at Whitsuntide.

Cousin Maud bided at home, where there was much to be done in preparing fitting cheer for the noble fellowship who were to be lodged in the Schopperhof; nay, the old house was to be decked outside with a festal dress, in obedience to the behest of the town-council that every citizen should do his utmost so to cleanse and adorn his house, that it should please the eyes of his Majesty the Emperor.

Towards evening on Saint Liborius' day,—[July 23rd.]—my lord the Duke came forth on horseback to the forest lodge, and as I write, I can see the beaming countenance of Junker Henning as he greeted Ann; she, however, took his devoted demeanor coolly and courteously, yet could she not hinder him from coming between her and the other gentlemen in an over-marked way. The company was a large one for us two maidens, and there was none other with us save Elsa Ebner, our best-beloved schoolmate, and on her young Master Jorg Loffelholz had cast his eyes.

Not long after dinner Akusch came to me with the tidings that Herdegen had ridden into Nuremberg yestereve. My grand-uncle, to whom he had sent word of his coming, had gone forth to meet him on the way, and, with him Jost Tetzel and his daughter Ursula. My brother had alighted at the Im Hoff's house, and had waited on Cousin Maud this morning early. In the afternoon it was his intent to come out to the forest with my uncle's leave, to see me.

When I repeated all this to Aunt Jacoba, she was mightily disturbed and bid me stand by Ann, and in all points obey the counsel she might find it good to give her. She desired I would fetch my friend to her July 23rd. forthwith, and then made a plan for all the young folks to go forth to the fair garden of a certain bee-keeper, one Martein, where flowers grew in great abundance, and where we might wind the wreaths which Uncle Christian would need to grace the Empress' chambers withal. Thither, quoth she, would she send Herdegen on his coming; for she knew full well that the tidings brought by Akusch could not remain hid.

Whereas Ann turned a little paler, my aunt shook her head in displeasure, and admonished her to remain calm; albeit she had charges to bring against that wild youth, yet, for the present, she must keep them to herself. Least of all was she to let him suppose that his faithlessness had caused her any bitter heart-ache; if she desired that matters end rightly she must command herself to receive the home-comer no more than kindly, and to demean her as though his denying of her had touched her but lightly; nay, as though it were a pleasure to her vanity to be courted by the Brandenburg Junker and other noble gentlemen. If she could but seem to rate him as less than either of them, she would have won a great part of the victory.

Such subtlety had no charm for Ann; howbeit, my aunt gave no place to her doubting, and once more her urgent eloquence prevailed on the sorrowing maid to govern the yearning of her soul; and when I promised my friend to support her, she gave the wise lady, who had shown her such plain proofs of her devoted friendship, her word that she would in every point obey her.

Many a time have we seen, in the churches of Nuremberg, certain acting of plays wherein right honest and worthy persons have appeared as Judas Iscariot, or even as the very Devil himself; and at Venice likewise have I seen such plays, called there Boinbaria, wherein men and women, innocent of all guilt, were made to stand for Calumny, Cruelty, and Craft; and that so cunningly that a man might swear that they were reprobate Knaves full ripe for the gallows. From this it may be seen that men are fit and able to seem other than they are by nature; nay, such feigning is a pleasure to most folks, as we plainly see from the delight taken by great and small alike in mummery at Carnival tide. Howbeit, they can scarce have their heart in such sport; and for my part, meseemeth that to play such a part as my aunt had set before Ann is one of the hardest that can be laid upon a pure-hearted and truthful maid. At the time I wist not clearly what was the end of such rash trifling; but now, when I know men better, meseems it was well conceived, and could not fail of its intent, albeit the course of events made it plain to my understanding how little the thoughts and plans of the wisest can avail when Heaven rules otherwise.

The gentlemen in the hall were more than ready to agree to our bidding; yet none but I could guess what made Ann's lip to quiver from time to time, while her gay spirit charmed the young men who bore us company through the woods to the beekeeper's garden.

I and Elsa cut the flowers helped by Jorg Loffelholz, while Ann sat under a shady lime-tree hard by an arbor of honeysuckle, and showed the others, who lay on the grass about her; how to wind a garland. Each one was ready to be taught by lips so sweet, and in guiding of fingers and words of praise or blame, there was right merry laughing and chatter and pastime.

Junker Henning lay at her feet, and near him my Hans' brother Paulus, and young Master Holzschuher. The Knight von Eberstein had fetched him a stool out from the beekeeper's house, and twisted and tied with great zeal; the Italian Conte, Fagio di Puppi, struck the mandoline, which he called "the lady of his heart" from whom he never parted even on the longest journey.

When Elsa and I had flowers enough, we sat down with the others, and it was pleasant there to rest in the shade of the lime-tree, whose leaves fluttered in a soft air, while bees and butterflies hovered above the flowers in the warm sunshine. The birds sang no more; they had finished nesting long ago; but we, with our young hearts overfull of love, were in the right mind for song, and when Puppi had charmed us with a sweet Italian lay, and I had decked his lute with a rose as a guerdon, my lord of Eberstein took example from him, and they then besought Ann and me to do our part; but Junker Henning was the more eager. Whereupon Ann smiled on him so graciously that I was in pain for him, and she signed to me, and, I taking the lower part as was our wont, we gave Prince Wizlav's "Song to Dame Love." It rang out right loud and clear from our throats over the gentlemen's heads as they sat at our feet, and through the garden close:

> *"Earth is set free and flowers*
> *In all the meads are springing,*
> *The balmy noontide hours*
> *Are sweet with odors rare;*
> *The hills for joy are leaping.*
> *The happy birds are singing,*
> *And now, while winds are sleeping,*
> *Sour through the sunny air.*

> *Now hearts begin to kindle*
> *And burn with love's sweet anguish*
> *As tapers blaze and dwindle.*
> *Love, our lady! lend thine ear!*
> *Would'st thou but spoil our pleasure?*
> *Ah, leave us not to languish!*
> *Who vows to thee his treasure,*
> *Haughty lady, must beware."*

We had sung so much as this when the sound of hoofs, of which we had already been aware on the soft soil of the woods, gave us pause. Then, behold! Ann turned pale and pressed her hands, full of the roses she had chosen for her garland, tightly to her bosom, as though in pain.

Junker Henning, who, while she sang, had gazed at her devoutly, nay, in rapture, marked this gesture and leaped to his feet to succour her; but she commanded herself with wonderful readiness, and laughed as she showed him her finger, from which two drops of blood had fallen on her white gown. And while the garden-gate was opening, she held out her hand to the young man, saying in haste: "Pricked,—a thorn!—would you please to take it out for me, Junker?"

He seized her hand and held it long in his own, as some jewel or marvel, before he remembered that he was required to take out the thorn. The other gentle men, and among them my brother-in-law Paulus, had likewise sprung forward to lend their aid; he, indeed, had snatched his lace neck-tie off and dipped it in the fountain.

Meanwhile the new-comers had joined the circle: First, Duke Rumpold, then Jost Tetzel, and lastly Herdegen with Ursula.

I flew to meet him, and when he held me in his arms and kissed me, and wished me joy of my betrothal right heartily, I forgot all old grievances and only rejoiced at having him home once more; till Ursula greeted me, and Herdegen came in sight of Ann. She had remained sitting under the lime-tree, on a saddle cushion of blue velvet, as on a throne; and in truth meseemed she might have been a queen, as she graciously accepted the service of the gentlemen who had been so moved by her pricked finger. The Junker wrapped it with care in a green leaf which, as his lady grandmother had taught him, had a healing gift; Paulus held forth the laced kerchief, and the Italian was striking wailing tones from his lute.

All this to-do, at any other time would, for a certainty, have made sport for me, but now laughing was far from me, and I had no eyes but for Ann in her little court, and for my brother.

At first she feigned as though she saw him not; and whereas the Junker still held her hand, she hit his fingers with a pink, albeit she was never apt to use such unseemly freedom.

Then she first marked my lord the duke, and rose to greet him with a courteous reverence, and not till she had bowed coldly and curtly to Tetzel and his daughter did she seem to be aware that Herdegen was of the company. At that moment I minded me of the morning when Love had thrown her into his arms, and it was with pain and wonder that I marked her further demeanor. In truth it outdid all I could have dreamed of: she held out her hand with an inviting smile, bid him welcome home and to the forest, reproved him for staying so long away from me, his dear little sister, and our good cousin, and then turned her back upon him to desire the Junker to place her cushions aright. Therewith she gave this young gentleman her hand to support her to her seat, and asked him whether, in his country, they did not do service and devoir to the divine Dame Musica? And whereas he replied that verily they did, that in his own land he had heard many a sweet ditty sung by noble ladies to the harp and lute, that the children would ever sing at their sports, and that he, too, had oftentimes uplifted his voice in singing of madrigals, she besought him that he would make proof of some ballad or song. The rest of the company joining in her entreaties she left him no peace till he gave way to her desire, and after that he had protested that his singing was no better than the twitter of a starling or a bullfinch, and his ditty only such as he remembered from his boyhood's time, he sang the song "It rained on the bridge and I was wet" in a voice neither loud nor fine, but purely, and with great modesty.

Ann highly lauded this simple and right childish ditty, and said that she felt certain that she, by her teaching, could make a fine singer of the Junker.

The others were of the same opinion, and Herdegen, meanwhile, who was standing somewhat apart, with Ursula, looked on, marvelling greatly as though he could not believe what his ear heard and his eye beheld.

Then, inasmuch as my lord duke desired to hear more music made, we were ready enough to obey and uplifted our voices, while he leaned on an easy couch, listening diligently, and gave us the guerdon of his gracious praise.

Still, as heretofore, many were obedient to Ann's lightest sign, but never till now had I seen her proud of her power and so eager to use it. Now and again she would turn to Herdegen with some light word and a free demeanor, yet he, it was plain, would not vouchsafe to take his seat before her with the rest.

Nay, meseemed that he and Ursula had no part with us; inasmuch as that she was arrayed in velvet and rich brocade, and a bower, as it were, of yellow and purple ostrich plumes curled above her riding-hat.

Herdegen likewise was in brave array, after the fashion of the French, and a bunch of tall feathers stood up above his head, being held in a silken fillet that bound his hair. His cross-belt was set with gems and hung with little bells, tinkling as he moved and jarring with our song; and in this hot summer-tide it could not have been for his easement that he wore the tagged lappets, which fell, a hand-breadth deep, from his shoulders over the sleeves of his velvet tunic.

The more gleefully we sang and the more it was made plain that we, to all seeming, were only to obey the wishes of Ann and of his highness the duke, the less could my brother refrain himself to hide his ill-pleasure; and when presently the Junker besought Ann that she would sing "Tanderadei," which she very readily did, Herdegen could bear no more; he asked the Italian to lend him his mandoline, and struck the strings as though merely for his own good pleasure. Whereupon Ann turned to him and courteously entreated him for a song, and he asking her which song she would have, she hastily replied: "Your old ditties are already known to me, Junker Schopper; and, to judge by your seeming, you now take no pleasure save in French music. Let us then hear somewhat of the latest Paris fashion."

To this he replied, however: "Here, in my own land, I would like better to sing in my own tongue, by your gracious leave, fair mistress."

Then bowing to Ursula and to me, without even casting a glance at Ann, he went on to say: "And seeing that methinks you love madrigals, I will sing a Franconian ditty after the Junker's Brandenburg ballad."

He boldly struck the strings, and the little birds, which by this time had gone to rest in the linden-tree, again uplifted their little heads, and all that had ears and soul, near and far, Ann not the least, hearkened as he began with his clear voice and noble skill.

> *"To all this goodly company*
> *I sing as best I may,*
> *A madrigal of ladies fair*
> *And damsels soote and gay.*
> *Through many countries great and small*
> *I roam, and ladies fair I see*
> *Many! but fairest of them all*
> *The maidens of my own countree.*
> *The maidens of Franconia*
> *I ever love to meet,*
> *They dwell in fond remembrance*
> *A vision ever sweet.*
> *Of maids they are the crown and pearl!*
> *And if I might but spin them*
> *I would make the spindle whirl!"*

My lord duke clapped hearty praise of the singer, and we all did the same; all save Junker Henning, who had not failed to mark that Herdegen had striven to out-do his modest warble, and likewise the ardent eyes he turned on the lady of his choice. Hence he moved not. Ann clapped her hands but lightly, sat looking into her lap, and for some time could say not a word; indeed, if she had trusted herself to speak the game would of a certainty have been lost.

The knight of Eberstein it was, who ere long, albeit unwittingly, came to her aid; he challenged Ursula to give us a song in thanks to Junker Herdegen's praise of the maids of Franconia.

The damsel thought to do somewhat fine by making choice, instead of a German song, of a French lay by the Sieur de Machault "J'aim la flour," which was well known to all of us by reason that she had learnt it from old Veit Spiesz, Ann's grandfather; and she had no need to fear to uplift her voice, inasmuch as it was strong and as clear as a bell. But she sang over-loud and with a mode of speech which made Herdegen smile, and I can see her now as she stood upright in her fine yellow and purple garb, singing the light-tripping ditty,

> "*J'aim la flour*
> *De valour*
> *Sans falour*
> *Et l'aour*
> *Nuit et jour.*"

with all her might, as though stirring them to battle. The folly of so wrong-headed a fashion of singing such words was plain to Ann, in whose very blood, as it were, lay all that was most choice in musical feeling, and Herdegen's smile brought her a calmer mind again. When, presently, Ursula, believing that she had done somewhat marvellous, boldly turned upon Ann and besought her to sing—as though there had never been a breach between the twain—Ann refused, as not caring but yet firm in her mind. Then the Duke, who was even yet a fine singer and bore in mind how Ursula had demeaned herself towards Ann at the great dance, desired to have the lute and sang the song as follows:

> "*Behold a lady sweet and fair*
> *In simple dress,*
> *But right well clothed upon is she*
> *With seemliness.*
> *By her do flowers seem less bright,*
> *And she is such a glorious sight*
> *As, on May morns, the golden sun which lights up hill and lea—*
> *But froward maids delight us not, with all their bravery.*"

And he sang the little verse to Ann as though it were in her praise, till at the last line, which fell from his lips as it were in scorn, he cast a reproving glance at Ursula, and many an one might see and feel how well the song befitted one and the other of the hostile damsels.

Yet was it hard to guess what Ursula was thinking of all this; she thanked the Duke right freely for his fine song which held up the mirror to all froward ladies. At the same time she looked steadfastly at Ann, and led both Herdegen and the Knight of Eberstein to talk with herself; yet how often all the time did my brother cast his eyes at his heart's beloved, whom he had betrayed.

As for myself, I can call to mind little enough of all that was said, for the most part concerning the flowers and trees in the garden. Only Ann and my brother dwell in my memory, each feigning neither to see nor to hear the other, while covertly each had not eyes nor ears for any other. Yes, and I mind me how my brother's unrest and distress so filled me now with joy and now with pity, that I longed to cry out to the Junker that this was a base trick they were playing on him, inasmuch as Ann poured oil and more oil on the flame of his love.

And there stood old Tetzel and his daughter, and it was plain to see that they deemed that they had Herdegen safe in their toils; nay, it seemed likely enough that he had done his uncle's bidding and was already betrothed to her. Howbeit this strange lover had up to that moment cast not one loving look on his lady love.

What should come of it all? How could I ever find peace and comfort in so perverse a world, and amid this feigning which had turned upside down all that heretofore had seemed upright? Whichever way I turned there were things which I did not crave to see, and the saints know full well that I gazed not round about me; nay, that my eyes were set on two small specks plain to be seen—the two drops of blood which had fallen from Ann's finger, and which were now two dark, round spots on her white gown; and, as it grew dusk, meseemed they waxed blacker and greater.

At length, to my great joy, my lord the Duke rose and made as though he were departing; whereupon the false image vanished, and I beheld Ann giving her hand with a witching smile to Junker Henning, that he might help her to rise.

Supper was waiting for us at the Forest lodge. My Aunt Jacoba placed the Duke in the seat of honor at her right hand, with Ann and Junker Henning next to him. Herdegen she sent to the other end of the table to sit near his uncle, and Ursula far from him near the middle; to the end that it might be clearly seen that she knew naught of any alliance between that damsel and her nephew.

During that meal my squire had little cause to be pleased with his lady. The foolish sport begun in the garden was yet carried on and I liked it not, no more than my brother's French bravery; at table he appeared in a long red and blue garment of costly silken stuff, with a cord round the middle instead of a belt, so that it was for all the world like the loose gown which was worn by our Magister and by many a worthy citizen when taking his easement in his own home.

Besides all this, my heart was heavy with longing for my own true love, and my eyes filled with tears a many times, also I thanked the Saints with all my heart when at length my aunt left the table.

When we were outside she asked me privily whether Ann had rightly played her part; to which I answered "Only too well."

Herdegen, also, so soon as he had bid good night to Ursula, led me aside and desired to know what had come upon Ann. To this I hastily replied that of a surety he could not care to know, inasmuch as he had broken troth with her. Thereat he was vexed and answered that as matters were, so might they remain; but that he was somewhat amazed to mark how lightly she had got over that which had spoiled many a day and night for him.

Then I asked him whether he had in truth rather have found her in woe and grief, and would fain have had her young days saddened for love of him? He broke in suddenly, declaring that he knew full well that he had no right to hinder her in any matter, but that one thing he could not bear, and that was that she, whom he had revered as a saint, should now demean herself no more nobly nor otherwise than any other maid might. On this I asked him wherefor he had denied his saint; nay, for the sake—as it would seem—of a maid who was, for sure, the worldliest of us all. And, to end, I boldly enquired of him how matters stood betwixt him and Ursula; but all the answer I got was that first he must know whether Ann were in earnest with the Junker. On this I said in mockery that he would do well to seek out the truth of that matter to the very bottom; and running up the steps by which we were standing, I kissed my hand to him from the first turning and wished him a good night's rest.

Up in our chamber I found Ann greatly disturbed.

She, who was commonly so calm, was walking up and down the narrow space without pause or ceasing; and seeing how sorely her fears and her conscience were distressing her, pity compelled me to forego my intent of not giving her any hopes; I revealed to her that I had discovered that my Herdegen's heart was yet hers in spite of Ursula.

This comforted her somewhat; but yet could it not restore her peace of mind. Meseemed that the ruthless work she had done that day had but now come home to her; she could not refrain herself from tears when she confessed that Herdegen had privily besought her to grant him brief speech with her, and that she had brought herself to refuse him.

All this was told in a whisper; only a thin wall of wood parted Ursula's chamber from ours. As yet there was no hope of sleep, inasmuch as that the noise made, by the gentlemen at their carouse came up loud and clear through the open window and, the later it grew, the louder waxed Herdegen's voice and the Junker's, above all others. And I knew what hour the clocks must have told when my brother shouted louder than ever the old chorus:

> *"Bibit heres, bibit herus*
> *Bibit miles, bibit clerus*
> *Bibit ille, bibit illa*
> *Bibit servus cum ancilla.*
> *Bibit soror, bibit frater*
> *Bibit anus, bibit mater*
> *Bibit ista, bibit ille:*
> *Bibunt centem, bibunt milee."*

> *[The heir drinks, the owner drinks,*
> *The soldier and the clerk,*
> *He drinks, she drinks,*
> *The servant and the wench.*
> *The sister drinks and eke the brother,*
> *The grand dam and the gaffer,*
> *This one drinks, that one drinks,*
> *A hundred drink—a thousand!]*

Nor was this the end. The Latin tongue of this song may peradventure have roused Junker Henning to make a display of learning on his part, and in a voice which had won no mellowness from the stout Brandenburg ale— which is yclept "Death and murder"—or from the fiery Hippocras he had been drinking he carolled forth the wanton verse:

> *"Per transivit clericus*
> *[Beneath the greenwood shade;]*
> *Invenit ibi stantent,*
> *[A fair and pleasant maid;]*
> *Salve mi puella,*
> *[Hail thou sweetest she;]*
> *Dico tibi vere*
> *[Thou my love shalt be!]"*

The rest of the song was not to be understood whereas Herdegen likewise sang at the same time, as though he would fain silence the other:

> *"Fair Lady, oh, my Lady!*
> *I would I were with thee,*
> *But two deep rolling rivers*
> *Flow down 'twixt thee and me."*

And as Herdegen sang the last lines:

> *"But time may change, my Lady,*
> *And joy may yet be mine,*
> *And sorrow turn to gladness*
> *My sweetest Elselein!"*

I heard the Junker roar out "Annelein;" and thereupon a great tumult, and my Uncle Conrad's voice, and then again much turmoil and moving of benches till all was silence.

Even then sleep visited us not, and that which had been doing below was as great a distress to me as my fears for my lover. That Ann likewise never closed an eye is beyond all doubt, for when the riot beneath us waxed so loud she wailed in grief: "Oh, merciful Virgin!" or "How shall all this end?" again and again.

Nay, nor did Ursula sleep; and through the boarded wall I could not fail to hear well-nigh every word of the prayers in which she entreated her patron saint, beseeching her fervently to grant her to be loved by Herdegen, whose heart from his youth up had by right been hers alone, and invoking ruin on the false wench who had dared to rob her of that treasure.

I was right frightened to hear this and, in truth, for the first time I felt honest pity for Ursula.

BOOK 2

CHAPTER I

The Imperial Diet in Nuremberg!—the Imperial Advent!

The next day their Majesties were to enter into the town, and with them my Hans.

A messenger had brought the tidings, and now we must use all diligence; Ann and Elsa and I, with one and twenty more, had been chosen among all the daughters of the worshipful gentlemen of the council, to go forth to greet the Emperor and Empress with flowers and a discourse. This Ursula was to speak, by reason that she was mistress of all such arts; likewise was she by birth the chiefest of us all, inasmuch as that her late departed mother was daughter to the great Reynmar, lord of Sulzbach. Nor need Ann and I seek far for the flowers. The Hallers' garden had not its like in all Nuremberg, and my dear parents-in-law had promised that we should pluck all we needed for our posies.

Or ever I mounted my horse, I had tidings that Herdegen and Junker Henning had, last evening, come to bitter strife, nay, well-nigh to bloodshed; for that when my brother had sung the ditty in praise of one Elselein and the other had called upon him to put in the name of Ann, Herdegen had cried: "An if you mean red-haired Ann, the tapster wench at the Blue Pike, well and good!" Whereupon the Junker sprang up and flung the tankard he had just emptied at Herdegen's head. Herdegen had nimbly ducked, and had rushed on the drunken fellow sword in hand; but Duke Rumpold had put a word in, and by this morning Junker Henning seemed to have forgotten the matter. In Brandenburg, verily, such frays were common at the drinking-bouts of the lords and gentlemen, and by dawn all offence given over-night in their cups was wiped out of mind.

My brother lodged again at our grand-uncle's, while the Junker dwelt at the Waldstromer's townhouse. My Lord Duke found quarters at the Hallerhof, and his Highness the Prince Elector, and Archbishop Conrad of Mainz likewise lodged there, with a great following. Cousin Maud had made ready to welcome the Margrave of Baden and the Count von Henneberg under our roof. The upper floor of the Pernhart's house was given up to his Eminence Cardinal Branda, the most steadfast friend at Rome of Master Ulman's brother the bishop. His Holiness the Pope had sent that right-reverend prelate as his legate to the assembly, and he presently celebrated mass with great dignity in the presence of their Majesties and of the assembled lords and princes.

To this day my memory is right good in all ways; and of what followed on these events much is yet as clear and plain in my mind as though I saw and heard it all at this present time; albeit I, an old woman, would fain hide my face in my hands and weep thereat. For, notwithstanding there were certain hours in those days which brought me sweet love-making, and others of sheer mirth and vanity, yet is the spirit of man so tempered that, when great sorrow follows hard on the greatest joy it sufficeth to darken it wholly. And thus we may liken heaviness of heart to the chiming of bells, which hurts the ear if they sound over near, but at a distance make a sweet and devout music. Now, in sooth, inasmuch as I must make record of the deepest woe of my life, the brazen toll is a sad one, and the long-healed wounds ache afresh.

Those two months of the Imperial Diet! They lie behind me like distant hills. I can no more discern them apart, albeit certain landmarks, as it were, stand forth plainly to be seen, like the church-tower, the windmill, and the old oak on the ridge on the horizon.

How the night sped after our return from the forest and the morning next after—the 27th of July in the year of our Lord 1422—I can no longer call to mind; but I can see myself now as, the afternoon of that day, I set forth with Ann, attired in silk and lace—all white and new from head to foot, as it were for a wedding—to go to the open place between St. James' Church and the German House, within the Spital Gate. Whichever way we looked, behold flowers, green garlands, hangings, pennons, and banners; it was as though all the gardens in Franconia had been stripped of their blossoms. Never had such a brave show been seen, and with every breath we drank in the odors of the leaves and flowers which were already withering in the July sunshine. A finer Saint Pantaloon's day I never remember; the very sky seemed to share the city's gladness and was fair to see, in spotless blue. A light wind assuaged the waxing heat, and helped the flags and banners to unfurl: Our fine churches were decked all over and about with garlands, boughs, and banners, and meseemed were like happy brides awaiting their marriage in holiday array. The market-place was a scene of high festival, the beautiful fountain was a mighty bower of flowers, the triumphal arches, methought, were such as the gods of wood and garden might have joined to raise. Every balcony was richly hung, and even the crested gables and the turrets on the roofs displayed some bravery. All, so far as eye could see, was motley-hued and spick and span for brightness. The tiniest pane in the topmost dormer-window glittered without a spot. The poorest were clad in costly finery; the patrician folk were in the dress of knights and nobles; every craftsman was arrayed as though he were a councillor, every squire like his lord. You would have weened that day that there were none but rich folk in Nuremberg. The maidens' pearl chaplets gleamed in the sun, and the golden jewels in their fur bonnets; and what did their mothers care for the heat as they went to and fro to display the costly fur turbans which crowned their heads as it were with a glory of fur? How carefully had they dressed the little ones! They were to see the Emperor and Empress with their own eyes, and their Majesties might even, by good hap, see them!

Presently we saw the procession of the guilds with their devices and banners; never had they come forth in such goodly bravery. They were to form in ranks, on each side of the streets and the highway, a long space outside the gate.

At last it was nigh the hour when their Majesties should arrive. We maids had all assembled. Albeit we had agreed all to be clad in white, Ursula had decked her head-gear with Ostrich feathers of rose-pink and sky-blue; right costly plumes they were, but over many. Now would she look into her parchment scroll, and for us she had brief words and few. The nosegay which her servant in scarlet livery bore in his hand was a mighty fine one; and Akusch and a gardener's boy presently came up with the posies culled for Ann and me in the Hallers' garden. We, and many another maid, clasped our hands in sheer delight, but Ursula cast a look on them which might, if it could, have robbed the roses and Eastern lilies of their sweetness.

The Emperor, it was said, would keep to the hour fixed on; then all the bells began to ring. I knew them all well, and one I liked best of all; the Benedicta in Saint Sebalds Church, which had been cast by old Master Grunewald, Master Pernhart's closest friend. Their brazen voices stirred my soul and heart, and presently the cannon in the citadel and on the wails rattled out a thundering welcome to the Emperor, rending the summer air. My heart beat higher and faster. But suddenly I meseemed that all the bravery of the town and the holiday weed of the folks, the chiming of bells and the roaring of cannon were not meant to do honor to the Emperor, but only to my one true love who was coming in his train.

All my thoughts and hopes were set on him. And when the town-pipers struck up with trumpets and kettledrums, bagpipes and horns, when the far-away muttering and roll of voices swelled to a roaring outcry and an uproarious shout, when from every mouth at every window the cry rose: "They are corning!" —yet did I not gaze at their Majesties, to whom the day and festival belonged, but only sought him who was mine—my own.

There they are! close before us.—The Emperor and his noble wife, Queen Barbara, the still goodly daughter of the great Hungarian Count of Cilly.

Aye! and he looks the man to rule six realms; worthy to stand at the head of the great German nation. He might be known among a thousand for an Emperor, and the son of an Emperor! How straight he sits in his saddle, how youthful yet is the fire in his eye, albeit he has past his fiftieth birthday! High spirit and contentment in his look; and meseems he has forgotten that he ever summoned the Diet to meet at Ratisbon and is entering the gates of Nuremberg against his will, by reason that the Electors and German princes have chosen to assemble there. His wife likewise is of noble mien, and she rides a white palfrey which, as she draws rein, strives to turn its pink nostrils to greet the bay horse on which her lord is mounted.

Yet do my eyes not linger long on the lordly pair; they wander down the long train of Knights wherein he is coming, though among the last. For a moment they rest on the stalwart forms of the Hungarian nobles, all blazing with jewels even to the harness of the steeds; and glance unheedingly at the Electors and Princes, the Dukes, Counts and Knights-all in velvet and silk, gold and silver; at the purple and scarlet of the prelates; at the solemn black with gold chains of the town councillors; on and beyond all the magnificent train which has come with his Majesty from Hungary or gone forth to meet him.

Hereupon Ursula steps forth to speak the address; but sooner may a man hear a cricket in a thunderstorm than a maid's voice amid that pealing of bells and shouting and cries of welcome. Meseems verily as though the fluttering handkerchiefs, the flying pennons, and the caps waved in the air had found voice; and Ursula turns her head to this side and that as though seeking help.

Emperor Sigismund signs with his hand, and the two heralds who head the train uplift their trumpets with rich embroidered banners. A rattling blast procures silence: in a moment it is as though oil were poured on a surging sea. Men and guns are hushed; the only sounds to be heard are the brazen tongue of the bells, the whinnying of a horse, the dull mutter of men's voices in the far-off lanes and alleys, and the clear voice of a young maid.

Ursula made her speech, her voice so loud at the last that it might have seemed that the honeyed verses were words of reproof. The imperial pair gave each other a glance expressing surprise rather than pleasure, and vouchsafed a few words of thanks to the speaker. His Majesty spoke in German; but in his Bohemian home and Hungarian Kingdom he had caught the trick of a sharper accent than ours.

A chamberlain now gave the signal, and we maidens all went forth towards our Sovereign lord and lady. Two and two—Tucher and Schilrstab—Groland and Stromer; and the sixth couple were Ann and I—Ann as the daughter of a member of the council—and my godfather it was, besides her sweet face, who had done most to get her chosen.

Noble youths clad as pages in velvet and silks had received the flowers offered by the damsels; but as Ann and I stood forth, the Emperor and Empress looked down on us. I could see that they gazed upon us graciously, and heard them speak together in a language I knew not; and Porro, the King's fool—and I say the King's, inasmuch as it was not till later that Sigismund was crowned Emperor at Rome, and by the same token it was at that time that my Hans' brothers, Paul and Erhart, were dubbed Knights—Porro, who rode at his lord's side on a piebald pony spotted black and yellow, cried out: "May we all be turned into drones, Nunkey, if the flowers which have given this town the name of the Bee-garden are not of the same kith and kin as these!"

And he pointed to us; whereupon the King asked him whether he meant the damsels or the posies. But the jester, rolling on his nag after a merry fashion, till the bells in his cap rang again, answered him: "Nay, Nunkey, would you tempt a Christian to walk on the ice? An if I say the damsels, I shall get into trouble by reason of your strict morality; but if I say the posies, I shall peril my poor soul's health by a foul lie."

"Then choose thee another shape," quoth the Queen, "for I fear lest the bees should take thee for a stinging wasp, Porro."

"True, by my troth," said the fool, thinking. "Since Eve fell into sin, women's counsel is often the best. You, Nunkey, shall be turned into a butterfly, and not into a drone, and grace the flowers as you flutter round them."

And he waved his arms as they were wings and rode round about us on his pony with right merry demeanor, like a moth fluttering over us. Ann looked down, reddening for shame, and the blood rose to my cheeks likewise for maiden shyness; nevertheless I heard the King's deep, outlandish tones, and his noble wife's pleasant voice, and they lauded our posies and made enquiry as to our names, and straitly enjoined Ann and me not to fail of appearing at every dance and banquet; and I remember that we made answer with seemly modesty till the King's grand-master came up and so ended our discourse.

And I fancy I can see the multitude coming on; the motley hues of velvet and silk, the housings and trappings of the horses, the bright sheen of polished metal, and the sparkle of cut gems dazzle my eyes, I ween, to this day. But on a sudden it all fades into dimness; the cries and voices, the bells, the neighing, the crash and clatter are silent—for he is come. He waves his hand, more goodly, more truly mine and dearer to my heart than ever. But not here do we truly meet again; that joy is to come later in his own garden.

That garden could already tell a tale of two happy human creatures, and of hours of the purest bliss ever vouchsafed to two young hearts; but what thereafter befell I remember as bright, hot, summer days, full of mirth and play-acting, of tourneys and courtly sports, of music and song, dancing and pleasuring. The gracious favor of the King and Queen and the presence of many princes ceased not to grace it, and went to our brain like heady wine. Things that had hitherto seemed impossible now came true. Out of sheer joy in those intoxicating pleasures, and for the sake of the manifold demands that came upon us in these over-busy days, we forgot those nearest and dearest to our hearts. Yet never was I given to self-seeking, neither before nor since that time.

Ann's beguiling of the Junker, the homage paid to her by all, even the highest, Herdegen's seething ire, his strivings to win back the favor of the maid he had slighted, his strange and various and high-handed demeanor, his shameless ways with Ursula, to whom he paid great court when my grand-uncle was present, albeit at other times he would cast dark glances at her as if she were a foe—all this glides past me as in a mist, and concerning me but little. Then, in the midst of this turmoil and magnificence, this love-making and royal grace, now and again meseemed I was suddenly alone and forlorn; even at the tourney or dance; nay, even when the King and Queen would vouchsafe to discourse with me, I would be filled with longing for peace and silent hours—notwithstanding that the mighty Sovereign himself took pleasure in questioning me and moving me to those quick replies whereof I never found any lack. Queen Barbara would many a time bid me to her chamber, and keep me with her for hours; sometimes would Ann also be bidden, and she bestowed on us both many costly jewels.

Then, no sooner had we quitted the castle, where their Majesties lodged, than we must think of our own noble guests; for Markgraf Bernhard of

Baden, who was quartered on us, would often ask for me, and Cardinal Branda would desire Ann to attend him. The larger half of our days was given to arranging our persons, and while Cousin Maud and Susan would dress me I was already thinking of making ready the weed, the ribbons, and the feathers needed for the next day. My Hans was now a Knight. The same honor was promised to Herdegen—honor on honor, pleasure on pleasure, bravery and display! In the stead of our old sun twenty, meseemed, were blazing in the heavens. Many a time it was as though my breath came so lightly that I could float on air, and then again a nightmare load oppressed me. Even through the night, in my very dreams, the sounds of music and singing ceased not; but when I awoke the question would arise: "To what end is this?"

Hans held the helm, and was ever the same, thoughtful yet truly loving. Also he never forgot to keep a lookout for the surety of the bark, and if the pace seemed too great, or he saw rocks ahead, he did his part and likewise guarded me with faithful care from heedless demeanor or over-weariness. Margery the rash, who was wanted everywhere, and was at all times in the foremost rank, at the behest of the King and Queen, did her devoir in all points and nought befell which could hurt or grieve her—and she knew full well whom she had to thank for that.

Likewise I discerned with joy that my lover kept the Junker's ardors in check, for he would fain have courted Ann as hotly as though he were secure of her love; and Hans called upon my brother Herdegen to quit himself as a man should and make an end of this double game by choosing either Ann or Ursula, once for all.

In the forest Uncle Conrad had bidden this noble company to the Lodge. After the hunt was over we went forth once more to the garden of Martin the bee-keeper, by reason that Duke Ernest of Austria, and Count Friedrich of Meissen, and my Lord Bishop of Lausanne, and other of the noble lords, desired to see somewhat of the far-famed bee-keeping huts in our Lorenzer-Wald. My uncle himself led the way, and Herdegen helped him do the honors.

Presently, as he over-hastily opened a hive, some bees stung his hand badly; I ran to him and drew the stings out. Ann was close by me, and Herdegen tried to meet her eyes, and sang in a low voice a verse of a song, which sounded sad indeed and strange, somewhat thus:

"*Augustho pirlin pcodyas.*"

Whereupon Ann asked of him in what tongue he spoke; for it was not known to her. He, however, replied that of a certainty it was known to her, and when she looked at him, doubtful yet, he laughed bitterly and said that he could but be well-content if she had forgotten the sound of those words, inasmuch as to him they were bound up with the first great sorrow he had known.

I saw that she was ill-at-ease; but as she turned away he held her back to put the words into German, saying, in so dull and low a voice that I scarce could hear him, while he stirred up the earth with the point of his sword, purposing to lay some on his swollen hand.

"A froward bee hath stung my hand;
Mother Earth will heal the smart.
But when I lie beneath the turf,
Say, Will she heal my broken heart?"

Then I saw that Ann turned pale as she said somewhat stiffly: "There are other remedies for you against even the worst!" and he replied: "But yours, Ann, work the best cure."

By this time she was herself again, and answered as though she cared not: "I learnt them from a skilled master.—But in what tongue is your song, Junker Schopper, and who taught you that?"

To which he hastily answered: "A swarthy wench of gipsy race."

And she, taking courage, said: "One peradventure whom you erewhile met in the forest here?" Herdegen shook his curly head, and his eye flashed lovingly as he spoke: "No, Ann, and by all the Saints it is not so! It was of a gipsy mother that I learnt it; she sang it to a man in despair—in despair for your sake, Ann—in the forest of Fontainebleau."

Whereupon Ann shook her head and strove to speak lightly as she said "Despair! Are you not like the man in the fable, who deemed that he was burnt whereas he had thrust another into the fire? The cap fits, methinks, Junker Schopper."

He replied sadly, and there was true grief in his voice: "Is a hard jest all you have to give me now?" quoth he, "Nay, then, tell me plainly, Ann, if there is no hope for me more."

"None," said she, firm and hard. But she forth with added more gently. "None, Herdegen, none at all so long as a single thread remains unbroken which binds you to Ursula."

On this he stepped close up to her and cried in great emotion: "She, she! Aye, she hath indeed cast her devil's tangle of gold about me to ensnare all that is vain and base in me; but she has no more room in my heart than those bees have. And if you—if my good angel will but be mine again I will cry 'apage'—I tear her toils asunder."

He ceased, for certain ladies and gentlemen came nigh, and foremost of them Ursula; aye, and I can see her now drawing off her glove and stooping to gather up some earth to lay on the burning hand of the man whom in truth she loved, while he strove to forestall her and not to accept such service. That night we stayed at the lodge, and Ursula again had the chamber next to ours; and again I heard her appealing to her Saints, while Ann poured out to me her overflowing heart in a low whisper, and confessed to me, now crying and now laughing, how much she had endured, and how that she was beginning to hope once more.

CHAPTER II

Our grand-uncle and guardian, the old knight Im Hoff, had ever, so long as I could remember, demeaned himself as a penitent, spending his nights, and not sleeping much, in a coffin, and giving the lion's share of his great revenues to pious works to open unto himself the gates of Heaven; but what a change was wrought in him by the Emperor's coming! This straight-backed and stiff necked man, who had never bowed his head save only in church and before the holy images of the saints, learnt now to stoop and bend. His bloodless face, which had long ceased to smile, was now the very home of smiles. His great house was filled, for there lodged Duke Ernst of Austria, the Hungarian Count of Gara—who through his wife was near of kin to the Emperor, and his Majesty's trusty secretary, Kaspar Slick, and all their people. And so soon as either of these came, a gleam as of starlight lighted up his old features, or, if it fell that the sovereign granted to him to attend him, it was broad sunshine that illumined it. And whereas the other gentlemen of the council, hereditary and elected, albeit they were ever ready to shake hands with a common workman, would stand face to face with their Majesties or the dukes and notables, upright and duly mindful of their own worth, my guardian would cast off his gravity and dignity both together; and verily we all knew full well to what end. He, who had been defrauded of his life's happiness by a Baron's daughter, yearned to move the King to raise him to the rank of Baron. He loaded the Secretary Slick with gifts and favors, and seeing that his Majesty was graciously pleased to smile on me, his ward, he would be at much pains to flatter me, calling me his "golden hair" or "Blue-eyes;" and enjoin it on me that I should make mention of him to the King as his Majesty's most faithful servant, ever ready for any sacrifice in his service, at the same time he asked with a grin how it would pleasure me to hear Herdegen called by the name and title of Baron von Schopper-Im Hoff?

Our own honest and honorable name I weened was good enough for us three; yet, for my brother's sake and for Ann's, I held my peace, and took occasion while he was in so friendly a mood to urge him to release Herdegen, and grant him to choose another than Ursula. But how wroth he waxed, how hastily he put on the icy, forbidding bearing he was wont to wear, as he rated me for a wilful simpleton who would undo her brother's weal!

It was now St. Susannah's day—[August 11th]—We were bidden to the tourney. Duke Ernest of Austria had challenged Duke Kanthner of Oels in Silesia to meet him in the lists and, besides the glory to be gained, there was a prize of sixty and four gold pieces. Other knights also were to joust in the ring.

Queen Barbara, of her grace, had bidden me attend with her ladies. At the jousting-place I found Ann; her mother had remained at home by reason that the old mother was sick. My faithful Uncle Christian Pfinzing, who played the host to the Emperor and Empress at the Castle as representing the town council, had brought his "dear watchman" hither and placed her in the keeping of certain motherly dames. Presently, seeing a moment when she might speak with me, Ann said in my ear: "I will end this sport, Margery; I can no longer endure it. He hath sworn to renounce all and everything that may keep us apart!" There was no time for more. Each one had to take his seat. As yet their Majesties were not come, and there was time to gaze about.

The lists were in the midst of the market-place. The benches were decked with hangings, the lords and ladies who filled them, the feathers waving, the sparkle of jewels, the glitter of gold and silver, the sheen of silk and velvet, the throng of common folk, head over head in the topmost places, the music and uproar, nay, the very savor of the horses dwell still in my mind; yet far be it from me to write of things well-known to most men.

Then my grand-uncle came forth. He had Ursula on his arm as he walked through the gate-way into the lists and across the sanded ring to his seat on the far side. This was in truth forbidden, but the unabashed old man defied the rules, and as for Ursula she was well pleased to be gazed at. The old knight was smiling; how stately was his mien, and how well the silver breast plate beseemed him, with the golden lion rampant of the Im Hoffs! That helmet and breastplate had been forged for his special use of the finest silver and gold plate, and were better fit to turn the point of my pen-knife than that of sword and lance. Yet many an one admired the stalwart gait of the old man in his heavy harness. Even Tetzel's dull face was less dull than its wont, and Ursula's eyes sparkled as though her knight had carried off the prize.

Presently my grand-uncle saw where I was sitting, and waved and bowed to me as though he had some good tidings to give me. Tetzel did likewise, seeming like the old man's pale and creeping shadow. Ursula's triumphing eyes proclaimed that now she had indeed gained her end; the dullest wit might not miss her meaning. In spite of Ann, Herdegen had pledged his troth to Ursula. The lists and seats, meseemed, whirled round me in a maze, and scarce had they settled down again, as it were, when Cousin Maud sat down heavily in her place, and by her face made me aware that some great thing had befallen; for now and again she drew in her cheeks and pursed her lips as though she would fain blow out a light. When my eyes met hers she privily pointed with her fan to show me Herdegen and Ursula, and shrugged her shoulders so high that her big head with its great feathered turban sank between them. And if there was surging and wrath in her breast not less was there in mine. Howbeit I had to put on a guise of content, nay of gladness, for the Royal pair had bidden me to their side and it was my task to explain all they desired to learn.

A sunny blue sky bent over the ground; albeit dark clouds came up from the west, and I found it hard to make fitting answer to their Majesties' questions.

While the horses were pawing and neighing, and the lances rattled on the shields, nay, even when the Dukes of Austria and Schleswig rushed on each other and the Austrian unhorsed his foe, I scarce looked on the jousting-place on which all other eyes were fixed as though held by chains and bonds. Mine were set on the spot where Ursula and Ann were sitting, and with them the young knight from Brandenburg, Sir Apitz of Rochow, and my brother Herdegen. Junker Henning had his part to play in the tournament. To Rochow the tourney was all in all; Herdegen gazed only at Ann. She, to be sure, made no return, but still he would fix his eyes on her and speak with her. Ursula had turned paler, and meseemed she had eyes only for him and his doings. What went forward in the pauses of the tilting I could not mark, inasmuch as my eyes and ears were their Majesties' alone.

Now, two more knights sprang forth. What cared I of what nation they were, what arms they bore and what they and their horses might do; I had somewhat else to think of. Ursula and I had long been at war, but to-day I felt nought but compassion for her: and indeed, on this very day, when she believed she had won the victory, she more needed pity than when she had so besought Heaven to grant her Herdegen's love, inasmuch as my brother sat whispering to Ann with his hand on his heart. And Ann herself had put away all false seeming; and while she gazed into her lover's eyes with soft passion, Ursula sat bending her fan as though she purposed to break it.

To think of Ursula as ruling in our house, and of Ann pining with heart sickness was cruel grief, and yet were these two things almost less hard to endure than the shameless flightiness and strange demeanor of my noble brother, the pride of my heart.

The town council had voted eight hundred gulden to King Sigismund, and four hundred to the Queen; two hundred and thirty to Porro the jester, and great gifts to many of the notables and knights as a free offering from the city; and now, in a pause in the jousting, his Majesty announced his great delight at the faithful, bountiful, and overflowing hand held out to him by his good town of Nuremberg, which had ever been dear to his late beloved father King Charles. And then he pointed to the gentlemen of the council, who made a goodly and reverend show indeed in their long flowing hair and beards, their dark velvet robes bordered with fine fur, and thin gold chains; and he spoke of their noble and honorable dealing. I heard him say that each one of them was to be respected as joint ruler with him over that which was his own, and likewise in greater matters. Each one was his equal in manly virtue, and the worthy peer of his Imperial self. Then he pointed out to the Queen certain noble and goodly heads, and it was my part to make known whatsoever I could tell of their possessions and their manner of trade. The Hallers were well known to him, and not alone my best beloved, inasmuch as they did great trading with his kingdom of Hungary; and he was well pleased to see my Hans with his father as one of the council.

His gracious wife was pleased to compare the good order, and cleanness, and comfort of Nuremberg with the cities in their native country. Whereas she had already been into some of our best houses, and indeed into our own, she spoke well of the wealth, and art, and skill in all crafts of the Nuremberg folk, saying they had not their like in all the world so far as she knew. And then again she spoke her pleasure at the honorable seemliness of the councillors, and asked me many questions concerning this one and that, and, among the rest, concerning Master Ulman Pernhart. The royal pair marked, in one his noble brow, in another his long flowing hair, in a third his keen and shrewd eye, till presently King Sigismund asked his Fool, Porro, which of all the heads in the ranks opposite he might judge to be the wisest and weightiest. The jester's twinkling eyes looked along the rows of folk, and whereas they suddenly fell on little Dame Henneleinlein, the Honey-wife, who sat, as was her wont, with her head propped on her hands, he took the King's word up and answered in mock earnest: "Unless I am deceived it is that butter-cup queen, Nuncle, seeing that her head is so heavy that she is fain to hold it up with both hands."

And he pointed with his bauble to the old woman, who, as the bee-master's widow, had boldly thrust herself into the front rank with those of knight's degree; and there she sat, in a gown of bright yellow brocade which Cousin Maud had once given her, stretching her long neck and resting her head on her hands. The King and Queen, looking whither the Fool pointed, when they beheld a little old woman instead of a stately councillor, laughed aloud; but the jester bowed right humbly towards the dame, and, she, so soon as she marked that the eyes of his Majesty and his gracious lady were turned upon her, and that her paltry person was the object of their regard, fancied that I had peradventure named her as being Ann's cousin, or as the widow of the deceased bee-master who, long years ago, had led the Emperor Charles to see the bee-gardens, so she made reverence again and again, and meanwhile laid her head more and more on one side, ever leaning more heavily on her hand, till the King and Queen laughed louder than ever and many an one perceived what was doing. The cup-bearer and chamberlain drew long faces, and Porro at last ended the jest by greeting the old woman with such dumbshow as no one could think an honor. The cunning little woman saw now that she was being made game of, and whereas not their Majesties alone, but all the Court about them were holding their sides, and she saw that I was in their midst, she believed me to be at the bottom of their mischief, and cast at me such vengeful glances as warned me of evil in store.

After this tourney there was to be a grand dance in the School of Arms, to which their Majesties were bidden with all the princes, knights, and notables of the Diet, and the patricians of the town. Next day, being Saint Clara's day, there would be a great feast at the Tetzels' house by reason that it was the name-day of Dame Clara, Ursula's grandmother, and the eldest of their kin. At this banquet Herdegen's betrothal was to be announced to all their friends and kindred—this my uncle whispered to me as he went off after the jousting to attend the King, who had sent for him. The old man had seen nought of Herdegen's doings with Ann, by reason that he and old Tetzel had both been seated on the same side of the lists, and the tall helmets and feathers had hidden the young folks from his sight. So assurance and contentment even yet beamed in his eye.

The tourney had lasted a long time. I scarce had time enough to change my weed for the dance. Till this day I had sported like a fish in this torrent of turmoil and pleasure; but to-day I was weary. My body was in pain with my spirit, and I would fain have staid at home; but I minded me of the Queen who, albeit she was so much older, and was watched by all—every one expecting that she should be gracious—in her heavy royal array, went through all this of which I was so weary.

Meanwhile a great storm had burst upon us and passed over; all creatures were refreshed, and I likewise uplifted my head and breathed more freely. The fencing school—a great square chamber, as it is to this day, with places all round for the folk to look on—was lighted up as bright as day. My lover and I, now in right good heart once more, paced through the Polish dance led by the King and Queen. Ann's mother had been compelled to stay at home, to tend the master's old mother, and my friend had come under Cousin Maud's protection. She was led out to dance by Junker Henning; his fellow country-man, Sir Apitz von Rochow, walked with Ursula and courted her with unfailing ardor. Franz von Welemisl, who was wont to creep like her shadow, and who was again a guest at the Tetzels' house, had been kept within doors by the cough that plagued him. Likewise I looked in vain for Herdegen.

The first dance indeed was ended when he came in with my great-uncle; but the old knight looked less confidently than he had done in the morning.

Ann was pale, but, meseemed fairer than ever in a dress of pomegranate-red and white brocade, sent to her from Italy by her step-father's brother, My lord Bishop, by the hand of Cardinal Branda. As soon as I had presently begun to speak with her, she was carried off by Junker Henning, and at that same moment my grand-uncle came towards me to ask who was that fair damsel of such noble beauty with whom I was but now speaking. He had never till now beheld Ann close at hand, and how gladly did I reply that this was the daughter of Pernhart the town Councillor and she to whom Herdegen had plighted his faith.

The old man was startled and full wroth yet, by reason of all the fine folk about us, he was bound to refrain himself, and he presently departed.

The festival went forward and I saw that Herdegen danced first with Ursula and then with Ann. Then they stood still near the flower shrubs which were placed round about the hall to garnish it, and it might have been weened from their demeanor that they had quarrelled and had come to high words. I would fain have gone to them, but the Queen had bid me stay with her and never ceased asking me a hundred questions as to names and other matters.

At last, or ever it was midnight, their Majesties departed. I breathed more freely, put my hand on my Hans' arm, and was minded to bid him take me to Herdegen and speak out my mind, but my brother, as it fell, prevented me. He came up to me and with what a mien! His eyes flashing, his cheeks burning, his lips tight-set. He signed to me and Hans to follow whither he went, and then passionately besought us that we would depart from the dance for a while with him and his sweetheart, that was Ann. Such an entreaty amazed us greatly, yet, when he told us that she would go no whither with him save under our care, and that everything depended on his learning this very hour how he stood with her, we did his will. And he likewise told us that he had not indeed given his word that morning to my grand-uncle and Jost Tetzel, but had only pledged his word that he would give them his answer next day.

So presently Hans and I stole out behind the pair, out into the road. I, for my part, was well content and thankful and, when we beheld them accuse and answer each other right doughtily, we laughed, and were agreed that Aunt Jacoba's counsel had led to a good issue; and I told my Hans that I should myself take a lesson from all this and let the smart Junkers and Knights make love to me to their hearts' content, if ever I should be moved to play him a right foolish trick.

Presently, when we had many times paced the road to and fro the Pernharts' house, Ann was minded to knock at the door; but behold she was saved the pains. Mistress Henneleinlein just then came out whereas she had been helping Dame Giovanna to tend the sick grandmother. The lantern Eppelein carried in front of us was not so bright as the sun, yet could I see full plainly the old woman's venomous eye; and what high dudgeon sounded in her voice! Each one had his meed, even my Hans, to whom she cried: "Keep thy bride out of Porro's way, Master Haller. It ill-beseems the promised wife of a worshipful Councillor to be casting her lot in with a Fool! Howbeit, to laugh is better than to weep, and he laughs longest who laughs last!" And thereupon she herself laughed loudly and, with a scornful nod to Ann, turned her back on us.

All was still in Master Pernharts' house; he himself had gone to rest. At Herdegen's bidding we followed him into the hall, and there he clasped Ann to his heart, and declared to us that now, and henceforth for ever, they were one. Whereupon we each and all embraced; but my friend clung longest to me, and whispered in my ear that she was happier than ever she could deserve to be. Herdegen asked me whether now he had made all right, and whether I would be the same old Margery again? And I right gladly put up my lips for his to kiss; and the returned prodigal, who had come back to that which was his best portion, was like one drunk with wine. He was beside himself with joy, so that he clasped first me and then Hans in his arms, and slapped Eppelein, who carried a lantern to show us the pools left by the storm of rain, again and again on the shoulder, and thrust a purse full of money into his free hand, albeit there was an end now of my grand-uncle's golden bounty. Nought would persuade him to go back to the dancing-hall, to meet Ursula and her kin; and when he presently departed from us we heard him along the street, singing such a love song as no false heart may imagine, as glad as the larks which would now ere long be soaring to the sky.

We got back to the great hall. The dancing and music were yet at their height; our absence we deemed had scarce been marked; howbeit, as soon as we entered, my grand-uncle made enquiry "where Herdegen might be," and when I looked about me at haphazard I beheld—my eyes did not cheat me—I beheld Mistress Henneleinlein in one of the side-stalls.

No man told me, yet was I sure and certain that she was saying somewhat which concerned me, and presently I discerned in the dim background the feathered plume which Ursula had worn at the dance. My heart beat with fears; every word spoken by the old Dame would of a surety do us a mischief. Hans mocked at my alarms and at a maid's folly in ever taking to herself matters which concern her not.

Then Ursula came forth into the hall again, and how she swept past us on Junker Henning's arm.

A young knight of the Palatinate now led me out to a dance I had erewhile promised him.

We stopped for lack of breath. The festival was over; yet did Ursula and the Junker walk together. He was hearkening eagerly to all she might say, and on a sudden he clapped his hand into hers which she held out to him, and his eyes, which he had held set on the floor, fired up with a flash. Presently he and the Knight von Rochow made their way, arm in arm through the press, and both were laughing and pulling their long red beards.

I still clung to my lover's arm and entreated him to take me to speak with Junker Henning, inasmuch as I sorely wanted to question him; but the Junker diligently kept far from us. Nevertheless we at last stayed him, and after that I had enquired, as it were in jest, whether he had healed his old feud with Mistress Ursula and concluded a truce, or peradventure made peace with her, he answered me, in a tone all unlike his wonted frank and glad manner, that this for a while must remain privy to him and her, and that we should scarce be the first to whom he should reveal the matter; and forthwith he bid us farewell with a courtly reverence. But my lover would not let him thus depart, and asked him, calmly, what was the interpretation of this speech, whereupon Rochow spoke for his young fellow-countryman, and enquired, in the high-handed and lordly tone which ever marked his voice and manner, whether here, in the native land of Nuremberg playthings, love and faith were accounted of as toys.

Junker Henning however, broke in, and said, casting a warning look at me: "Far be it from him to break friendship with an honorable gentleman, such as my Hans, before having an explanation." And he held out his hand somewhat more readily than before, bowed sweetly to me and led away his cousin.

At last we got out with the Haller parents and Cousin Maud. The old folks got into litters, and the serving men were lighting the way before me to mine, when my lover stayed me, saying: "It is already grey in the East. Never before were we together so well betimes, Margery, and happy hours are few. If thou'rt not too weary, let us walk home together in this fresh morning air."

I was right well-content and we went gently forward, I clinging to him closely. He felt how high my heart was beating and, when he asked me whether it was for love that it beat so fast, I confessed in truth that, whereas the Brandenburgers outdid all other knights in the kingdom, in defiance and hotheadedness, I feared lest there should be a passage of arms betwixt Junker Henning and my brother Herdegen. But Hans made answer that, if it were the Brandenburgers intent to challenge him, he could not hinder it; yet be trowed it would be to their own damage; that Herdegen had scarce found his match at the Paris school of arms; and at least should we not mar this sweet morning walk by such fears.

And he held me closer to him, and while we slowly wandered on he poured forth his whole heart to me, and confessed that through all his lonely life in foreign lands he had ever lacked a great matter; that even with the gayety of his favorite comrades, even when his best diligence had been crowned with great issues, yet had he never had full joy in life. Nor was it till my love had made him a complete and truly happy man that he had felt, as it were, whole, inasmuch as that alone had stilled the strange craving which till then had made his heart sick.

Yea, and I could tell him that it had been the same with me; and as for what more we said, verily it should rather have been sung to sweet and lofty music on the lute and mandoline. Two rightly matched souls stood revealed each to each, and Heaven itself, meseemed, was opened in the strait ways of our town.

We kissed as we stood on the threshold of the Schopper-house, and when at length we must need part he held me once more to his heart, longer than ever he had before, and tore himself away; and laying his hands on my shoulders, as he looked into my eyes in the pale light of dawn, he said: "Come what may, Margery, we love each other truly and have learned through each other what true happiness means; and nevertheless we are as yet but in the March-moon of our love, and its May days, which are sweeter far, are yet to come. But even the March-joy is good—right good to me."

CHAPTER III

I had forgotten my fears and gloomy forebodings by the time I climbed into bed in my darkened chamber. Sleep forthwith closed my eyes, and I lay without even a dream till Cousin Maud waked me. I turned over by reason that I was still heavy with slumber; yet she stood by my bed, and scarce half a quarter of an hour after, lo, again I felt her hand on my shoulder and woke up quaking, with a cold sweat on my brow. I had dreamed that I was riding out in the Lorenzer-wald with Hans and my grand-uncle and other some; but we went slowly and softly, by reason that all our horses fell lame. And it fell that on the very spot where Ann had flown into Herdegen's arms I beheld a high, yellow grave-stone, and on it was written in great black letters: "HANS HALLER."

Hereupon I had started up with a loud cry, and it was long or ever my brain was clear as to the world about me. Cousin Maud laughed to see me so drunk asleep, as was not my wont; yet could she not deny that my dream boded no good. Nevertheless, quoth she, it was small marvel that such a heathen Turkish turmoil as we had been living in should beget monstrous fancies in a young maid's brain. She would of set purpose have left me to sleep the day through, to give me strength; howbeit Herdegen had twice come to ask for me, and so likewise had Ann and Hans, and it wanted but an hour and a half of noon. This made me laugh; nevertheless I minded me then and there of all that had befallen last night at Pernhart's house-door and in the school of arms, and, moreover, that we were bidden this day to eat with the Tetzels; also that they, and eke my grand-uncle, were still in the belief that Herdegen's betrothal to Ursula might be at once proclaimed to their friends.

I began to dress in haste and fear, and Susan was in the act of plaiting my hair when Cousin Maud flew in to say that Queen Barbara had sent her own litter to carry me to her. Thus had I to make all speed.

The royal quarters in the castle had been newly ordered by the town at his Majesty's desire, and they were indeed bravely decked; yet never had the like show pleased me less. The Queen was giving audience to the Pope's Legate, to their excellencies the envoys from the Greek Emperor, to my Lord Conrad the Elector of Maintz, and many more nobles. She had made so bold as to declare that the German maidens were no less skilled in the art of song than the damsels of Italy, and had bidden me to her in such hot haste that I might let the notables there assembled hear a few lays. I might not say nay to the royal behest; for better, for worse, I must fain take my lute and sing, at first alone, and then with my lord Conte di Puppi. Our voices presently brought the King to the chamber, and in truth I won praise enough if I had best cared to hear it. Nay, for the first time it was a torment to me to sing, and when the notables had all been sent forth, and I was alone with the Queen and her ladies, I knew not what ailed me but I burst into tears, hot and bitter tears. The gracious Queen took me in her arms with womanly sweetness, but while she gave me her phial of vinegar to smell, and spoke words of comfort, I was suddenly scared at hearing close behind me right woeful sobbing and sighing, as from a woman's breast. I looked about me, and beheld Porro, the jester, who had cast himself on a couch and was mocking me, pulling such a grimace the while that his smooth, long, thin face seemed grown to the length of two lean faces. The sight was so merry that I was fain to laugh. Whereas he nevertheless ceased not from sobbing, the Queen reproved him and bid him not carry his fooling too far. Whereupon he sobbed out: "Nay, royal and gracious Coz, thou art in error. Never have I so shamelessly forgotten to play my part as Fool, as at this moment. Alack, alack! what a thing is life! Were we not one and all born fools, and if we did but measure it as it is now and ever shall be, with the wisdom of the sage, we should never cease to bewail ourselves, from the nurse's rod to the scythe of death."

Whether Porro were in earnest I could not divine; his face, like a mystic oracle, might bear manifold interpretations; verily his speech went to my heart. And albeit hitherto life had brought me an hundredfold more reasons for thanksgiving than sorrow, meseemed that it had many griefs in store. The Queen indeed replied full solemnly: "Peradventure it is true. Yet forget not that it is not as Sage that you attend us.—Moreover I, as a good Hungarian, know my Latin, and the great Horatius Flaccus puts your dismal lore to shame; albeit, as a Christian woman, I am fain to confess that it is wiser and more praiseworthy to bewail our own sins and the sins of the world, and to meditate on the life to come, than to live only for present joys. As for thee, sweet maid, for a long time yet thou may'st take pleasure in the flowers, even though venom may be hidden in their cups."

"Men are not wont to eat them," replied the fool. "And I have often marvelled wherefor the flighty butterfly wears such gay and painted wings, while every creature that creeps and grubs is grey or brown and foul to behold."

Whereupon he burst into loud laughter and such boisterous mirth that we fairly wept for merriment, and my lady Queen bid him hold his peace.

On my departing I had need to pass through the King's audience-chamber. He was bidding my Hans depart right graciously, and I went forth into the castle yard with Masters Tucher, Stromer, and Schurstab, all members of the Council. I fancy I hear them now thanking Hans for his fearless manfulness in saying to his Majesty that the treasure-chest must ever be empty if the old disorder were suffered to prevail. Likewise they approved the well-devised plan which he had proposed for the bettering of such matters, and my heart beat high with pride as I perceived the great esteem in which the worshipful elders of our town held their younger fellow.

Hans might not part company from them; but when I got into the litter he whispered to me: "Be not afraid—as to Herdegen and the Junker—you know. Farewell till we meet at the Tetzels'."

When I came home I learnt that my brother, and Ann, and then Eppelein had come to ask for me; now must I change my attire for the feast, and my heart beat heavy in my bosom. The bold Brandenburger and my brother were perchance at this very hour crossing swords.

Cousin Maud, who now knew all, and I stepped out of our litters at the Tetzels' door. Eppelein was standing by the great gate, booted and spurred, holding two horses by their bridles. My lord who spoke with him was my dear Hans. We went into the hall together, and as our eyes met, I wist that there was evil in the air. The letter he held bid him ride forthwith to Altenperg. Junker Henning and my brother were minded to have a passage of arms, and with sharp weapons. This, however, they might not do within the limits of the city save at great risk, inasmuch as that the town was within the King's peace, and by a severe enactment knight or squire, lord or servant, in short each and every man was threatened by the Emperor with outlawry, who should make bold to provoke another to challenge him, or to lift a weapon against another with evil intent, be he who he might, throughout the demesne of Nuremberg or so long as the diet was sitting. Hence they would go forth to Altenperg, inasmuch as it was the nearest to arrive at of any township without the limits of the city.

All this my lover had heard betimes that morning; but Herdegen had told him that Master Schlebitzer and a certain Austrian Knight would attend him. Now the letter was to say that they had both played him false; the former in obedience to the stern behest of his father, the town-councillor; the second by reason that his Duke commanded his attendance. And Herdegen hereby urgently besought my Hans that he would take the place thus left unfilled and ride forthwith to Altenperg.

Nor was this all the letter. In it my brother set forth that he had pledged his word solemnly and beyond recall to Ann and her parents, and entreated my lover to declare to the Tetzels and to his grand-uncle that henceforth and forever he renounced Ursula. He would speak of the matter at greater length at the place of meeting.

Cousin Maud and Hans and I held a brief council, and we were of one mind: that this message should not be given to the Tetzels till after the great dinner and when we should know the issue of the combat. My heart urged me indeed to desire my lover to forego this ride, and I mind me yet how I implored him with uplifted hands and how he forced himself to put them from him with steadfast gentleness. And when he told me that he for certain, if any one, could pacify the combatants or ever blood should be shed, I gazed into his brave and manful and kind face, and methought whither he went all must be for the best, and I cried with fresh assurance: "Then go!" Every word do I remember as though it were graven in brass.

Eppelein cracked his whip against his leathern boot-tops; old Tetzel's leaden voice cried out to enquire where we were lingering, and a silken train came rustling down the stairs. My lover kissed his hand to me, and I went forth with him into the court-yard. His fiery horse gave him so much to do that he never marked my farewell. On a sudden it flashed through my brain that this was that very horse which my grand-uncle had given to Herdegen, and herein again, meseemed, was an omen of ill. Likewise I noted that Hans was in silken hose with neither spurs nor riding-boots. Howbeit the Hallers had many horses; and as a lad he had been wont to ride with or without a saddle, and was a rider whom none could unhorse, even in the jousting-ring.

He had soon quelled his steed and was trotting lightly over the stones, followed by Eppelein; but as he vanished round the first corner meseemed that the bourn stone, as he rode past it, was turned into the yellow gravestone I had seen in my dream, and that again I saw the great black letters of the name "Hans Haller."

I passed my hands across my eyes to chase away the hideous vision, and I was young enough and brave enough to return Ursula's greeting without any quaking of my knees. Cousin Maud, meanwhile, had walked up the stairs, snorting and fuming like a boiling kettle; nor could she be at peace, even among the company who were awaiting the bidding to table. Many an one marked that something more than common was amiss with her. I refrained myself well enough, and I excused my brother's and my lover's absence with a plea of weighty affairs. My grand-uncle, however, guessed the truth, and when I gave true answer to his short, murmured questions he wrathfully cried: then these were the thanks he got? Henceforth he would plainly show how he, who had been a benefactor, could deal with the youth who had dared to mock his authority. Hereupon I besought him first to grant me a hearing for a few words; but he waved me away in ire, and signed to Ursula, who hung on his arm, and she set her lips tight when he presently with wrathful eyes whispered somewhat in her ear whereof I believed I could guess the intent. And when I beheld her call Sir Franz von Welemisl to her side and give him her hand, speaking a few words in a low voice, I discerned that, in truth she knew all.

She presently led her father aside and told him somewhat which brought the blood to his ashy face, and led him to say her nay right vehemently. But, as she was wont, she made good her own will and he shrugged his shoulders, wrathful indeed, but overmastered by her.

During this space the great door of the refectory had been thrown open, and when Tetzel with his old mother moved that way, desiring the guests to follow him, my Uncle Christian, Ann's faithful friend, whispered to me that Herdegen had told him that he was now pledged to his "dear little warder," and likewise what was on hand between him and the Junker von Beust. I might be easy, quoth he; the Brandenburger would have a bitter taste of Nuremberg steel, of that he was fully assured. And he ended his speech with a merry: "Hold up your head, Margery."

Then we all sat down at the laden table, Dame Clara sitting at the top, albeit she looked but sullen and ill to please.

Ursula had chosen to set Sir Franz by her side. Herdegen's seat, at her left hand, was vacant; and she bid her white Brabant hound, as though in jest, to leap into it. The meal was served, but it all went in such gloomy silence that Master Muffel, of the town-council, whom they named Master Gall-Muffel, whispered across the table to my Uncle Christian "was it not strange to give a funeral feast without ever a corpse." Again I shuddered. My jovial uncle had already lifted his glass, and stretching himself at his ease he nodded to me, and drank, saying loud enough for all to hear: "To the last pledged couple, and the faithfullest pair of lovers."

I nodded back to him, for I wist what he meant, and drank with all my heart. Ursula had meanwhile kept her ears and eyes intent on us, and she now signed to her father and he slowly rose, clinked on his glass, and seeing that many were hearkening for what he should say, he declared to his guests that he had bidden them to this banquet not alone to do honor to the name-day of his venerable mother, whose praises his friend Master Tucher had eloquently spoken, but rather that he might announce to them the betrothal of his daughter Ursula to the noble knight and baron Franz von Welemisl. Then was there shouting and clinking and emptying of wine cups, whereat old Dame Clara Tetzel, who was deaf and had failed to gather the purport of her son's address, cried aloud "Is young Schopper come at last then?"

Hereupon Sir Franz turned pale; he had gone up to the old woman, glass in hand, with Ursula, and she now spoke into her grand-dame's ear to explain the matter. The old woman looked first at her son and then at my grand-uncle, and shook her head; nevertheless she put a good face on a bad case, gave Sir Franz her hand to kiss, and was duly embraced by Ursula; yet she sat nodding her head up and down, and ever more shrewdly as she heard the bridegroom cough. Amazement sat indeed on the faces of all the guests; howbeit the ice was broken, and the silent and gloomy company had on a sudden turned right mirthful. Cousin Maud, meseemed, was the most content of all. Ursula's betrothal had rescued her favorite from great peril, and henceforth her plumed head-gear was at rest once more.

All about me was talk and laughter, glasses ringing, voices uplifted in set speeches, and many a shout of gratulation. When a betrothal is in the wind, folks ever believe that they have hold of the guiding clue to happiness, even if it be between a simpleton and a deaf mute.

The seat on my left hand, which my lover should have filled, remained empty; on my right sat his reverence Master Sebald Schurstab, the minorite preacher and prior who, so soon as he had spoken in honor of one toast, fixed his eyes on the board and thought only of the next. Thus, in the midst of all this mirthful fellowship, there was nought to hinder my fears and hopes from taking their way. Each time that a cry of "Hoch!" was raised, I roused me and joined in; scarce knowing, however, in whose honor. Likewise the hall waxed hotter and hotter, and the air right heavy to breathe.

To-day again, as yesterday, a storm burst over us. Albeit the sun was not yet set, it was presently so dark that lights had been brought in and fifty tapers in the silver candlesticks added to the heat. The lightning flashes glared in at the curtained windows like a flitting lamp, and the roar of the thunder shook the panes which rattled and clanked in their leaden frames. The reverend Prior called on the blessed saints whose special protection this house had never neglected to secure, and crossed himself. We all did the same, and had soon forgotten the storm without. The glasses ere long were clinking once more. I watched the numberless dishes borne in and out-roasted peacocks, with showy spread tails and crested heads raised as it were in defiance: boars' heads with a lemon in their mouth and gaily wreathed; huge salmon lying in the midst of blue trout, with scarlet crawfish clinging to them; pasties and skilfully-devised sweetmeats; nay, now and again, I scarce consciously put forth my hand and carried this or that morsel to my mouth but whether it were bread or ginger my tongue heeded not the savor. Silver tankards and Venetian glasses were filled from flasks and jugs; I heard the guests praising the wines of Furstenberg and Bacharach, of Malvoisie and Cyprus, and I marked the effects of the noble and potent grape-juice, nay, now and then I played the part of "warder" to Uncle Christian; yet meseemed that it was only by another's will or ancient habit that I raised a warning finger. Was I in truth at a banquet or was I only dreaming that I sat as a guest at the richly spread board? The only certain matter was that the storm was overpast, and that no hail nor rain now beat upon the window panes. How wet must my Hans be, who had ridden forth in court array, without a cloke to cover him.

To judge by the voices and demeanor of the menfolk the end of the endless meal must surely be not far off, and indeed dishes were by this time being served with packets of spices and fruits and pies and sweetmeats for the little ones at home. I drew a deeper breath, and methought the company would soon rise from the table, forasmuch as that Jost Tetzel had already quitted his seat. Then I beheld his pale face through a curtain and his lean hand beckoning to my grand-uncle. He likewise rose, and Ursula followed him. Forthwith, from without came a strange noise of footsteps to and fro and many voices. A serving man came to hail forth Master Ebner and Uncle Tucher, and the muttering and stir without waxed louder and louder. The guests sat in silence, gazing and enquiring of each other. Somewhat strange, and for certain somewhat evil, had befallen.

My heart beat in my temples like the clapper of an alarm-bell. That which was going forward, and to which one after another was called forth, was my concern; it must be, and mine alone. I felt I could not longer keep my place, and I had pushed back my seat when I saw Uncle Tucher standing by Cousin Maud, and his kind and worthy face, still ruddy from the wine he had drunk, was a very harbinger of horror and woe. He bent over my cousin to speak in her ear.

My eyes were fixed on his lips, and lo! she, my second mother, started up hastily as any young thing and, clasping her hand to her breast she well-nigh screamed: "Jesu-Maria! And Margery!"

All grew dark before my eyes. A purple mist shrouded the table, the company, and all I beheld. I shut my eyes, and when presently I opened them once more, close before me, as it were within reach, behold the yellow headstone with black letters thereon, as in my dream; and albeit I closed my eyes again the name "Hans Haller" was yet there and the letters faded not, nay, but waxed greater and came nigher, and meseemed were as a row of gaping werewolves.

I held fast by the tall back of my heavy chair to save me from falling, on my knees; but a firm hand thrust it aside, and I was clasped in a pair of old yet strong arms to a faithful heart, and when I heard Cousin Maud's voice in mine ear, though half-choked with tears, crying: "My poor, poor, dear good Margery!" meseemed that somewhat melted in my heart and gushed up to my eyes; and albeit none had told me, yet knew I of a certainty that I was a widow or ever I was a wife, and that Cousin Maud's tears and my own were shed, not for Herdegen, but for him, for him....

And behold, face to face with me, who was this? Ursula stood before me, her blue eyes drowned in tears—tears for me, telling me that my woe was deep enough and bitter enough to grieve even the ruthless heart of my enemy.

CHAPTER IV

The storm had cleared the air once more. How fair smiled the blue sky, how bright shone the sun, day after day and from morning till night; but meseemed its splendor did but mock me, and many a time I deemed that my heart's sorrow would be easier to bear with patience if it might but rain, and rain and rain for ever. Yea, and a grey gloomy day would have brought rest to eyes weary with weeping. And in my sick heart all was dark indeed, albeit I had not been slow to learn how this terror had come about.

That was all the tidings I had craved; as to how life should fare henceforth I cared no more, but let what might befall without a wish or a will. Sorrow was to me the end and intent of life. I spurned not my grief, but rather cherished and fed it, as it were a precious child, and nought pleased me so well as to cling to that alone.

Howbeit I seldom had the good hap to be left to humor this craving. I was wroth with the hard and bitter world for its cruelty; yet it was in truth that very world, and its pitiless call to duty, which at that time rescued me from worse things. Verily I now bless each one who then strove to rouse me from my selfish and gloomy sorrow, from the tailor who cut my mourning weed to Ann, whose loving comfort even was less dear to me than the solitude in which I might give myself up to bitter grieving. All I cared for was to hear those who could tell of his last hours and departing from this life, till at last meseemed I myself had witnessed his end.

From all the tidings I could learn, I gathered that old Henneleinlein, whose gall had been raised against me by the Court Fool, had no sooner parted from us at Master Pernhart's door than she had hastened to the school of arms to make known to Ursula that my brother had plighted his troth anew to his cast-off sweetheart. Hereupon Ursula had dared to say to the Junker that Herdegen was her knight, who would pick up his glove which he had cast down at the former dance; but that he nevertheless was playing a two-fold game, and had treacherously promised Ann to wed her, to win her favor likewise. Hereupon the Brandenburger had been filled with honest ire, had sworn to Ursula that he would chastise her false lover, and was ready, not alone to accept my brother's defiance, but to fight with ruthless fury.

Thus Ursula's plot had prospered right well, inasmuch as, so long as she hoped to win Herdegen, she had been in deathly fear lest the Junker should fall out with him; whereas, now that in her wrath she only desired that the faithless wight should give an account to the Junker's sword, she thought fit in her deep and malignant fury to brand my brother as the challenger, knowing that if the combat had a bloody issue he would of a surety suffer heavy penalty. And in truth she had not reckoned wrongly when she declared that my brother, whom she knew only too well, would be her ready, champion.

On the morning next after the great dance she had addressed a brief letter to Herdegen beseeching him, for the friendship's sake which had bound them from their youth up, and by reason that she had no brother, to teach Junker von Beust that a patrician's daughter of Nuremberg should not lack a true knight, when Brandenburg pride dared to cast scorn on her in the face of all the world. My brother's response to this letter was a challenge to the Junker; yet had he not perchance been in such hot haste, save that he had long burned to punish the overweening young noble who had given him many an uneasy hour. He scarce, indeed, would have drawn his sword at Ursula's behest, inasmuch as he could plainly see that what she had most at heart was to make their breach wear such seeming to other folks as though he, who had been looked upon by the whole city as her pledged husband, had not quitted her, but had been ready rather to shed his heart's blood in her service.

Verily Ursula believed that she had found a sure instrument of vengeance, whereas she had heard say that Junker Henning von Beust was one of the most dreaded swordsmen in the Marches. Herdegen, to be sure, was likewise famed in Nuremberg as a doughty champion; yet it is ever the way in Franconia, nay, and in all Germany, to esteem outlandish means more highly than the best at home. Moreover she had many a time heard my grand-uncle declare that the gentlemen of our patrician families were not above half knights, and her intent was to sacrifice Herdegen to the Brandenburger's weapon.

Howbeit she had reckoned ill. Hans, who did service to my brother as his second at Altenperg, after striving faithfully to make peace between the two, was witness how our Nuremberg swordsman, who had had the finest schooling at Erfurt, Padua, and Paris, not merely withstood the Brandenburger, but so far outdid him in strength and swiftness that the Junker fell into the arms of his friends with wounds in the head and breast, while Herdegen came forth from the fray with no more hurt than a slight scratch on the arm.

The witnesses saw what he could do with amazement, and Sir Apitz von Rochow avowed that at my brother's first thrust he foresaw his cousin's evil plight; and they said that during the combat the supple blade of the Nuremberger's bedizened sword was changed into a raging serpent, which wound in everywhere, and bit through iron and steel. Afterwards he set forth that perchance Junker Schopper, who was said to be even better versed in all manner of writing than in the use of his weapon, had made use of some magic art, whereat a pious Knight of the Marches would fain cross himself.

Now whereas Junker von Beust had been in attendance on the King's person, the end of the fray could not be hidden from his Majesty, and so soon as the wounded man had been carried into the priest's house at Altenperg for shelter and care, it was needful to remove his fortunate foe into surety from King Sigismund's wrath. In this matter both Rochow and Muschwitz, who were the Junker's seconds, demeaned them as true nobles, inasmuch as they offered my brother refuge and concealment in their castles, albeit they accused him between themselves of some secret art; but he who was so soon to die counselled him to bide a while with Uncle Conrad at the forest lodge, and see what he himself and other of his friends might do to win his pardon.

When, at length, my lover was about to depart, the storm had burst; wherefore the Brandenburgers besought him to tarry in the priest's house till it should be overpast. This he would not do, by reason that his sweetheart looked for him with a fearful heart, knowing that her brother was in peril; and forthwith he rode away. Herdegen gave him Eppelein to attend him, and to bring back to him such matters as he had need of, and so my beloved set forth for the town, the serving man riding behind him.

It rained indeed and lightened and thundered, yet all was well till, nigh to Saint Linhart, the hail came down, beating on them heavily. At that moment a burning flash, with a terrible crash of thunder, reft a tree asunder by the road-way; his powerful horse was maddened with fear, stood upright, fell back, and crushed his rider against the trunk of a poplar tree. Never more did I look on the face of the true lover to whom I was so closely knit—save only in dreams; and I thank those who held me back from beholding his broken skull. To this day he rises before me, a silent vision, and I see him as he was in that hour when he gave me a parting kiss on our threshold, in the pale gleam of early morning, solemnly glad and in his festal bravery. Yet they could not hinder me from pressing my lips to the hands of the beloved body in its winding-sheet.

It was on a fair and glorious morning—the day of the Assumption of the Blessed Virgin—when Hans Haller, Knight, Doctor, and Town councillor, the eldest of his ancient race, my dear lord and plighted lover, was carried to the grave. The velvet pall wherewith his parents covered the bier of their beloved and firstborn son was so costly, that the price would easily have fed a poor household for years. How many tapers were burnt for him, how many masses said! Favor and good-will were poured forth upon me, and wherever I might go I was met with the highest respect. Even in my own home I was looked upon as one set apart and dedicated, whose presence brought grace, and who should be spared all contact with the common and lesser troubles of life. Cousin Maud, who was ever wont to mount the stair with an echoing tread and a loud voice, now went about stepping softly in her shoes, and when she called or spoke it was gently and scarce to be heard.

As for me I neither saw nor heard all this. It did not make me thankful nor even serve to comfort me.

All things were alike to me, even the Queen's gracious admonitions. The diligent humility of great and small alike in their demeanor chilled me in truth; sometimes meseemed it was in scorn.

To my lover, if to any man, Heaven's gates might open; yet had he perished without shrift or sacrament, and I could never bear to be absent when masses were said for his soul's redemption. Nay, and I was fain to go to churches and chapels, inasmuch as I was secure there from the speech of man. All that life could give or ask of me, I had ceased to care for.

If, from the first, I had been required to bestir myself and bend my will, matters had not perchance have gone so hard with me. The first call on my strength worked as it were a charm. The need to act restored the power to act: and a new and bitter experience which now befell was as a draught of wine, making my heavy heart beat high and steady once more. Nought, indeed, but some great matter could have roused me from that dull half-sleep; nor was it long in coming, by reason that my brother Herdegen's safety and life were in peril. This danger arose from the fact that, not long ere the passage of arms at Altenperg, in despite of strait enactments, the peace of the realm had many times been broken under the very eyes of his Majesty by bloody combats, and the Elector Conrad of Maintz had gone hand in hand with him of Brandenburg to entreat his Majesty to make an example of this matter. These two were likewise the most powerful of all the electors; the spiritual prince had, at the closing of the Diet, been named Vicar of the Empire, and he of Brandenburg was commander-in-chief of all the Imperial armies. And his voice was of special weight in this matter, inasmuch as the great friendship which had hitherto bound him to the Emperor had of late cooled greatly, and both before and during the sitting of the Diet, his

Majesty had keenly felt what power the Brandenburger could wield, and with what grave issues to himself.

Thus, when my lord the Elector and the high constable Frederick demanded that the law should be carried out with the utmost rigor in the matter of Herdegen, it was not, as many deemed, by reason that the King was not at one with our good town and the worshipful council, and that he was well content to vent his wrath on the son of one of its patrician families, but contrariwise, that his Majesty, who hated all baseness, had heard tidings of Herdegen's bloody deeds at Padua and his wild ways at Paris. Likewise it had come to his Majesty's ears that he had falsely plighted his troth to two maidens. Nay, and my grand-uncle had made known to King Sigismund that Ursula, who had been known to the Elector from her childhood up, had been driven by despair at Herdegen's breach of faith to give her hand to the sick Bohemian Knight, Sir Franz von Welemisl.

Moreover the Knight Johann von Beust, father of Junker Henning, had journeyed to Nuremberg to visit his wounded son; and whereas he learnt many matters from his son's friends around his sick-bed, he earnestly besought the Elector so to bring matters about that due punishment should overtake the Junker's foeman.

My lord the Elector had many a time showed his teeth to the knighthood of Brandenburg, appealing to law and justice when he had taken part with the citizens and humbled the overbearing pride of the nobles. It was now his part to show that he would not suffer noble blood to be spilt unavenged, though it were by the devilish skill of a citizen; forasmuch as that if indeed he should do so all men would know thereby that he was the sworn foe of the nobles of Brandenburg and kept so tight a hand on them, not for justice' sake, but for sheer hatred and ill-will.

When at a later day, I saw the old knight, with his ruddy steel-eaters' face and great lip-beard, and was told that in his youth he had been a doughty free booter and highway robber, who by his wealth and power had made himself to be a mainstay of the Elector in Altmark, I could well imagine how his threats had sounded, and that all men had been swift to lend ear to his words. Yet that just King to whom he accused Herdegen gave a hearing to von Rochow and the other witnesses; they could but declare that all had been done by rule, and that Rochow had said from the first that of a certainty the devil himself guided Herdegen's sword. Muschwitz, indeed, was sure that he had seen his blade flash forth fire. Hereupon the father was urgent on the King's Majesty that he should seek to seize my brother, pronounce him a banished outlaw, and that whenever his person should be taken he was to be punished with death.

All this I learnt not till some time after, inasmuch as folks would not add new cause of grief to my present sorrow.

The way I was going could lead no-whither save to madness or the cloister; I had so lost my wits in self, that I weened that I had done my part for my brother when I had humbly entreated their Majesties to vouchsafe him their gracious pardon, and had signed my name to certain petitions in favor of the accused. Of a truth I wist not yet in what peril he stood, and rarely enquired for him when Uncle Conrad had assured me that he lay in safe hiding.

Sometimes, indeed, meseemed as though Ann and the others kept somewhat privy from me; but even all care to enquire was gone from me, nor cared I for aught but to be left in peace. And thus matters stood till rumor waxed loud and roused me from my leaden slumber.

I had passed the day for myself alone, refusing to see our noble guests; I was sitting in silence and dreaming by my spinning-wheel, which I had long ceased to turn, when on a sudden there were heavy steps and wrathful voices on the stairs. The door of the room was thrown open and, in spite of old Susan's resistance, certain beadles of the city came in, with two of the Emperor's men-at-arms. My cousin was not within doors, as had become common of late, and I was vexed and grieved to be thus unpleasantly surprised. I rose to meet the strangers, making sharp enquiry by what right they broke the peace of a Nuremberg patrician's household. Hereupon their chief made answer roundly that he was here by his Majesty's warrant, and that of the city authorities, to make certain whether Junker Herdegen Schopper, who had fled from the Imperial ban, were in hiding or no in the house of his fathers. At first it was all I could do to save myself from falling; but I presently found heart and courage. I assured the bailiffs that their search would be vain, albeit I gave them free leave to do whatsoever their office might require of them, only to bear in mind that great notables were guests in the house; and then I drew a deep breath and meseemed I was as a child forgotten and left in a house on fire which sees its father pressing forward to rescue it.

Hitherto no man had told me what fate it was that threatened my brother, and now that I knew, I hastily filled up the meaning of many a word to which I had lent but half an ear. My cousin's frequent absence in court array, Ann's tear-stained eyes and strange mien, and many another matter was now full plain to me.

My newly-awakened spirit and restored power asserted their rights, and, as in the days of old, neither could rest content till it knew for a certainty what it might do.

While Susan and the other serving folks, with certain of the retainers brought by our guests, were searching the house through, I hastily did on my shoes and garments for out-door wear, and albeit it was already dusk, I went forth. Yea, and I held my head high and my body straight as I went along the streets, whereas for these weeks past I had crept about hanging my head; meseemed that a change had come over my outward as well as my inner man. And as I reached Pernhart's house, with long swift steps, more folks would have seen me for what in truth I was: a healthy young creature, with a long span of life before me yet and filled with strength and spirit enough to do good service, not to myself alone, but to many another, and chiefest of all to my dearly beloved brother.

And when I was at my walk's end and stood before the old mother,— who was now recovered from her sickness and sitting upright and sound in her arm-chair with her youngest grandchild in her lap,—I knew forthwith that I had come to the right person.

The worthy old dame had not been slow to mark what ailed me; nay, if Cousin Maud had not besought her to spare my sorrowing soul, she long since had revealed to me what peril hung over Herdegen. She had not failed to perceive that my weary submission to ills which might never be remedied, had broken my power and will to fulfil what good there was in me. And now I stood before her, freed from that sleepwalking dulness of will, eager to know the whole truth, and declared myself ready to do all that in me lay to attain one thing alone, namely to rescue my brother. On this I learnt from the venerable dame's lips that now I was indeed the old Margery, albeit Cousin Maud had of late denied it, and with good reason; and the old woman was right, inasmuch as that the more terrible and unconquerable the danger seemed, the more my courage rose and the greater was my spirit. Now, too, I heard that what I had taken for love-sick weakness in Ann was only too-well founded heart-sickness; and that she likewise, on her part, had not been idle, but, under the guidance of Cousin Maud and Uncle Christian, had moved heaven and earth to succor her lover, albeit alas! in vain.

In truth the cause was as good as lost; and Uncle Christian, who ever hoped for the best, made it no secret that, in the most favorable, issue Herdegen must begin life afresh in some distant land. Yet was neither Ann nor I disposed to let our courage fail, and it was at that time that our friendship put forth fresh flowers. We fought shoulder to shoulder as it were, comrades in the struggle, full of love towards each other and of love for my brother; and when I bid her farewell and she would fain walk home with me, all those who dwelt in the coppersmith's house were of the same mind as men might be in a beleaguered town, who had been about to yield and then, on a sudden, beheld the reinforcements approaching with waving banners and a blast of trumpets.

In truth there was a shrewd fight to be waged; and the stronghold which day by day waxed harder to conquer was my lord chief Constable, the Elector Frederick; his peer, the Elector of Maintz, put all on him when Cardinal Branda, who was Ann's kind patron, besought his mercy.

Until I had been roused to this new care in life I had never been to court, in spite of many a gracious bidding from my lady, the Queen. My supplications found no answer, and when Queen Barbara granted me audience at my entreaty, though she received me graciously, yet would she not hear me out. She would gladly help, quoth she, but that she, like all, must obey the laws; and at last she freely owned that her good will would come to nought against the demands of the Elector of Brandenburg. The greatness of that wise and potent prince was plainly set before our eyes that same day, for on him, as commander-in-chief of the crusade to be sent forth against the Hussite heresy, the Emperor's own sword was solemnly bestowed in the church of Saint Sebald. It was girt on to him by reverend Bishops, after that he had received from the hand of the Pope's legate a banner which his Holiness had himself blessed, and which was borne before him by the Count of Hohenlohe as he went forth.

That it would be a hard matter to get speech with so potent a lord at such a time was plain to see; howbeit I was able to speak privily at any rate with his chamberlain, and from him I learned in what peril my brother was, inasmuch as not the Junker's father alone was bent on bringing him to extreme punishment, but likewise no small number of Nuremberg folk, who had of yore been aggrieved by my brother's over-bearing pride.

Every one who had ever met him in the streets with a book under his arm, or had seen him, late at night, through the lighted window-pane, sitting over his papers and parchments, was ready to bear witness to his study of the black arts. Thus the diligence which he had ever shown through all his wild ways was turned to his destruction; and it was the same with the open-handed liberality which had ever marked him, by reason that the poor, to whom he had tossed a heavy ducat instead of a thin copper piece, would tell of the Devil's dole he had gotten, and how that the coin had burnt in his hand. Nay and Eppelein's boasting of the gold his young lord had squandered in Paris, and wherewith he had filled his varlet's pockets, gave weight to this evil slander. Many an one held it for a certainty that Satan himself had been his treasurer.

Thus a light word, spoken at first as a figure of speech by the Knight von Rochow, had grown into a charge against him, heavy enough to wreck the honor and freedom of a man who had no friends, and even to bring him to the stake; and I know full well that many an one rejoiced beforehand to think that he should see that lordly youth with all his bravery standing in the pointed cap with the Devil's tongue hung round his neck, and gasping out his life amid the licking flames.

CHAPTER V

The Diet was well-nigh over, yet had we not been able to gain aught in Herdegen's favor. One day my Forest Aunt, who had marked all our doings with wise counsel and hearty good-will, sent word that he on whose mighty word hung Herdegen's weal or woe, the Elector Frederick himself, had promised to visit at the Lodge next day to the end that he might hunt, and that we should ride thither forthwith.

By the time we alighted there his Highness had already come and gone forth to hunt the deer; wherefor we privily followed after him, and at a sign from Uncle Christian we came out of the brushwood and stood before him. Albeit he strove to escape from us with much diligence and no small craftiness, we would not let him go, and kept up with him, pressing him so closely that he afterwards declared that we had brought him to bay like a hunted beast. Of a truth no bear nor badger ever found it harder to escape the hounds than he, at that moment, to shut his eyes and ears against bright eyes and women's tongues made eloquent by Dame Love herself. Moreover my mourning array, worn as it was for a youth who had stood above most others in his love, would have checked any hard words on his lips; thus was he once more made to know that Eve's power was not yet wholly departed. Yet were we far from believing in any such power in ourselves, as we appeared before that great and potent sovereign, whose manly, calm, and withal fatherly dignity made him, to my mind, more majestic than the tall but unresting Emperor.

I can see him as he stood with his booted foot on the hart's neck, and turned his noble head, with its long, smooth grey hair, gazing at us with his great blue eyes, kindly at first, but presently with vexation and well-nigh in wrath.

We held our hands tight on our hearts, striving to call to mind some few of the words we had meditated with intent to speak them in defence of Herdegen. And our love, and our steadfast purpose that we would win grace and mercy for him came to our aid; and whereas my lord's first enquiry was to know whether I were that Mistress Margery Schopper who had been betrothed to his dear Hans Haller, too soon departed, my eyes filled with tears, but the memory of the dead gave me courage, so that I dared to meet the great man's eye, and was right glad to find that the words which in my dread I had forgot, now came freely to my mind. Likewise meseemed that, in overriding my own fears, I had conquered Ann's; whereas she had been pale and speechless, clinging to the folds of my dress, she now stood forth boldly by my side.

Then, when I had presented her to his Highness as Herdegen's promised bride, to whom he had been plighted in love from their childhood, I made known to his lordship that it was not my brother's desire, but that of my grand-uncle, that Ursula should be his wife. Likewise I strove to release my brother from the charge of making gold, by diligently showing that the old Knight had ever showered ducats on him to beguile him to his will. Then I spoke at length of Herdegen's skill with the sword, and hereupon Ann made bold to say that it would be well to bid her lover return in safe-keeping to Nuremberg, and there let him give proof of his skill with a weapon specially blessed by my lord Cardinal Julianus Caesarinus, the Pope's legate, which could have no taint of devilish arts.

Thus did we give utterance to everything we had meditated beforehand; and albeit the Elector at first made wrathful answer, and even made as though he would turn his back on us, each time we made shift to hold him fast. Nay, or ever we had ceased he had taken his foot from the stag's neck, and at length we walked with him back to the forest lodge, half amused, yet half grieved, with the mocking words he tormented us with. Then he bid us quit him, promising that he would once more examine into the matter of that young criminal.

Within doors supper was now ready, but we, as beseemed us, kept out of the way. My brother's case was now in safe hands, inasmuch as my Uncle Conrad and Christian sat at table with my lord. Likewise we were much comforted, whereas my aunt told us that the elder Knight, Junker Henning von Beust's father, who was here in the Elector's following, had, of his own free will, said to her that he now rued his deed in so violently accusing Herdegen, by reason that his son, who was now past all danger, had earnestly besought him to save this man, whose skill was truly a marvel, and had likewise said that he whom Hans Haller had honored with his friendship could not have practised black arts. Also he held me dear as the widowed maid to whom his friend was to have been wed, and he could never forgive himself if fresh woe came upon me through him or his kith and kin.

All this was glad tidings indeed, not alone for Herdegen's sake, but also by reason that there are few greater joys than that of finding good cause to approve one whom we respect, and yet whom we have begun to doubt.

Ann and I went to our chamber greatly comforted, and in such good heart as at that time I could be, and when from thence I heard Uncle Christian's great voice, as full of jollity as ever, I was certain that matters were all for the best for Herdegen. Our last fears and doubts were ere long cleared away; while the gentlemen beneath were still over their cups a heavy foot tramped up the stairs, a hard finger knocked at our chamber door, and Uncle Christian's deep voice cried: "Are you asleep betimes or still awake, maidens?"

Whereupon Ann, foreboding good, answered in the gladness of her heart that we were long since sleeping sweetly, and my uncle laughed.

"Well and good," quoth he, "then sleep on, and let me tell you what meseems your very next dream will be: You will be standing with all of us out in a green mead, and a little bird will sing: 'Herdegen is freed from his ban.' At this you will greatly rejoice; but in the midst of your joy a raven shall croak from a dry branch: 'Can it be! The law must be upheld, and I will not suffer the rascal to go unpunished.' Whereupon the little bird will twitter again: 'Well and good; 't will serve him right. Only be not too hard on him.' And we shall all say the same, and thereupon you will awake."

And he tramped down the stair again, and albeit we cried after him, and besought him to tell us more of the matter, he heard us not at all.

When we were at home again, lo, the Elector had done much to help us. I found a letter waiting for me, sealed with the Emperor's signet, wherein it was said that, by his Majesty's grace and mercy, my brother Herdegen was purged of his outlawry, but was condemned in a fine of a thousand Hungarian ducats as pain and penalty.

Thus the little bird and the raven had both been right. Howbeit, when I presently betook me to the castle to speak my thanks to the Empress, I was turned away; and indeed it had already been told to me that at Court this morning that sorrowful Margery, with her many petitions, was looked upon with other eyes than that other mirthful Margery, who had come with flowers and songs whensoever she was bidden. None but Porro the jester seemed to be of the same mind as ever; when he met me in the castle yard he greeted me right kindly and, when I had told him of the tidings in the Emperor's letter, he whispered as he bid me good day: "If I had a fox for a brother, fair child, I would counsel him to lurk in his cover till the hounds were safe at home again. In Hungary once I met a certain fellow who had been kicked by a highway thief after he had emptied his pockets. I tell you what. A man may well pawn his last doublet, if he may thereby gain a larger. He need never redeem the first, and it is given some folks to coin gold ducats out of humbler folks' sins. Ah! If I had a fox for a brother!"

He sang the last words to himself as it were, and vanished, seeing certain persons of the Court.

Now I took this well-meant warning as it was intended; and albeit Ann and I were heartsick with longing to see Herdegen and to release him from his hiding, we nevertheless took patience. The legal guardians of our estate, having my uncle's consent, took my Cousin Maud's suretyship, and expressed themselves willing to pay the fine out of the moneys left by our parents, into the Imperial treasury. And that which followed thereafter showed us how wise the Fool's admonition had been.

The knight, Sir Apitz von Rochow, who had served as Junker Henning's second in the fight, tarried yet in Nuremberg, and this rude, arrogant youth had devoted himself with such true loving-kindness to the care of his young cousin, at first in the priest's house at Altenpero and afterwards in the Deutsch-haus in the town, that he had taken no rest, day nor night, until the Junker's father came, and then he fell into a violent fever. It was but of late that the leech had granted him to go out of doors, and his first walk was to our house to show me his sorrow for my grief, and to thank my cousin for many pleasant trifles which she had sent to him and the Junker during their sickness, to refresh them. At the same time he broke forth in loud and unstinted wrath against Sir Franz von Welemisl, and gave us to wit that with his whole heart he grudged him the fair Ursula, whose favor he himself had so diligently sued for since the first days of the Diet. From our house he went to the Tetzels', and then he and the Bohemian forthwith came to high words and defiant glances.

Shortly after this, and a few hours only after my brother's penalty had been paid into the Treasury, the two young gentlemen met in the nobles' wine-room by the Frohnwage, and von Rochow, heated by wine and heeding neither moderation nor manners, began to taunt Ursula's betrothed. After putting it to him that he had left the task to Herdegen of picking up the glove, "which peradventure he had thought was of too heavy leather," to which the other made seemly reply, he enquired, inasmuch as they were discoursing of marriage, whether the Church, which forbids the joining of those who are near of kin, hath not likewise the power to hinder a young and blooming maid from binding herself for life to a sickly husband. Such discourse was ill-pleasing by reason of the Bohemian's presence there: and the Junker went yet further, till to some speech made by old Master Grolaud, he made answer by asking what then might be a priest's duty, if the sick bridegroom failed to say "yes" at the altar by reason of his coughing? And as he spoke he cast a challenging look at Welemisl.

The hot blood of the Bohemian flew to his brain; or ever any one could hinder him, his knife was buried to the hilt in the other's shoulder. All hastened to help the Brandenburger, and when presently some turned to seize the criminal he was no more to be seen.

This dreadful deed caused just dismay, and most of all at Court, inasmuch as the chamberlain and the maid of honor in close attendance on their Majesties' persons were near kin to the Bohemian, whose mother was of the noble Hungarian house of Pereny.

As to the Emperor, he flew into great fury and threatened to cancel the murderer's coat of arms and punish him with death. Never within the peace of his realm, nay and under his very eyes, had so much noble blood been shed in base brawling as here in our sober city, and he would forthwith make an example of the guilty men. He would make young Schopper pay some penalty yet more than a mere fine, to that he pledged his royal word, and as for young Welemisl, he was minded to devise some punishment that should hinder many an over-bold knight from drawing his sword! And he commanded that not only his own constables and men-at-arms, but likewise the town bailiffs, should forthwith seek and take both those young men.

Only two days later Sir Franz was brought in by the city watch; he had dressed himself in the garments of a waggoner, but had betrayed himself in a tavern at Schwabach by his coughing. Howbeit his Majesty had by this time come to another mind; nay, Queen Barbara left him less peace than even the court-folks, for indeed her father, Count Cilly, was near of kin to the Perenys, and through them to the Welemisl.

The Emperor Sigismund was a noble-minded and easy-living prince, who once, when forty thousand ducats had been poured into his ever-empty treasure chest, divided it forthwith among his friends, saying: "Now shall I sleep well, for that which broke my rest you bear away with you." And this light-hearted man, who was ever tossed hither and thither against his will, now saw that his peace was in evil plight by reason of Sir Franz. This was ill to bear; and whereas his royal wife called to mind in a happy hour that Welemisl had been provoked out of all measure by Rochow's scorn, and had done the deed out of no malice aforethought but, being heated with wine, in a sudden rage, and that he was in so far more worthy of mercy than young Schopper, who had shed noble blood with a guilty intent, counting on his skill as a swordsman, the Emperor surrendered at discretion. In this he was confirmed by his privy secretary, Caspar Slick, whom the Queen had beguiled; and this man, learned in the law, was ready with a decision which the Imperial magistrate gladly agreed to forthwith, as mild yet sufficient. Matters in short were as follows: About ten years ago the Knight Sir Endres von Steinbach had slain a citizen of Nuremberg in a fray with the town, and had made his peace afterwards with the council under the counsel of the Abbot of Waldsassen: by taking on himself, as an act of penance, to make a pilgrimage to Vach and to Rome, to set up stone crosses in four convents, and henceforth to do service to the town in every quarrel, in his own person, with a fellowship of ten lances for the space of two years. All this he had duly done, and it came about that the Emperor now condemned the Bohemian and my brother both alike to make a pilgrimage, not only to Rome—inasmuch as their guilt was greater than Steinbach's—but likewise to Jerusalem, to the Holy Sepulchre and other sacred places. Welemisl was to pay the same penalty in money as Herdegen had paid, and in consideration of their having thus made atonement for the blood they had shed, and as their victims had escaped death, they were released from the doom of outlawry. On returning from their pilgrimage they were to be restored to their rank and estates, and to all their rights, lordships, and privileges.

Not long after this sentence was passed the Court removed from Nuremberg through Ratisbon, where the Emperor strove to make up his quarrel with the Duke Bavaria and then to Vienna; but ere his departing he gave strait orders to the chief magistrate to see that the two criminals should fare forth on their pilgrimage not longer than twenty-four hours after the declaration of their doom.

CHAPTER VI

Shall I now set forth how that Ann and I found Herdegen in his hiding-place, a simple little beekeeper's but in the most covert part of the Lorenzer wald, a spot whither no horseman might pass; how that even in his poor peasant's weed my brother was yet a goodly man, and clasped his sweetheart in his arms as ardently as in that first day on his homecoming from Italy— and how that the dear, hunted fellow, beholding me in mourning dress, took his sister to his heart as soon as his plighted love had left the place free? Yea, for the dead had been dear to him likewise, and his love for me had never failed.

When we presently gave ourselves up in peace to the joy of being all together once more, I weened that his eye was more steadfast, and his voice graver and calmer than of old; and whensoever he spoke to me it was in a soft and heartfelt tone, which gave me comforting assurance that he grieved for my grief. And how sweetly and gravely did he beguile Ann to make the most of this sad meeting, wherein welcome and God-speed so closely touched. In the house once more I rejoiced in the lofty flight which lifted this youth's whole spirit above all things common or base; and his sweetheart's eyes rested on him in sheer delight as he talked with my uncle, or with the magistrate who had come forth with us to the Forest. And albeit it was in truth his duty to the Emperor his master, to fulfil his behest, nevertheless he gave us his promise that he would put off the announcement of the sentence till we should return to the town next day, and prolong our time together and with Cousin Maud as much as in him lay.

My aunt's eyes shone with sheer joy when they fell on her darling with Herdegen at her side, and she could say to herself no doubt that these two, who, as she conceived, were made for each other, would hardly have come together again but for her help. Or ever we set forth on the morrow, she called Herdegen to her once more to speak with him privily, and bid him bear in mind that if ever in his wanderings he should meet another youth— and he knew who—he might tell him that at home in the Lorenzerwald a mother's heart was yet beating, which could never rest till his presence had gladdened it once more.

My uncle rode with us into the town. It was at the gate that the magistrate told Herdegen what his fate should be: that he must leave Nuremberg on the morrow at the same hour; and to my dying day I shall ever remember with gladness and regret the meal we then sat down to with our nearest and dearest.

Cousin Maud called it her darling's condemnation supper. She had watched the cooking of every dish in the kitchen, and chosen the finest wine out of the cellar. Yet the victual might have been oatmeal porridge, and the noble liquor the smallest beer, and it would have been no matter to our great, albeit melancholy gladness. And indeed, no man could have gazed at the pair now come together again after so many perils, and not have felt his heart uplifted. Ah! and how dear to me were those twain! They had learnt that life was as nothing to either of them without the other, and their hearts meseemed were henceforth as closely knit as two streams which flow together to make one river, and whose waters no power on earth can ever sunder. They sat with us, but behind great posies of flowers, as it were in an isle of bliss; yet were they in our midst, and showed how glad it made them to have so many loving hearts about them. Notwithstanding her joy and trouble Ann forgot not her duty as "watchman," and threatened Uncle Christian when he would take more than he should of the good liquor. He, however, declared that this day was under the special favor of the Saints, and that no evil could in any wise befall him. My Forest-uncle and Master Pernhart had been found in discourse together, and the matter of which they spoke was my Cousin Gotz. And how it gladdened the father to speak of his far-off son! More especially when Pernhart's lips overflowed with praise of the youth to whom his only child owed her early death.

Most marvellous of all was the Magister. Herdegen's return to his beloved robbed Master Peter of his last hope; nevertheless his eyes had never rested on her with fonder rapture. Verily his faithful heart was warmed as it were by the happiness which surrounded her as with a glory, and indeed it was not without some doubts that I saw the worthy man, who was wont to be so sober, raise his glass again and again to drink to Ann, whether she marked him or not, and drain his glass each time in her honor. My Uncle Christian likewise filled his cup right diligently, and seeing him quaff it with such lusty good will I feared lest he should keep us all night at table, when the time was short for Ann and my brother to have any privy speech together. But that good man forgot not, even over the wine-jar, what might pleasure other folks; and albeit it was hard for him to quit a merry drinking-bout he was the first to move away. We were alone by sundown. The Magister had been carried to bed and woke not till noon on the morrow.

The plighted couple sat once more in the oriel where they had so often sat in happier days, and seeing them talking and fondling in the gathering dusk, meseemed for a while that that glad winter season had come again in which they had rejoiced in the springtide of their love.

Thus the hours passed, and I was in the very act of enquiry whether it were not time to light the lamps, when we heard voices on the stairs, and Cousin Maud came in saying that Sir Franz had made his way into the house, and that he declared that his weal or woe, nay and his life lay in Herdegen's hand, so that she had not the heart to refuse to suffer him to come in. Hereupon my brother started up in a rage, but the chamber door was opened, and with the maid, who brought the lamp in, the Bohemian crossed the threshold. We maids would fain have quitted them; but the knight besought us to remain, saying, as his eyes humbly sued to mine, that rather should I tarry and speak a good word for him. Then, when Herdegen called upon him to speak, but did not hold forth his hand, Sir Franz besought him to suffer him to be his comrade in his pilgrimage. Howbeit so doleful a fellow was by no means pleasing in my brother's eyes, and so he right plainly gave him to understand; then the Bohemian called to mind their former friendship, and entreated him to put himself in his place and not to forget that he, as a man sound of limb, would have avenged the scorn put on him by Rochow in fair fight instead of with a dagger-thrust. They were condemned to a like penance and, if Herdegen would not suffer him and give him his company, this would be the death-blow to his blighted honor.

Hereupon I appealed to my brother right earnestly, beseeching him not to reject his former friend if it were only for love of me. And inasmuch as on that day his whole soul was filled with love, his hardness was softened, and how gladly and thankfully my heart beat when I beheld him give his hand to the man who had endured so much woe for my sake.

Presently, while they were yet speaking of their departing, again there were voices without; and albeit I could scarce believe my ears I mistook not, and knew the tones for Ursula's. Ann likewise heard and knew them, and she quitted the chamber saying: "None shall trouble me in such an hour, least of all shall Ursula!" The angelus had long since been tolled, and somehap of grave import must have brought us so rare a guest at so late an hour. My cousin, who would fain have hindered her from coming in, held her by the arm; and her efforts to shake off the old lady's grasp were all in vain till she caught sight of Herdegen. Then at length she freed herself and, albeit she was gasping for breath, her voice was one of sheer triumph as she cried: "I had to come, and here I am!"

"Aye, but if you come as a Mar-joy I will show you the way out, my word for that!" my cousin panted; but the maid heeded her not, but went straight toward Herdegen and said: "I felt I must see you once more ere you depart—I must! Old Jorg attended me, and when I am gone forth again Dame Maud will speak my 'eulogium'. Only look at her! But it is all one to me. Find me a place, Herdegen, where I may speak with you and Ann Spiesz alone. I have a message for you."

Hereupon my cousin broke in with a scornful laugh, such as I could never have looked to hear from her, with her kind and single heart; and my brother told Ursula shortly and plainly that with her he had no more to do. To this she made answer that it would be a sin to doubt that, inasmuch as he was now a pious pilgrim and honorably betrothed, nevertheless she craved to see Ann. That, too, was denied her, and she did but shrug her shoulders; then she turned to the Bohemian, who had gone towards her, and asked him with icy politeness to remove from her presence, inasmuch as he was an offence to her. Hereupon I saw the last drop of red blood fade away from the young Knight's sickly cheek, and it went to my heart to see him uplift his hands and implore her right humbly: "You know, Ursula, all that hath befallen me for your sake, and how hard a lot awaits me. Three times have I been plighted to you, my promised bride, and as many times cast off...."

"To spare you the like fate a fourth time; all good things being in threes!" she put in, mocking him. "Verily you have cured me of any desire ever to be your Dame, Sir Knight. And since meseems this day our speech is free and truthful, I am fain to confess that such a wish was ever far enough from me, and even when we stood betrothed. A strange thing is love! 'Here's to fair Margery!' one day, on every noble gentleman's lips; and on the morrow: 'Here's to sweet Ursula!' In some folks it grows inwardly, as it were a polypus, and of such, woe is me, am I. My love, if you would know the truth, my lord Baron von Welemisl, love such I have known I gave once for all to that man Herdegen Schopper; it has been his from the time when, in my short little skirts, I learnt to write; and so it has ever been, till the hour when worthy Dame Henneleinlein, the noble Junker's new cousin—it is enough to make one die of laughing!—when that illustrious lady whispered the truth in my ear that her intending kinsman had thrown me over, and, with me, old Im Hoff's wealth, for the sake of a scrivener's wench. And to think that as a boy he was wont to bring me posies, and wear my colors! Nay, and since that time he has shot many a fiery glance at me. Only lately he wrote to his uncle from Paris that he was minded to make me his wife. Ah, you may open your eyes wide, most respected every-one's-cousin Maud, and you likewise, prim and spotless Mistress Margery! Cross yourselves in the name of all the Saints! A dead wolf cannot bite, and as for my love for that man, I may boldly declare that it is dead and buried. But mark me," and she clapped her hand to her heaving bosom, "mark me, somewhat else hath made entrance here, with drums and trumpets and high jubilee: Hate!—I hate you, Herdegen, as I hate death, pestilence, and hell; and I hate you twice as much since your skill with the rapier brought the combat with the Brandenburger, into which I entrapped you, to so perverse an end."

Hereupon Cousin Maud, wild with rage herself, gripped her again by the arm to draw her forth from the chamber, but Ursula went on in a milder tone:

"Only a few moments longer, I pray you; for by the Blessed Virgin and all the Saints I swear that I would not have come hither at so late an hour but to deliver my message to Herdegen."

My cousin released her, and she drew forth a written paper and again enquired for Ann; howbeit my brother said that he did not purpose to call her in, and desired that she would give him the paper, if indeed it concerned him. To this she answered that he would presently know that much, inasmuch as it was her intent to read it to the company, only she would fain have had his fair mistress among the hearers. Howbeit she had a good loud voice, she thanked the Saints, and the doors in the Schoppers' house were scarce thicker than in other folks' houses. The letter in her hand had been given to her to deliver to Herdegen by the newlymade vicar of his Highness the Elector and Archbishop of Treves, who was lodged with the Tetzels. He had not been able to find him, no more than the Emperor's men-at-arms; so he had bidden her take good heed that she gave it into Junker Schopper's own hand. But verily she would do yet more, and spare him the pains of reading it.

Hereupon my brother, in great ire, bid her no longer keep that which was not her own; yet she refused, and whereas Herdegen seized her hand to wrench away the paper she shrieked out to the Bohemian: "Give him his due, for a knave who offends maidens; that outcast for whom I scorned and misprized you! Help, help, if you are no churl!"

My brother nevertheless had already snatched the letter from her, and the Bohemian, who had laid his hand on his dagger, thought better of it as his eye met my look of warning.

It was a fearful moment of terror, and Ursula, whose hair had fallen loose, while her flashing blue eyes, full of hate, shot lightnings on one and another, stood clinging to the heavy dresser whereon our silver and glass vessels were displayed, and cried out as loudly as she could shout: "The letter is from his lady-love in Padua, the Marchesa Bianca Zorzi. That cunning swordsman's blade made her a widow, and now she bids him return to her embrace. The fond and ardent lady is in Venice, and her intent is to revel there in love and pleasure with her husband's murderer. And he—though he may have sworn a thousand vows to the scrivener's hussy—he will do the Italian Circe's bidding, and if he may escape her snares he will fall into those of another. Oh! I know him; and I feel in my soul that his fate will be to dally with one and another in delights and raptures, till the Saints fulfil my heart's chiefest desire, and he comes to despair and anguish and want, and the scrivener's wench breaks her heart under my very eyes with pining and sheer shame. Away, away, Herdegen Schopper! Go forth to joy and to misery! Go-with your pale black-haired mate. Revel and wallow, till you, who have trampled on this heart's true love, are brought low—as loathsome in the eyes of men as a leper and a beggar."

And she shook the dresser so that the precious glass cup which the German merchants of the Fondaco at Venice had given to my father at his departing, fell to the floor and was broken to pieces with a loud crash.

We had hearkened to her ravings as though spellbound and frozen; and when we at last took heart to put an end to her wild talk, lo, she was gone, and flying down the stairs with long strides.

Herdegen, who had turned pale, struggled to command himself. Cousin Maud, who had lost her breath with dismay, burst into loud weeping; the wild maid's curse had fallen heavy on her soul. I alone kept my senses, so far as to go to the window and look out at her. I saw her walking along, hanging her head; the serving man carried the lantern before her, and the Bohemian was speaking close in her ear.

When I came back into the chamber Cousin Maud had her arm round Herdegen, and was saying to him, with many tears, that the curse of the wicked had no power over a pious and faithful Christian; yet he quitted her in haste to seek Ann, who doubtless would have stayed in the next chamber, and perchance needed his succor. Howbeit the door was opened, and we could scarce believe our eyes when she came in with that same roguish smile which she was wont to wear when, in playing hide-and-seek, she had stolen home past the seeker, and she cried: "Thank the Virgin that the air is clear once more! You may laugh, but in truth I fled up to the very garret for sheer dread of Mistress Tetzel. Did she come to fetch her bridegroom?"

Herdegen could not refrain from smiling at this question, and we likewise did the same; even Cousin Maud, who till this moment had sat on the couch like one crushed, with her feet stretched out before her, made a face and cried: "To fetch him! Ursula who has caught the Bohemian! She is a monster! Were ever such doings seen in our good town?—And her mother was so wise, so worthy a woman! And the hussy is but nineteen!—Merciful

Father, what will she be at forty or fifty, when most women only begin to be wicked!" And thus she went on for some while.

Ere long we forgot Ursula and all the hateful to-do, and passed the precious hours in much content, till after midnight, when the Pernharts sent to fetch Ann home. Herdegen and I would walk with her. After a grievous yet hopeful leave-taking I came home again, leaning on his arm, through the cool autumn night.

When I now admonished Herdegen as we walked, as to the fair Marchesa and her letter, he declared to me that in those evil weeks he had spent in bitter yearning as a serving man in the bee-keeper's hut, he had learned to know his own mind. Neither the Marchesa, whom he scorned from the bottom of his heart, inasmuch as, with all her beauty, she was full of craft and lies, no, nor event Dame Venus herself could now turn him aside from the love and duty he had sworn to Ann. He would, indeed, take ship from Genoa rather than from Venice, were it not for shame of such fears of his own weakness, and that he longed once more to set eyes on our brother Kunz whom he had not seen for so long a space.

I found it hard to see clear in this matter. Yet could I not deem it wise to deny him the first chance of proving himself true and honest; likewise meseemed that our younger brother's presence would be a safe guard against temptation. Under the eye of our parent's pictures I bid him good night for the few hours till he should depart, and when I pointed up to them he understood me, and clasped me fondly in his arms saying: "Never fear, little mother Margery!"

We were with Herdegen again or ever it was morning. While we had been sleeping he had written a loving letter to my grand-uncle, who had yesterday forbidden him his presence, to bear witness to his duty and thankfulness.

The cocks still were crowing in the yards, and the country-folk were coming into town with asses and waggons, when I mounted my horse to ride forth with my brother. He was busied in the courtyard with the new serving-man he had hired, by reason that Eppelein, who for safety's sake had not been suffered to go with him into hiding, had vanished as it were from the face of the earth. Nay, and we knew for what cause and reason, for Dame Henneleinlein had counselled the King's men to seize him, to the end that he might be put on the rack to give tidings of where his master lay hid. If they had caught him his stout limbs would have fared ill indeed; but the light-hearted varlet was a favorite with the serving men and wenches of the court-folk, jolly at the wine cup and all manner of sport, and thus they had bestowed him away. And so, while we were living from day to day in great fear, an old charcoal wife would come in from the forest twice or thrice in every week and bring charcoal to the kitchen wench to sell, and albeit she was ever sent away, yet would she come again and ask many questions.

While we were yet tarrying for Herdegen to be ready the old wife came by with her cart, and when she had asked of some needful matters she pulled off her kerchief with a loud laugh, and lo, in her woman's weed, there stood Eppelein and none other. Hereupon was much rejoicing and, in a few minutes, the crafty fellow was turned again into a sturdy riding man, albeit beardless.

Eppelein's return helped Cousin Maud over the grief of leave-taking. Yet, when at last we must depart, it went hard with her. At the gate we were met by the Pernharts with Ann and Uncle Christian. My lord the chief magistrate likewise was there, to bear witness to Herdegen's departing; also Heinrich Trardorf, his best beloved schoolmate, who had ever been his faithful friend.

We had left the walls and moat of the town far behind us, when we heard swift horses at our heels, and Sir Franz, with two serving-men, joined the fellowship. My brother had soon found a place at Ann's side, and we went forward at an easy pace; and if they were minded to kiss, bending from their saddles, they need fear no witness, for the autumn mist was so thick that it hid every one from his nearest neighbor.

Thus we went forth as far as Lichtenhof, and while we there made halt to take a last leave, meseemed that Heaven was fain to send us a friendly promise. The mist parted on a sudden as at the signal of a magician, and before us lay the city with its walls, and towers, and shining roofs, over-topped by the noble citadel. Thus we parted in better cheer than we had deemed we might, and the lovers might yet for a long space signal to each other by the waving of hat and of kerchief.

CHAPTER VII

Herdegen's departing marks my life's way with another mile-stone. All fears about him were over, and a great peace fell upon me.

I had learnt by experience that it was within my power to be mistress of any heart's griefs, and I could tell myself that dull sufferance of woe would have ill-pleased him whose judgment I most cared for. To remember him was what I best loved, and I earnestly desired to guide my steps as would have been his wish and will. In some degree I was able to do so, and Ann was my great helper.

My eyes and ears were opened again to what should befall in the world in which my lover had lived; all the more so as matters now came about in the land and on its borders which deeply concerned my own dear home and threatened it with great peril.

After the Diet was broken up, the Elector Frederick of Brandenburg was forced to take patience till the princes, lords, and mounted men-at-arms sent forth by the townships, five or six from each, could muster at his bidding to pursue the Hussites in Bohemia. One year was thus idly spent; albeit the Bohemian rebels meanwhile could every day use their weapons, and instead of waiting to be attacked marched forward to attack. Certain troops of the heretics had already crossed the borders, and our good town had to strengthen its walls and dig its moat deeper to make ready for storm and siege. Or ever the Diet had met, many hands had already been at work on these buildings; and in these days every man soul in Nuremberg, from the boys even to the grey-haired men, wielded the spade or the trowel. Every serving-man in every household, whether artisan or patrician—and ours with the rest—was bound to toil at digging, and our fine young masters found themselves compelled to work in sun or rain, or to order the others; and it hurt them no more than it did the Magister, whose feebleness and clumsiness did the works less benefit than the labor did to his frail body.

Wheresoever three men might be seen in talk, for sure it was of state-matters, and mostly of the Hussites. At first it would be of the King's message of peace; of the resistance made by the Elector Palatine, Ludwig, in the matter of receiving the ecclesiastical Elector of Mainz as Vicar-general of the Empire; of the same reverend Elector's loss of dignity at Boppard, and of the delay and mischief that must follow. Then it was noised abroad that the Margrave Frederick of Meissen, who now held the lands of the late departed Elector Albrecht of Saxony in fief from the King, and whose country was a strong bulwark against the Bohemians, was about to put an end to the abomination of heresy. Howbeit, neither he nor Duke Albrecht of Austria did aught to any good end against the foe; and matters went ill enough in all the Empire.

The Electors assembled at Bingen made great complaints of the King tarrying so far away, and with reason; and when he presently bid them to a Diet at Vienna they would not obey. The message of peace was laughed to scorn; and how much blood was shed to feed the soil of the realm in many and many a fight!

And what fate befell the army whereon so great hopes had been set? The courage and skill of the leader were all in vain; the vast multitude of which he was captain was made up of over many parts, all unlike, and each with its own chief; and the fury of the heretics scattered them abroad. Likewise among our peaceful citizens there was no small complaining, and with good cause, that a King should rule the Empire whose Realm of Hungary, with the perils that beset it from the Ottoman Turks, the Bohemians, and other foes, so filled his thoughts that he had neither time, nor mind, nor money to bestow due care on his German States. His treasury was ever empty; and what sums had the luckless war with Venice alone swallowed up! He had not even found the money needful to go to Rome to be crowned Emperor. He had failed to bring the contentious Princes of the Empire under one hat, so to speak; and whereas his father, Charles IV., had been called the Arch-stepfather of the German Empire, Sigismund, albeit a large-hearted, shrewd, and unresting soul, deserved a scarce better name, inasmuch as that he, like the former sovereign, when he fell heir to his Bohemian fatherland, knew not how to deal even with that as a true father should.

Not a week passed after Herdegen's departing but a letter by his own hand came to Ann, and all full of faithful love. I, likewise, had, not so long since, had such letters from another, and so it fell that these, which brought great joy to Ann, did but make my sore heart ache the more. And when I would rise from table silent and with drooping head, the Magister would full often beg leave to follow me to my chamber, and comfort me after his own guise. In all good faith would he lay books before my eyes, and strive to beguile me to take pleasure in them as the best remedy against heaviness of soul. The lives of the mighty heathen, as his Plutarch painted them, would, he said, raise even a weak soul to their greatness and the Consolatio Philosophiae of Boetius would of a surety refresh my stricken heart. Howbeit, one single well-spent hour in life, or one toilsome deed fruitful for good, hath at all times brought me better comfort than a whole pile of pig-skin-covered tomes. Yet have certain verses of the Scripture, or some wise and verily right noble maxim from the writings of the Greeks or Latins dropped on my soul now and again as it were a grain of good seed.

Sad to tell, those first letters from Herdegen, all dipped in sunshine, were followed by others which could but fill us with fears. The pilgrims had been over-long in getting so far as Venice, by reason that Sir Franz had fallen sick after they had passed the Bienner, and my brother had diligently and faithfully tended him. Thus it came to pass that another child of Nuremberg, albeit setting forth after them, passed them by; and this was Ursula Tetzel, whose father deemed it well to send her forth from the city, where, of a truth, the ground had waxed too hot for her, inasmuch as she had given cause for two bloody frays; and Cousin Maud, to be sure, had not kept silence as to her unbridled demeanor in our house.

Now Mistress Mendel, her aunt, had many years ago gone to the city of St. Mark, and albeit it was there against the laws for a noble to marry with a stranger maiden, she had long since by leave of the Republic, become the wife of Filippo Polani, with whom she was still living in much ease and honor. In Augsberg, in Ulm, and in Frankfort, there were many noble families of the Tetzels' kith and kin, yet she had chosen to go to this aunt in Venice; and doubtless the expectation of meeting Herdegen there, whether in love or hate, had had its weight with her.

Thus it came to pass that she found him at Brixen, where he tarried with the sick knight; and he wrote that, as it fell, he had had more to do with her and her father than he had cared for, and that in a strange place many matters were lightly smoothed over, whereas at home walls and moats would have parted them; nay, that in Italy the Nuremberger would even call a man of Cologne his countryman.

For my part, I could in no wise conceive how those two should ever more speak a kind word to each other, and this meeting in truth pleased me ill. Howbeit, his next letter gave us better cheer. He had then seen Kunz, meeting him right joyfully, and was lodged in the Fondaco, the German Merchants' Hall, where likewise Kunz had his own chamber.

Herdegen's next letter from Venice brought us the ill tidings that the plague had broken out, and that he could find no fellowship to travel with him, by reason that, so long as the sickness raged in Venice, her vessels would not be suffered to cast anchor in any seaport of the Levant. And a great fear came over me, for our dear father had fallen a prey to that evil.

In his third or fourth letter our pilgrim told us, with somewhat of scorn, that the Marchesa Zorzi, who had in fact removed thither from Padua, and had made friends with Ursula in the house of Filippo Polani, had bidden him to wait on her, by one of her pages; yet might he be proud—he said—of the high-handed and steadfast refusal he had returned, once for all. In truth I was moved to deeper fears by what both my brothers wrote of the black barges, loaded to the gunwale with naked corpses, which stole along the canals in the silent night, to cast forth their dreadful freight in the grave yards on the shore, or into the open sea. The plague was raging nigh to the Fondaco, and my two brothers were living in the midst of the dead; nay, and Ann knew that Ursula would not depart from her lover, although the Palazzo Polani, where she had found lodging, lay hard by the Fondaco.

Yet, hard as as it is to conceive of it, never had the music sounded with noisier delights in the dancing-halls of Venice, nor had the money been more lightly tossed from hand-to-hand over the gaming-tables, nor, at any time, had there been hotter love-making. It must be that each one was minded to enjoy, in the short space of life that might yet be his, all the delights of long years.—And foremost of these was the Marchesa Bianca Zorzi.

As for Herdegen, not long did he brook the narrow chambers of the Fondaco-house; driven forth by impatience and heart-sickness, from morning till night he was in his boat, or on the grand Piazza, or on the watery highways; and inasmuch as he ever fluttered to where ladies of rank and beauty were to be found, as a moth flies to the light, that evil woman was ever in his path, day after day, and whensoever her hosts would suffer it, Ursula would be with her. Nay, and the German maiden, who had learned better things of the Carthusian sisters, was not ashamed to aid and abet that sinful Italian woman. Thus my brother was in great peril lest Ursula's prophecy should be fulfilled by his own fault. Indeed he already had his foot in the springe, inasmuch as that he could not say nay to the Marchesa's bidding that he would go to her house on her name-day. It was a higher power that came betwixt them, vouchsafing him merciful but grievous repentance; the plague, Death's unwearied executioner, snatched the fair, but sinful lady, from among the living. Ursula lamented over her as though it were her own sister that had died; and it seemed that the Marchesa was fain to keep up the bond that had held them together even beyond the grave, for it was at her funeral that the son of one of the oldest and noblest families of the Republic first saw Mistress Ursula Tetzel, and was fired with love for the maiden. She had many a time been seen abroad with the Marchesa, or with the Polanis, and the young gentlemen of the Signoria, the painters, and the poets, had marked her well; the natural golden hue of her hair was an amazement and a delight to the Italians; indeed many a black-haired lady and common hussy would sit on her roof vainly striving to take the color out of her own locks. It was the same with her velvet skin, which even at

Nuremberg had many a time brought to men's minds the maid in the tale of "Snow-white and Rose-red."

Thus it fell that Anselmo Guistiniani had heard of her during the lifetime of his cousin the Marchesa Zorzi, while he was absent from Venice on state matters. And when he beheld her with his own eyes among the mourners, there was an end to his peace of heart; he forthwith set himself to win her for his own. Howbeit Ursula met her noble suitor with icy coldness, and when he and Herdegen came together at the Palazzo Polani, where she was lodging, she made as though she saw my lord not at all, and had no eyes nor ears save for my brother; till it was more than Guistinani would bear, and he abruptly departed. Herdegen's letter, which told us all these things, was full of kindly pity for the fair and hapless damsel who had demeaned herself so basely towards him, by reason that her fiery love had turned her brain, and that she still was pining for him to whom she had ever been faithful from her childhood up. She had freely confessed as much even under the very eyes of so lordly a suitor as Anselmo Giustiniani; and albeit Ann might be sure of his constancy, even in despite of Ursula, yet would he not deny that he could forgive Ursula much in that she had loved much, as the Scripture saith. Every shadow of danger for him was gone and overpast; he had already bid Ursula farewell, and was to ride forth next morning to Genoa, leaving the plague-stricken city behind him, and would take ship there. It was well indeed that he should be departing, inasmuch as yestereve, when he bid Ursula good night, Giustiniani had given him to understand that he, Herdegen, was in his way; at home he would have shown his teeth, and with good right, to any man who had dared to speak to him, but in Venice every man who lodged in the Fondaco was forbid the use of weapons, and he had heard tell of Anselmo Giustiniani that he, unlike the rest of his noble race, who were benevolent men and patrons of learning, albeit he was a prudent statesman and serviceable to the city, was a stern and violent man. This much in truth a man might read in his gloomy black eyes; and many a stranger, for all he were noble and a Knight, who had fallen out with a Venetian Signor of his degree had vanished forever, none knew whither.

As we read these words the blood faded from Ann's cheek; but I set my teeth, for I may confess that Herdegen's ways and words roused my wrath. In Ann's presence I could, to be sure, hide my ire; but when I was alone I struck my right fist into my left hand and asked of myself whether a man or a woman were the vainer creature? For what was it that still drew my brother to that maid who had ever pursued him and the object of his love with cruel hate—so strongly, indeed, that he would have been ready to cherish and comfort her—but joy at finding himself—a mere townbred .Junker—preferred above that grand nobleman? For my part, I plainly saw that Ursula was playing the same game again as she had carried on here with Herdegen and the Brandenburger. She spoke the man she hated fair before the jealous Marchese, only to rouse that potent noble's fury against my brother.

After all this my heart rejoiced when we received Herdegen's first letter written from Genoa, nay, on board of the galleon which was to carry him, Sir Franz and Eppelein to Cyprus. In this he made known that he had departed from Venice without let or hindrance, and he bid us farewell with such good cheer, and love, and hope, that Ann and I forgot and forgave with all our hearts everything that had made us wroth. This last greeting came as a fragrant love-posy, and it helped us to think of Herdegen's long pilgrimage as he himself did—as of a ride forth to the Forest. From this letter we were likewise aware that he had never known what peril he had escaped; for ere long I learned from Kunz that paid assassins had fallen on him the very next evening after Herdegen's departing, in the crooked street called of Saint Chrysostom, at the back part of the German Merchants' House; yea, and they would easily have overpowered him but that certain great strong Tyrolese bale-packers of the Fondaco came to his succor or ever it was too late. And it was right certain that these murderers were in Giustiniani's pay, and in the dusk had taken Kunz for his brother, who was some what like him. The younger had come off unharmed by the special mercy of the Saints, but it might well have befallen that, as of old in his schooldays, he should have borne the penalty for Herdegen's misdoings. And whereas I mind me here of the many ways in which my eldest brother prospered and got the best of it over the younger, and of other like cases, meseems it is the lot of certain few to suffer others, not their betters, to stand in their sun, and eat the fruit that has ripened on their trees.

Howbeit, Herdegen had by good hap escaped a sharp fray; and when Ann and I, kneeling side by side in Saint Laurence's church, had offered up a thanksgiving from the bottom of our hearts, meseemed we were as some Captain who sings Te Deum after a victory.

Yet, as ofttimes in the month of May, when for a while the sun bath shone with summer heat and glory, there comes a gloomy time with dark days and sharp frost at nights, so did we deem the long space which followed after that glad and pious church-going. Days grew to weeks and weeks to months and we had no tidings, no word from our pilgrims, for good or for evil.

Verily it was well-nigh a comfort and a help when those who were on the look-out, Kunz and other friends, gave it as certain tidings that the galleon which was carrying Herdegen to Cyprus, and which belonged to the Lomellini of Genoa, had been lost at sea. Saracen pirates, so it was told, had seized the ship; but further tidings were not to be got, as to what had befallen the crew and the travellers, albeit Kunz forthwith betook himself to Genoa and the Futterers, who had a house and trade of their own there, did all they might to find their traces. The eldest and the finest link of the Schopper chain had, we deemed, been snatched away, peradventure for ever; the death of her lover had made life henceforth bitter to the third and least, and only the middle one, Kunz, remained unhurt and still such as it might have gladdened his parents' hearts to behold him. Thus I deemed, at least, when after long parting I set eyes on him once more, a goodly man, tall and of a fair countenance. All that had ever been good and worthy in him had waxed and sped well at Venice, that high school of the merchant class; but where was the smiling mirthfulness which had marked him as a youth? The same earnest calm shone in his wise and gentle gaze, and rang in the deep voice he had now gotten.

My grand-uncle had esteemed him but lightly, so long as Herdegen was his delight; but whereas Kunz had done good service at Venice and the master of the Im Hoff house there was dead, and our guardian himself, on whom a grievous sickness had fallen, gave himself up day and night to meet his end, he had, little by little, given over the whole business of the trade to his young nephew; thus it came to pass that Kunz, when he was but just twenty, was called upon to govern matters such as are commonly trusted only to a man of ripe years. But his power and wisdom grew with the weight of his burthens. Whether it were at Nuremberg or at Venice, he was ever early to rise and ready, if need should be, to give up his night's rest, sitting over his desk or travelling at great speed; and he seemed to have no eyes nor ears for the pleasures of youth. Or ever he was four and twenty I found the first white hair in his brown locks. Many there were who deemed that the uncommon graveness of his manners came of the weight of care which had been laid on him so young, and verily not without reason; yet my sister's heart was aware of another cause. When I chanced to see his eye rest on Ann, I knew enough; and it was a certainty that I had not erred in my thought, when old Dame Pernhart one day in his presence spoke of Ann as her poor, dear little widow, and the blood mounted to his brow.

I would fain have spoken a word of warning to Ann when she would thank him with heartfelt and sisterly love for all the pains he had been at, with steadfast patience, to find any token of our lost brother. And how fair was the forlorn bride in these days of waiting and of weary unsatisfied longing!

Poor Kunz! Doubtless he loved her; and yet he neither by word nor deed gave her cause to guess his heart's desire. When, at about this time, old Hans Tucher died, one of the worthiest and wisest heads of the town and the council, Kunz gave Ann for her name-day a prayer-book with the old man's motto, which he had written in it for Kunz's confirmation, which was as follows:

"God ruleth all things for the best
And sends a happy end at last."

And Ann took the gift right gladly; and more than once when, after some disappointment, my spirit sank, she would point to the promise "And sends a happy end at last."

Whereupon I would look up at her, abashed and put to shame; for it is one thing not to despair, and another to trust with steadfast confidence on a happy outcome. She, in truth, could do this; and when I beheld her day by day at her laborious tasks, bravely and cheerfully fulfilling the hard and bitter exercises which her father-confessor enjoined, to the end that she might win the favor of the Saints for her lover, I weened that the Apostle spake the truth when he said that love hopeth all things and believeth all things.

Notwithstanding it was not easy to her, nor to us, to hold fast our confidence; now and again some trace of the lost man would come to light which, so soon as Kunz followed it up, vanished in mist like a jack-o' lantern. And often as he failed he would not be overweary; and once, when he was staying at Nuremberg and tidings came from Venice that a certain German who might be Herdegen was dwelling a slave at Joppa, he made ready to set forth for that place to ransom him forthwith. My grand-uncle, who in the face of death was eagerly striving to win the grace of Heaven by good works, suffered him to depart, and at my entreaty he took my squire Akusch with him, inasmuch as he could still speak Arabic, which was his mother-tongue. Likewise I besought Kunz to make it his care to restore the lad to his people, if it should befall that he might find them, albeit hitherto we had made enquiry for them in vain. This he promised me to do; yet, often as that good youth had longed to see his native land once more, and much as he had talked in praise of its hot sun, in our cold winter seasons, it went hard with the good lad to depart from us; and when he took leave of me he could not cease from assuring me that in his own land he would do all that in him lay to find the brother of his beloved mistress.

Thus they fared forth to the Levant; and this once again we were doomed to vain hopes. Kunz found not him he sought, but a wild Swiss soldier who had fallen into the hands of the Saracens. Him he ransomed, as being a Christian man, for a small sum of money; and as for Akusch he left him at Joppa, whereas his folk were Egyptians and he deemed he had found some track of them there.

Kunz did not go thither with him, inasmuch as in Alexandria all had been done that might be done to discover and ransom a Frankish captive. Nor was Akusch idle there, and moreover fate had brought another child of Nuremberg to that place.

Ursula had become the wife of the Marchese Anselmo Giustiniani, by special favor of the great council, and had come with him to Egypt, whither he was sent by the Republic as Consul. There she now dwelt with her noble lord, and in many letters to my granduncle she warmly declared to him that, so far as in her lay, all should be done to discover where the lover of her youth might be. Her husband was the most powerful Frank in all the Sultan's dominions, and it was a joy to her to see with what diligence he made search for the lost youth. Herdegen, indeed, had ill-repaid her childish love, yet she knew of no nobler revenge than to lay him under the debt of thanks to her and her husband for release and ransom. These words doubtless came from the bottom of her heart; she were no true woman if she could not forgive a man in misfortune for the sins of a happier time. And above all she was ever of a rash and lawless mind, and truthful even to the scorn of modesty and good manners, rather than crafty and smooth of tongue.

Yet she likewise failed to find the vanished wanderer, and the weeks and months grew to be years while we waited in vain. It was on the twenty-second day of March in the second twelve month after Herdegen's departing that the treasures of the realm, and among them a nail from the Cross and the point of the spear wherewith they pierced the Lord's side, were to be brought into the town in a solemn procession, and I, with many others, rode forth to meet it. They were brought hither from Blindenberg on the Danube, and the Emperor sent them in token of his grace, that we might hold them in safe keeping within our strong walls. They had been brought thus far right privily, under the feint that the waggon wherein they were carried bore wine vats, and a great throng gathered with shouts of joy to hail these precious things. Prisoners were set free in honor of their coming; and for my own part I mind the day full well, by reason that I put off my black mourning weed and went forth in a colored holiday garb for the first time in a long while.

If I had, in truth, been able by good courage to shake off in due time the oppressing weight of my grief, I owed it in no small measure to the forest-whither we went forth, now as heretofore, to sojourn in the spring and autumn seasons—and to its magic healing. How many a time have I rested under its well-known trees and silently looked back on the past. And, when I mind me of those days, I often ask myself whether the real glad times themselves or those hours of calmer joy in remembrance were indeed the better.

As I sat in the woods, thinking and dreaming, there was plenty for the eye to see and the ear to hear. The clouds flew across in silence, and the soft green at my feet, with all that grew on tree and bush, in the grass, and by the brink of the pool, made up a peaceful world, innocently fair and full of precious charm. Here there was nought to remind me of the stir of mankind, with its haste and noise and fighting and craving, and that was a delight; nor did the woodland sounds.—The song of birds, the hum of chafers and bees, the whisper of leaves, and all the rush and rustle of the forest were its mother-tongue.

Yet, not so! There was in truth one human soul of whom I was ever minded while thinking and dreaming in these woods through whom I had first known the joy of loving, and that was the youth whose home was here, for whose return my aunt longed day and night, whose favorite songs I was ever bidden to sing to my uncle when he would take the oars in his strong old hands of an evening, and row us on the pool-he who peradventure had long since followed my lover, and was dead in some far-off land.

Ann, who was ever diligent, took less pleasure in idle dreaming; she would ever carry a book or some broidery in her hand. Or she would abide alone with my aunt; and whereas my aunt now held her to be her fellow in sorrow, and might talk with her of the woe of thinking of the dearest on earth as far away and half lost, they grew closer to each other, and there was bitter grief when our duty took us back to the town once more. At home likewise Herdegen was ever in our minds, nevertheless the sunshine was as bright and the children's faces as dear as heretofore, and we could go about the tasks of the hour with fresh spirit.

If now and again grief cast a darker shade over Ann, still the star of Hope shone with more comfort for her than for me and Cousin Maud; and it was but seldom that you might mark that she had any sorrow. Truly there were many matters besides her every-day duties, and her errands within and without the house to beguile her of her fears for her lost lover. First of all there came her stepfather's brother, his Eminence Cardinal Bernhardi—for to this dignity had his Holiness raised the Bishop—from Rome to Nuremberg, where he lodged in the house of his fathers. Now this high prelate was such a man as I never met the like of, and his goodly face, beardless indeed, but of a manly brown, with its piercing, great eyes, I weened was as a magic book, having the power to compel others, even against their will, to put forth all that was in them of grace and good gifts. Yet was he not grave nor gloomy, but of a happy cheer, and ready to have his jest with us maidens; only in his jests there would ever be a covert intent to arouse thought, and whensoever I quitted his company I deemed I had profited somewhat in my soul.

He likewise vouchsafed the honor of knowing him to the Magister; and whereas he brought tidings of certain Greek Manuscripts which had been newly brought into Italy, Master Peter came home as one drunk with wine, and could not forbear from boasting how he had been honored by having speech with such a pearl among Humanists.

My lord Cardinal was right well pleased to see his home once more; but what he loved best in it was Ann. Nay, if it had lain with him, he would have carried her to Rome with him. But for all that she was fain to look up to such a man with deep respect, and wait lovingly on his behests, yet would she not draw back from the duty she had taken upon her to care for her brothers and sisters, and chiefly for the deaf and dumb boy. And she deemed likewise that she was as a watchman at his post; it was at Nuremberg that all was planned for seeking Herdegen, and hither must the first tidings come that could be had of him. The old grand dame also was more than ever bound up in her, and so soon as my lord Cardinal was aware that it would greatly grieve his old mother to lose her he renounced his desire.

As for me, I was dwelling in a right happy life with Cousin Maud; never had I been nearer to her heart. So long as she conceived that her comforting could little remedy my woe, she had left me to myself; and as soon as I was fain to use my hands again, and sing a snatch as I went up and down the house, meseemed her old love bloomed forth with double strength. Meseemed I could but show her my thankfulness, and my ear and heart were at all times open when she was moved to talk of her best-beloved Herdegen, and reveal to me all the wondrous adventures he had gone through in her imagination. And this befell most evenings, from the hour when we unclothed till long after we had gone to rest; and I was fain to keep my eyes open while, for the twentieth time, she would expound to me her far-fetched visions: that the Mamelukes of Egypt, who were all slaves and whose Sultan was chosen from among themselves, had of a surety set Herdegen on the throne, seeing him to be the goodliest and noblest of them all. And perchance he would not have refused this honor if he might thereby turn them from their heathenness and make of them good Christians. Nay, nor was it hard for her to fancy Ann arrayed in silk and gems as a Sultana. And then, when I fell asleep in listening to these fancies, which she loved to paint in every detail, behold my dreams would be of Turks and heathen; and of bloody battles by land and sea.

No man may tell his dreams fasting; but as soon as I had eaten my first mouthful she would bid me tell her all, to the veriest trifle, and would solemnly seek the interpretation of every vision.

CHAPTER VIII

My lord Cardinal had departed from Nuremberg some long while, by reason that he was charged by his holiness the Pope with a mission which took him through Cologne and Flanders to England. Inasmuch as he was not suffered to have Ann herself in his company, he conceived the wish to possess her likeness in a picture; and he sent hither to that end a master of good fame, of the guild of painters in Venice. We owed this good limner thanks for many a pleasant hour. Sir Giacomo Bellini was a youth of right merry wit, knowing many Italian ditties, and who made good pastime for us while we sat before him; for I likewise must be limned, inasmuch as Cousin Maud would have it so, and the painter's eye was greatly pleased by my yellow hair.

Whereas he could speak never a word of German, it was our part to talk with him in Italian, and this exercise to me came not amiss. Also I could scarce have had a better master to teach me than Giacomo Bellini, who set himself forthwith to win my heart and turn my head; nay, and he might have done so, but that he confessed from the first that he had a fair young wife in Venice, albeit he was already craving for some new love.

Thus through him again I learned how light a touch is needed to overthrow a man's true faith; and when I minded me of Herdegen and Ann, and of this Giacomo—who was nevertheless a goodly and well-graced man—and his young wife, meseemed that the woman who might win the love of a highly-gifted soul must ofttimes pay for that great joy with much heaviness and heartache.

Howbeit, I mind me in right true love of the mirthful spirit and manifold sportiveness which marked our fellowship with the Italian limner; and after that I had once given him plainly and strongly to understand that the heart of a Nuremberg damsel was no light thing or plaything, and her very lips a sanctuary which her husband should one day find pure, all went well betwixt us.

The picture of Ann, the first he painted, showed her as Saint Cecelia hearkening to music which sounds from Heaven in her ears. Two sweet angel babes floated on thin clouds above her head, singing hymns to a mandoline and viol. Thus had my lord Cardinal commanded, and the work was so excellent that, if the Saint herself vouchsafed to look down on it out of Heaven, of a certainty it was pleasing in her eyes.

As to mine own presentment; at first I weened that I would be limned in my peach-colored brocade gown with silver dolphins thereon, by reason that I had worn that weed in the early morn after the dance, when Hans spoke his last loving farewell at the door of our house. But whereas one cold day I went into Master Giacomo's work-chamber in a red hood and a green cloak bordered with sable fur, he would thenceforth paint me in no other guise. At first he was fain to present me as going forth to church; then he deemed that he might not show forth my very look and seeming if I were limned with downcast head and eyes. Therefor he gave me the falcon on my hand which had erewhile been my lover's gift. My eyes were set on the distance as though I watched for a heron; thus I seemed in truth like one hunting—"chaste Diana," quoth the painter, minding him of the reproofs I had given him so often. But it would be a hard task to tell of all the ways whereby the painter would provoke me to reprove him. When the likeness was no more than half done, he painted his own merry face to the falcon on my wrist gazing up at me with silly languor. Thereupon, when he presently quitted us, I took the red chalk and wrote his wife's name on a clear place in front of the face and beneath it the image of a birch rod; and on the morrow he brought with him a right pleasant Sonnet, which I scarce had pardoned had he not offered it so humbly and read it in so sweet a voice. And, being plainly interpreted, it was as follows:

"Upon Olympus, where the gods do dwell
Who with almighty will rule earth and heaven,
Lo! I behold the chiefest of them all
Jove, on his throne with Juno at his side.
A noble wedded pair. In all the world
The eye may vainly seek nor find their like.
The nations to his sanctuary throng,
And kings, struck dumb, cast down their golden crowns.

"Yet even these are not for ever one.
The god flies from the goddess.—And a swan
Does devoir now, the slave of Leda's charms.

"Thus I behold the beams of thy bright eye,
And bid my home farewell,—I, hapless wight,
Fly like the god, fair maid, to worship thee!"

Albeit I suffered him to recite these lines to the end I turned from him with a countenance of great wrath, and tore the paper whereon they were writ in two halves which I flung behind the stove. Nor did I put away my angry and offended mien until he had right humbly besought my forgiveness. Yet when I had granted it, and he presently quitted the chamber, I did, I confess, gather up the torn paper and bestow it in my girdle-poke. Nay, meseems that I had of intent rent it only in twain, to the end that I might the better join it again. Thus to this day it lieth in my chest, with other relics of the past; yet I verily believe that another Sonnet, which Sir Giacomo found on the morrow, laid on his easel, was not so treasured by him. It was thus:

> "There was one Hans, and he was fain to try,
> Like to Olympian Jove, the magic arts
> Of witchcraft upon some well-favored maid.
> Bold the adventure, but the prize how sweet!
> 'Farewell, good wife,' quoth he, 'Or e'er the dawn
> Hath broke I must be forward on my way.
> Like Jupiter I will be blessed and bless
> With love; and in the image of a swan.'
>
> "The magic spell hath changed him. With a wreath
> About his head he deems he lacketh nought
> Of what may best beguile a maiden's soul.
>
> "Thus to fair Leda flies the hapless wight.—
> With boisterous mirth the dame beholds the bird.
> 'A right fine goose! Thou'lt make a goodly roast.'"

Howbeit Giacomo would not leave this verse without reply; and to this day, if you look close into the picture, you may see a goose's head deep in shade among the shrubs in the back part of it, but clearly to be discerned.

Notwithstanding many such little quarrels we liked each other well, and I may here note that when, in the following year, which was the year of our Lord one thousand four hundred and twenty-six, a little son was born to him, since grown to be a right famous painter, known as Giambellini— which is to say Giovanni, or Hans, Bellini, I, Margery Schopper, stood his sponsor at the font. Yea and I was ever a true godsib to him, and that painter might indeed thank my kith and kin when he was charged with a certain office in the Fondaco in Venice, which is worth some hundreds of ducats yearly to him, to this day.

Thus were the portraits ended, and when I behold my own looking from the wide frame with so mirthful and yet so longing a gaze, meseems that Giacomo must have read the book of my soul and have known right well how to present that he saw therein; at that time in truth I was a happy young creature, and the aching and longing which would now and again come over me, in part for him who was gone, and in part I wist not for what, were but the shadow which must ever fall where there is light. And verily I had good cause to be thankful and of good cheer; I was in health as sound as a trout in the brook, and had good chances for making the most of those humble gifts and powers wherewith I was blessed.

As to Herdegen, it was no small comfort to us to learn that my lord Cardinal Bernhardi had taken that matter in hand, and had bidden all the priests and friars in the Levant to make enquiry for tidings of him.

The good prelate was to be nine months journeying abroad, and whereas five months were now spent we were rejoicing in hope of his homecoming; but there was one in Nuremberg who looked for it even more eagerly than we did, and that was my grand-uncle Im Iloff. The old knight had, as I have said, done us thank-worthy service as our guardian; yet had he never been dear to me, and I could not think of him but with silent wrath. Howbeit he was now in so sad and cruel a plight that a heart of stone must have melted to behold him. Thus pity led me to him, although it was a penance to stay in his presence. The old Baron,—for of this title likewise he could boast, since he had poured a great sum into the Emperor's treasury,—this old man, who of yore had but feigned a false and evil show of repentance— as that he would on certain holy days wash the feet of beggar folk who had first been cleansed with care, now in sickness and the near terror of death was in terrible earnest, and of honest intent would fain open the gates of Heaven by pious exercises. He had to be sure at the bidding of Master Ulsenius the leech, exchanged the coffin wherein he had been wont to sleep for a common bedstead of wood; yet in this even he might get no rest, and was fain to pass his sleepless nights in his easy chair, resting his aching feet in a cradle which, with his wonted vain-glory, he caused to be made of the shape and color of a pearl shell. But his nights in the coffin, and mockery of death, turned against him; he had ever been pale, and now he wore the very face of a corpse. The blood seemed frozen in his veins, and he was at all times so cold that the great stove and the wide hearth facing him were fed with mighty logs day and night.

In this fearful heat the sweat stood on my brow so soon as I crossed the threshold, and if I tarried in the chamber I soon lacked breath. The sick man's speech was scarce to be heard, and as to all that Master Ulsenius told us of the seat of his ill, and of how it was gnawing him to death I would fain be silent. Instead of that Lenten mockery of the foot washing he now would do the hardest penance, and there was scarce a saint in the Calendar to whom he had not offered gifts or ever he died.

A Dominican friar was ever in his chamber, telling the rosary for him and doing him other ghostly service, especially in the night season, when he was haunted by terrible restlessness. Nothing eased him as a remedy against this so well as the presence of a woman to his mind. But of all those to whom, on many a Christmas eve, he had made noble gifts, few came a second time after they had once been in that furnace; or, if they did, it would be no more than to come and depart forthwith. Cousin Maud could endure to stay longest with him; albeit afterwards she would need many a glass of strong waters to strengthen her heart.

As for me, each time when I came home from my grand-uncle's with pale cheeks she would forbid me ever to cross his threshold more: but when his bidding was brought me she likewise was moved to compassion, and suffered me to obey.

Nevertheless, if I had not been more than common strong, thank the Saints, long sitting with the sick man would of a certainty have done me a mischief, for body and soul had much to endure. Meseemed that pain had loosened the tongue of that hitherto wordless old man, and whereas he had ever held his head high above all men, he would now abase himself before the humblest. He would stay any man or woman who would tarry, to tell of all his sufferings, and of what he endured in mind and body. His confessor had indeed forbidden him to complain of the evil wherewith Heaven had punished him, but none could hinder him from bewailing the evil he had committed in his sinfulness and vanity. And his self-accusings were so manifold and fearful, that I was fain to believe his declaration that all he had ever thought or done that was good was, as it were, buried; and that nought but the ill he had suffered and committed was left and still had power over him. The death-stroke he had dealt all unwittingly, in heedless passion, rose before his soul day and night as an accursed and bloody deed; and every moment embittered by his wife's unfaith, even to the last hour when, on her death-bed, she cursed him, he lived through again, night after night. Whereupon he would clasp his thin hands, through which you might see the light, over his tear-stained face and would not be still or of better cheer till I could no longer hide my own great grief for him.

Howbeit, when I had heard the same tale again and again it ceased from touching me so deeply; so that at last, instead of such deep compassion, it moved me only to dull gloom and, I will confess, to unspeakable weariness. The tears came not to my eyes, and the only use for my kerchief was to hide my yawning and vinaigrette. Thus it fell that the old penitent took no pleasure in my company, and at last weeks might pass while he bid me not to his presence.

Now, when the pictures were ended, whereas he heard that they were right good likenesses, and moreover was told that my lord Cardinal was minded to come home within no long space, he fell into a strange tumult and desired to behold those pictures both of me and of Ann. At this I marvelled not: he had long since learned to think of Councillor Pernbart's step-daughter in all kindness; nay, he had desired me to beg her to forgive a dying old man. We were well-disposed to do his will, and the Pernharts no less; on a certain Wednesday the pictures were carried to his house, and on the morrow, being Thursday, I would go and know whether he were content. And behold my likeness was set in a corner where he scarce could see it; but that of Ann was face to face with him and, as I entered the chamber, his eyes were fixed thereon as though ravished by the vision of a Saint from Heaven. And he was so lost in thought that he looked not away till the Dominican Brother spoke to him.

Thereupon he hastily greeted me, and went on to ask of me whether I duly minded that he had been a faithful and thankworthy guardian. And when I answered yes he whispered to me, with a side-look at the friar, that of a surety my lord Cardinal must hold Ann full dear, if he would bid so famous a master to Nuremberg that he might possess her image. Now inasmuch as I wist not yet to what end he sought to beguile me by these questions, I confirmed his words with all prudence; and then he glanced again at the monk, and whispered hastily in my ear, and so low that I scarce might hear him:

"That fellow is privily drinking up all my old Cyprus wine and Malvoisie. And the other priests, the Plebian here—do you know their worldly and base souls? They take up no cross, neither mortify the flesh by holy fasting, but cherish and feed it as the lost heathen do. Are they holy men following in the footsteps of the Crucified Lord? All that brings them to me is a care for my oblations and gifts. I know them, I know them all, the whole lot of them here in Nuremberg. As the city is, so are the pastors thereof! Which of them all mortifies himself? Is there any high court held here? To win the blessing of a truly lordly prelate, a man must journey to Bamberg or to Wurzburg. Of what avail with the Blessed Virgin and the Saints are such as these ruddy friars? Fleischmann, Hellfeld, nay the Dominican prior himself—what are they? Why, at the Diet they walked after the Bishop of Chiemsee and Eichstadt. In the matters of the city—its rights, alliances, and dealings—they had indeed a hand; there is nought so dear to them—in especial to Fleischmann—as politics, and they are overjoyed if they may but be sent on some embassy. Aye, and they have done me some service, as a merchant trader, whensoever I have desired the safe conduct of princes and knights; but as to charging them with the safe conduct of my soul, the weal or woe of my immortal spirit!—No, no, never! Aye, Margery, for I have been a great sinner. Greater power and more mighty mediation are needed to save and deliver me, and behold, my Margery, meseems—hear me Margery—meseems a special ruling of Heaven hath sent.... When is it that his Eminence Cardinal Bernhardi will return from England?"

Hereupon I saw plainly what was in the wind. I answered him that his Eminence purposed to return hither in three or four months' time; he sighed deeply: "Not for so long—three months, do you say?"

"Or longer," quoth I, hastily; but he, forgetting the Friar, cried out as though he knew better than I "No, no, in three months. So you said."

Then he spoke low again, and went on in a confident tone: "So long as that I can hold out, by the help of the Saints, if I.... Yea, for I have enough left to make some great endowment. My possessions, Margery, the estate which is mine own—No man can guess what a well-governed trading-house may earn in half a century.—Yes, I tell you, Margery, I can hold out and wait. Two, or at most three months; they will soon slip away. The older we grow and the duller is life, the swifter do the days fly."

And verily I had not the heart to tell him that he might have to take much longer patience, and, whereas I noted how hard he found it to speak out that which weighed on his mind, I gave him such help as I might; and then he freely confessed that what he most desired on earth was to receive absolution and the Viaticum from the hands of the Cardinal. Meseemed he believed that his Eminence's prayers would serve him better in Heaven than those of our simple priests, who had not even gained a bishop's cope; just as the good word of a Prince Elector gains the Emperor's ear sooner than the petition of a town councillor. Likewise it soothed his pride, doubtless, to think that he might turn his back on this world under the good guidance of a prelate in the purple. Hereupon I promised that his case should be brought to the Cardinal's knowledge by Ann, and then he gave me to understand that it was his desire that Ann should come to see him, inasmuch as that her presentment only had brought him more comfort than the strongest of Master Ulsenius' potions. He could not be happy to die without her forgiveness, and without blessing her by hand and word.

And he pointed to my likeness, and said that, albeit it was right well done, he could bear no more to see it; that it looked forth so full of health and hope, that to him it seemed as though it mocked his misery, and he straitly desired me to send Ann to him forthwith; the Saints would grant her a special grace for every hour she delayed not her coming.

Thereupon I departed; Ann was ready to do the dying man's bidding, and when I presently went with her into his presence he gazed on her as he had on her portrait, as it were bewitched by her person and manners; and ever after, if she were absent for more than a day or two, he bid her come to him, with prayers and entreaties. And he found means to touch her heart as he had mine; yet, whereas I, ere long, wearied of his complaining, Ann's compassion failed not; instead of yawning and being helpless to comfort him, she with great skill would turn his thoughts from himself and his sufferings.

Then they would often talk of Herdegen, and of how to come upon some trace of him, and whereas the old man had in former days left such matters to other folks, he now showed a right wise and keen experience in counselling the right ways and means. Hitherto he had trusted to Ursula's good words and commended us to the same confidence; now, however, he remembered on a sudden how ill-disposed she had ever been to my lost brother, and whereas it was the season of the year when the trading fleet should set sail from Venice for Alexandria in the land of Egypt, he sent forth a messenger to Kunz, charging him to take ship himself and go thither to seek his brother. This filled Ann and me likewise with fresh hope and true thankfulness. Yet, in truth, as for my grand-uncle, he owed much to Ann; her mere presence was as dew on his withered heart, and the hope she kept alive in him, that her uncle, my lord Cardinal, would ere long reach home and gladly fulfil his desires, gave him strength and will to live on, and kept the feeble spark of life burning.

CHAPTER IX

The month of October had come; the Forest claimed us once more, and indeed at that season I was needed at the Forest lodge. A pressing bidding had likewise come to Ann; yet, albeit her much sitting in my grand-uncle's hot chamber had been visited on her with many a headache, she had made her attendance on him one of her duties and nought could move her to be unfaithful.

Moreover, it was known to us that by far the greater half of the Venetian galleons had sailed from the Lido between the 8th and 25th of the past month, and were due to be at home again by the middle of October or early in November. A much lesser fleet went forth from Venice late in the year and came to anchor there again, loaded with spices, in the month of March or not later than April. Hence now was the time when we might most surely look for tidings from the Levant, and Ann would not be out of the way in case any such might come to Nuremberg.

I rode forth on Saint Dionysius' day, the 9th day of October, alone with Cousin Maud; other guests were not long in following us and among them my brothers-in-law and the young Loffelholz pair; Elsa Ebner having wed, some months since, with young Jorg Loffelholz.

Uncle Christian would come later and, if she would consent, would bring Ann with him, for he held himself bound to give his "little watchman" some fresh air. Also he was a great friend in the Pernharts' house, and aught more happy and pleasant than his talks with the old Dame can scarce be conceived of.

Never had the well-beloved home in the Forest been more like to a pigeon cote. Every day brought us new guests, many of them from the city; still, none had any tidings yet of the Venice ships or of our Kunz, who should come home with them. And at this my heart quaked for fear, in despite of the hunting-sports, and of many a right merry supper; and Aunt Jacoba was no better. The weeks flew past, the red and yellow leaves began to fall, the scarlet berries of the mountain ash were shrivelled, and the white rime fell of nights on the meadows and moor-land.

One day I had ridden forth with my Uncle Conrad, hawking, and when we came home in the dusk I could add a few birds to the gentlemen's booty. All the guests at that time present were standing in the courtyard talking, many a one lamenting or boasting of the spite or favor of Saint Hubert that day, when the hounds, who were smelling about the game, suddenly uplifted their voices, and the gate-keeper's horn blew a merry blast, as though to announce some right welcome guest.

The housekeeper's face was seen at Aunt Jacoba's window, and so soon as tidings were brought of who it as that came, the dog-keeper's whips hastily silenced the hounds and drove them into the kennel. The serving-men carried off the game, and when the courtyard was presently cleared, behold, a strange procession came in.

First a long wain covered in by a tilt so high I trove that meseemed many a town gate might be over low to let it pass; and it was drawn by four right small little horses, with dark matted coats and bright, wilful eyes. A few hounds of choice breed ran behind it. From within the hangings came a sharp, shrill screaming as were of many gaudy parrots.

In front of this waggon two men rode, unlike in stature and mien, and a loutish fellow led the horses. Now, we all knew this wain right well. Heretofore, in the life-time of old Lorenz Waldstromer, the father of my Uncle Conrad, it had been wont to come hither once or twice a year, and was ever made welcome; if it should happen to come in the month of August it was at that season filled with noble falcons, to be placed on Board ships at Venice, inasmuch as the Sultan of Egypt and his Emirs were so fain to buy them that they would give as much as a hundred and fifty sequins for he finest and best.

Old Jordan Kubbeling of Brunswick, the father of he man who had now come hither, was wont to send the birds to Alexandria by the hand of dealers, to sell them for him there; but his son Seyfried, who was to this day called Young Kubbeling, albeit he was nigh on sixty, would carry his feathered wares thither himself. Verily he was not suffered to sell any other goods in the land, inasmuch as the Republic set strait bounds to the dealings of German traders. If such an one would have aught from the Levant he may get it only through the Merchants' Hall or Fondaco in Venice; and much less is a German suffered to carry his wares, of what kind soever, out of Venice into the East, inasmuch as every German trader is bound to sell by the hand of the syndicate all which his native land can produce or make in Venice itself. And in no other wise may a German traffic in any matters, great or small, with the Venice traders; and all this is done that the Republic may lose nought of the great taxes they set on all things.

As to Seyfried Kubbeling, the great Council, by special grace, and considering that none but he could carry his birds over seas in good condition, had granted to him to go with them to the land of Egypt. For many and many a year had the Kubbelings brought falcons to the Waldstromers, and whensoever my uncle needed such a bird, or if he had to provide one for our lord constable and prince elector the Duke of Bavaria, or any other great temporal or spiritual prince, it was to be had from Seyfried—or Young Kubbeling. To be sure no man better knew where to choose a fine bird, and while he journeyed between Brunswick, Italy, and the Levant, his sons and brothers went as far as to Denmark, and from thence to Iceland in the frozen Seas, where the royal falcon breeds. Yet are there right noble kinds likewise to be found in the Harz mountains, nigh to their native country.

The man who was ever Kubbeling's fellow, going with him to the Levant now, as, erewhile to the far North, was Uhlwurm, who, albeit he had been old Jordan's serving-man, was held by Seyfried as his equal; and whoso would make one his guest must be fain to take the other into the bargain. This was ever gladly done at the Forest-lodge; Uhlwurm was a man of few words, and the hunting-lads and kennel-men held him to be a wise man, who knew more than simply which side his bread was buttered. At any rate he was learned in healing all sick creatures, and in especial falcons, horses, and hounds, by means of whispered spells, the breath of his mouth, potions, and electuaries; and I myself have seen him handle a furious old she-wolf which had been caught in a trap, so that no man dared go nigh her, as though it were a tame little dog. He was taller than his master by a head and a half, and he was ever to be seen in a hood, on which an owl's head with its beak and ears was set. Verily the whole presence of the man minded me of that nightbird; and when I think of his Master Seyfried, or Young Kubbeling, I often remember that he was ever wont to wear three wild-cats' skins, which he laid on his breast and on each leg, as a remedy against pains he had. And the falcon-seller, who was thick-set and broad-shouldered, was in truth not unlike a wild-cat in his unkempt shagginess, albeit free from all craft and guile. His whole mien, in his yellow leather jerkin slashed with green, his high boots, and ill-shaven face covered with short, grey bristles, was that of a woodsman who has grown strange to man in the forest wilds; howbeit we knew from many dealings that he was honest and pitiful, and would endure hard things to be serviceable and faithful to those few whom he truly loved.

All the creatures he brought with him were for sale; even the Iceland ponies, which he but seldom led home again, by reason that they were in great favor with the Junkers and damsels of high degree in the castles where he found shelter; and my uncle believed that his profits and savings must be no small matter.

Scarce had Kubbeling and his fellow entered the court-yard, when the house wife appeared once more at my aunt's window, and bid him come up forthwith to her mistress. But the Brunswicker only replied roughly and shortly: "First those that need my help." And he spoke thus of a wounded man, whom he had picked up, nigh unto death, by the road-side. While, with Uhlwurm's help, he carefully lifted the youth from under the tilt, my uncle, who had long been hoping for his advent, gave him a questioning look. The other understood, and shook his head sadly to answer him No. And then he busied himself with the stricken man, as he growled out to my uncle: "I crossed the pond to Alexandria, but of your man—you know who—not a claw nor a feather. As to the Schopper brothers on the other hand.... But first let us try to get between this poor fellow and the grave. Hold on, Uhlwurm!" And he was about to lift the sick man in doors. Howbeit, I went up to the Brunswicker, who in his rough wise had ever liked me well, and whereas meseemed he had seen my brothers, I besought him right lovingly to give me tidings of them; but he only pointed to the helpless man and said that such tidings as he had to give I should hear only too soon; and this I deemed was so forbidding and so dismal that I made up my mind to the worst; nay, and my fears waxed all the greater as he laid his big hand on my sleeve, as it might be to comfort me, inasmuch as that he had never yet done this save when he heard tell of my Hans' untimely end.

And then, since he would have none of my help in attending on the sick man, I ran up to my aunt to tell her with due care of the tidings I had heard; but my uncle had gone before me, and in the doorway I could see that he had just kissed his beloved wife's brow. I could read in both their faces that they were bereft of another hope, yet would my aunt go below and herself speak with Young Kubbeling. My uncle would fain have hindered her, but she paid no heed to his admonitions, and while her tiring-woman arrayed her with great care to appear at table, she thanked the saints for that Ann was far away on this luckless day.

Thus the hours sped between our homecoming from the chase and the evening meal, and we presently met all our guests in the refectory. Aunt Jacoba, as was her wont, sat on her couch on which she was carried, at the upper end of the table near the chimneyplace, next to which a smaller table was spread, where Kubbeling and Uhlwurm took their seats as though they had never sat elsewhere in their lives; and in truth old Jordan had taken his meals in that same place, and whenever they came to the Lodge the serving people knew right well what was due to them and their fellows. And whereas they did not sit at the upper table, it was only by reason that old Jordan, sixty years ago, had deemed it a burthensome honor, and more than his due; and Young Kubbeling would in all things do as his father had done before him. My seat was where I might see them, and an empty chair stood between me and my aunt; this was left for Master Ulsenius, the leech. This good man loved not to ride after dark, by reason of highway robbers and plunderers, and some of us were somewhat ill at ease at his coming so late. Notwithstanding this, the talk was not other than cheerful; new guests had come to us from the town at noon, and they had much to tell. Tidings had come that the Sultan of Egypt had fallen upon the Island of Cyprus, and that the Mussulmans had beaten King Janus, who ruled over it, and had carried him beyond seas in triumph to Old Cairo, a prisoner and loaded with chains. Hereupon we were instructed by that learned man, Master Eberhard Windecke, who was well-read in the history of all the world—he had come to Nuremberg as a commissioner of finance from his Majesty, and Uncle Tucher had brought him forth to the Forest—he, I say, instructed us that the forefather of this King Janus of Cyprus had seized upon the crown of Jerusalem at the time of the crusades, during the lifetime of the mighty Sultan Saladin, by poison and perjury, and had then bartered it with the English monarch Richard Coeur de lion, in exchange for the Kingdom of Cyprus. That ancestor of King Janus was by name Guy de Lusignan, and the sins of the fathers, so Master Windecke set forth with flowers of eloquence, were ever visited on the children, unto the third and fourth generation.

I, like most of the assembled company, had hearkened with due respect to this discourse; yet had I not failed to note with what restless eyes my aunt watched the two men when, after hardly staying their hunger and thirst, they forthwith quitted the hall to tend the sick man; she truly—as I would likewise—would rather have heard some present tidings than this record of sins of the Lusignans dead and gone. Presently the two men came back to their seats, and when Master Windecke, who, in speaking, had forgotten to eat, fell to with double good will, Uncle Conrad gravely bid Kubbeling to out with what he had to say; and yet the man, who was lifting the leg of a black-cock to his mouth, would reply no more than a rough, "All in good time, my lord."

Thus we had to wait; nor was it till the Brunswicker had cracked his last nut with his strong teeth, and the evening cup had been brought round, that he broke silence and told us in short, halting sentences how he had sailed from Venice to Alexandria in the land of Egypt, and all that had befallen his falcons. Then he stopped, as one who has ended his tale, and Uhlwurm said in a deep voice, and with a sweep of his hand as though to clear the crumbs from the table "Gone!"—And that "Gone" was well-nigh the only word that ever I heard from the lips of that strange old man. As he went on with his tale Kubbeling made free with the wine, and albeit it had no more effect on him than clear water, still meseemed he talked on for his own easement; only when he told how and where he had vainly sought the banished Gotz he looked grievously at my aunt's face. And Kunz, who had crossed the sea in the same ship with him, had helped him in that search.

When I then asked him whether Kunz had not likewise come home with him to Venice, and Kubbeling had answered me no, Uhlwurm said once more, or ever his master had done speaking, "Gone!" in his deep, mournful voice, and again swept away crumbs, as it might be, in the air. Hereupon so great a fear fell upon me that meseemed a sharp steel bodkin was being thrust into my heart; but Kubbeling had seen me turn pale, and he turned upon Uhlwurm in high wrath, and to the end that I might take courage he cried: "No, no, I say no. What does the old fool know about it! It is only by reason that the galley tarried for Junker Schopper and weighed anchor half a day later, that he forbodes ill. The delay was not needed. And who can tell what young masters will be at? They get a fancy in their green young heads, and it must be carried out whether or no. He swore to me with a high and solemn oath that he would not rest till he had found some trace of his brother, and if he kept the galleon waiting for that reason, what wonder? Is it aught to marvel at? And you, Mistress Margery, have of a surety known here in the Forest whither a false scent may lead.—Junker Kunz! Whither he may have gone to seek his brother, who can tell? Not I, and much less Uhlwurm. And young folks flutter hither and thither like an untrained falcon; and if Master Kunz, who is so much graver and wiser than others of his green youth, finds no one to open his eyes, then he may—I do not say for certain, but peradventure, for why should I frighten you all?—he may, I say, hunt high and low to all eternity. The late Junker Herdegen...."

And again I felt that sharp pang through my heart, and I cried in the anguish of my soul: "The late Junker—late Junker, did you say? How came you to use such a word? By all you hold sacred, Kubbeling, torture me no more. Confess all you know concerning my elder brother!"

This I cried out with a quaking voice, but all too soon was I speechless again, for once more that dreadful "Gone!" fell upon my ear from Uhlwurm's lips.

I hid my face in my hands, and sitting thus in darkness, I heard the bird-dealer, in real grief now, repeat Uhlwurm's word of ill-omen: "Gone." Yet he presently added in a tone of comfort: "But only perchance—not for certain, Mistress Margery."

Albeit he was now willing to tell more, he was stopped in the very act. Neither he nor I had seen that some one had silently entered the hall with my Uncle Christian and Master Ulsenius, had come close to us, and had heard Uhlwurm's and Kubbeling's last words. This was Ann; and, as she answered to the Brunswicker "I would you were in the right with that 'perchance'. How gladly would I believe it!" I took my hands down from my face, and behold she stood before me in all her beauty, but in deep mourning black, and was now, as I was, an unwedded widow.

I ran to meet her, and now, as she clung to me first and then to my aunt, she was so moving a spectacle that even Uhlwurm wiped his wet cheeks with his finger-cloth. All were now silent, but Young Kubbeling ceased not from wiping the sweat of anguish from his brow, till at last he cried: "'Perchance' was what I said, and 'perchance' it still shall be; aye, by the help of the Saints, and I will prove it...."

At this Ann uplifted her bead, which she had hidden in my aunt's bosom, and Cousin Maud let drop her arms in which she held me clasped. The learned Master Windecke made haste to depart, as he could ill-endure such touching matters, while Uncle Conrad enquired of Ann what she had heard of Herdegen's end.

Hereupon she told us all in a low voice that yestereve she had received a letter from my lord Cardinal, announcing that he had evil tidings from the Christian brethren in Egypt. She was to hold herself ready for the worst, inasmuch as, if they were right, great ill had befallen him. Howbeit it was not yet time to give up all hope, and he himself would never weary of his search: Young Kubbeling, who had meanwhile sent Uhlwurm with the leech to see the sick man and then taken his seat again with the wine-cup before him, had nevertheless kept one ear open, and had hearkened like the rest to what Ann had been saying; then on a sudden he thrust away his glass, shook his big fist in wrath, and cried out, to the door, as it were, through which Uhlwurm had departed, "That croaker, that death-watch, that bird of ill-omen! If he looks up at an apple-tree in blossom and a bird is piping in the branches, all he thinks of is how soon the happy creature will be killed by the cat! 'Gone! gone' indeed; what profits it to say gone! He has befogged even my brain at last with his black vapors. But now a light shines within me; and lend me an ear, young Mistress, and all you worshipful lords and ladies; for I said 'perchance' and I mean it still."

We listened indeed; and there was in his voice and mien a confidence which could not fail to give us heart. My lord Cardinal's assurance that we were not to rest satisfied with the evil tidings he had received, Kubbeling had deemed right, and what was right was to him a fact. Therefore had he racked his brain till the sweat stood on his brow, and all he had ever known concerning Herdegen had come back to his mind and this he now told us in his short, rude way, which I should in vain try to set down.

He said that, since the day when they had landed in Egypt, he had never more set eyes on Kunz, but that he himself had made enquiry for Herdegen. Anselmo Giustiniani was still the Republic's consul there, and lodging at the Venice Fondaco with Ursula his wife; but the serving men had said that they had never heard of Schopper of Nuremberg; nor was it strange that Kunz's coming should be unknown to them, inasmuch as, to be far from Ursula, he had found hospitality with the Genoese and not with the Venetians. When, on the eve of sailing for home, the Brunswicker had again waited on the authorities at the Fondaco, to procure his leave to depart and fetch certain moneys he had bestowed there, he had met Mistress Ursula; and whereas she knew him and spoke to him, he seized the chance to make enquiry concerning Herdegen. And it was from her mouth, and from none other, that he had learned that the elder Junker Schopper had met a violent death; and, when he had asked where and how, she had answered him that it was in one of those love-makings which were ever the aim and business of his life. Thus he might tell all his kith and kin in Nuremberg henceforth to cease their spying and prying, which had already cost her more pains and writing than enough.

This discourse had but ill-pleased Kubbeling, yet had he not taken it amiss, and had only said that she would be doing Kunz—who had come to Egypt with him—right good service, if she would give him more exact tidings of how his brother had met his end.

"Whereupon," said the bird-seller, "she gave me a look the like of which not many could give; for inasmuch as the lady is, for certain, over eyes and ears in love with Junker Kunz...."

But I stopped him, and said that in this he was of a certainty mistaken; Howbeit he laughed shortly and went on. "Which of us saw her? I or you? But love or no love—only listen till the end. Mistress Ursula for sure knew not till then that Junker Kunz was in Alexandria, and so soon as she learnt it she began to question me. She must know the day and hour when he had cast anchor there, wherefor he had chosen to lodge in the Genoa Fondaco, when I last had seen him, nay, and of what stuff and color his garments were made. She went through them all, from the feather in his hat to his hose. As for me, I must have seemed well nigh half witted, and I told her at last that I had no skill in such matters, but that I had ever seen him of an evening in a white mantle with a peaked hood. Hereupon the blood all left her face, and with it all her beauty. She clapped her hand to her forehead like one possessed or in a fit, as though caught in her own snare, and she would have fallen, if I had not held her upright. And then, on a sudden, she stood firm on her feet, bid me depart right roughly, and pointed to the door; and I was ready and swift enough in departing. When I was telling of all this to Uhlwurm, who had stayed without, and what I had heard concerning Junker Herdegen, he had nought to say but that accursed 'Gone!' And how that dazes me, old mole that I am, you yourselves have seen. But the demeanor of Mistress Tetzel of Nuremberg, I have never had it out of my mind since, day or night, nor again, yesterday."

He rubbed his damp brow, drank a draught, and took a deep breath; he was not wont to speak at such length. But whereas we asked him many questions of these matters, he turned again to us maidens, and said "Grant me a few words apart from the matter you see, in time a man gets an eye for a falcon, and sees what its good points are, and if it ails aught. He learns to know the breed by its feathers, and breastbone, and the color of its legs, and many another sign, and its temper by its eye and beak;—and it is the same with knowing of men. All this I learned not of myself, but from my father, God rest him; and like as you may know a falcon by the beak, so you may know a man or a woman by the mouth. And as I mind me of Mistress Ursula's face, as I saw it then, that is enough for me. Aye, and I will give my best Iceland Gerfalcon for a lame crow if every word she spoke concerning the death of Junker Herdegen was not false knavery. She is a goodly woman and of wondrous beauty; yet, as I sat erewhile, thinking and gazing into the Wurzburg wine in my cup, I remembered her red lips and white teeth, as she bid me exhort his kin at home to seek the lost man no more. And I will plainly declare what that mouth brought to my mind; nought else than the muzzle of the she-wolf you caught and chained up. That was how she showed her tusks when Uhlwurm wheedled her after his wise, and she feigned to be his friend albeit she thirsted to take him by the throat.—False, I say, false, false was every word that came to my ears out of that mouth! I know what I know; she is mad for the sake of one of the Schoppers, and if it be not Kunz then it is the other, and if it be not with love then it is with hate. Make the sign of the cross, say I; she would put one or both of them out of the world, as like as not. For certain it is that she would fain have had me believe that the elder Junker Schopper had already come to a bad end, and it is no less certain that she had some foul purpose in hand."

The old man coughed, wiped his brow, and fell back in his seat; we, indeed, knew not what to think of his discourse, and looked one at the other with enquiry. Jung Kubbeling was the last man on earth we could have weened would read hearts. Only Uncle Christian upheld him, and declared that the future would ere long confirm all that wise old Jordan's son had foretold from sure signs.

The dispute waxed so loud that even our silent Chaplain put in his word, to express his consent to the Brunswicker's opinion of Ursula, and to put forward fresh proofs why, in spite of her statement, Herdegen might yet be in the land of the living.

At this moment the door flew open, and the housekeeper—who was wont to be a right sober-witted widow—rushed into the refectory, followed by my aunt's waiting-maid, both with crimson cheeks and so full of their matter that they forgot the reverence due to our worshipful guests, and it was hard at first to learn what had so greatly disturbed them. So soon as this was clear, Cousin Maud, and Ann and I at her heels, ran off to the chamber where Master Ulsenius still tarried with the sick traveller, inasmuch as that if the women were not deceived, the poor fellow was none other than Eppelein, Herdegen's faithful henchman. The tiringwoman likewise, a smart young wench, believed that it was he; and her opinion was worthy to be trusted by reason that she was one of the many maids who had looked upon Eppelein with favor.

We presently were standing by the lad's bedside; Master Ulsenius had just done with bandaging his head and body and arms; the poor fellow had been indeed cruelly handled, and but for the Brunswicker's help he must have died. That Kubbeling should not have known him, although they had often met in past years, was easy to explain; for I myself could scarce have believed that the pale, hollow-eyed man who lay there, to all seeming dying, was our brisk and nimble-witted Eppelein. Yet verily he it was, and Ann flung herself on her knees by the bed, and it was right piteous to hear her cry: "Poor, faithful Eppelein!" and many other good words in low and loving tones. Yet did he not hear nor understand, inasmuch as he was not in his senses. For the present there was nought of tidings to be had from him, and this was all the greater pity by reason that the thieves had stripped off his clothes, even to his boots, and thus, if he were the bearer of any writing, he might now never deliver it. Yet he had come with some message. When the men left us there Ann bent over him and laid a wet kerchief on his hot head, and he presently opened his eyes a little way, and pointed with his left hand, which was sound, to the end of the bed-place where his feet lay, and murmured, scarce to be heard and as though he were lost: "The letter, oh, the letter!" But then he lost his senses; and presently he said the same words again and again. So his heart and brain were full of one thing, and that was the letter which some one—and who else than his well-beloved Master—had straitly charged him to deliver rightly.

Every word he might speak in his fever might give us some important tidings, and when at midnight my aunt bid us go to bed, Ann declared it to be her purpose to keep watch by Eppelein all night, and I would not for the world have quitted her at such a moment. And whereas she well knew Master Ulsenius, and had already lent a helping hand of her own free will to old Uhlwurm, the tending the sick man was wholly given over to her; and I sat me down by the fire, gazing sometimes at the leaping flames and flying sparks, and sometimes at the sick-bed and at all Ann was doing. Then I waxed sleepy, and the hours flew past while I sat wide awake, or dreaming as I slept for a few minutes. Then it was morning again, and there was somewhat before my eyes whereof I knew not whether it were happening in very truth, or whether it were still a dream, yet meseemed it was so pleasant that I was still smiling when the house-keeper came in, and that chased sleep away. I thought I had seen Ann lead ugly old Uhlwurm to the window, and stroke down his rough cheeks with her soft small hand. This being all unlike her wonted timid modesty, it amused me all the more, and the old man's demeanor likewise had made me smile; he was surly, and notwithstanding courteous to her and had said to her I know not what. Now, when I was wide-awake, Ann had indeed departed, and the house-wife had seen her quit the house and walk towards the stables, following old Uhlwurm.

Hereupon a strange unrest fell upon me, and when Kubbeling presently answered to my questioning that old Uhlwurm had craved leave to be absent till noon, to the end that he might go to the very spot where they had found Eppelein, and make search for that letter which he doubtless had had on his person, I plainly saw wherefor Ann had beguiled the old man.

CHAPTER X

"The old owl! I will give him somewhat to remember me by till some one else can say 'Gone' over him!" This was what my Uncle Christian growled a little later, out near the stables, where Matthew was putting the bridle on my bay nag, while the other serving-men were saddling the horses for the gentlemen. I had stolen hither, knowing full well that the old folks would not have suffered me to ride forth after Ann, and my good godfather even now ceased not from railing, in his fears for his darling. "What else did we talk of yestereve, Master leech and I, all the way we rode with the misguided maid, but of the wicked deeds done in these last few weeks on the high roads, and here in this very wood? With her own ears, she heard us say that the town constable required us to take seven mounted men as outriders, by reason that the day before yesterday the whole train of waggons of the Borchtels and the Schnods was overtaken, and the convoy would of a certainty have been beaten if they had not had the aid, by good-hap, of the fellowship marching with the Maurers and the Derrers.—And it was pitch dark, owls were flitting, foxes barking; it was enough to make even an old scarred soldier's blood run cold. It is a sin and a shame how the rogues ply their trade, even close under the walls of the city! They cut off a bleacher's man's ears, and when I wished that young Eber of Wichsenstein, and all the rout that follows him might come to the gallows, Ann made bold to plead for them, by reason that he only craved to visit on the Nurembergers the cruel death they brought upon his father the famous thief. As if she did not know full well that, since Eppelein of Gailingen was cast into prison, our land has never been such a den of murder and robbery as at this day. If there is less dust to be seen on the high-ways, said the keeper, it is by reason that it is washed away in blood. And notwithstanding all this the crazy maid runs straight into the Devil's arms, with that old dolt."

Then, when I went into the stable to mount, Uncle Conrad turned on Kubbeling in stormy ire for that he had suffered Uhlwurm to lead Ann into such peril; howbeit the Brunswicker knew how to hold his own, and declared at last that he could sooner have looked to see a falcon grow a lion's tail in place of feathers, than that old death-watch make common cause with a young maiden. "He had come forth," quoth he, "to counsel their excellencies to take horse." But my uncle's question, whether he, Kubbeling, believed that they had come forth to the stables to hear mass, put an end to his discourse; the gentlemen called to the serving-men to make speed, and I was already in the saddle. Then, when I had commanded Endres to open the great gate, I bowed my head low and rode out through the stable door, and bade the company a hearty good-day. To this they made reply, while Uncle Conrad asked whether I had forgotten his counsels, and whither it was my intent to ride; whereupon I hastily replied: "Under safe guidance, that is to say yours, to follow Ann."

My uncle slashed his boot with his whip, and asked in wrath whether I had considered that blood would perchance be shed, and ended by counselling me kindly: "So stay at home, little Margery!"

"I am as obedient as ever," was my ready answer, "but whereas I am now well in the saddle, I will stay in the saddle."

At this the old man knew not whether to take a jest as a jest, or to give me a stern order; and while he and the others were getting into their stirrups he said: "Have done with folly when matters are so serious, madcap child! We have enough to do to think of Ann, and more than enough! So dismount, Margery, with all speed."

"All in good time," said I then, "I will dismount that minute when we have found Ann. Till then the giant Goliath shall not move me from the saddle!"

Hereupon the old man lost patience, he settled himself on his big brown horse and cried out in a wrathful and commanding tone: "Do not rouse me to anger, Margery. Do as I desire and dismount."

But that moment he could more easily have made me to leap into the fire than to leave Ann in the lurch; I raised the bridle and whip, and as the bay broke into a gallop Uncle Conrad cried out once more, in greater wrath than before: "Do as I bid you!" and I joyfully replied "That I will if you come and fetch me!" And my horse carried me off and away, through the open gate.

The gentlemen tore after me, and if I had so desired they would never have caught me till the day of judgment, inasmuch as that my Hungarian palfrey, which my Hans had brought for me from the stables of Count von Cilly, the father of Queen Barbara, was far swifter than their heavy hook-nosed steeds; yet as I asked no better than to seek Ann in all peace with them, and as my uncle was a mild and wise man, who would not take the jest he could not now spoil over seriously, I suffered them to gain upon me and we concluded a bargain to the effect that all was to be forgotten and forgiven, but that I was pledged to turn the bay and make the best of my way home at the first sign of danger. And if the gentlemen had come to the stables in a gloomy mood and much fear, the wild chase after me had recovered their high spirits; and, albeit my own heart beat sadly enough, I did my best to keep of good cheer, and verily the sight of Kubbeling helped to that end. He was to show us the way to the spot where he had found Eppelem, and was now squatted on a very big black horse, from which his little legs, with their strange gear of catskins, stuck out after a fashion wondrous to behold. After we had thus gone at a steady pace for some little space, my confidence began to fail once more; even if Ann and her companion had been somewhat delayed by their search, still ought we to have met them by this time, if they had gone to the place without tarrying, and set forth to return unhindered. And when, presently, we came to an open plot whence we might see a long piece of the forest path, and yet saw nought but a little charcoal burner's cart, meseemed as though a cold hand had been laid on my heart. Again and again I spied the distance, while a whole army of thoughts and terrors tossed my soul. I pictured them in the power of the vengeful Eber von Wichsenstein and his fierce robber fellows; methought the covetous Bremberger had dragged them into his castle postern to exact a great ransom—nor was this the worst that might befall. If Abersfeld the wildest freebooter of all the plundering nobles far or near were to seize her? My blood ran cold as I conceived of this chance. Ann was so fair; what lord who might carry her off could she fail to inflame? And then I minded me of what I had read of the Roman Lucretia, and if I had been possessed of any magic art, I would have given the first raven by the way a sharp bodkin that he should carry it to her.

In my soul's anguish, while I held my bridle and whip together in my left hand, with the right I lifted the gold cross on my breast to my lips and in a silent heartfelt prayer I besought the Blessed Virgin, and my own dear mother in Heaven to have her in keeping.

And so we rode on and on till we came to the pools by Pillenreuth. Hard by the larger of these, known as the King's pool, was a sign-post, and not far away was the spot where they had found Eppelein, stripped and plundered; and in truth it was the very place for highwaymen and freebooters, lying within the wood and aside from the highway; albeit, if it came to their taking flight, they might find it again by Reichelstorf. Nor was there any castle nor stronghold anywhere nigh; the great building with walls and moats which stood on the south side of the King's pool was but the peaceful cloister of the Augustine Sisters of Pillenreuth. All about the water lay marsh-ground overgrown with leafless bushes, rushes, tall grasses, and reeds. It was verily a right dismal and ill-boding spot.

The boggy tract across which our path lay was white with fresh hoar-frost, and the thicket away to the south was a haunt for crows such as I never have seen again since; the black birds flew round and about it in dark clouds with loud shrieks, as though in its midst stood a charnel and gallows, and from the brushwood likewise, by the pool's edge, came other cries of birds, all as full of complaining as though they were bewailing the griefs of the whole world.

Here we stayed our horses, and called and shouted; but none made answer, save only toads and crows. "This is the place, for certain," said Young Kubbeling, and Grubner the head forester, sprang to his feet to help him down from his tall mare. The gentlemen likewise dismounted, and were about to follow the Trunswicker across the mead to the place where Eppelein had been found; but he bid them not, inasmuch as they would mar the track he would fain discover.

They, then, stood still and gazed after him, as I did likewise; and my fears waxed greater till I verily believed that the crows were indeed birds of ill-omen, as I saw a large black swarm of them wheel croaking round Kubbeling. He, meanwhile, stooped low, seeking any traces on the frosted grass, and his short, thick-set body seemed for all the world one of the imps, or pixies, which dwell among the roots of trees and in the holes in the rocks. He crept about with heedful care and never a word, prying as he went, and presently I could see that he shook his big head as though in doubt, nay, or in sorrow. I shuddered again, and meseemed the grey clouds in the sky waxed blacker, while deathly pale airy forms floated through the mist over the pools, in long, waving winding-sheets. The thick black heads of the bulrushes stood up motionless like grave-stones, and the grey silken tufts of the bog-grass, fluttering in the cold breath of a November morning, were as ghostly hands, threatening or warning me.

Ere long I was to forget the crows, and the fogs, and the reed-grass, and all the foolish fears that possessed me, by reason of a real and well-founded terror; again did Kubbeling shake his head, and then I heard him call to my Uncle Conrad and Grubner the headforester, to come close to him, but to tread carefully. Then they stood at his side, and they likewise stooped low and then my uncle clasped his hands, and he cried in horror, "Merciful Heaven!"

In two minutes I had run on tip-toe across the damp, frosted grass to join them, and there, sure enough, I could see full plainly the mark of a woman's dainty shoe. The sole and the heel were plainly to be seen, and, hard by, the print of a man's large, broad shoes, with iron-shod heels, which told Kubbeling that they were those of Uhlwurm's great boots. Yet though we had not met those we sought, the forest was full of by-ways, by which they might have crossed us on the road; but nigh to the foot-prints of the maid and the old man were there three others. The old woodsman could discern them only too well; they had each and all been made in the hoar-frost by men's boots. Two, it was certain, had been left by finely-cut soles, such as are made by skilled city cordwainers; and one left a track which could only be that of a spur; whereas the third was so flat and broad that it was for sure that of the shoe of a peasant, or charcoal burner.

There was a green patch in the frost which could only be explained as having been made by one who had lain long on the earth, and the back of his head, where he had fallen, had left a print in the grass as big as a man's fist. Here was clear proof that Ann and her companion had, on this very spot, been beset by three robbers, two of them knights and one of low degree, that Uhlwurm had fought hard and had overpowered one of them or had got the worst of it, and had been flung on the grass.

Alas! there could be no doubt, whereas Kubbeling found a foot-print of Ann's over which the spurred mark lay, plainly showing that she had come thither before those men. And on the highway we found fresh tracks of horses and men; thus it was beyond all doubt that knavish rogues had fallen upon Ann and Uhlwurm, and had carried them off without bloodshed, for no such trace was to be seen anywhere on the mead.

Meanwhile the forester had followed the scent with the bloodhounds, starting from the place where the man had lain on the grass, and scarce were they lost to sight among the brushwood when they loudly gave tongue, and Grubner cried to us to come to him. Behind a tall alder bush, which had not yet lost its leaves, was a wooden lean-to on piles, built there by the Convent fisherman wherein to dry his nets; and beneath this shelter lay an old man in the garb of a serving-man, who doubtless had lost his life in the struggle with Uhlwurm. But Kubbeling was soon kneeling by his side, and whereas he found that his heart still beat, he presently discovered what ailed the fellow. He was sleeping off a drunken bout, and more by token the empty jar lay by his side. Likewise hard by there stood a hand-barrow, full of such wine-jars, and we breathed more freely, for if the drunken rogue were not himself one of the highway gang, they must have found him there and seized the good liquor.

Now, while Kubbeling fetched water from the pool, Uncle Christian tried the quality of the jars in the barrow, and the first he opened was fine Malvoisie. Whether this were going to the Convent or no the drunken churl should tell, and a stream of cold November-water ere long brought him to his wits. Then was there much mirth, as the rogue thus waked on a sudden from his sleep let the water drip off him in dull astonishment, and stared at us open-mouthed; and it needed some patience till he was able to tell us of many matters which we afterwards heard at greater length and in fuller detail.

He was a serving-man to Master Rummel of Nuremberg, who had been sent forth from Lichtenau to carry this good liquor to the nuns at Pillenreuth; the market-town of Lichtenau lieth beyond Schwabach and had of yore belonged to the Knight of Heideck, who had sold it to that city, of which the Rummels, who were an old and honored family, had bought it, with the castle.

Now, whereas yestereve the Knight of Heideck, the former owner of the castle, a noble of staunch honor, was sitting at supper with Master Rummel in the fortress of Lichtenau, a rider from Pillenreuth had come in with a petition from the Abbess for aid against certain robber folk who had carried away some cattle pertaining to the convent. Hereupon the gentlemen made ready to go and succor the sisters, and with wise foresight they sent a barrow-load of good wine to Pillenreuth, to await them there, inasmuch as that no good liquor was to be found with the pious sisters. When the gentlemen had, this very morning, come to the place where the highwaymen had fallen on Eppelein, they had met Ann who was known to them at the Forest lodge, where she was in the act of making search for Herdegen's letter, and they, in their spurred boots, had helped her. At last they had besought her to go with them to the Convent, by reason that the men-at-arms of Lichtenau had yesternight gone forth to meet the thieves, and by this time peradventure had caught them and found the letter on them. Ann had consented to follow this gracious bidding, if only she might give tidings of where she would be to those her friends who would for certain come in search of her. Thereupon Master Rummel had commanded the servingman, who had come up with the barrow, to tarry here and bid us likewise to the Convent; the fellow, however, who had already made free on his way with the contents of the jars, had tried the liquor again. And first he had tumbled down on the frosted grass and then had laid him down to rest under the fisherman's hut.

Rarely indeed hath a maiden gone to the cloister with a lighter heart than I, after I had heard these tidings, and albeit there was yet cause for fear and doubting, I could be as truly mirthful as the rest, and or ever I jumped into my saddle again I had many a kiss from bearded lips as a safe conduct to the Sisters. My good godfather in the overflowing joy of his heart rushed upon me to kiss me on both cheeks and on my brow, and I had gladly suffered it and smiled afterwards to perceive that he would allow the barrow-man to tarry no longer.

In the Convent there was fresh rejoicing. The mist had hidden us from their sight, and we found them all at breakfast: the gentlemen and Ann, the lady Abbess and a novice who was the youngest daughter of Uncle Endres Tucher of Nuremberg, and my dear cousin, well-known likewise to Ann. Albeit the Convent was closed to all other men, it was ever open to its lord protector. Hereupon was a right happy meeting and glad greeting, and at the sight of Ann for the second time this day, though it was yet young, the bright tears rolled over Uncle Christian's round twice-double chin.

Now wheresoever a well-to-do Nuremberg citizen is taking his ease with victuals and drink, if others join him they likewise must sit down and eat with him, yea, if it were in hell itself. But the Convent of Pillenreuth was a right comfortable shelter, and my lady the Abbess a woman of high degree and fine, hospitable manners; and the table was made longer in a winking, and laid with white napery and plates and all befitting. None failed of appetite and thirst after the ride in the sharp morning air, and how glad was my soul to have my Ann again safe and unharmed.

We were seated at table by the time our horses were tied up in the stables, and from the first minute there was a mirthful and lively exchange of talk. For my part I forthwith fell out with the Knight von Heideck, inasmuch as he was fain to sit betwixt Ann and me, and would have it that a gallant knight must ever be a more welcome neighbor to a damsel than her dearest woman-friend. And the loud cheer and merrymaking were ere long overmuch for me; and I would gladly have withdrawn with Ann to some lonely spot, there to think of our dear one.

At last we were released; Jorg Starch, the captain of the Lichtenau horsemen, a tall, lean soldier, with shrewd eyes, a little turned-up cock-nose, and thick full beard, now came in and, lifting his hand to his helmet, said as sharply as though he were cutting each word short off with his white teeth: "Caught; trapped; all the rabble!"

In a few minutes we were all standing on the rampart between the pools and the Convent, and there were the miserable knaves whom Jorg Starch and his men-at-arms had surrounded and carried off while they were making good cheer over their morning broth and sodden flesh. They had declared that they had been of Wichsenstein's fellowship, but had deserted Eber by reason of his over-hard rule, and betaken themselves to robbery on their own account. Howbeit Starch was of opinion that matters were otherwise. When he had been sent forth to seek them he had as yet no knowledge of the attack on Eppelein; now, so soon as he heard that they had stripped him of his clothes, he bid them stand in a row and examined each one; in truth they were a pitiable crew, and had they not so truly deserved our compassion their rags must have moved us to laughter. One had made his cloak of a woman's red petticoat, pulling it over his head and cutting slits in it for arm-holes, and another great fellow wore a friar's brown frock and on his head a good-wife's fur turban tied on with an infant's swaddling band. Jorg Starch's enquiries as to where were Eppelein's garments made one of them presently point to his decent and whole jerkin, another to his under coat, and the biggest man of them all to his hat with the cock's feather, which was all unmatched with his ragged weed. Starch searched each piece for the letter, and meanwhile Uhlwurm stooped his long body, groping on the ground in such wise that it might have seemed that he was seeking the four-leaved clover; and on a sudden he laid hands on the shoes of a lean, low fellow, with hollow cheeks and a thrifty beard on his sharp chin, who till now had looked about him, the boldest of them all; he felt round the top of the shoes, and looking him in the face, asked him in a threatening voice: "Where are the tops?"

"The tops?" said the man in affrighted tones. "I wear shoes, Master, and shoes are but boots which have no tops; and mine...."

"And yours!" quoth Uhlwurm in scorn. "The rats have made shoes of your boots and have eaten the tops, unless it was the mice? Look here, Captain, if it please you...."

Starch did his bidding, and when he had made the lean knave put off his left shoe he looked at it on all sides, stroked his beard the wrong way, and said solemnly: "Well said, Master, this is matter for thought! All this gives the case a fresh face." And he likewise cried to the rogue: "Where are the tops?" The fellow had had time to collect himself, and answered boldly: "I am but a poor weak worm, my lord Captain; they were full heavy for me, so I cut them away and cast them into the pool, where by now the carps are feeding on them." And he glanced round at his fellows, as it were to read in their faces their praise of his quick wit. Howbeit they were in overmuch dread to pay him that he looked for; nay, and his bold spirit was quelled when Starch took him by the throat and asked him: "Do you see that bough there, my lad? If another lie passes your lips, I will load it with a longer and heavier pear than ever it bore yet? Sebald, bring forth the ropes. — Now my beauty; answer me three things: Did the messenger wear boots? How come you, who are one of the least of the gang, to be wearing sound shoes? And again, Where are the tops?"

Whereupon the little man craved, sadly whimpering, that he might be asked one question at a time, inasmuch as he felt as it were a swarm of humble-bees in his brain, and when Starch did his will he looked at the others as though to say: "You did no justice to my ready wit," and then he told that he had in truth drawn off the boots from the messenger's feet and had been granted them to keep, by reason that they were too small for the others, while he was graced with a small and dainty foot. And he cast a glance at us ladies on whom he had long had an eye, a sort of fearful leer, and went on: "The tops—they... " and again he stuck fast. Howbeit, as Starch once more pointed to the pear-tree, he confessed in desperate terror that another man had claimed the tops, one who had not been caught, inasmuch as they were so high and good. Hereupon Starch laughed so loud and clapped his hand with such a smack as made us maidens start, and he cried: "That's it, that is the way of it! Zounds, ye knaves! Then the Sow—[Eber, his name, means a boar. This is a sort of punning insult]—of Wichsenstein was himself your leader yesterday, and it was only by devilish ill-hap that the knave was not with you when I took you! You ragged ruffians would never have given over the tops in this marsh and moorland, to any but a rightful master, and I know where the Sow is lurking—for the murderer of a messenger is no more to be called a Boar. Now then, Sebald! In what hamlet hereabout dwells there a cobbler?"

"There is crooked Peter at Neufess, and Hackspann at Reichelstorf," was the answer.

"Good; that much we needed to know," said Starch. "And now, little one," and he gave the man another shaking, "Out with it. Did the Sow—or, that there may be no mistake—did Eber of Wichsenstein ride away to Neufess or to Reichelstorf? Who was to sew the tops to his shoes, Peter or Hackspann?"

The terrified creature clasped his slender hands in sheer amazement, and cried: "Was there ever such abounding wisdom born in the land since the time of chaste Joseph, who interpreted Pharaoh's dreams? The man who shall catch you asleep, my lord Captain, must rise earlier than such miserable hunted wretches as we are. He rode to Neufess, albeit Hackspann is the better cobbler. Reichelstorf lies hard by the highway by which you came, my lord; and if Eber does but hear the echo of your right glorious name, my lord Baron and potent Captain...."

"And what is my name—your lord Baron and potent Captain?" Starch thundered out.

"Yours?" said the little man unabashed. "Yours? Merciful Heaven! Till this minute I swear I could have told you; but in such straits a poor little tailor such as I might forget his own father's honored name!" At this Starch laughed out and clapped the little rogue in all kindness behind the ears, and when his men-at-arms, whom he had commanded to make ready, had mounted their horses, he cried to Uhlwurm: "I may leave the rest to you,

Master; you know where Barthel bestows the liquor!—Now, Sebald, bind this rabble and keep them safe.—And make a pig-sty ready. If I fail to bring the boar home this very night, may I be called Dick Dule to the end of my days instead of Jorg Starch!"

And herewith he made his bow, sprang into his saddle, and rode away with his men.

"A nimble fellow, after God's heart!" quoth Master Rummel to my Uncle Conrad as they looked after him. And that he was in truth; albeit we could scarce have looked for it, we learned on the morrow that he might bear his good name to the grave, inasmuch as he had taken Eber of Wichsenstein captive in the cobbler's work-place, and carried him to Pillenreuth, whence he came to Nuremberg, and there to the gallows.

Starch had left a worthy man to fill his place; hardly had he departed when old Uhlwurm pulled off the tailor's right shoe, and now it was made plain wherefor Eppelein had so anxiously pointed to his feet; the letter entrusted to him had indeed been hid in his boot. Under the lining leather of the sole it lay, but only one from Akusch addressed to me. Howbeit, when we had threatened the now barefoot knave with cruel torture, he confessed that, having been an honest tailor till of late, he had soft feet by reason that he had ever sat over his needle. And when he pulled on the stolen shoes somewhat therein hard hurt his sole, and when he made search under the leather, behold a large letter closely folded and sealed. This had been the cause and reason of his being ill at ease, and he had opened it, being of an enquiring mind, and, inasmuch as he was a schoolmaster's son he could read with the best. Howbeit, at that time the gang were about to light a fire to make their supper, and whereas it would not burn by reason of the wet, they had taken the dry paper and used it to make the feeble flame blaze up.

Thus there was nought more to be hoped for, save that the tailor might by good hap remember certain parts of the letter; and in truth he was able to tell us that it was written to a maid named Ann, and in it there were such words of true love in great straits and bitter parting as moved him to tears, by reason that he likewise had once had a true love.

While he spoke thus he perceived that Ann was the maiden to whom the letter had been writ, and he forthwith poured forth a great flow of fiery love-vows such as he may have learned from his Amadis, but never, albeit he said it, from that letter.

One thing at least he could make known to us from Herdegen's letter; and that was that the writer said much concerning slavery and a great ransom, and likewise of a malignant woman who was his foe, and of her husband, whose wiles could by no means be brought to nought unless it were by cunning and prudent craft. This, indeed, he could repeat well-nigh word for word, by reason that he had conceived the plan of urging Eber to set forth for the land of Egypt with his robber-band, and deliver that guiltless slave from the hands of the misbelieving heathen. Albeit he had made himself a highway thief, it was only by reason that he had been told that von Wichsenstein had no other end than to restore to the poor that of which the rich had robbed them, and to release the oppressed from the power of the mighty. All this had not suffered him to rest on his tailor's bench till he had laid down the needle and seized the cook's great roasting spit. Ere long he had discovered that, like master like man, each man cared for himself alone. He himself had been forced to do many cruel and knavish deeds, sorely against his will and all that was good in him. From his pious and gentle mother he had come by a soft and harmless soul, so that in the winter season he would strew sugar for the flies when they were starving, and it had even gone against him to stick his needle into a flesh-colored garment for sheer fear of hurting it. When the others had left the messenger-lad stripped on the road, he had gone back alone and had bound up the wound in his head with his own kerchief, and more by token that he spoke the truth the kerchief bore his Christian name in the corner of it, "Pignot," which his good mother, God rest her, had sewn there. He was but a poor orphan, and if... Here his voice failed him for sobs. But ere long he recovered his good cheer; for Ann had indeed marked the letter P on the cloth about Eppelein's head, and the poor wight was of a truth none other than he had declared. Hereupon we made bold to speak for him, and it was to his own act of mercy and the letters set in his kerchief by that pious mother that he owed it. He afterwards came to be an honest and worthy master-tailor at Velden, and instead of taking up the cudgels for his oppressed fellow men, he suffered stern treatment in much humility at the hands of the great woman whom he chose to wife, notwithstanding he was so small a man.

CHAPTER XI

Herdegen's letter was burnt with fire, and the letter from Akusch was to me, and contained little besides thanks and assurances of faithfulness due to me his "beloved mistress," with greetings to Cousin Maud, who had ever with just reproofs kept him in the right way, and to every member of the household. The Pastscyiptum only contained tidings of great import; and it was as follows:

"Moreover I declare and swear to you, my gracious lady, that my kindred take as good care of my Lord Kunz as though he were at home in Nuremberg. His wounds are bad, yet by faithful care, and by the grace and help of God the all-merciful, they shall be healed. He lacks for nothing. In the matter of my lord Herdegen's ransom there are many obstacles.

"Had God the all-merciful but granted to my dear father to hold his high estate a few weeks longer, it would have been a small matter to him to release a slave; but now he is cast into a dungeon by the evil malice of his enemies. Oh! that the all-wise God should suffer such malignant men to live as his foes and as that shameless woman whom you have long known by the name of Ursula Tetzel! But you will have learnt by my lord Herdegen's letter all I could tell, and you will understand that your humble servant will daily beseech the Most High God to prosper you, and cause you to send hither some wise and potent captain to the end that we may be delivered; inasmuch as the craft and fury of our foes are no less than their power. They are lions and likewise poisonous serpents."

These lines were signed with the name of Akusch, and the words, Ibn Tagri Verdi al-Mahmudi, which is to say: Akusch, Son of Tagri Verdi al-Mahmudi.

We were at home at the Forest-lodge or ever the sun had set; there we found Aunt Jacoba more calm than we had hoped for, inasmuch as that not only had her husband sent her brief tidings of us, but likewise she had heard more exactly all that had kept us away. Kubbeling, albeit the lady Abbess had bidden him to her table, had privily stolen forth to send a messenger to the grieving lady, whereas the thought of her gave him no peace among the feasters. Eppelein was neither better nor worse. But, in his stead, Master Windecke the Imperial Councillor, who was learned in the trading matters of all the world and who, in our absence, had wholly won the heart of the other women and, above all, of Cousin Maud by his good discourse, was able to interpret somewhat which had been dark to us in Akusch's letter. When I showed it to him he started to his feet in amazement and declared that my squire's father, Tagri Verdi al-Mahmudi, had been one of the most famous Captains of the host who had struck the great blow in Cyprus and carried off King Janus to the Sultan at Cairo. Nay, and he could likewise tell us what had led to the overthrow of this same Tagri Verdi, inasmuch as he had heard the tale from a certain noble gentleman of Cyprus, who had come to the court of Emperor Sigismund to entreat him to provide moneys for the ransom of King Janus, as follows: When Akusch's glorious father was raised to the dignity of a chief Mameluke, together with Burs Bey, now the Sultan of Egypt, they were both cast into prison during a certain war and lay in the same dungeon. There had Tagri Verdi dreamed one night that his fellow, Burs Bey, would in due time be placed on the throne, and had revealed this to him. Then, when this prophecy was fulfilled, and Burs Bey was Sultan, Tagri Verdi rose step by step to high honor, and had won many glorious fights as his Sovereign's chief Emir and Captain. The Sultan heaped him with honors and treasure, until he learned that his former companion had dreamed another dream, and this time that it was to be his fate to mount the throne. Hereupon Burs Bey was sore afraid; thus he had cast the victorious Captain into prison, and many feared for Tagri that his life would not be spared.

And Master Windecke could tell us yet more of the matter; and whereas from him we heard that our Emperor, by reason that his coffers were empty, could do nought to ransom King Janus, and that the Republic of Venice was fain to take it in hand, we were in greater fear than ever, inasmuch as this must need add yet more to the high respect already enjoyed by the Republic in the land of Egypt, and to that in which its Consul Giustiniani was held; and thereby his wife Ursula might, with the greater security, give vent to that malice she bore in her heart against Herdegen.

Thus we went to our beds silent and downcast; and after we had lain there a long time and found no sleep the words would come, and I said: "My poor, dear Kunz! to be there in that hot Moorish land, wounded and alone! Oh, Ann, that must be full hard to bear."

"Hard indeed!" quoth she in a low voice. "But for a free man, and so proud a man as Herdegen, to be a slave to a misbelieving Heathen, far away from all he loves, and chidden and punished for every unduteous look; Oh, Margery! to think of that!" And her voice failed.

I spoke to her, and showed that we had much to make us thankful, inasmuch as we now at last knew that he we loved was yet alive.

Then was there silence in the chamber; but I minded me then of what Akusch had written, that he besought some wise and mighty gentleman to set forth from Nuremberg to overpower the foe, and now I racked my brain to think whom we might send to take my brothers' cause in hand—yet still in vain. None could I think of who might conveniently quit home for so long, or who was indeed fit for such an enterprise.

Which of us twain first fell asleep I wist not; when I woke in the morning Ann had already quitted the chamber; and while Susan braided my hair, all I had been planning in the night grew plainer to me, and I went forth and down stairs full of a great purpose which made my heart beat the faster. When I entered the ball, behold, I saw the same thing, albeit I was now awake, as I had seen yestermorn in my half-sleep. Yet was it not Uhlwurm, but Kubbeling, to whom Ann was paying court. As he stood facing her, she looked him trustfully in the eyes, and held his great hand in hers; nay, and when she saw me she did not let it go, but cried out in a clear and thankful voice: "Then so it is, Father Seyfried; and if you do as I beseech you, all will come to a good end and you will remember so good a deed with great joy all your life long."

"As to 'great joy' I know not," replied he. "For if I be not the veriest fool in all the land from Venice to Iceland, my name is not Kubbeling. I scarce know myself! Howbeit, let that pass: I stand by my word, albeit the pains I shall endure in the winter journey."

"The Saints will preserve you on so pious an errand," Ann declared. "And if they should nevertheless come upon you, dear Father, I will tend you as your own daughter would. And now again your hand, and a thousand, thousand thanks."

Whereupon Kubbeling, with a melancholy growl, and yet a smile on his face, held forth his hand, and Ann held it fast and cried to me: "You are witness, Margery, that he has promised to do my will. Oh, Margery, I could fly for gladness!"

And verily meseemed as though the wings had grown, and her eyes sparkled right joyfully and thankfully. And I had discerned from her very first words whereunto she had beguiled Kubbeling; and verily to me it was a marvel, inasmuch as I myself had imagined the self-same thing in the watches of the night, and while my hair was doing: namely, to beseech Kubbeling to be my fellow and keeper on a voyage to Egypt. Who but he knew the way so well? Howbeit, Ann had prevented me, and now, whereas

I heard the sound of voices on the stair, I yet found time to cry to her: "We go together, Ann; that is a settled matter!"

Hereupon she looked at me, at first in amazement and then with a blissful consenting smile, and said "You had imagined the same thing, I know. Yes, Margery, we will go."

The others now trooped in, and I had no more time but hastily to clasp her hand. Howbeit, when most of our guests had gone into the refectory, where the morning meal was by this time steaming on the board, none were left with us save Cousin Maud and Uncle Conrad and Uncle Christian; and Uncle Conrad enquired of the Brunswicker whether he purposed indeed to set forth this day, and the man answered No, if so be that his lordship the grand-forester would grant him shelter yet awhile, and consent to a plan to which he had been just now beguiled.

And my uncle gave him his hand, and said the longer he might stay the better. And then he went on to ask with some curiosity what that plan might be. Howbeit, I took upon me to speak, and I told him in few words how that we had been thinking whom we might best send forth to help my brethren, and that, with the morning sun, light had dawned on our minds, and that whereas we had found a faithful and experienced companion, it was our firm intent....

Here Cousin Maud broke in, having come close to me with open ears, crying aloud in terror: "What?" Howbeit I looked her in the eyes and went on:

"When our mind is set, Cousin, the thing will be done, of that you and all may make certain—that stands as sure as the castle on the rock. And be it known to you all, with all due respect, that this time I will suffer none to cross my path. Once for all, I, Margery, and Ann with me, are going forth to the land of Egypt in Kubbeling's company, and to Cairo itself!"

The worthy old woman gave a scream, and while the Brunswicker shut the dining-hall door, that we might not be heard, she broke out, with glowing eyes, beside herself with wrath: "Verily and indeed! So that is your purpose! Thanks be to the Virgin, to say and to do are not one and the same, far from it. Do you conceive that you hold all love for those two youths yonder in sole fief or lease? As though others were not every whit as ready as you to give their best to save them. A head that runs at a wall cracks its skull! Maids should never touch matters which do not beseem them! What next for a skittle-witted fancy!—That it should have come into the brain of a Schopper is no marvel, but Ann, prudent Ann! Would any man have dreamed of such a thing in our young days, Master Cousin? There they stand, two well born Nuremberg damsels, who have never been suffered to go next door alone after Ave Maria! And they are fain to cross the seas to a dark outlandish place, into the very jaws of the dreadful Heathen who butcher Christian people!" Whereupon she clapped her hands and laughed aloud, albeit not from her heart, and then raved on: "At least is it a new thing, and the first time that the like hath ever been heard of in Nuremberg!"

If the whole of the holy Roman Empire had risen up to make resistance and to mock us, it would have failed to move Ann or me, and I answered, loud and steadfast: "Everything right and good that ever was done in Nuremberg, my heart's beloved Cousin, was done there once for the first time; and it is right and good that we should go, and we mean to do it!" Whereupon Cousin Maud drew back in disgust and amazement, and gazed from one to the other of us with enquiring eyes, and as wondering a face as though she were striving to rede some dark riddle. Then her vast bosom began to heave up and down, and we, who knew her, could not fail to perceive that somewhat great and strange was moving her. And whereas she presently shook her heavy head to and fro, and set her fists hard on her hips, I looked for a sudden and dreadful storm, and my Uncle Conrad likewise gazed her in the face with expectant fear; yet it was long in breaking forth. What then was my feeling when, at last, she took her hands from her sides and struck her right hand in her left palm so that it rang again, and burst forth eagerly, albeit with roguish good humor and tearful eyes: "If indeed everything good and right that ever was done in Nuremberg must have once been done there for the first time, our good town shall now see that a grey-headed old woman with gout in her toes can sail over seas, from the Pegnitz even to the land of the barbarian Heathen and Cairo! Your hand on it, Young Kubbeling, and yours, Maidens. We will be fellow travellers. Signed and sealed. Strew sand on it!"

Hereupon Ann, who was wont to be still, shrieked loudly and cast herself first on my cousin's neck and then on mine and then on my uncle's; he indeed stood as though deeply offended, as likewise did my good godfather Christian. Yet they would not speak, that they might not mar our joy, albeit Uncle Pfinzing growled forth that our plan was sheer youthful folly, wilfulness, and the like. "At any rate it is an unlaid egg, so long as my wife has not added mustard to the peppered broth," Uncle Conrad declared, and he departed to carry tidings to my aunt of what mad folly these women's heads had brewed.

Even Kubbeling shook his head, albeit he spoke not, inasmuch as he knew that it was hard to contend with the powers beyond seas.

He and Cousin Maud had ever been on terms of good-fellowship with Uncle Christian, but to-day my uncle was ill to please; neither look nor word had he for his heart's darling, Ann; and when he presently recovered somewhat, he stormed around, with so red a face and such furious ire that we feared lest he should have another dizzy stroke, saying "that Kubbeling and Cousin Maud might be ashamed of themselves, inasmuch as they were old enough to know better and were acting like a pair of young madcaps." And thus he went on, till it was overmuch for the Brunswicker's endurance, and on a sudden he cried out in great wrath that that he had promised was in truth not wise, forasmuch as that he would gain nought but mischief thereby, yet that it concerned him alone and he took it all on himself, although Master Pfinzing might yet ask for why and to what end he should risk a hurt by it, whereas, to his knowledge, the ill-starred Junker Schopper could be little more to him than the man in the moon. He was wont, quoth he, to take good care not to risk his skin for other folks, but in this matter it seemed to him not too dear a bargain. Neither the stoutest will nor the strongest fist might avail against Mistress Ursula, the veriest witch in all the land of Egypt; a better head was needed for that, than the heavy brain-pan which God Almighty had set on his short neck, and yet he had sworn to bring her knavery to nought. Our faithful hearts and shrewd heads would be the aid he needed. He trusted to Cousin Maud to dare to dance with old Nick himself, if need should arise. And he was man enough to protect us all three. And now Master Pfinzing knew all about it and, if he yet craved to hear more, he would find him among the birds, whereas Uhlwurm was to depart on his way with them that very day, without him.

And he turned his back on my uncle, and quitted the chamber with a heavy tread; but he turned on the threshold and cried: "Yet keep your lips from telling what you have in your mind, Master, and in especial to those who are at their meal in there, as touching that Tetzel-adder; for the wind flies over seas faster than we can."

While he spoke thus Uncle Christian had recovered his temper, and he followed after Kubbeling with such a haste as his huge body would allow, nor was it to quarrel with him any more.

The rest, who had sat at breakfast, had by good hap heard nought of our disputing, by reason that Master Windecke had so much new matter for discourse that every ear hung on his words; and he, again, forgot to eat while he talked. In Cousin Maud, indeed, as she hearkened to my godfather's wrathful speech, certain doubts had arisen; yet even stronger resistance would never have turned her aside from anything she deemed truly good and right; howbeit she was more than willing to leave it to us to settle matters with Aunt Jacoba. We went up-stairs to her, and at her chamber door our courage failed us, inasmuch as we could hear through the door my uncle's angry speech, and that laugh which my aunt was wont to utter when aught came to her ears which she was not fain to hear.

"And if she were to say No?" said I to Ann. Hereupon a right sorrowful and painful cloud overspread her face, and it was in a dejected tone that she answered me that then indeed all must be at an end, and her fondest hopes nipped, by reason that she owed more to Mistress Waldstromer than ever she could repay, and whatsoever she might undertake against her will would of a certainty come to no good end. And we heard my aunt's laugh again; but then I took heart, and raised the latch, and Ann led the way into the chamber.

Howbeit, if we had cherished the smallest hope without, within it failed us wholly. As we went in my uncle was standing close by my aunt; his back was towards us, and he saw us not; but his mien alone showed us that he was wroth and provoked: his voice quaked as he cried aloud with a shrug of his shoulders and his hand uplifted: "Such a purpose is sheer madness and most unseemly!"

Then, when for the third time I coughed to make our presence known to him, he turned his red face towards us, and cried out in great fury: "Here you are to answer for yourselves; and come what may, this at least shall be said: 'If mischief comes of it, I wash my hands in innocence!'"

Whereupon he went in all haste to the door and had lifted his hand to slam it to, when he minded him of his beloved wife's sick health and gently shut it and softly dropped the latch.

We stood in front of Aunt Jacoba, and could scarce believe our eyes and ears when she opened wide her arms and, with beaming eyes, cried in a voice of glad content: "Come, come to my heart, children! Oh, you good, dear, brave maids! Why, why am I so old, so fettered, so sick a creature? Why may I not go with you?"

At her first words we had fallen on our knees by her side, and she fervently clasped our heads to her bosom, kissed our lips and foreheads, and cried, with ever-streaming eyes: "Yes, children, yes! It is brave, and the right way; Courage and true love are not dead in the hearts of the women of Nuremberg. Ah, and how many a time have I imagined that I might myself rise and fly after my froward, dear, unduteous exile, my own Gotz, be he where he may, over mountains and seas to the ends of the earth!—I, a hapless, suffering skeleton! Yet what is denied to the old, the young may do, and the Virgin and all the Saints shall guard you! And Kubbeling, Young-Kubbeling, that bravest, truest Seyfried! Bring him up to speak with me. So rough and so good!—My old man, to be sure, must storm and rave, but then his feeble and sickly nobody of a little wife can wind him round her finger. Leave him to me, and be sure you shall win his blessing." After noon Uhlwurm and the waggon of birds set forth to Frankfort, where Kubbeling's eldest son was tarrying to meet his father with fresh falcons. Or ever the grim old grey-beard mounted his horse, he whispered to Ann: "Truest of maidens, find some device to move Seyfried to take me in your fellowship to the land of Egypt, and I will work a charm which shall of a surety give your lover back to you, if indeed he is not..." and he was about to cry "gone" as was his wont; yet he refrained himself and spoke it not. Young Kubbeling tarried at the Forest-lodge; and as for my uncle, it was soon plain enough that my aunt had been in the right in the matter; nay, when we went home to the city, meseemed as though he and his wife had from the first been of one mind. Our purpose pleased him better as he learned to believe more surely that our little women's wits would peradventure be able to find his wandering son, and to tempt him to return to his father's forest home.

CHAPTER XII

We carefully obeyed Kubbeling's counsel that we should keep our purpose dark, and it remained hidden even from the guests at the lodge. On the other hand they had been told all that Herdegen's letter had contained, and that it was Ursula who was pursuing him with such malignant spite. Yet albeit we bound over each one to hold his peace on the matter in Nuremberg, no woman, nor perchance no man either, could keep such strange doings privy from near kith and kin; and whereas we might not tell what in truth it was which stood in the way of our brothers' homecoming, it was rumored among our cousins and gossips that some vast and unattainable sum was needed to ransom the two young Schoppers. And other marvellous reports got abroad, painting my brother's slavery in terrible colors.

At first this made me wroth, but presently it provoked me less, inasmuch as that great compassion was aroused; and those very citizens and dames who of old were wont to chide Herdegen as a limb of Satan, and would have gladly seen him led to the gallows, now remembered him otherwise. Yea, fellow-feeling hath kindly eyes, widely open to all that is good, and willing to be shut to all that is evil, and so it came to pass that the noble gifts of the poor slave now lost to the town, were lauded to the skies. Hereupon came a letter from my lord Cardinal with these tidings of good comfort: that he was willing to administer extreme unction to my grand-uncle Im Hoff, if his life should be in peril when his eminence returned from England. Our next letters were, by his order, to find him at Brussels, and when old Dame Pernhart had given her consent to our journeying to the land of Egypt—whereas Aunt Jacoba held her wisdom and shrewd wit in high honor,—and had moved her son and Dame Giovanna to do likewise, Ann wrote a long letter to my lord Cardinal, the venerable head of the Pernhart family, setting forth in touching words for what cause and to what end she had dared so bold a venture. She besought his aid and blessing, and declared that the inward voice, which he had taught her to obey, gave her assurance that the purpose she had in hand was pleasing in the eyes of God and the Virgin.

I, for my part, could never have writ so fair a letter; and how calmly would Ann now fulfil the duties of each day, while Cousin Maud, albeit her feet scarce might carry her, was here, there, and everywhere, like a Will-o'-the-Wisp.

Ann it was who first conceived the idea of going with Young Kubbeling to the Futterers' house and there making enquiries as to the roads to Genoa, and also concerning the merchants who might there be found ready and willing to ship his falcons for sale in Alexandria; inasmuch as that it was only by journeying in a galleon which sailed not from Venice that we could escape Ursula's spies; and that Kubbeling should suffer loss through us we could by no means allow. And whereas old Master Futterer himself was now in Nuremberg, he declared himself willing to buy the birds on account of his own house, at the same price as the traders in Venice; nor was the Brunswicker any whit loth, forasmuch as that he might presently get a better price on the Lido, when it should be known that he had other ways and means at his command. Also the journey by Genoa gave us this advantage: that we were bound to no time or season. Old Master Futterer pledged himself to find a ship at any time when Kubbeling should need it.

Whereas we purposed to set forth in the middle of December, we went to the forest-lodge early in that month, and as it was with me at that time, so, for sure, must it be with the swallows and the nightingales or ever they fly south over mountains and seas. Never had the pure air been sweeter, never had I looked forward to the future with greater hope and strength or higher purpose. And my feeble, sickly Aunt Jacoba, meseemed, was like-minded with me. In spirit, ever eager, she was with us already in that distant region, and albeit of old she ever had preferred Ann above me, now on a sudden the tables were turned; she could never see enough of me, and when at last Ann was fain to go home to town with Uncle Christian, she besought so pressingly that I would stay with her that I was bound to yield; and indeed I was well content to tarry there, the forest being now in all its glory.

The daintiest lace was hung over the frosted trees. They had been dipped, meseemed, in melted silver and crystal, and the whole forest was broidered over with shining enamel and thickly strewn with clear diamond sparks. And how brightly everything glittered when the sun rose up from the morning mist, and blazed down on all this glory from a blue sky! At night the moon lighted up the frosted forest with a softer and more loving ray, and till a late hour I would gaze forth at it, or up at the starry vault where the shooting stars came flying across from the dark blue deep. Now it is well-known to many who are still in their green youth that, whensoever it befalls that we are in the act of thinking of some heartfelt wish just as a star falls, it is sure of fulfilment; and behold, on the very next night, as I was gazing upwards and wondering in my heart whether indeed we might be able to rescue my brothers, and to find my Cousin Gotz as his sick mother so fervently hoped, a bright star fell, as it were right in front of me. Whereupon I went to bed in such good cheer and so sure of myself as I have rarely felt before or since that night.

And next morning, as I went to my aunt in high spirits and happy mood, she perceived that some good hap had befallen me. Then, when I had told her what I had had in my mind as the star fell which, as little children believe, is dropped from the hand of an angel blinded by the glory of Almighty God, she looked me in the face with a sad smile and bid me sit down by her side. And she took my hand in hers and opened her heart so wide as she had never done till this hour. It was plain to see that she had long been biding her time for this full and free discourse, and she confessed that she had never shown me such love and care as were indeed my due. The mere sight of me had ever hurt the open wound, inasmuch as long ago, or ever I first went to school, her fondest hopes had been set on me. She had looked on me ever as her only son's future wife, and Gotz himself had been of the same mind, whereas in his boyhood, and even when his beard was coming, he loved nought better than little Margery in her red hood.

And she reminded me now of many a kind act her son had done me, and how that once on a time, when my lord the High Constable had bidden him with other lads to Kadolzburg, which she and my uncle took as a great honor, he had said, No, he would not go from home, by reason that Cousin Maud was to come that day and bring me with her.

[Kadolzburg—A country lodge belonging to the High Constables of the city of Nuremberg, and their favourite resort, even after they had became Electors of Brandenburg. It was at about three miles and a half west of the town]

Whereupon arose his first sharp dispute with his parents, and when my uncle threatened that he would carry him thither by force he had stolen away into the woods, and stayed all night with some bee-keeper folk, and not come home till midday on the morrow, when it was too late to ride to the Castle in good time. 'To punish him for this he was locked up; but hearing my voice below he had let himself down by the gutter-pipe, seized my hand, and ran away to the woods with me, nor did he come back till Ave Maria. And hereupon he was soundly thrashed, albeit he was even then a great lad and of good counsel in all matters.

My uncle's wrath at that time had dwelt in my mind, but my share in the matter was new to me and brought the color to my face. Howbeit, I deemed it might have been better if my aunt had never told me; for though it was indeed good to hear and gladdened my soul, yet it would hinder me from looking Gotz freely in the face if by good hap I should meet him.

Then she went on to tell me in full all that had befallen my cousin until he had gone forth to wander. When they had parted in wrath, he had written to her from the town to say that if she were steadfast in her displeasure he should seek a new home for himself and his sweetheart in a far country; and she had sent him a letter to tell him that her arms were ever open to receive him, but that rather than suffer the only son and heir of the old and noble race of Waldstromer to throw himself away on a craftsman's daughter, she would never more set eyes on him whom she loved with all her heart. Never more, and she swore it by the Saviour's wounds with the crucifix in her hand, should his parents' doors be opened to him unless he gave up the coppersmith's daughter and besought his mother's pardon.

And now the sick old woman bewailed her stern hardness and her over-hasty oath with bitter tears; Gotz had been faithful to his Gertrude in despite of her letter, and when, three years later, the tidings reached him that his sweetheart had pined away for grief and longing, and departed this life with his name on her lips, he had written in the wild anguish of his young soul that, now Gertrude was dead, he had nought more to crave of his parents; and that whereas his mother had sworn with her hand on the image of the Saviour never to open her doors to him till he had renounced his sweet, pure love, he now made an oath not less solemn and binding, by the image of the Crucified Christ, that he would never turn homewards till she bid him thither of her own free will, and owned that she repented her of that innocent maid's early death, whereas there was not her like among all the noble maidens of Nuremberg, whatever their names might be.

This letter I read myself, and I plainly saw that these twain had sadly marred their best joy in life by over-hasty ire. Albeit, I knew full well how stubborn a spirit was Aunt Jacoba's, I nevertheless strove to move her to send a letter to her son bidding him home; yet she would not, though she bewailed herself sorely.

"Only one thing of those he requires of me can I in all truth grant him," quoth she. "If you find him, you may tell him that his mother sends her fondest blessing, and assure him of my heart's deepest devotion; nay, and let him understand that I am pining with longing for him, and that I obey his will inasmuch as that I truly mourn the death of his beloved; for that is verily the truth, the Virgin and the Saints be my witness. Yet I may not and I will not open my doors to him till he has craved my forgiveness, and if I did so he must think of his own mother as a perjured woman."

Hereupon I showed her—and my eyes overflowed—that his oath stood forth as against her oath, and that one was as weighty as the other in the sight of the Most High.

"Set aside that cruel vow, my dear aunt," cried I, "I will make any pilgrimage with you, and I know full well that no penance will seem overhard to you."

"No, no, of a surety, Margery, no!" she replied with a groan. "And the Chaplain said the like to me long ago; and yet I feel in my heart that you and he are in the wrong. An oath sworn by Christ's wounds!—Moreover I am the elder and his mother, he is the younger and my son. It is his part to come to me, and if he then shall make a pilgrimage it shall be to Rome and the Holy Sepulchre. He has time before him in which to do any penance the Holy Church may require of him. I—I would lay me on the rack only to see him once more, I would fast and scourge myself till my dying day; but I am his mother, and he is my son, and it is his part to take the first step, not mine who bore him."

How warmly I urged her again and again, and how often was she on the point of yielding to her heart's loud outcry! Yet she ever came back to the same point: that it ill-beseemed her to be the first to put forth her hand, albeit her every feeling drove her to it.

The letters sent to Gotz had reached him through a merchant's house in Venice. This his parents knew, and they had long since charged Kunz to inquire where he dwelt. Yet had his pains been for nought, inasmuch as the banished youth had forbidden the traders to tell any one, whosoever might ask. Howbeit my uncle had implored his son in many a letter to mind him of his mother's sickness, and come home; and in his answers Gotz had many a time given his parents assurance of his true and loving devotion; yet had he kept his oath, and tarried beyond seas. These letters likewise did my aunt show me, and while I read them she charged me to make it my duty not to quit that merchant's house and to take no rest until I had learned where her son was dwelling: saying that what an Italian might deny to a man a fair young maiden might yet obtain of him.

It was not yet dusk when Master Ulsenius came and broke off our discourse. He had come forth in part to see Eppelein, and presently, when a lamp was brought, as we stood by the faithful lad he called me by name, and then Uncle Conrad, and said that albeit he was weary of limb he was easy and comfortable; that he felt a smart now and then, and in especial about his neck, yet that troubled him but little, inasmuch as that it plainly showed him that the thought which had haunted him, that he was really killed and in a darksome hell, was but a horrible dream.

Then when he had spoken thus much, with great pains, his pale face turned red on a sudden, and again he asked, as he had many times in his sickness, where was his master's letter. Hereupon I hastily told him that we had hunted down the robbers and rescued it, and it was a joy to see how much comfort and delight this was to him. And when he had swallowed a good cup of strong Malvoisie, he could sit up, and enquired if the Baron von Im Hoff were minded to satisfy the Sultan's over-great demand. And to this I replied, to give him easement, that we had good reason to hope so. And was his mind now clear enough to enable him to remember how great a sum was demanded for ransom?

He smiled craftily, and said that even as a dead man he could scarce have forgotten that, by reason that he had muttered the words to himself on his way oftener than any old monk mumbles his Paternoster. And when Uncle Conrad laughed and bid him jestingly repeat it, he said, like a school boy who is sure of his task: "For Master Herdegen Schopper, slave of the said unbeliever Abou Sef—[Father of the scimitar]—in the armory of Sultan Burs Bey in the Castle of Cairo, a ransom is demanded of twenty-four thousand Venice sequins. George—Christina! Death and fire on the head of the misbelieving wretch!"

When we heard this we all believed that he had of a surety been wrong as to the sum or the coin, likewise we thought his last strange words were due to a wandering mind; howbeit, we were soon to learn that verily his tidings were the truth. He forthwith went on to say with some pains that his master had made him to use a means by which he might remember the number from all others in case, by ill-hap, the letter should be lost. And on this wise he gave us to know for certain that the vast sum demanded was not an error on his part. It was to this end that he had stamped on his memory the names of Saint George and Saint Christina, whose days in the calendar are on the 24th of April and the 24th of July, and the number of thousands named for the ransom was likewise four and twenty. Also Herdegen had bid him think of twice the twelve apostles, and of the twenty-four hours from midnight till midnight again. It would seem beyond belief to most folks, he said, yet it was indeed twenty-four thousand, and not hundred, sequins which that devilish Sultan has asked, as indeed we must know from the letter. Presently, when he had rested a while, we made him tell us more, and we learned that the Sultan had been minded to set Herdegen free without price, and he would have had him led forthwith to the imprisoned King Janus of Cyprus, to whom he thought he might thus do a pleasure, but that Ursula Tetzel, who was standing by with her husband, had whispered to the Sultan that she would not see him robbed of a great profit forasmuch as that yonder Christian slave—and she pointed to my brother—was of one of the richest families of her native town, who could pay a royal ransom for him and find it no great burthen; and that the same was true of Sir Franz, who was likewise to have been set free. Hereupon the Sultan, who at all times lacked moneys, notwithstanding the heavy tribute he levied on all merchandise, commanded that Herdegen and the Bohemian should be led away again and then he asked this overweening ransom. Then Ursula took upon herself of her own free will to send tidings of the Sultan's demands to the slaves' kith and kin, and of her deep malice had never done so.

That evening we might not hear how and on what authority Eppelein knew all this, for much talking had wearied him. All we could then learn was that it was Ursula, and none other, whom the lad would still speak of as the She-devil, who had plotted the snare which had well nigh cost my other brother his life. Yet had he left him so far amended that he, Eppelein, would be glad to be no worse.

Albeit these tidings of Kunz were good to cheer us, our hopes of ransoming Herdegen were indeed far away, or rather in the realm of nevermore; even if my grand-uncle were possessed of so great a sum, it was a question whether he would be willing to pay it; and as for us, we could never have raised it at the cost of all our fortune. At that time the Venice sequin and Nuremberg gulden were not far asunder in value, and what the sum of twenty-four thousand gulden meant any man may imagine when I say that, no more than twelve years sooner, the liberty of coining for the whole city was granted by the Emperor Sigismund to Herdegen Valzner for four thousand Rhenish gulden; and that Master Ulman Stromer purchased his fine dwelling-house behind the chapel of Our Lady, with the houses pertaining thereto, and his share in the Rigler's house for two thousand eight hundred gulden. For such a sum as was demanded a whole street in Nuremberg might have been sold; nay, the great castle of Malmsbach on the Pegnitz would lately have been bought by the city for a thousand Rhenish gulden, but that Master Ulrich Rummel, whose it was, would not part with it. And we were now required to pay the price of two dozen such strongholds! It was indeed an unheard-of and devilish extortion; and when Kubbeling came to hear of it he turned his wild-cat-skin pocket inside out, and fell to raging and storming.

Aunt Jacoba turned pale when she heard the great sum named, and she likewise was of opinion that old Im Hoff, who had of late been spending much money in vows and foundations, would never give forth so vast a sum. The richest families in Nuremberg might be moved to pay fifty, and at the most a hundred gulden for the ransom of a Christian and a fellow-countryman, but if even twenty might be found so open-handed, which was not to be looked for, and if my godfather Christian Pfinzing, and the

Waldstromers, and the Hallers should do their utmost, and we should give the greater part of all our possessions, we could scarce make it up to twenty-four thousand sequins if my grand-uncle did not help.

Thus after a day of hope came a first night of despairing, and many another must follow, and I was to know once more that misfortunes never come singly.

I had hoped of a surety to speak with Eppelein once more or ever I departed at noon, and to ask him of many matters; howbeit, when I went up to his chamber Master Ulsenius met me with a face of care and told me that the poor fellow was again wandering in his wits. When I presently went forth from the house, a bee-keeper's waggon was slowly moving from the court-yard. The housewife waved her hand, and from beneath the tilt the face of Dame Henneleinlein looked at me with a scornful grin. Since her evil demeanor at the Pernbarts' they had closed their house on her, and when she had dared once to go to the Schopperhof, thence likewise had she been shut out, and thus she felt no good-will towards us. Now when I enquired of the housekeeper what might be the end and reason for this visit, the woman hid beneath her apron a jar of honey which the old dame had given her as a sweetmeat for the children; and she gave me to understand that the worthy lady had come forth to the forest to collect her widow's dues of honey, and had tarried on her way for a little friendly discourse. But methought that "little" must have had some strange meaning, inasmuch as the housewife's withered cheeks were of the color of a robin's breast. Hereupon I threatened her with my finger, and enquired of her whether she had not betrayed more to the evil-tongued old woman than she ought, but she eagerly denied the charge.

My ride home to the town after noon was not altogether a pleasant one, by reason that icy rain poured from heaven in streams, mingled with snow. The further we went the worse the roads were, and yet when my companions turned at the city-gate to ride homewards again, a strange, fierce confidence came upon me. Whether it were that the wet which ran off from me and my stout horse had singularly refreshed me, or whether it was the steadfast purpose I had set as I rode along, to risk my all to the end that I might redeem my brethren, I know not. But to this hour I mind me that, as I rode in through the dark streets, my heart beat high with contentment, and that had I been such another man as Herdegen I might have been ready enough to pick a quarrel with the first who should have said me nay.

Thus I fared on past my grand-uncle's house; there I beheld from afar a lighted lantern, as it were a glow-worm at midsummer, moving along the street, and when I perceived that it was none other than old Henneleinlein who carried it, I put my horse, which till now had been wading through the mire step by step, to a swift gallop, as fast as he might go, and the servingman behind me, passing close by her. And what simple glee was mine when our horses splashed the old woman from head to foot, inasmuch as I wist for certain that she could have stolen to my grand-uncle's house at that late hour to no end but to reveal whatsoever she might have picked up from her friend and gossip at the forest-lodge.

Thus I reached home in better cheer than I had hoped; and when Susan told me that Cousin Maud was in the kitchen ordering the supper, I crept up-stairs, hastily changed my wet raiment, sent forth my man to tell Ann that she was to come to me, and then, in the best chamber, I fetched forth the elecampane wine which I had ever found the best remedy when my cousin needed some strength. Nor was my care in vain; for when I had told her, little by little, as it were in small doses, all the tidings I had heard yesterday, and ended with the great and cruel price demanded by the Sultan, she shrieked aloud and clasped her hands to her heart in such wise that I was verily in great fear. Then the elecampane wine did good service; yet was it not till she had drunk of it many times that her tongue spoke plainly again. And presently, when she was able to wag it, it went on for a long time with no pause nor rest, in sheer impatience and godless railing.

When she had thus relieved her mind, she began pacing up and down the floor on one and the same plank, like a lion in its cage, and to call to mind, one by one, all our earthly possessions, and to reckon at how we might attain to selling it for gold. The whole sum was not much to comfort us, for her worldly estate, like that of the Waldstromers, was in land, and in these days of peril from the Hussites it was hard enough to sell landed property, and her best portion was in meads and pasture and a few vineyards near Wurzburg.

It was from the first her fixed intent, as though it were a matter of course, to give everything she had, down to her jewels; and whereas she conceived, and rightly, that for Herdegen's sake I should be like-minded, she asked me no questions but added to it in her mind, the Schopper jewels which had come to me from my father and mother, and then began to count and reckon. It might perchance come to so much as eleven thousand sequins if we sold all we had to sell; yet our inheritance lay in Chancery, and, as she knew full well, not a farthing thereof might be given up but with the full and well-proven authority of Herdegen and Kunz. Nor might I even have that which was mine own, by reason that our inheritance had never been shared, and our houses and lands had not been valued at a price. Thus I must have long patience or ever I came by my own; all the more so whereas the gentlemen of the Chancery were required to answer for the wealth of orphans in their keeping with their own.

Hereupon we again thought of my grand-uncle, and Cousin Maud declared that he would of a certainty be ready to pay half the required ransom for a purpose so pleasing in the eyes of God, and that the other half might be raised by the help of our friends. Then she was fain to think of the future. And the longer she did so, even when Ann had come to us and had been told all our tidings, the better cheer she showed; nay, it might have been conceived that it would be a far more easy and delightful matter to live in narrow poverty than in superfluous riches, and thereupon she put me in mind how that many a time, when the men-folks were away from home, she and I had been content to make good cheer with some sweet porridge, and had very gladly dined without flesh-meat, which was so costly. We should be free from the vexation of so many serving-men and wenches; and whereas of late she had been forced to turn Brigitta out of the house, had she not herself scarce escaped a fever from sheer worry of mind. Susan would ever be true to us; she would be ready to share our poverty with us, and the unresting up-stairs and down had long been a torment to her old feet.

The Magister was a well-disposed man, and if he found it an over-hard matter to depart from us we might very gladly let him board with us, if he could be content to live with us in her little house in the Grassmarket, in which Rosmuller now dwelt. There was no lack of good home-spun cloth in Nuremberg; nay, and if we should never again have new garments that would be all the better for our souls' health. As for me, I might perchance have fewer suitors, but if one should pay his court to me, he would have no thought but for Margery, and how she looked and moved. Nay, take it for all in all, we owed much thanks to Ursula and the reprobate heathen Sultan if we were by their means brought low from ill-starred wealth and ease to God-pleasing poverty.

Ann was far less horror-struck at the fearful sum of the ransom than we had been, by reason that she was ever possessed by the assurance that Heaven had created her and Herdegen for each other, and would bring them together at last.

Moreover she had good cause to build her hopes on my grand-uncle's help. In a letter from the Cardinal to her he said that now, as of old, he could only counsel her to follow the voice of her heart; that he would put no hindrance in the way of our departing, albeit he urgently prayed us to put it off till after his homecoming, which should now be in a short space. She was to let Baron Im Hoff know that he was ready to do his will, albeit he hoped at his coming to find him in mended health. She had forthwith carried these good tidings to my grand-uncle, and they had so uplifted and comforted his heart that verily it seemed as though my lord Cardinal's good hopes might find fulfilment. And this very morning she had seen him, and a right strange mind had come over him; he had enquired of her straitly, and as though it was to him a great matter, all that she could tell him of my lord Cardinal's way of life, of the duties of his office and the like; and whereas she answered him that of all these matters she knew but little, yet had she heard from his own mouth that his eminence was bound in thankfulness to his Holiness the Pope, by reason that he had made him to be high Almoner of the Papal treasury and thus put it into his power to do many good works; and this she deemed, had brought great easement to my granduncle. Then when she rose to depart from him, he had sent his serving-man to bid Master Holzschuher, the notary, to come to him, and to bring with him two trustworthy witnesses duly sworn to secrecy. As he bid her farewell he had laughed, and whispered to her that his Eminence the Cardinal would be well-content with old Im Hoff, yea, and she likewise, and her lover.

All this gave us matter for thought, and also gave us good heart; only it weighed upon our souls that our departing was not to be yet for some weeks.

CHAPTER XIII

Next morning Cousin Maud let me see in a right pleasant way how truly she was in earnest in the matter of thrift henceforth; she would take but one small pat of butter from the country wench who brought it, she sent away the butcher's man and would have no flesh meat, and at breakfast she abstained from butter on her bread, as she was wont to eat it. Likewise the chain and the great gold pin which she ever wore from morning till night, flashing on her bosom like a watchman's lantern, were now laid aside, and while I was eating my porridge she showed me the coffer wherein she had bestowed all she possessed of rings, pins, and the like, which she would presently take to the weigh-house to be weighed and then to a goldsmith to be valued. Howbeit, when I was fain to do likewise with my jewels she would not have it so, inasmuch as youth, quoth she, needed such bravery, and first we must learn how great a portion of the ransom my grand-uncle would take upon himself to pay.

Hereupon, in fulfilment of my purpose yestereve, I made it my hard duty to carry the evil tidings to the old baron, and humbly to remind him of his promise to take care for Herdegen's ransom. It was raining heavily, and a wet west wind whistled along the miry streets. It was weariful to wade through them, and when at last I reached the Im Hoff house Master Ulsenius called to me down the stairs: "Silence, Mistress Margery; there is worse weather in here than without doors!"

Thus as I went into the overheated chamber, I saw there was no good to be hoped for: yet were matters worse than I had looked to find them. So soon as my grand-uncle set eyes on me he frowned darkly, his hollow eyes had an angry glare and, without answering my good-day, he croaked at me: "You hoped that the old man might have passed away into eternity or ever you set forth on your wild adventure? Hah, hah But you are mistaken. I shall yet be granted time enough to show you whom you have to deal with, as it has likewise been enough to show me what you truly are! Whereas I trusted to have found a faithful and wise brain, what have I seen? Loveless and malignant privity, miserable folly, and such schemes as might have been dreamed of in a mad-house!"

"But, uncle, only hearken," I tried to say, and forthwith the idea fell into my mind, which I afterwards found to be a true one, that either Henneleinlein, had yestereve betrayed to him or to her gossip his housekeeper, all she had heard at the Forest Lodge. He would not suffer me to speak to the end, but went on to chide and complain, and broke in again and again, even when at last I found words and made it plain to him that we had kept our purpose privy from him to no end but to save him from grieving so long as we might; and albeit he might be wroth with us, yet he must grant that heretofore we had ever been modest and seemly maidens; but now, when it was a matter of life and freedom for those who were nearest and dearest to our hearts....

Here he broke in with scornful laughter, and cried out that he, for his part, might not indeed hope to be numbered among those chosen few. He had ever known full well that when we did him any Samaritan service it had been to no end save to draw from his purse the money to ransom my brothers and Ann's lover. Every kind word had been pure lies and falseness; yea, and worse than either of us were that crafty witch out in the forest, and the old scarecrow who made boast of having been as a mother to me. Thus far had I suffered his railing in patience, but now it was too much for the hot blood of the Schoppers; I could refrain myself no longer, and broke out in great wrath and reproaches for so vile an accusation. If it were not that his age and infirmities claimed our compassion, I would, said I, after such evil treatment, desire of Ann that she should never more cross the threshold of a man who could so cruelly defame us, and those two good women to whom we owed so much.

I spoke right loudly, beside myself with rage, and my face aglow; nor was it till I marked that my uncle was staring at me as at some marvel that I recovered myself, and on a sudden held my peace, inasmuch as the thought flashed through my brain that I was denying my brother even as Peter denied the Lord, albeit not indeed through any fear of man, but by giving way to my angered pride. Howbeit I had not long ceased when the stern old man cried out in pitiful entreaty.

"Nay, Margery, in the name of the Saints I pray you! You will not make Ann my foe. How hardhearted you can be, and how wroth, and against an old man sick unto death on the edge of the grave!—what was it, in truth, that brought the bitter words to my tongue, but my care and fears for you, who are verily and indeed my only comfort and all I have to love on earth? And now when I say again: I will not suffer you to depart. I will sacrifice all, everything to keep you from running into certain death, will you even then threaten to leave me alone in my misery, and to beguile Ann to desert me likewise?"

Hereupon I spoke him fair and as lovingly as in truth I might, and pledged my word that Ann should not set foot without the city gates or ever my lord Cardinal had come into them, and had given him the comfort of his blessing. And then he was of better cheer, and of his own free will he minded me of his promise to pay certain moneys for Herdegen's ransom; and all this he spoke full lovingly and my heart overflowed with true and fervent thankfulness, so that I took his thin hand and kissed it. Howbeit, he knew not yet how great a sum was needed: and whereas I was about to prepare his mind for the worst, Ann came into the chamber, and as soon as my grand-uncle saw her he cried out in glad good cheer: "Thank God, sweet maid, all is peace between us again. You forego your mad purpose, and I—I will pay the ransom." At this Ann flew to his side and thanked him, with overflowing eyes, and little by little we led him on, till he cried out: "Well, well, children, they surely cannot set the price of a kingdom on that young scapegrace Schopper's head!"

So Ann took courage, and told him that Ursula had, of her deep malice, declared that Herdegen was one of the richest youths of Germany, and that by reason of this the Sultan had demanded the great price of twenty-four thousand sequins.

The truth was out; I marvelled to mark that my grand-uncle was not dismayed as I had looked to see him; nay, but he laughed aloud and said: "That would indeed be somewhat new and strange! You children would ever rack your brains over the Italian poets rather than over matters of mine and thine, albeit that is the axis on which the world turns. There would, in truth, be no justice in so vast a sum, but that in the markets of Egypt they reckon in Venice sequins with none but the Franks; nigh upon thirteen of their dirhems go to the gold sequin, and thus we have-let me reckon—the old trader has not forgotten his skill on his sick-bed—we have one thousand eight hundred and forty and six sequins; and that is a vast ransom still such as is never paid but for lords of the highest degree. Four and twenty thousand sequins!" And again he laughed aloud. "It is easily spoken, children, but you cannot even guess what it would mean. Believe me when I tell you that many a well-to-do merchant in Nuremberg, who is at the head of a fine trade, would be at his wits' end if he were desired to pay down half of your four and twenty thousand sequins in hard coin!"

Then I took up my parable and told him how Eppelein had stamped the sum on his mind, and that he for certain was in the right, both as to the sum and as to the Venice sequins, forasmuch as that Herdegen, to the end that he might know it rightly, had told him that they should be ducats such as he had three in a red stuff wrapper, and Kunz and I likewise each two, in our money-boxes as christening-gifts.

Now while I thus spoke the old man was sorely troubled, and his wax-white face turned paler at each word. He raised himself up, leaning on the arms of the great chair, so high that we were filled with amazement, and he gazed about him with his glassy eyes and then said, still holding himself up: "That, that.... And yesterday, only yesterday.... The captive himself.... Four and twenty thousand sequins, do you say?... and I—oh, what were my words?... But what old Im Hoff promises that he will do.... And yet.... If you maids had but been duteous children, if you had but come to me first, as trustful daughters.... Only yesterday I might—Yes, perchance I might...." And then he stormed forth: "But who is there indeed to care for me? Who ever comes nigh me with true love and honest trustfulness? Not one, no, not one!... Ursula—the lad whom from an infant—and you—both of you, what have you done?... Yesterday, only yesterday!... But to-day.... Four and twenty thousand sequins!" His arms on a sudden failed him, and he sank back in a deep swoon, his colorless face drooping on his shoulder. Now, while we did all in our power to revive him, and while one serving-man ran for the leech and another for the friar, meseemed that the old man's left side was strangely stiff and numb; yet the low flame of his feeble life was still burning.

Howbeit, when Master Ulsenius had let blood the old man opened his right eye; and when presently he was able to say: "Book," and then again "Book," we perceived by sundry signs that what he craved was water, and that he spoke one word for another. And thus it was till his chief confessor, Master Leonard Derrer, the reverend Prior of the Dominicans, came in with the sacristan, to administer to him extreme unction. But now, when the reverend Father came toward the dying man with the Body of the Lord, there was so dreadful and sorrowful a sight to be seen as I may never forget to my latter day. Instead of receiving that Holy Sacrament in all thankful humility, my grand-uncle thrust away my lord Prior—a whitebearded old man, of a venerable and commanding presence—with great fury and ungoverned rage, storming at him in strangely-mingled words, which for sure, he meant for others, but in a voice and with a mien which plainly showed that he would have nought of that Messenger of Grace. And from time to time he turned that eye he could use on Ann, and albeit he spoke one word for another, he made shift many times to repeat the Cardinal's name with impatient bidding, so that it was not hard to understand his meaning and his intent to receive the Viaticum from none other than that high prelate.

Howbeit, to us it seemed nothing less than treason to the dying man to interpret this to my lord Prior, in especial since my grand-uncle had, but now, shown us so much favor. Indeed we were moved to show him all loving kindness. Ann held his hand in hers, and whispered to him again and again that he should take patience, and that his Eminence was already on his way and would ere long be here. The reverend Prior showed indeed true Christian forbearance, thinking that the departing soul was more sorely troubled than was in truth the fact. He heeded not the old man's threats and struggles, but stood in silence at his post, and when presently the old Baron's hand dropped lifeless from Ann's grasp he sent us from the chamber.

We could hear through the door the good priest's voice in prayer and benediction, pronouncing absolution over the dying man, and at times my grand uncle's wrathful tones, feeble indeed, but terrible to hear. Each time he broke in on the Prior's pious words we shuddered, and when at last the priest rang his little bell a great terror fell upon us, whereas this ordinance is wont to bring comfort and edification to the soul.

We had been on our knees some long space, praying fervently for that hapless, imperilled soul, when the door was opened, and my lord Prior declared in a loud voice that the noble Baron and Knight Sebald Im Hoff had made a good end after receiving the most holy Sacrament.

Then thought I, a good end peradventure, by the grace of Christ and the Virgin, but a peaceful end alas! by no means. And this might be seen even in the dead man's face. In later years, whensoever it has been my lot to gaze on the face of the dead, I have ever perceived that death hath lent them an aspect of peaceful calm so that the saying of common folk, that the Angel of Death hath kissed them is right fitting; but my grand-uncle's face was as that of a man whose dignity is broken by a mightier than he, and who hath suffered it in silent, gloomy rebellion.

With all our might and soul we prayed for him again and again; howbeit, as must ever befall, other cares came crowding in, to swallow up that one. As soon as the tidings of the old noble's death were rumored abroad, those who had known him in life came pouring in, and messengers from the town-council, notaries with sealing-wax and seals, priests for the burying, neighbors, and other good folk, and among them many friars and nuns. Lastly came Doctor Holzschuher of the council, my grand-uncle's notary, and one of our own father's most trusted friends, in all points a man of such worth and honesty that no words befit him so well as the Cardinal's saying: that he reminded him of an oak of the German forests.

When, now, this man, who in his youth had been one of the goodliest in all Nuremberg, and who was still of noble aspect with his long silver-grey hair lying on his shoulders—when he now greeted us maids well-nigh gloomily, and with no friendly beck or nod, we knew forthwith that he must have great and well-founded fears for our concerns. Yea, and so it was. Presently, when he had held grave discourse with the High Treasurer and the other chief men of the council, he called to him Cousin Maud and me, and told us that old Im Hoff's latest dealing was such, to all seeming, as to take from us all hope that our inheritance from him should help us to pay the ransom for Herdegen. And on the morrow his will would be opened and read and we should learn thereby in what way that old man had cared for those who were nearest and dearest to him.

Hereupon we had no choice but to bury many a fair hope in the grave; and notwithstanding this, we might owe no grudge to the departed; for albeit he had cared first and chiefly for the salvation of his own sinful soul, he nevertheless had taken thought to provide for my brothers and likewise for Ann and to keep the pledge he had given. Never in all his days—and this was confessed even by his enemies, of whom he had many—had he broken his word, and it was plain to be seen from all his instructions that the true cause of the deadly blow which had killed him was the sudden certainty that, by his own act, he had bereft himself of the power to redeem Herdegen by paying the ransom as he had promised.

And this was my uncle's will:

When he had heard from Ann that my lord Cardinal was minded to hasten his home-coming and give him extreme unction, and had likewise had tidings that that high Prelate took great joy in his liberty of dealing with the Papal treasury for alms, he had bidden to him, that very evening, Doctor Holzschuher, his notary, and certain sworn witnesses, and had in all due form cancelled his former will, and in a fine new one had devised his estate as follows:

Ursula Tetzel was to have the five thousand gulden which he had promised her when he had unwittingly killed young Tetzel.

To Kunz he bequeathed the great trade both in Nuremberg and Venice, with all that pertained thereto and certain moneys in capital for carrying it on; likewise his fine dwelling-house, inasmuch as Herdegen would have our house for his own. And Kunz should be held bound to carry on the said trade in the same wise as my grand-uncle had done in his life-time, and pay out of it two-third parts of the profits to Herdegen and Ann; and that these two should wed was the dearest wish of his old age. Not a farthing was to be taken from the moneyed capital for twenty years to come, and this was expressly recorded; nor might the trade be sold, or cease to be carried on. If Kunz should die within that space, then he charged the head clerk of the house to conduct the business under the same pledge. And if and when Kunz should wed, then should he pay only half the profits to his brother instead of two-thirds.

The eldest son of Herdegen and Ann was to fall next heir to the business; but if this marriage came to nought, or they had no male issue, then Herdegen's son-in-law, or my son, or Kunz's.

Likewise he believed that he had made good provision for the maintenance of the young pair, inasmuch as though it could scarce be hoped that Herdegen would be able to take the lead of the trading house, yet his own fortune was not so great as to assure to Ann a life so free from burthens, and in all ways so easy as he desired for her, and as beseemed the mistress of so ancient a Nuremberg family.

His landed estates he had for the most part devised to the holy Church, and the remainder in equal halves to Herdegen and to me.

Three thousand gulden, which he had lent to the Convent of Vierzehnheiligen, and of which he might at any time require the repayment, he had set apart to ransom Herdegen and pay for his home-coming.

Of his possessions in hard coin, three thousand gulden were for Herdegen's share, and one thousand each for Ann and me as a bride-gift, and he had devised goodly sums of money to the hospitals and poor of the city, and the serving-folk and retainers of the household.

But then where was the great and well-nigh royal treasure of which old Im Hoff had, not so long since, been possessed; so that in the time of the Diet he had paid down in hard coin thirty thousand Hungarian ducats to buy himself a Baron's title? Master Holzschuher could tell us well enough. When that old man had once said to Ann that she could scarce believe how great profit might be gained in a few years by well-directed trading with Venice, he spoke not without book. After endowing many churches and convents in Franconia while he was yet living, with truly lordly generosity, and providing for masses for his soul and other pious offices, he had still a sum of forty and four thousand Hungarian ducats to dispose of. And these moneys, notwithstanding Master Holzschuher's entreaties that he would devise at least half of these vast possessions to his own town and near of kin, he had bequeathed to the alms-coffers of his Holiness the Pope, to be dealt with at the pleasure of his Eminence Cardinal Bernliardi, with this sole condition: that every year, on his name-day, mass should be said by some high Prelate for his miserable soul, which sorely needed such grace. Moreover he had provided that the document, duly attested by the notary and witnesses, should be sent to Rome on the morrow by a specially appointed messenger; thus it was long since far away and out of reach when my grand-uncle had learnt that all his remaining possessions were not enough to release Herdegen. And this, as I have already said, had fallen heavy on his soul.

Verily there hath been no lack of fervent prayers for his soul on our part; and at a later time, when I came to know to how many hapless wretches his testament had brought a blessing, little by little I forgave this strange bestowal of his wealth, and could pronounce over his grave a clear "Requiescat in pace!" May he rest in peace!

When we had presently duly weighed and reckoned with Master Holzschuher what we had indeed inherited from our rich kinsman, and how much we might ere long hope to collect of our own and from Cousin Maud, we had it before our eyes in plain writing that a large portion of the ransom was yet lacking. The trade of the Im Hoffs' was to be sure of great money value; but by my grand-uncle's will we might not touch it for twenty years. Likewise Master Holzschuher pointed out to us by many an example how wrong it would be, and in especial at this very time, to sell landed estate at any price, that is to say at about one-third of its real worth. And finally he told us that the Chancery guardians were not at that present time suffered to pay down one farthing of our inheritance from our father. Thus we were heavy at heart, while Doctor Holzschuher was discoursing in a low voice with Uncle Christian and Master Pernhart, and noting certain matters on paper.

Then those gentlemen rose up; and whereas I looked in the face of the worthy notary meseemed it was as withered grass well bedewed with rain; and glad assurance beamed on me from his goodly and noble features. And I read the same promise in the looks of Uncle Christian and Master Pernhart, and where three such men led the fray methought the victory was certain.

And now we were told what was the matter of their discourse. If they might find a fitting envoy, they might perchance move the Sultan to forego some portion of the ransom; yet would they bear in mind what the whole sum was. Much of our possessions we were indeed not suffered to sell, yet might we borrow on them or pledge them, and the good feeling of our friends and fellow citizens would, for sure, help us to the remainder. Nay, and these gentlemen methought had some privy purpose; yet, inasmuch as they told us nought of their own free will, we were careful to put no questions. As we took leave they besought us yet to delay our departing and to suffer them to be free to do what they would. And we were fain to yield, albeit the blood of the Schoppers boiled at the thought that I must tarry here idle, and others go round as it were with the beggars' staff, in our name, and for the sake of a son of our house who had done no good to any man. Howbeit, I knew full well that pride and defiance were now out of place; and while I was walking homewards with Ann and Cousin Maud, on a sudden my cousin asked me: If Lorenz Stromer were in Herdegen's plight would I not gladly give of my estate; and when I said yes, quoth she: "Then all is well." And inasmuch as she was of the same mind she could, without a qualm, suffer the gentlemen to ask from door to door in Herdegen's name and in her own. It was our part only to show that we, as his nearest and dearest, were foremost in giving. And on that same day Ann brought all she possessed in gold and jewels, even to her christening coins which she had kept in her money-box, and among them likewise a costly cross of diamonds which my lord Cardinal had given her a few months ago.

That evening, again, as dusk was falling, Ann once more knocked at our door, and the reason of her coming was in truth a sad one: her grand-uncle, old Adam Heyden the organist, our friend of the tower, felt that his last hour was nigh, and bid us go to see him. Thus it came to pass that in two following days we had to stand by a death-bed. On each lay an old man departing to the other world, and meseemed their end had fallen so close together to yield warning and meditation to our young souls. Now, as I toiled up the steep turret-stair, after flying, yesterday, up the matted steps of the wealthy house of the Im Hoffs, meseemed that the two men's lives had been like to these staircases, and, young as I was, I nevertheless could say to myself that the humbler man's steep stair, which of late he could not mount without much panting, led up to a higher and brighter home than the wide steps of the rich merchant's palace.

Howbeit, when I had presently closed that good old man's eyes, I would not suffer myself to think thus of the twain, by reason that I could not endure to mar my remembrance of that other, to whom, after all, we owed much thanks.

The old organist had received the Holy Sacrament at mid-day from the hand of his old friend Nikolas Laister, the Vicar of Saint Sebald's. He would have no one to see him save ourselves and Hans Richter the churchwarden, a man after his own heart, and the Pernharts; and at first he marked not our coming, inasmuch as he was just then giving a toy to the deaf-mute boy, which he had carved with his own hand, and Dame Giovanna had much pains to carry away the child, who had cast himself on the old man with passionate love. Everything that moved the little one's soul he was forced, as it were, to express with unreasoning violence; and now, when the child was so boisterous as to disturb the peace of the others, his mother took him by the hand to lead him away into another chamber; but the dying man signed to him with a look which none may describe, and that moment the little fellow set his teeth hard and stood in silence by the door. Whereupon the old man nodded to him as though the child had done him some kindness.

Then he shut his eyes for a good while, and presently asked for some of the fine Bacharach wine which Cousin Maud had sent him; but his voice could scarce be heard. Ann reached him the glass, and at a sign from him she tasted of it; then he drank it with much comfort while Dame Giovanna held him sitting. The old, sweet smile was on his lips, and as he yet held the stem of the glass with a shaking hand, and suffered that I should help him, he cried in a clear voice: "Once more, Prosit, Elsie! You have waited long enough up there for your old man. And Prosit, likewise, to my dear old home, the fair city of Nuremberg." Then he took breath and added according to his wont: "Prosit, Adam! Thanks, Heyden!" And emptied the cup which I tilted up for him, to the very bottom. Then, when he fell back and gazed before him in silence, I found speech, and noted, albeit it struck me in truth as somewhat strange, that he bore our good town in mind then, in drinking his old pledge. Hereupon he nodded kindly and added, with an enquiring glance at the churchwarden: "It is rightly the duty of every true Christian man to pray for all mankind! Well, well; but they are so many, so infinitely many; and I, like every other man, have my own little world, inside the great world, as it were, and that is my dear old, staunch town of Nuremberg. Never have I been beyond its precincts, and it contains all on earth that is dear and precious to me. To me the citizens of Nuremberg are all mankind, and our city and so much as the eye can see from this tower all my world, small though it may be. I could ever find some good matter for thought in Nuremberg, something noble and well-compact, a fine whole. I have never sought the boundaries of the other, greater world."

Yet, that his world was in truth wider than he weened, was plain to us from the prayer he murmured wherein we could hear my brothers' names, albeit land and seas parted them from him. And after that, for a space all were silent, and he lay gazing at the bone crucifix on the wall; and at last he besought Dame Giovanna to lift him somewhat higher, and he drank again a little more, and said right softly as he cast a loving glance upon us each in turn: "I have looked into my own heart and gazed on Him on the Cross! That is our ensample! And I depart joyfully—and if you would know what maketh death so easy to me; it is that I have needed but little, and kept little for myself; and whereas I was wont to give away what other men save, I came to know of a certainty that all the good we do to others is the best we can do for ourselves. It is that, it is that!"

And he stretched forth his hand, and when we had all kissed it, he cried out: "My God, I now can say I thank Thee! What to-morrow may bring, Thou alone canst know! Margery, Ann, my poor children! May the bright day of meeting dawn for you! May Heaven in mercy protect the youths beyond seas! Here, close at hand is Mistress Kreutzer with her orphan children, you know them—you and Master Peter—they are in sore need of help—and the good we do to others. But come close to me, come all of you—and the little ones likewise."

And we fell upon our knees by the bed, and he spread forth his hands and said in a clear voice: "The Lord bless you and keep you, the Lord lift up his countenance upon you and be merciful unto you."

And then he sighed deeply, and his hands fell, and Dame Giovanna closed his eyes.

Yea! Death had come easy to this simple soul. Never knew I any man who gave so much out of a little, and never have I seen a happier or more peaceful face on a death-bed.

My grand-uncle's burial was grand and magnificent. All the town-council, and many of the nobles joined in the funeral-train. Bells tolling and priests chanting, crape, tapers, incense and the rest of it—we had more than enough of them all. Only one thing was lacking, namely, tears—not those of the hirelings who attended it, but such as fall in silence from a sorrowing eye.

In the Im Hoffs' great house all was silence till the burying was done; up in the tower, where old Adam Heyden lay asleep, the bells rang out as they did every day, for wedding and christening, for mass and mourning; yet by the low door which led to the narrow turret-stair I saw a crowd of little lads and maids with their mothers; and albeit the leaves were off the trees and the last flowers were frozen to death, many a child had found a green twig or carried a little bunch of everlasting flowers in its little hand to lay on the bier of that kind old friend. It was all the sacristan could do to keep away the multitudes who were fain to look on his face once more; and when he was borne to the grave-yard, not above two hours after my grand-uncle, there was indeed a wondrous great following. The snow was falling fast in the streets, and the fine folks who had attended him to the grave were soon warming themselves at home after the burying of old Im Hoff. But there came behind Adam Heyden's bier many right honest and respected folk, and a throng, reaching far away, of such as might feel the wind whistling cold through the holes in their sleeves and about their bare heads. And among these was there many a penniless woman who wiped her eyes with her kerchief or her hand, and many a widow's child, who tightened its little belt as it saw him who had so often given it a meal carried to the grave.

CHAPTER XIV

Our good hope of going forth with good-speed into the wide world to risk all for our lover and brother was not to be yet. We were fain to take patience; and if this seemed hard to us maidens, it was even worse for Kubbeling; the man was wont to wander free whither he would, and during these days of tarrying at the forest-lodge, first he lost his mirthful humor, and then he fell sick of a fever. For two long weeks had he to be abed, he, who, as he himself told, had never to this day needed any healing but such as the leech who medicined his beasts could give him. We awaited the tidings of him with much fear; and at this time we likewise knew not what to think of those gentlemen who heretofore had been such steadfast and faithful friends to us, inasmuch as that Doctor Holzschuher gave no sign, and soon after my grand-uncle's burying Uncle Christian and Master Pernhart had set forth for Augsburg on some privy matters of the town council. Yet we could do nought but submit, by reason that we knew that every good citizen thinks of the weal of the Commonwealth before all else.

Even our nearest of kin had laid our concerns on the shelf, while day and night alike it weighed on our souls, and we made ready for a long time to come of want and humble cheer. The Virgin be my witness that at that time I was ready and willing to give up many matters which we were forced to forego; howbeit, we found out that it was easier to eat bread without butter and no flesh meat, than to give up certain other matters. As for my jewels, which Cousin Maud would not sell, but pledged them to a goldsmith, I craved them not. Only a heart with a full great ruby which I had ever worn as being my Hans' first lovetoken, I would indeed have been fain to keep, yet whereas Master Kaden set a high price on the stone I suffered him to break it out, notwithstanding all that Cousin Maud and Ann might say, and kept only the gold case. It was hard likewise to send forth the serving-folk and turn a deaf ear to their lamenting. Most of the men, when they heard how matters stood, would gladly have stayed to serve us for a lesser wage, and each and all went about looking as if the hail had spoilt their harvest; only old Susan held her head higher than ever, by reason that we had chosen her to share our portion during the years of famine. Likewise we were glad to promise the old horse-keeper, who had served our father before us, that we would care for him all his days; he besought me eagerly that I would keep my own Hungarian palfrey, for, to his mind, a damsel of high degree with no saddle nor steed was as a bird that cannot rise on its wings. Howbeit, we found those who were glad to buy the horse, and never shall I forget the hour when for the last time I patted the smooth neck of my Bayard, the gift of my lost lover, and felt his shrewd little head leaning against my own. Uncle Tucher bought him for his daughter Bertha, and it was a comfort to me to think that she was a soft, kind hearted maid, whom I truly loved. All the silver gear likewise, which we had inherited, was pledged for money, and where it lay I knew not; yet of a truth the gifts of God taste better out of a silver spoon than out of a tin one. Cousin Maud, who would have no half measures, carried many matters of small worth to the pawn-broker; yet all this grieved us but lightly, although the sky hung dark over the town, by reason that other events at that time befell which gave us better cheer.

The Magister, as soon as he had tidings of our purpose, came with right good will to offer us his all, and declared his intent to share our simple way of life, and this was no more than we had looked for, albeit we steadfastly purposed only to take from him so much as he might easily make shift to spare. But it was indeed a joyful surprise when, one right dreary day, Heinz Trardorf, Herdegen's best-beloved companion in his youth, who had long kept far from the house, came to speak with us of Herdegen's concerns. He had now followed his father, who was dead, as master in his trade, and was already so well thought of that the Council had trusted his skilled hands to build a new great organ for the Church of Saint Laurence. I knew full well, to be sure, that when Herdegen had come back from Paris in all his bravery, he had cared but little for Trardorf's fellowship; but I had marked, many a time in church, that his eyes were wont to rest full lovingly on me.

And now, when I gave him my hand and asked him what might be his will, at first he could scarce speak, albeit he was a man of substance to whom all folks would lift their hat. At last he made bold to tell me that he had heard tidings of the sum demanded to ransom Herdegen, and that he, inasmuch as that he dwelt in his own house and that his profits maintained him in more than abundance, could have no greater joy than to pay the moneys he had by inheritance to ransom my brother.

And as the good fellow spoke the tears stood in his eyes, and mine likewise were about to flow; and albeit Cousin Maud here broke in and, to hide how deeply her heart was touched, said, well-nigh harshly, that without doubt the day was not far off when he would have a wife and family, and might rue the deed by which he had parted with his estate, never perchance to see it more, I freely and gladly gave him my hand, and said to him that for my part his offering would be dearest to me of any, and that for sure Herdegen would be of the same mind. And a beam as of sunshine overspread his countenance, and while he shook my hand in silence I could see that he hardly refrained himself from betraying more. After this, I came to know from his good mother that this offer of moneys had cost him a great pang, but only for this cause: that he had loved me from his youth up, and his noble soul forbid him to pay court to me when he had in truth done me so great a service.

Still, and in despite of these gleams of light, I must ever remember those three weeks as a full gloomy and sorrowful time.

Kubbeling's eldest son and his churlish helpmate had fared forth to Venice instead of himself. They might not sail for the land of Egypt, and this chafed Uhlwurm sorely, by reason that he was sure in himself that he, far better than his master or than any man on earth, could do good service there to Ann, on whom his soul was set more than on any other of us.

Towards the end of the third week we rode forth to spend a few days again at the lodge, and there we found Young Kubbeling well nigh healed of his fever, and Eppelein's tongue ready to wag and to tell us of his many adventures without overmuch asking. Howbeit, save what concerned his own mishaps, he had little to say that we knew not already.

The Saracen pirate who had boarded the galleon from Genoa which was carrying him and his lord to Cyprus, had parted him from Herdegen and Sir Franz, and sold him for a slave in Egypt. There had he gone through many fortunes, till at last, in Alexandria, he had one day met Akusch. At that time my faithful squire's father was yet in good estate, and he forthwith bought Eppelein, who was then a chattel of the overseer of the market, to the end that the fellow might help his son in the search for Herdegen. This search they had diligently pursued, and had discovered my brother and Sir Franz together in the armory of the Sultan's Palace, in the fort over against Cairo, whither they had come after they had both worked at the oars in great misery for two years, on board a Saracen galley.

But then Herdegen had made proof, in some jousting among the young Mamelukes, of how well skilled he was with the sword, and thereby he had won such favor that they were fain to deliver sundry letters which he wrote to us, into the care of the Venice consul. Whereas he had no answer he had set it down to our lack of diligence at home, till at last he was put on the right track by Akusch, and it was plainly shown that those letters had never reached us, and that by Ursula's malice. To follow up these matters Akusch had afterwards betaken himself again to Alexandria; notwithstanding by this time his father had fallen on evil days. And behold, on the very evening after their return, as they were passing along by the side of the Venice Fondaco, whither they had gone to see the leech who attended the

Consul—having heard that he was a German by birth—they were aware of a loud outcry hard by, and presently beheld a wounded man, whom they forthwith knew for Kunz.

At first they believed that their eyes deceived them; and that it should have been these two, of all men, who found their master's brother lying in his blood, I must ever deem a miracle. To be sure, any man from the West who was fain to seek another in the land of Egypt, must first make enquiry here at the Fondaco.

A few hours later Kunz was in bed and well tended in the house of Akusch's mother, and it was on their return to Cairo, to speak with my eldest brother of these matters, that Eppelein was witness to Ursula's vile betrayal and the vast demand of the Sultan. Then my brother, by the help of some who showed him favor, had that letter conveyed to Akusch of which Eppelein had been robbed hard by Pillenreuth. More than this the good fellow had not to tell.

As I, on my ride home through the wood, turned over in my mind who might be the wise and trusty friend to whom we could confide our case and our fears, if Kubbeling should leave us in the lurch, verily I found no reply. If indeed Cousin Gotz—that wise and steadfast wayfaring man, rich with a thousand experiences of outlandish life—if he were willing to make common cause with his Little Red-riding-hood, and the companion of his youth! But a terrible oath kept him far away, and where in the wide world might he be found?

Ann likewise had much to cause her heaviness, and I thanked the Saints that I was alone with Eppelein when he told me that his dear lord was sorely changed, albeit having seen him only from afar, he could scarce tell me wherein that change lay.

Thus we rode homewards in silence, through the evening dusk, and as we came in sight of the lights of the town all my doubting and wandering fears vanished on a sudden in wonderment as to who should be the first person we might meet within the gate, inasmuch as Cousin Maud had ever set us the unwise example of considering such a meeting as a sign, or token, or Augury.

Now, as soon as we had left the gate behind us, lo, a lantern was lifted, and we saw, by the light twinkling dimly through the horn, instead of old Hans Heimvogel's red, sottish face, a sweet and lovely maiden's; by reason that he had fallen into horrors, imagining that mice were rushing over him, so that his fair granddaughter Maria was doing duty for him. And I greeted her right graciously, inasmuch as Cousin Maud held it to be a good sign when a smiling maid should be the first to meet her as she came into the city gates.

As for Ann, she scarce marked that it was Maria; and when, after we were come home, I spoke of this token of good promise, she asked me how, in these evil days, I could find heart to think of such matters; and she sighed and cried: "Oh, Margery, indeed I am heavy at heart! For three long years have I taken patience and with a right good will. But the end, meseems, is further than ever, and he who should have helped us is disabled or ever he has stirred a finger, and even my lord Cardinal's home-coming is put off, albeit all men know that Herdegen is as a man in a den of lions—and I, my spirit sinks within me. And even my wise grandmother can give me no better counsel than to 'wait patiently' and yet again 'Wait'..."

Whereupon Susan, who had taken off from us our wet hoods, broke in with: "Aye, Mistress Ann, and that has ever from the days of Adam and Eve, been the best of all counsel. For life all through is but waiting for the end; and even when we have taken the last Sacrament and our eyes are dim in death then most of all must we take Patience, waiting for that we shall find beyond the grave. Here below! By my soul, I myself grew grey waiting in vain for one who long years ago gave me this ring. Others had better luck; yet if the priest had wed us, would that have made an end of Patience? I trow not! It might have been for weal or it might have been for woe. A wife may go to mass every day in the month. But is that an end of Patience? Will the storks bring her a babe or no? Will it be a boy or a maid? And if the little one should come, after the wife has told her beads till her fingers are sore, what will the waiting babe turn out? Such an one as Junker Herdegen grows up to be the delight of every eye and heart, and if that make less need of Patience meseems we know full well! And Mistress Waldstromer, out in the forest, a lady, she, of stern stuff, she could tell a tale; and I say, Mistress Ann, if old Dame Pernhart's answer sinks into your heart, God's blessing rest on it!—I am waiting, as you are waiting. We each and all are waiting for one; if by the merciful help of the Saints he ever comes home, yet never dream, Mistress Ann, that Patience will be out of court."

And with such comfort as this the old woman hung our garments to dry while we bowed our heads and went up-stairs.

Up in the guest-chamber we heard loud voices, and as we went in a strange sight met our eyes. Uncle Christian and Doctor Holzschuher were sitting face to face with Cousin Maud, and she was laughing so heartily that she could not control herself, but flung up her arms and then dropped them on her knees, for all the world as she had taught us children to play at a game of "Fly away, little birds."

When she marked my presence she forgot to greet me, and cried to me well nigh breathless:

"A drink of wine, Margery, and a morsel of bread. I am ready to split—I shall die of laughing!"

Then, when I heard my good Godfather Christian's hearty laughing, and saw that Master Holzschuher had but just ceased, I was fain to laugh likewise, and even Ann, albeit she had but now been so sad, joined in. This lasted a long while till we learned the cause of such unwonted mirth; and this was of such a kind as to afford great comfort and new assurance, and we were bound to crave our good friends' pardon for having deemed them lacking in diligence. Master Holzschuher had indeed made the best use of the time to move every well-to-do man in Nuremberg who had known our departed father, and the Abbots of the rich convents, and many more, to give of their substance as they were able, to redeem Herdegen from the power of the heathen; and the other twain had worked wonders likewise, in Augsburg.

But that which had moved Cousin Maud to mirth was that my Uncle Christian had related how that he and Master Pernhart, finding old Tetzel, Ursula's father, at Augsburg, had agreed together to make him pay a share towards Herdegen's ransom; and my godfather's face beamed again now, with contentment in every feature, as he told us by what means he had won the churlish old man over to the good cause.

Whereas the three good gentlemen had considered that all of Jost Tetzel's great possessions must presently fall to his daughter, and that it would be a deed pleasing to God to bring some chastisement on that traitorous quean, they had laid a plot against her father; and it was for that alone that Uncle Christian, who could ill endure the ride in the winter-season, had set forth, with Master Pernhart, for Augsburg. And there he had achieved a rare masterpiece of skill, painting Dame Ursula's reprobate malice in such strong colors to her father that Master Pernhart was in fear lest he should bring upon himself another fit. And he had furthermore sworn to lay the whole matter before the Emperor, with whom, as all men knew, he enjoyed much privilege, inasmuch as he had been as it were his host when his Majesty held his court at Nuremberg. Ursula, to be sure, was no subject now of his gracious Majesty's; yet would he, Christian Pfinzing, know no rest till the Emperor had compelled her father, Jost Tetzel, to cut off from her who had married an Italian, the possessions she counted on from a German city.

Thereupon Pernhart had spoken in calm but weighty words, threatening that his brother, the Cardinal, would visit the heaviest wrath of the Pope on the old man and his daughter, unless he were ready and willing to make amends and atonement for his child's accursed sin, whereby a Christian man had fallen into the hands of the godless heathen. And when at last they had conquered the churlish old man's hardness of heart and stiff-necked malice, they drove him to a strange bargain. Old Tetzel was steadfast in his intention to give up as little as he might of his daughter's inheritance, while his tormentors raised their demands, and claimed a hundred gulden and a hundred gulden more, up to many hundreds, which Tetzel was forced to yield; till at last he gave his bond, signed and sealed, to renounce all his daughter's estate, and to add thereto two thousand gulden of his own moneys, and to hold the sum in readiness to ransom Herdegen.

Thus, at one stroke, all our fears touching the moneys were at an end; and when the notary showed us the parchment roll on which each one had set down the sum he would give, we were struck dumb; and when we reckoned it all together, the sum was far greater than that which had cost us so many sleepless nights.

By this time we scarce could read for tears, and our souls were so moved to thankfulness as we marked the large sums set forth against the names of the noble families and of the convent treasurers, that we had never felt so great a love for our good city and the dear, staunch friends who dwelt therein. Nay, and many simple folk had promised to pay somewhat of their modest store; and although my soul overflowed with thankful joy over the great sums to be given by our kith and kin, I rejoiced no less over the five pounds of farthings promised by a cordwainer, whom we had holpen some years ago when he had been sick and in debt.

And then was there hearty embracing and kissing, and the men, as was befitting after a deed so well done, craved to drink. Cousin Maud hastened with all zeal to do honor to friends and guests so dear; but as she reached the door she stood still as in doubt, and signed to me so that I perceived that somewhat had gone wrong. And so indeed it had, inasmuch as our silver vessels, down to the very least cup, had gone to the silversmith in pledge, and Uncle Tucher, the Councillor, who had bought my palfrey, had also been fain to have all our old wine, whereof many goodly rows of casks, and jars sealed with pitch, lay in our cellars. A few hams still hung in the chimney by good luck; and there were chickens and eggs in plenty; but of all else little enough, even of butter. When Cousin Maud set forth all this with a right lamentable face I could not refrain my mirth, and I promised her that if she could send up a few dainty dishes from the kitchen, I would make shift to please our beloved guests. That as for the wine, I would take that upon myself, and no Emperor need be ashamed of our Venice glasses. And herewith I sent her down stairs; but I then frankly confessed to our friends how matters stood; and when they had heard me, now laughing heartily, and now in amazement and shaking their heads, I enquired of Doctor Holzschuher, as a man of law, how I might deal with the wine, inasmuch as it had already found a purchaser? Hereupon arose much jocose argument and discussion, and at last the learned notary and doctor of laws declared that he held it to be his duty, as adviser to the Council and administrator of the Schopper estates, to taste and prove with all due caution whether the price promised by Tucher, and not yet paid down, were not all too little for the liquor, inasmuch as his clients, being but women-folk, had no skill in the good gifts of Bacchus, and could not know their value. To abstain from such testing he held would be a breach of duty, and whereas he did not trust his own skill alone, he must call upon Master Christian Pfinzing as a man of ripe experience, and Master Councillor Pernhart, who, as brother to a great prelate, had doubtless drunk much good liquor, in due form to proceed with him to the Schoppers' cellar, and there to mark those vessels or jars out of which the wine should be drawn for the testing. Moreover, to satisfy all the requirements of the case, a serving-man should be sent to call upon Master Tucher, as the purchaser, to be present in his own person at the ceremony. Inasmuch as it yet lacked two hours of midnight, he would, without doubt, be found in the gentlemen's tavern; and it might be enjoined on the messenger to add, that if Master Tucher were fain to bring with him one skilled in such matters to bear him witness on his part, such an one would be made right welcome at the Schopperhof.

Thus within a quarter of an hour the three worthy gentlemen, and Ann and I, were seated with the winejars before us, they having chosen for themselves of the best our cellar could afford; and when the meats which Cousin Maud sent up were set on the table, albeit there were but earthen plates and crocks, and no silver glittered on the snow-white cloth, yet God's good gifts lacked not their savor.

And presently Uncle Tucher came in, and with him, as his skilled witness, old Master Loffelholz; and when they likewise had sat down with us, and when we had bidden the Magister to join us, there was such hearty and joyful emptying of glasses and friendly discourse that Master Tucher declared that the happy spirit of our father, the singer, still dwelt within our walls. Howbeit, Ann had to do her duty as watcher over my uncle more often that evening than for a long time past.

In the course of that right joyful supper many weighty matters were discussed, and the gentlemen, meseemed, were greatly more troubled than Cousin Maud or I that we should so hastily have parted with sundry matters which should not be lacking in a house of good family, but which, as we had learned by experience, were in no wise needful in life. And many a jesting word was spoken concerning our poor platters and dishes, and tin spoons, and empty stables. The bargain over the wine was declared to be null and void, and my cousin took heart to assure the gentlemen, in right seemly speech, that now again she was happy, when she knew that what she had set before such worshipful and welcome guests was indeed our own, and not another's.

By the time of their departing it was nearer to cockcrow than to midnight; and when, on the morrow, I went into the chamber in the morning, to look forth into the street, the sun was shining brightly in a blue sky. I minded me with silent thanksgiving of all the good cheer yestereve had brought us, and of the wisdom and faithfulness of our good friends. Many a wise and a witty word uttered over their wine came back to me then; and I was wondering to myself what new plot had been brewing between my godfather and Uncle Tucher, whereas I had marked them laying their heads together, when behold, the stable-lad from the Tuchers' coming down the street, leading my own dear bayhorse; and as I saw him closer I beheld that his mane and flowing tail were plaited up with fine red ribbons. He stood still in front of our door and, when I flew down to greet the faithful beast, the lad gave me a letter wherein nought was written save these Latin words in large letters: "AMICITIA FIDEI" which is to say: "Friendship to Fidelity."

Thus the pinch and sacrifice were on a sudden ended; and albeit a snow-storm ere long came down on us, yet the sunshine in my bosom was still as bright as though Spring had dawned there in the December season, and all care and fear were banished.

CHAPTER XV

It was noon. Master Peter could not come to table for a bad headache, and Cousin Maud scarce opened her lips. The sudden turn of matters had upset her balance, and so dazed her brain that she would answer at cross-purposes, and had ordered so many pats of butter from the farm wench as though she had cakes to bake for a whole convent full of sisters. Likewise a strange unrest kept her moving to and fro, and this was beginning to come upon me likewise, by reason that Ann came not, albeit in the morning she had promised to be here again at noon.

I was about to make ready to seek her, when I was stopped, first by a message from the forest bidding me, albeit I had scarce left the lodge, to return thither no later than on the morrow; and next by an unlooked-for guest, who had for long indeed been lost to sight. This was Lorenz Abenberger, the apothecary's son, erewhile a companion of Herdegen in his youth, and he who, after he had beguiled the other pueri to dig for treasure, had been turned out of the school. Since those days, when likewise he had cast nativities for us maidens, and many a time amused us with his magic arts, we had no knowledge of him but that, after his parents' death, he had ceased to ply the apothecary's trade, and had given himself up to the study of Alchemy. If folks spoke truth he had already discovered the philosopher's stone, or was nigh to doing so: but notwithstanding that many learned men, and among them the Magister had assured me, that such a thing was by no means beyond the skill of man, Lorenz Abenberger for certain had not attained his end, inasmuch as that, when he appeared in my presence, his aspect was rather that of a beggar than of a potent wise-head at whose behest lead and copper are transmuted into gold.

He had heard of the great sum needed for Herdegen's ransom, and he now came to assure me of the warm friendship he had ever cherished for his old school-mate, and that he had it in his power to create the means of releasing him from bondage. Then, marking that I gazed pitifully on his thread-bare, meagre, and by no means clean raiment, whence there came a sour, drug-like smell, he broke into a foul laugh and said that, to be sure, it would seem strange that so beggarly a figure should make bold to promise so great a treasure; howbeit, he stood to his word. So sure as night follows day, he could reach the goal for which he had consumed all his father's and mother's estate, nay all he had in the world, if he might but once have three pounds of pure gold to do whatsoever he would withal. If I would yield to his entreaties and be moved to grant what he needed, he was ready to pledge his body and soul to death and damnation, and sign the bond with his heart's blood, if by the end of the thirteenth day he had not found the red Lion, and through its aid 'Aurum potabile' and the panacea against every evil of body or soul. This would likewise give him the power of turning every mineral, even the most worthless, into pure gold, as easily as I might turn my spinning-wheel or say a Paternoster.

All this he poured forth with rolling eyes and panting breath, and that he spoke every word in sacred earnest none could doubt; and indeed the fervent, eager longing which appealed to my compassion and charity from every fibre of his being, might have moved me to bestow on him that which he craved, if I had possessed such wealth; but, as it was, I was forced to say him nay; and whereas at this minute Susan came in with the tidings that a man had come from the Pernharts', bidding me go forthwith to Ann, I threw over me my cloak and gave him to understand how matters stood with me, bidding him farewell with all gentleness yet of set purpose.

The blood mounted into his pale cheeks; he came close up to me, and set his teeth, and said wrathfully that I must and I should save him, and with him my own brother, if I did but clearly understand the sense and purpose of his entreaty. And he began with a flood of speech to tell me how near he was to his end, with a number of outlandish, magical words such as "the great Magisterium," "the Red Lion," "the Red Tincture," and the like, till meseemed my brain reeled with the sinful gibberish; notwithstanding, to this day I believe that in all truth he was nigh attaining his purpose; and he might have done so at last were it not that, a short space after this, he was choked by the vapor from an alembic which burst.

But whence might I at that day procure the means to succor him?

Again and again I strove to check his fiery zeal, but in vain, till I told him plainly that I had not at my command three pounds of brass farthings, much less three pounds of gold, and that he must apply elsewhere and no longer keep me tarrying.

And I gave him my hand to bid him farewell; howbeit he seized it with both of his, and wrung and shook my arm till it ached; and being beside himself with rage, he admonished me with threatening words and gestures not to ruin his life's work, and him, and those dear to me, by my base avarice. When I had got over my first fear I snatched myself free from the miserable little man, and turned my back upon him; but he leaped in front of me, spread forth his arms to bar the doorway, and shrieked, foaming with fury:

"Away, away, down to the depths! Away with us all! Woe unto thee, mean, blind fool that thou art! Woe unto us all! Take away that hand! Verily even if my mouth were gagged, yet shouldst thou hear what is coming upon thee and all thy race! I could have hindered it, and I would have hindered it; but now it shall be fulfilled. Oh, it was not for nothing that we were young together! I read thy horoscope and that arrogant brawler thy brother's long ago, and when I interpret it to thee, if the blood does not curdle in thy veins...."

Hereupon the blood of the Schoppers surged up; I laid hands on the mad wight, whose strength was scarce greater than mine, but he hit and stamped about like one bereft, crying: "Your planets stand over the houses of Death, Captivity, and Despair. The fulfilment thereof began on Saint Lazarus' day, and on this day it falls first on thee; and thus the doom shall run its course till it hath an end on Saint John's eve, by reason that ye will then have nought left to lose!"

Here Abenberger's raving came to a sudden end. His outcry had brought up Cousin Maud, and when she opened the door behind him and saw a man standing in my way, she clutched him from behind, throwing her arms about him, and dragged him out of the chamber. Meanwhile she shrieked aloud "Fire!" and "Murder!" and again "Fire!" and all the men and wenches ran up in hot haste and had the gold-maker down the stairs fast enough.

Howbeit, I felt truly grieved for him; yet, as I gazed down on him from the window, I saw that he had taken his stand without in the street, and was shaking his fist up at me till a constable saw it and sent him homewards.

Then I must first comfort Cousin Maud for this untoward scene, and suffer her to rub my wrists with wine and spirit of balm, forasmuch as they tingled like fire and were scratched by the hapless wight's nails. She was beside herself with rage, and the evil prediction of the master of the black arts and of star-gazing filled her with unbounded terrors. Thus it was my part, though; the younger, to give her courage, notwithstanding the awful curse haunted me likewise, and rang in my ears even when at last I made my way through the dark streets, followed by the serving-man, to do Ann's bidding. My heart was heavier than it had been for many a day; for my fears were mingled with pity for that hapless soul, so skilled in much learning. I had learned to feel other woes and joys besides my own, and I could full well picture in my mind the despair which at this hour, must wring the soul of that poor fellow. I was glad to think that the serving-man might believe that

I put my kerchief to my eyes only to wipe away the whirling snow. At the same time, methought that for certain some new and terrible sorrow hung over us nay, never so clearly as then, after Abenberger's violent attack, had I perceived how much alone and without protection I stood in the world. And wherefor had Ann not come to me? For what reason or matter had she sent for me at so late an hour?

Then, when I looked up at the Pernharts' house; saw that the windows of the first floor which had been made ready as guest chambers some days ago, for my lord Cardinal, were lighted up, so he must have come home and now be lodging there again.

But Ann knew full well how truly I honored the reverend and illustrious uncle, and for sure if he had brought her good tidings she would forthwith have sent me word, or have come to me herself.

What then was now the matter? In what form had the misfortune come upon us which Abenberger had read in the stars?

I lifted the knocker with a faint heart, and could scarce breathe when I had to knock three times or ever the door was opened.

How swiftly my Ann was wont to fly to me when she heard my tap! Was she then afraid to meet me with the message of woe which my lord Cardinal had perchance received from Cairo through his chaplains there? We had the ransom ready to be sure; yet Ursula would be almost forced, after her treacherous deed, to pursue Herdegen to his death; what could she look for if he ever came home again? Come what might then, and were it the worst, I must set out, and that forthwith, even if I found no fellowship but Cousin Maud and Eppelein. And to this purpose I had come, when at last the door was opened.

Below stairs nought was stirring. I hastily flung my wet mantle to Mario, the deaf-mute, who had let me in, and ran up stairs. Hardly had I reached the second floor when Ann met me, well and of good cheer; and when I began, in the outer chamber, to beseech her to be no less steadfast than I was in departing for the East, she nodded consent, and pointed the way into the inner chamber, where we might be more at our ease. I was amazed to see her in such good heart, and all the more so when she told me that my lord Cardinal had come home that morning.

There was above stairs, she hastily told me, a noble Italian Knight, who had desired to see our pictures; so we went into the guest chamber, which was all lighted up as when company was bidden. Nay, it was of such festal aspect as well nigh dazzled me, and I discerned at once that my portrait, which only a few days ago had been hanged on the wall by the side of Ann's for my lord Cardinal, was now placed on two chairs and leaning against the high backs.

All this and more I perceived in a few hasty glances, and when I enquired where might this stranger from Italy be, I was told that he had gone with Master Pernhart into the chamber which had been fitted for his Eminence with the magnificent stuffs from Rome and Florence which he had brought as a gift for his old mother. The finest of these were certain hangings of fine tissue and of many colors, which hung over the wide opening between the great guest chamber and that next to it. And the Italian must likewise have seen these, inasmuch as that they hung down, whereas they were wont to be drawn to the sides. Behind them, all was dark; thus the Master and his wife, with their strange guest, must have withdrawn into the chamber at the back of the house, where the Cardinal had loved to work, and wherein there were sundry works of art to be seen, and choice Greek manuscripts which he had brought with him to show to the learned doctors in his native town; as being rare and precious.

None was here save the old grandam, and her countenance beamed with joy as she held out her hands to me from her arm-chair, in glad and hearty greeting. She was dressed in her bravest array, and there was in her aspect likewise somewhat solemn and festal.

Albeit I was truly minded at all times to rejoice with those who were rejoicing, all this bravery, at this time, was sorely against the grain of my troubled heart and its forebodings of ill. I could not feel at ease, and meseemed that all this magnificence and good cheer mocked my hapless and oppressed spirit.

In truth, I could scarce bring myself to return the old dame's greeting with due gladness; and her keen eyes at once discerned how matters were with me. She held me by the hand, and asked me in a hearty voice whence came the clouds that darkened my brow. When her bright, high-spirited Margery, whom she had never known to be in a gloomy mood, looked like this, for sure some great evil had befallen.

Whereupon what came over me I know not. Whether it were that the blackness and the terror in my bosom were too great a contrast with the gladness and splendor about me, or what it was that so tightly gripped my heart, I cannot tell to this day; but I know full well that all which had oppressed me since Abenberger denounced me came rushing down on my soul as it were, and that I burst into tears and cried out "Yes, grandmother dear, I have gone through a dreadful, terrible hour! I have had to withstand the attack of a madman, and hear a horrible curse from his lips. But it is not that alone, no, verily and indeed! I can, for that matter, make any man to know his place, were he twice the man that little Abenberger is; and as to curses, I learnt from a child to mind my dear father's saying: 'Curse me if you will! What matters it if I may earn God's blessing!'"

"And you have earned it, honestly earned it," quoth she, drawing me down to kiss my forehead. Hereupon I ceased weeping and bid my heart take fresh courage, and went on, still much moved: "It is nought but a woman's shameless craft that troubles me so sorely. Ursula's hate hangs over my brothers like a black storm-cloud; and on my way hither meseemed I saw full plainly that the ransom is not the end of the matter. Nay, if we had twice so much, yet Herdegen will never come home alive if we fail to cross Ursula's scheming; has she not cause to fear the worst, if ever he comes home in safety? But where is the envoy who would dare so much? Kunz lies wounded in a strange land, Young Kubbeling would doubtless be ready to cross the seas, notwithstanding his fever, but good-will would not serve him, so little is he skilled in such matters. Our other friends are over old, or forced to stay in Nuremberg. Thus do matters stand. What then is left to us—to Ann and me, Grandmother? I ask you—what, save to act on our first and only wise intent? And that which it is our part to do, which we may not put off one day longer than we need, is to take ship, under the grace of the Blessed Virgin, and ourselves to carry fresh courage to those who are nearest and dearest to us. Of a truth I am but an orphaned maid; my lover and my guardian are both dead; and yet do I not fear to depart for a land beyond seas; true and faithful love is the guiding-star which shall lead us, and we have seen in Ann how true is the Apostle's saying that love conquereth all things. Any creature who stands straight on a pair of strong legs, and who is sound in soul and body, and who looks up to Heaven and trusts in God's grace with joyful assurance, even if it be but a weak maiden, may rescue a fellow-creature in need; and I, thank God, am sound and whole. Nay, and I will even pledge my word that I will tear asunder the subtlest web which Ursula may spin, in especial if I have Ann's keen wit to aid me. So I will go forth, and away, through frost and snow, to find my brethren; and if his pains keep Kubbeling at home in spite of his catskins, and if Master Ulsenius should forbid Eppelein to ride so far, yet will we find some other to be our faithful squire."

And with this I drew a deep breath; and when I turned to seek Ann, with a lighter heart, to the end that she should signify her consent, on a sudden me seemed as though the floor of the chamber rose up beneath my feet, and I was nigh falling, by reason that the fine hangings which hid the Cardinal's chamber from my eyes were drawn asunder, and a tall man, tanned brown by the sun, came forth, and said in a deep voice: "Wilt thou trust these hands, Margery? They are ready and willing to serve thee faithfully."

Hereupon a cry of joy broke from me: "Gotz," and again "Gotz!"

And albeit meseemed as though the walls, and tables, and chairs were whirling round me, and as though the ceiling, nay and the blue sky above it had yawned above me, yet I fell not, but hastened to meet this new-comer, and grasped his kind, strong hand.

Yet was not this all; or ever I was rightly aware how it befell, he had clasped me in his arms, and I was leaning on his breast, and his warm bearded lips were for the first time set on mine.

Master Pernhart and his wife had come out of the further chamber with my cousin, and Ann, and the grandam, and the elder children gazed at us; yet neither he nor I paid heed to them and, as each looked into the other's eyes, and I saw that his face was the same as of old, albeit of a darker brown, and more well-favored and manly; then my heart sang out in joyful triumph, and I made no resistance when he held me closer to him and whispered in my ear: "But Margery, how may a cousin, who is not an old man, go forth as squire to a fair young maid, and so further on through a lifetime, and not rouse other folks to great and righteous wrath?"

At this the blood mounted to my face; and albeit I by no means doubted of my reply, he spared my bashfulness and went on with deep feeling: "But if he did so as your wedded husband, what aunt or gossip then might dare to blame him and his honored wife, Dame Margery Waldstromer?"

Whereat I smiled right gladly up at my new lover, and answered him in a whisper: "Not one, Gotz, not one."

Thus I plighted my troth to him that very evening; and as for the costly jewels which he had bought on the Rialto at Venice to bring to his dear Red-riding-hood, and now gave me as his first love-tokens, what were they to me as compared with the joyful news wherewith he could rejoice our hearts? So presently we sat with the Pernharts after that Cousin Maud and Uncle Christian Pfinzing, my dear godfather, had been bidden to join us. Gotz sat with his arm round me, and my hand rested in his.

For how long a space had lands and seas lain betwixt us, how swift and sudden had his wooing been and my consent! And yet, meseemed as though I had but now fulfilled the purpose of Providence for me from the beginning; and there was singing and blossoming in my breast and heart, as though they were an enchanted garden wherein fountains were leaping, and roses and tulips and golden apples and grapes were blooming and ripening among pine-trees and ivy-wreaths.

Nevertheless I lost no word of his speech, and could have listened to him till morning should dawn again. And while we thus sat, or paced the room arm-in-arm, I heard many matters, and yet not enough of Gotz's adventurous fate, and of the happy turn my brothers' concerns had taken with his good help. And what we now learned from his clear and plain report, answering our much questioning, was that, after separating from his home, he had taken service as a soldier of the Venice Republic, and had done great deeds under the name of Silvestri, which is to say "of the Woods." Of all the fine things he had done before Salonica and elsewhere, fighting against Sultan Mourad and the Osmanli, yea, and in many fights against other infidels, thereby winning the favor of his general, the great Pietro Loredano—of all this he would tell us at great length another day. Not long since he had been placed as chief, at the head of the armed force on board the fleet sent forth by the Republic to Alexandria to treat with the Sultan as concerning the King of Cyprus, who was held a prisoner. With him likewise, on the greatest of the galleys, were there sundry great gentlemen of the most famous families of Venice, and chief of them all, Marino Cavallo, Procurator of Saint Mark; inasmuch as that the Council desired to ransom the King of Cyprus with Venice gold, and to that end had sent Angelo Michieli with the embassy, he being the Senior of one of the most powerful and wealthy merchants' houses in the East.

With all of these Gotz, as a hero in war, was on right friendly terms, and when they landed at Alexandria, Anselmo Giustiniani, the Consul, had given them all fine quarters in the Fondaco.

Here, then, my new lover had met Ursula; howbeit, he made not himself known to her, by reason that already he had heard an evil report of her husband's dealings as Consul, and of her deeds and demeanors. Yet was there one man dwelling in the Fondaco to whom he confessed his true name, and that was Hartmann Knorr, a son of Nuremberg and of good family, who, after gaining his doctor's degree at Padua, had taken the post of leech to the Consul, provided and paid by the Republic. In this, his fellow countryman's chamber, the two, who had been schoolmates, had much privy discourse, and inasmuch as that Master Knorr knew of old that Gotz was near of kin to the Schoppers, he forthwith made known to him that he had been bidden to the house of Akusch's parents to tend and heal Kunz, and had learnt from him many strange tidings; accusing Ursula of the guilt of having concealed and kept back the letters written by Herdegen and Sir Franz to their kindred at home, of having set her husband's hired knaves on himself, to murder him, and lastly, of having maliciously increased the sum for his brother's ransom. Hereupon the worthy leech was minded to sail to Venice in the next homeward-bound galleon, to do what he might for his countrymen in sore straits; howbeit, Gotz might now perchance work out their release from grief and slavery in some other wise. And whereas Master Knorr could give him tidings of other criminal deeds committed by Giustiniani, my new lover had forthwith written a petition of accusation to the Council at Venice, and forthwith Marino Cavallo, in his rights as procurator of Saint Mark, had commanded the Consul and his wife to depart for Venice and present themselves before the Collegium of the Pregadi, which hath the direction of the Consuls beyond seas.

Likewise Gotz had taken in hand the cause of Herdegen and Sir Franz and forasmuch as he was held in great respect, Master Angelo Michieli was not hardly won to do what he might for them, taking Gotz and Kunz for surety. The Venice embassy went forth to Cairo, and whereas Master Michieli, who was skilled in such matters, beat down the ransom demanded for King Janus to the sum of two hundred thousand ducats, and paid it down for the royal captive, he likewise moved the Sultans to be content with fifteen thousand ducats each for Herdegen and Sir Franz, and my brother and his fellow in misfortune were set free.

All through this tale my heart beat higher; I secretly hoped that peradventure my brothers had come home with Gotz, and were hiding themselves away, only for some reason privy to themselves. Howbeit, I presently heard that they had set forth with their faces to Jerusalem; to the end that they might, at their homecoming, tell the Emperor with the greater assurance, that they had taken upon themselves the penance of going at last to the Holy Places whither they had been bidden to go.

When Gotz had ended these great and comforting tidings, and I enquired of him what then had at last brought him homewards, he freely confessed that my brothers' discourse had recalled to him so plainly his fathers' house, his parents, and all that was dear and that he had left, that he could no longer endure to stay away beyond seas. Then he looked me in the eyes and whispered: "The images of my sick mother and my grey-headed father drew me most strongly; yet was a third; a dear, sweet, childish face; the very same as now looks into mine so gladly and lovingly. Yes, it is the very face I had hoped to find it; and when, erewhile, I saw your likeness in the red hood, and heard your speech as you poured forth your inmost soul to grandmother Pernhart, I knew my own mind."

How dear the newcomer was, in truth, to all in the Pernhart household I might mark that evening. The old grandam's eyes rested on him as though he were a dear son, and Master Pernhart would come close to him now and again, and stroke his arm. Twice only did he hastily turn away and privily wipe his eyes. Nevertheless he saw our love-making with no jealousy; nay, when Gotz could scarce tear himself away from my picture, Master Pernhart whispered to him that if ever a maid should stand in his Gertrude's place it should be Margery, and the grandam had cried Amen.

It was already midnight when horses' hoofs were heard in the street, and when they stopped Gotz rose, and then presently all the others vanished from the chamber. Yet were we not long suffered to enjoy each other's fellowship, inasmuch as he himself had ordered his horse, to the end that he might ride forth spite of the lateness of the hour to the forest. His servingman, himself the son of a forester, had been there already to desire Grubner, the headman, to bid my uncle to his dwelling early on the morrow, and the good son purposed there to gladden himself by meeting his father, after that he had greeted the house unseen in the darkness.

But how hard it was to part after so brief a meeting from this newly-found and best-beloved lover, and to see the weary traveller fare forth once more into the dark night. And how few words in secret had we as yet spoken, how little had we discussed what might befall on the morrow, and how he should demean himself to his mother!

To my humble entreaty that he would set aside the unnatural and sinful oath which forbade him to enter his parents' house he had turned a deaf ear. Yet how lovingly had he given me to understand his stern refusal, which I justly deserved, inasmuch as I knew full well the meaning of an oath; and yet I besought him with all my heart to send away his horse, and bid me not farewell when welcome had scarce been spoken. On the morrow it would be a joy to me to ride forth with him, and my uncle could never chafe at a few short hours' delay.

All this poured from my lips smoothly and warmly enough, and he calmly heard me to the end; but then he solemnly declared to me that, sweet as he might deem it to have me by his side to keep him company, it might not be; and he set forth clearly and fully how he had ordered the matter yestereve, and I looked up at him as to a general who foresees and governs all that may befall, to the wisest ends. So steadfast and clear a purpose I had never met; howbeit, Mother Eve's part in me was ill-content. It was too much for me to suffer that he should depart, and, like the fool that I was, the desire possessed me to bend to my will this man of all men, whose stiff-necked will was ever as firm as iron.

I began once more to beseech him, and this time he broke in, declaring that, say what I would, he must depart, and therewith he pulled the hood of his cloak over his head so that his well-favored, honest brown face, with its pointed beard, framed as it were in the green cloth, looked down on me, the very image of manly beauty and mild gravity.

My heart beat higher than ever for joy and pride at calling the heart of such a man mine own, and therewith my desire waxed stronger to exert my power. And I knew right well how to get the upper-hand of my lovers. My Hans had never said me nay when I had entreated him with certain wiles. And whereas I had in no wise forgotten my tricks, I took Gotz by the hem of his hood and drew his dear head down to my face. Then I rubbed my nose against his as hares do when they sniff at each other, put up my lips for a kiss, stood on tip-toe, offered him my lips from afar, and whispered to him right sweetly and beseechingly:

"And, in spite of all, now you are to be my good, dear heart's treasure, and will do Margery's bidding when she entreats you so fondly and will give you a sweet kiss for your pains."

But I had reckoned vainly. The reward for which my Hans modestly served me, this bold warrior cared not to win. His bearded lips, to be sure, were ready enough to meet mine, nor was he content with one kiss only; but, as soon as he had enjoyed the last, he took both my hands tight in his own, and said solemnly but sweetly:

"Do you not love me, Margery?" And when I had hastily declared that I did, he went on in the same tone, and still holding my bands: "Then you must know, once for all, that I could refuse you nought, neither in great matters nor small, unless it were needful. Yet, when once I have said," and he spoke loud, "nothing can move me in the very least. You have known me from a child, and of your own free will you have given yourself over to this iron brain. Now, kiss me once more, and bear me no malice! Till to-morrow. Out in the forest, please God, we will belong to each other for many a long day!"

Therewith he clasped me firmly and truly in his arms, and I willingly and hotly returned his kiss, and or ever I could find a word to reply he had quitted the chamber. I hastened to the window, and as he waved his hand and rode off down the street facing the snow-storm, I pressed my hand to my breast, and rarely has a human being so overflowed with pure gladness at being twice worsted in the fray, albeit I had forced it on myself.

How I returned home I know not; but I know that I had rarely knelt at my prayers with such fervent thanksgiving, and that meseemed as though my mother in Heaven and my dead Hans likewise must rejoice at this which had befallen me.

As I lay in bed, or ever I slept, all that was fairest in my past life came back to me as clearly as if it were living truth, and first and chiefest I saw myself as little Red-riding-hood, under the forest-trees with Gotz, who did me a thousand services and preferred me above all others till, for Gertrude's sake, he departed beyond seas, and set my childish soul in a turmoil.

Then came the joy and the pain I had had by reason of the loves of Herdegen and Ann, and then my Hans crossed my path, and how glad I was to remember him and the bliss he had brought me! But or ever I had come to the bitterest hour of my young days, sleep overcame me, and the manly form of Gotz, steeled by much peril and strife for his life, came to me in my dreams; and he did not, as Hans would have done, give me his hand; Oh no! He snatched me up in his arms and carried me, as Saint Christopher bears the Holy Child, and strode forward with a firm step over plains and abysses, whithersoever he desired; and I suffered him to go as he would, and made no resistance, and felt scarce a fear, albeit meseemed the strong grip of his iron arm hurt me. And thus we went on and on, through ancient mountain-forests, while the boughs lashed my face and I could look into the nests of the eagles and wood-pigeons, of the starlings and squirrels. It was a wondrous ramble; now and then I gasped for breath, yet on we went till, on the topmost bough of an oak, behold, there was Lorenz Abenberger, and the evil words he spoke made me wake up.

After this I could sleep no more, and in thought I followed Gotz through the snow-storm. And in spirit I saw Waldtrud, the fair daughter of Grubner, the chief forester, bidding him welcome, and giving him hot spiced wine after his cold ride, and sipping the cup with her rosy lips. Hereupon a pang pierced my heart, and methought indeed how well favored a maid was the forester's daughter, and not more than a year older than I, and by every right deemed the fairest in all the forest. And the evil fiend jealousy, which of yore had had so little hold over me that I could bear to see my Hans pay the friendliest court to the fairest maidens, now whispered wild suspicions in mine ear that Gotz, with his bold warrior's ways, might be like enough to sue for some light love-tokens from the fair and mirthful Waldtrud.

Howbeit, I presently called to mind the honest eyes of my new heart's beloved, and that brought me peace; and how I was struck with horror to think that I had known the sting of that serpent whom men call jealousy. Must it ever creep in where true love hath found a nest? And if indeed it were so, then—and a hot glow thrilled through me—then the love which had bound me to Hans Haller had been a poor manner of thing, and not the real true passion.

No, no! Albeit it had worn another aspect than this brand new flame, which I now felt burning and blazing up from the early-lighted and long smouldering fire, nevertheless it had been of the best, and faithful and true. Albeit as the betrothed of Hans Haller I had been spared the pangs of jealousy, I owed it only to the great and steadfast trust I had gladly placed in him. And Gotz, who had endured so much anguish and toil to be faithful to his other sweetheart, was not less worthy of my faith, and it must be my task to fight against the evil spirit with all the strength that was in me.

Then again I fell asleep; and when, as day was breaking, I woke once more and remembered all that had befallen me yestereve, I had to clutch my shoulders and temples or ever I was certain that indeed my eyes were open on another day. And what a day! My heart overflowed as I saw, look which way I might, no perils, none, nothing, verily nothing that was not well-ordered and brought to a good end, nothing that was not a certainty, and such a blessed certainty!

I rose as fresh and thankful as the lark, my Cousin Maud was standing, as yet not dressed and with screws of paper in her hair, in front of the pictures of my parents, casting a light on their faces from her little lamp; and it was plain that she was telling them, albeit without speech, that her life's labor and care had come to a happy issue, and I was irresistibly moved to fly to her brave and faithful heart; and although, while we held each other in an embrace, we found no words, we each knew full well what the other meant.

After this, in all haste we made ready to set forth, and the Magister came down to us in the hall, inasmuch as my cousin had called him. He made his appearance in the motley morning gabardine which gave him so strange an aspect, and to my greeting of "God be with 'ee!" he gaily replied that he deemed it wasted pains to ask after my health.

Then, when he had been told all, at first he could not refrain himself and good wishes flowed from his lips as honey from the honey-comb; and he was indeed a right merry sight as, in the joy of his heart, he clapped his arms together across his breast, as a woodhewer may, to warm his hands in winter. On a sudden, however, he looked mighty solemn, and when Cousin Maud, bethinking her of Ann, spoke kindly to him, saying that matters were so in this world, that one who stood in the sun must need cast a shadow on other folks, the Magister bowed his head sadly and cried: "A wise saying, worthy Mistress Maud; and he who casts the shade commonly does so against his will, 'sine ira et studio'. And from that saying we may learn— suffer me the syllogism—that, inasmuch as all things which bring woe to one bring joy to another, and vice-versa, there must ever be some sad faces so long as there is no lack of happy ones. As to mine own poor countenance, I may number it indeed with those in shadow—notwithstanding"—here his flow of words stopped on a sudden. Howbeit, or ever we could stay him, he went on in a loud and well-nigh triumphant voice. "Notwithstanding I am no wise woeful—no, not in the least degree. I have found the clue, and who indeed could fail to see it: Your shadow can fall so black on me only by reason that you stand in the fullest sunshine! As for me, it is no hard matter for me to endure the blackness of night; and may you, Mistress Margery, for ever and ever stand in the glory of light, henceforth till your life's end."

As he spoke he upraised his eyes and hands to heaven as in prayer, and without bidding us "Vale," or "Valete," as was his wont, he gathered his gaudy robe and fled up-stairs again.

The storm was yet as heavy as it had been yestereve; howbeit, though Bayard sank into the snow so deep that I swept it with the hem of my kirtle, yet the ride to the forest-lodge meseemed was as short as though I had flown. Cousin Maud would ride slowly in the sleigh, so I suffered her to creep along, and presently outstripped her.

Gotz and I had yestereve agreed that I should first see Aunt Jacoba, and then meet him at Grubner's lodge to report of what mind she might seem to be. Ann had no choice but to stay at home, inasmuch as she must be in attendance at the Cardinal's homecoming.

No one in all the dear old forest home was aware of my coming save the gate warden. My uncle had ridden forth at an early hour, and was not yet returned, but my aunt I found below stairs, strange to say, against her wont, dressed and in discourse with the chaplain. Peradventure then her husband had already made known to her what had taken him forth to Grubner's dwelling, and if so he had lifted a heavy task from me, for indeed my whole soul yearned to this dearly-beloved aunt, yet meseemed it was no light matter to prepare her, who was so feeble and yet so self-willed, for the joy and the strife of soul which awaited her. The board was spread for them as it were, and yet she and Gotz, by their baleful oath, had barred themselves from tasting of that bread and that cup.

I crossed the threshold in trembling, and as soon as she beheld me she cried out, with burning cheeks, which glowed not so, for sure, from the blaze in the chimney: "Margery, Margery! And so happy as she looks! You have seen your uncle, child, and can tell me wherefor he is gone forth?"

I told her truly that I had not; and then bid her rejoice with me, inasmuch as that all the price of Herdegen's ransom had been paid and, best of all, that we had good tidings of our brothers' well-being.

Then she was fain to know when and through whom, and made enquiry in such wise as though she had some strong suspicion; and I answered her as calmly as I might, that a pilgrim from the East had come to us yestereve, a right loyal and worthy gentleman, whom, indeed, I hoped to bring to her knowledge.

But I might say no more by reason that her eyes on a sudden flashed up brightly, and she vehemently broke in:

"Chaplain, Chaplain! Now what do you say? When the old man rode forth so early this morning, and bid me farewell in so strange a wise, then—hear me, Margery—he likewise spoke to me of a messenger from the East who rode into the city yestereve—just as you say. But it was not of Herdegen that he brought tidings, but of him—of him—of Gotz that he had sure knowledge. And when the old man told me so much as that, for certain somewhat lay behind it.—And now, Margery—when I see you—when I consider...." Here, as I cast a meaning glance at the Chaplain, on a sudden she shrieked with such a yell as pierced my bones and marrow; and or ever I saw her, her weak, lean hand had clutched my wrist, and she cried in a hoarse voice:

"Then you, you have hid somewhat from me! The look wherewith you warned the Chaplain, oh! I marked it well.—And you hesitate—and now—you—Margery—Margery! By Christ's wounds I ask you, Margery. What is it?—What of Gotz? Has he... out with it—out with the truth.... Has he written?—No.—You shake your head.... Merciful Virgin! He—he—Gotz is on his way Home wards." And she clapped her hands over her face. I fell on my knees by her side, dragged first her left hand and then her right hand away from her eyes, covered them with kisses, and whispered to her: "Yes, yes, Aunt, Mother, sweet, dear little mother! Only wait—You shall hear all. Gotz is weary of wandering; he had not forgotten his father and mother, nor me, his little Red-riding-hood—I know it, I am sure of it. Patience! only a little patience and he will be here—in Germany, in Franconia, in Nuremberg, in the forest, in the house, in this hall, here, here where I am kneeling, at your feet, in your arms!"

Then the deeply-moved dame, who had listened to me breathless, flung her hands high in the air as if she were seeking somewhat, and it was as though her eyes turned inside out; and I was seized with sudden terror, inasmuch as I deemed that she had drunk death out of the overfull cup of joy that my hand had put to her lips. Howbeit, it was but a brief swoon which had come upon her, and as soon as she had come to herself again and I had told her the whole truth, little by little and with due caution, even that Gotz and I had found each other and both fervently and earnestly longed for her motherly blessing, she gave it me in rich abundance.

Now was it my part to make known to her that her returned son held fast to his oath; and I had already begun to tell her this when she waved her hands, and eagerly broke in: "And do you think I ever looked that he, who is a Waldstromer and a Behaim both in one, should ever break a vow? And of a truth he hath given me time enough to consider of it!—But to-day, this very day, early in the morning I found the right way out of the matter, albeit it is as like a trick of woman's craft as one egg is like another.—You know that reckless oath. It requires me never, never to bid Gotz home again; but yet,"—and now her eyes began to sparkle brightly with gladness—"what my oath does not forbid is that I should go forth to meet Gotz, and find him wheresoever he may be."

Hereupon the Chaplain clapped his hands and cried:

"And thus once more the love of a woman's heart hath digged a pit for Satan's craft."

And I ran forth to bid them harness the sleigh, whereas I knew full well that no counsel would avail.

And now, as of yore when she had fared into the town for love of Ann, she was wrapped in a mountain of warm garments, so we clothed her to-day in a heap of such raiment, and Young Kubbeling would suffer no man but himself to drive the horses. Thus we went at a slow pace to Grubner's lodge, and all the way we rode we met not a soul save Cousin Maud, and she only nodded to me, by reason that she could not guess that a living human creature was breathing beneath the furs and coverlets at my side. Young Kubbeling on the box, and the ravens and tomtits and redbreasts in the woods had not many words from us. While I was thinking with fear and expectation of the outcome of this meeting of the mother and son, I scarce spoke more than a kind word of good cheer now and again to my aunt, to which Kubbeling would ever add in a low voice: "All will come right!" or "God bless thee, most noble lady!" And each time we thus spoke I was aware of a small movement about my knees, and would then press my lips to the outermost cover of the beloved bundle by my side.

At about two hundred paces from the Forester's but the path turned off from the highway, so that we might be seen from the windows thereof; and scarce had the sleigh turned into this cross-road, when the door of the lodge was opened and my uncle and Gotz came forth.

The son had his arm laid on his father's shoulder and they gazed at us. And indeed it was a noble and joyful sight as they stood there, the old man and the young one, both of powerful and stalwart build, both grown strong in wind and weather, and true and trustworthy men. The slim young pine had indeed somewhat overtopped the gnarled oak, but the crown of the older tree was the broader. Such as the young man was now the old man must have been, and what the son should one day be might be seen—and I rejoiced to think it—in his father's figure and face. Howbeit, as a husband Gotz gave no promise of treading in his father's footsteps, and when I thought of this, and of the lesson I had yestereve received, my cheeks grew redder than they had already turned in the sharp December air, or under the gaze of my new lover.

Howbeit I had no time for much thought; the sleigh was already at the door, and or ever I was aware the old man had me in his arms and kissed my lips and brow, and called me his dear and well-beloved daughter. Then the younger man pressed forward to assert his claims, and when he bent over me I threw my arms round his neck, and he lifted me up, for all that I was none of the lightest in my winter furs and thick raiment, out of the sleigh like a child, and again his lips were on mine. But we might not suffer them to meet for more than a brief kiss. Uncle Conrad had discovered my aunt's face among all her wrappings, and gave loud utterance to his well-founded horror, while my aunt cried out to her long-lost son by name again and again, with all the love of a longing and long-robbed mother's heart.

I gladly set my lover free, and at the next minute he was on his knees in the snow and his trembling hands removed wrap after wrap from the beloved head, Kubbeling helping him from the driving-seat with his great hands, purpled by the cold.

And again in a few minutes the mother was covering her only son's head with tender kisses, so violently and so long that her strength failed her and she fell back on the pillows, overdone.

Hereupon Gotz bowed over her, and as he had erewhile lifted his sweetheart out of the sleigh, so now he lifted his mother; and while he held her thus in his arms and bore her into the house, not heeding the kerchiefs which dropped off by degrees and lay in a long line covering the ground behind her, as coals do which are carried in a broken scuttle, she cried in a trembling voice: "Oh you bad, only boy, you my darling and heart-breaker, you noble, wicked, perverse fellow! Gotz my son, my own and my All!"

And when she had found a place in the warm room, in the head forester's wife's arm-chair by the fire, I removed her needless raiment and Gotz sank down at her feet, and she took his head in her hands, and cried:

"I did not wait for you to come, but flew to meet you, my lad, by reason that, as you know—I took a sinful oath never to bid you to come home. But oath and vow are nought; they are null and void! I have learned from the depths of my heart that Heaven had nought to do with them—that it was pure pride and folly; and I bid you home with my whole heart and soul, and beseech your forgiveness for all the sorrow we have brought upon each other, and I will have and keep you henceforth, and nought else here on earth! Ah, and Gertrude, poor maid! She would have been heartily, entirely welcome to me as at this day, were it not that there is another maiden who is dearest to my heart of all the damsels on earth!"

Then was there heartfelt embracing and kissing on both parts, and, as I saw her weep, I made an unspoken vow that if the eyes of this mother and her son should ever shed tears again I would be the last to cause them, and that I would ever be ready and at hand to dry them carefully away.

I mind me likewise that I then beheld fair Waldtrud, the forester's daughter, inasmuch as she full heartily wished me joy; yet I remember even better that I felt no pang of jealousy, and indeed scarce looked at the wench, by reason that there were many other matters of which the sight gave me far greater joy.

It was a delightful and never-to-be-forgotten hour, albeit over-short; by my uncle's desire we ere long made ready to go homewards. Now when Gotz was carrying his mother from the hot chamber to the sleigh, and I was left looking about me for certain kerchiefs of my aunt's, I perceived, squatted behind the great green-tiled stove, Young Kubbeling in a heap, and with his face hidden in his hands. He moved not till I spoke to him; then he dried his wet eyes with his fur hood, and when I laid my hand on his shoulder he drew a deep breath, and said:

"It has been a moving morning, Mistress Margery. But it will all come right. It has come upon me as a sharp blow to be sure; and I have no longer any business here in the forest, all the more so by reason that I have children and grandchildren at home who have looked over-long for the old man's home-coming. I will set forth to-morrow early. To tell the truth to none but you, I cannot endure to be away from the old place a longer space than it takes to go to Alexandria and back. My old heart is grown over-soft and weary for an absence of two journeys. And yet another matter for your ear alone: You will be the wife of a noblehearted man, but mind you, he has long been free to wander whithersoever he would. Take it to heart that you make his home dear and happy, else it will be with you as it is with my old woman, who hath never mastered that matter, and who lives alone for more days in the year than ever we dreamed the morning we were wed."

Hereupon we went forth together; and I took his counsel to heart, and Gotz never left me for any long space of time, save when he must.

As for Kubbeling, he kept his word and departed from us on the morrow morning; yet we often saw him again after that time, and the finest falcon in our mews is that he sent us as a wedding gift; and after our marriage Ann received a fine colored parrot as a gift from old Uhlwurm, and the old man had made it speak for her in such wise that it could say right plainly: "Uhlwurm is Ann's humble servant."

We now spent two days at the forest lodge in bliss, as though paradise had come down on earth; and albeit it is a perilous thing to rejoice in the love of a man who has wandered far beyond seas, yet has it this good side: that many matters which to another seem far away and out of reach, he deems near at hand, and half the world is his as it were. And how well could Gotz make me to feel as though I shared his possession!

On the morning of the third day after his coming, my lord Cardinal rode forth to the forest with Ann; and, inasmuch as the duties of his office now led, him to sojourn in Wurzberg and Bamberg, he could promise us that he would bless our union or ever he departed to Italy. Albeit methought it would be a happy chance if we might stand at the altar at the same time with Herdegen and Ann, Gotz's impatience, which had waxed no lesser even during his journeyings, was set against our waiting for my brother's coming. Likewise he desired that we might live together a space as man and wife, before he should go to Venice to get his release from the service of the Republic.

At the same time he deemed it not prudent to take me with him on that journey, howbeit, after that we were wed, when he was about to depart, I made so bold as to beseech him; and he plainly showed me that I had not made him wroth or troubled him whereas he willingly granted me to journey with him, and without reproof. Thus I fared with him to the great and mighty city of Saint Mark, which I had ever longed to behold with my bodily eyes. I never went beyond seas, yet we journeyed as far as Rome, and there, under the protection and guidance of my lord Cardinal, I spent many never-to-be-forgotten days by the side of my Gotz.

But one thing at a time; some day, if my many years may suffer, I will write more concerning these matters.

How well my aunt and the Cardinal were minded towards each other would be hard to describe, albeit now and again they fell to friendly strife; the reverend prelate found it hard to depart from the lodge and from that strange woman, whose clear and busy brain in her sickly body came, in after times, to be accounted as one of the great marvels of her native town. Howbeit, it was his duty to pass Christmas-eve with his venerable mother. He plighted Gotz and me as he had promised us, and to his life's end he was ever a kind and honored friend and patron to us and to our children.

Ann was ever his favorite, and ere he quitted Nuremberg, he bestowed on her a dowry such as few indeed of our richest nobles could give with their daughters.

Christmas-eve, which we spent at the lodge with our parents and the Chaplain and my dear godfather, uncle Christian Pfinzing, was a right glorious festival, bringing gladness to our souls; yet was it to end with the first peril that befell our love's young joy. After the others had gone to their chambers, and Gotz had indeed given me a last parting kiss, he stayed me a moment and besought me to be ready early in the morning to ride with him to the hut of Martin the bee keeper, whose wife had been his nurse. On many a Christmas morning had he greeted the good woman with some little posy, and now he had not found one hour to spare her since his home-coming. Now I would fain have granted this simple request but that I had privily, with the Chaplain's help, made the school children to learn a Christmas carol wherewith to wake the parents and Gotz from their slumbers. Thus, when he bid me hold myself in readiness at an early hour, I besought him to make it later. This, however, by no means pleased him; he answered that the good dame was wont of old to look for him full early on Christmas morning, and he had already too long deferred his greeting. Yet the surprise I had plotted was uppermost in my mind, and I craved of him right duteously that he would grant me my will. Whereupon his eyebrows, which met above his nose, were darkly knit, and he gave me to wit, shortly and well-nigh harshly, that he would abide by his own.

At this the blood rose to my head, and a wrathful answer was indeed on my tongue when I minded me of the evening when we had come together, and I asked of him calmly whether he verily deemed that I was so foolish or evil-minded as to hinder him in a pious and kindly office if I had not some worthy reason. And herein I had hit on the right way; he recovered himself, his brow cleared, and saying only "Women, women!" he shook his head and clasped me to him; and as I fervently returned his kiss, and opened my chamber door, he called after me: "We will see in the morning, but as early as may be."

When I presently was in my bed I minded me of the carol the little ones were to sing; and then I remembered my own school-days, and how the Carthusian Sisters had explained to us those words of Scripture: "And the times shall be fulfilled." They were written, to be sure, of a special matter, of the birth of our Saviour and Redeemer; yet I applied them to myself and Gotz, and wondered in my heart whether indeed anything that had ever befallen me in life, whether for joy or for sorrow, had been in vain, and how matters might have stood with me now if, as a young unbroken thing, or ever I had gone through the school of life, I had been plighted to this man, whom the Almighty had from the first fated to be my husband. If the wilful blood of the Schoppers, unquelled as it had then been, had come into strife with Gotz's iron will, there would have been more than enough of hard hitting on both sides, and how easily might all our happiness have been wrecked thereby.

It was past midnight when at last I slept; and in the dim morning twilight the Christmas chorus rang through the house in the words the Shepherds heard in Angels' voices: "Glory to God in the highest, and on earth peace." It woke Gotz, and when we presently got into the sleigh, he whispered to me: "How piously glad was your hymn, my sweetheart! And you were right yestereve, and peace shall indeed reign on earth, and above all betwixt you and me, everywhere and at all times till the E N D."

A POSTSCRIPTUM BY KUNZ SCHOPPER

The children entreat me to write more of Margery's unfinished tale. Howbeit I am nigh upon eighty years of age, and how may I hope to win favor in the exercise of an act to which I am unskilled save in matters of business? Yet, whereas I could never endure to say nay to any reasonable prayer of those who are dearest to my heart, I will fulfil their desire, only setting down that which is needful, and in the plainest words.

They at whose bidding I sit here, all knew my dear sister well. Margery, the widow of the late departed Forest-ranger, the Knight Sir Gotz Waldstromer, Councillor to his Imperial Majesty and Captain of the men-at-arms in our good city; and each profited during a longer or shorter space by her loving-kindness, and her wise and faithful counsel.

Many of them can likewise remember the late Anna Spiesz, sometime wife of Herdegen Schopper; and as to the said Herdegen Schopper, my dear brother, Margery's book of memorabilia right truly shows forth the manner of his life and mind in the bloom of his youth, and verily it is a sorrowful task for me to set forth the decay and end of so noble a man.

As to myself, the last remaining link of the Schopper chain whereof Margery hath many times made mention, I am still with you, my dear ones; and I remain but little changed, inasmuch as that my life has ever flowed calmly and silently onward.

How it came to pass that Margery should so suddenly have brought her memories to an end most of you know already; howbeit I will set it down for the younger ones.

Till she reached the age of sixty and seven years, she never rode in a litter, but ever made her journeyings on horseback. For many years past she and her husband abode in the forest during the summer months only, and dwelt in their town-house the winter through. Now on a day, when in her written tale she had got as far as the time when she and Gotz, her dear husband, were wed, she besought him to ride forth with her to the forest, inasmuch as that she yearned once more to see the spot in the winter season which had seen the happiest days of her life in that long-past December.

Thus they fared forth on horseback, although it was nigh on Christmas-tide, and when they waved their hands to me as they passed me by in sheer high spirits and mirthfulness, meseemed that in all Nuremberg, nay in Franconia or in the whole German Empire a man might scarce find an old white-haired pair of lovers to match these for light-heartedness and goodly mien. Some few happy and glad days were at that time vouchsafed to them in the old well-known forest; but on the ride home Margery's palfrey stumbled close without the city gates on the frozen ground. Her arm-bone was badly broken and her right hand remained so stiff, notwithstanding Master Hartmann Knorr's best skill, that she could no more use the pen save with great pain, albeit she often after this rode on horseback. Thus the little book lay aside for a long space; and while she was yet diligently striving to write with her left hand death snatched from her Ann Schopper, the widow of our late dear brother Herdegen Schopper and her heart's best friend, and this fell upon her soul as so cruel a grief that she never after could endure to take up the pen.

Then, when she lost her dearly-beloved husband, a few months after their golden wedding day, all was at an end for her; the brave old woman gave up all care for life, and died no more than three months after him. And indeed often have I seen how that, when one of a pair, who have dwelt together so many years in true union of hearts, departs this life, this earth is too lonely for the other, so that one might deem that their hearts had grown to be as it were one flesh, and the one that is left hath bled to death inwardly from the Reaper's stroke.

Then I read through this book of memories once more, and meseemed that Margery had written of herself as less worthy than of a truth she was in her life's spring-tide.

Most of you can yet remember how that my lord the Mayor spoke of the bride with the golden chaplet crowning her thick silver hair, as the pride of our city, the best friend and even at times the wisest counsellor of our worshipful Council, the comforter and refuge of the poor; and you know full well that Master Johannes Lochner, the priest, spoke over her open grave, saying that, as in her youth she had been fairest, so in old age she was the noblest and most helpful of all the dames of the parish of Saint Sebald; and you yourselves have many a time been her almoners, or have gazed in silence to admire her portrait.

And at Venice I have heard from the lips of the very master who limned her, and who was one of the greatest painters of the famous guild to which he belonged, that such as she had he imagined the stately queen of some ancient German King defeated by the Romans, or Eve herself, if indeed one might conceive of our cold German fatherland as Paradise. Yea, the most charming and glowing woman he had ever set eyes on was your mother and grandmother.

And whensoever she went to a dance all the young masters of noble birth, and the counts and knights, yea even at the Emperor's court, were of one mind in saying that Margery Schopper was the fairest and likewise the most happy-tempered maid and most richly endowed with gifts of the mind, in all Nuremberg. None but Ann could stand beside her, and her beauty was Italian and heavenly rather than German and earthly.

Margery's manuscript ends where she had reached a happy haven; howbeit there were others of whom she makes mention who were not so happy as to cast anchor betimes, and if I am to set forth my own tale I must go back to Alexandria in the land of Egypt.

The dagger hired by Ursula to kill Herdegen struck me; howbeit, by the time when my cousin Gotz brought my dear brother to see me, himself a free man, I was already healed of my wound and ready to depart. The worthy mother of Akusch had tended me with a devotion which would have done honor to a Christian woman, and it was under her roof that first I saw Herdegen and my cousin once more. And how greatly was I surprised to see Gotz, taller than of old, appear before me in the magnificent array and harness of a chief captain in the army of the all-powerful Republic of Venice! Instead of an exiled adventurer I found him a stalwart gentleman, in every respect illustrious and honored, whose commanding eye showed that he was wont to be obeyed, albeit his voice and mien revealed a compassionate and friendly soul. Yea, and meseemed that at his coming a fresher, purer air blew about me; and as soon as he had made Herdegen's cause his own and stood surety for him, the chief of the great trading house of Michieli paid the ransom, which to me, knowing the value of money, must have seemed never to be compassed, unless my grand-uncle had been fain to help us. Howbeit, my cousin would not do the like service for the Knight of Welemisl, in whose mien and manners he put less trust, wherefore I became his surety, out of sheer pity and at Herdegen's prayer.

Here you will ask of me wherefore I do not first speak of my meeting again with my dear long-suffering brother. And indeed my heart beat high with joy and thanksgiving, when we held each other clasped; but alack what changes had come over him in these years of slavery! When he came into my chamber, his head bowed and his hands behind his back, after that we had greeted I turned from him and made as though I had some matter to order, to the end that he might not see me dry my tears; inasmuch as that he who stood before me was my Herdegen indeed, and yet was not.

For eighteen long months had he plied the oars on board of a Saracen galley, while Sir Franz, who was overweak for such toil, served as keeper of slaves on the benches, himself with chains on his feet. And it was this long, hard toil which had made my brother diligently to hide his hands behind his back, as though he were ashamed of them; whereas those strong hands of his with their costly rings he had ever been wont to deem a grace, and now of a truth they were grown coarse and as red as a brick, and were like to those of a hewer in the woods. And whereas men are apt often to pay less heed to another's face than to the shape and state of his hands, I ever mind me of Herdegen's as I saw them on that day, and a star and a crescent were branded in blue on the back of his right, so that all men must see it.

Likewise his deep breast had lost some of its great strength, and he held himself less stately than of old. Meseemed as though the knight had laid some part of his sickness upon him, inasmuch that many a time he coughed much. Likewise the long golden hair, which had flowed in rich abundance down over his shoulders, had been shorn away after the manner of the unbelievers, and this gave to his well-favored face a narrow and right strange appearance. Only the shape of his countenance and his eyes were what they had ever been; nay, meseemed that his eyes had a brighter and moister light in them than of yore.

One thing alone was a comfort to me, and that was that my heart beat with more pitiful and faithful love for him than ever. And when evening fell, as we brethren sat together with Gotz and Master Knorr and Akusch, drinking our wine, which only Akusch would not touch, this comforting assurance waxed strong within me, by reason that Herdegen's voice was as sweet as of old, both in speech and in song; and when he set forth all the adventures and sufferings he had gone through in these last past years I was fain to listen, and even so was Gotz; and first he drew tears from our eyes and presently made us laugh right mirthfully. And what had he not gone through?

I betook me to bed that night in hope and contentment; howbeit, on the morrow Master Knorr told me privily that whereas my brother's lungs had never been of the strongest, if now, in the cold December season, he should fare north of the Alps after such long sojourning under a warmer sky, it could not fail to do him a serious mischief, as it likewise would to Sir Franz. Thus it must be my part to delay our homecoming; and albeit the leech's tidings made me heavy at heart I was fain to yield, inasmuch as that Herdegen might not appear in the presence of his sweetheart in his present guise.

To this end we made him to believe that he might not come home in safety unless he had performed the penance laid upon him by the Emperor; and albeit felt it a hard matter to refrain the craving of his heart, nevertheless he gave way to our pressing admonitions.

Now, while Gotz fared back to Venice, the galleon which carried Don Jaime, Prince of Catalonia, as far Joppa, brought us likewise to the Promised Land to the holy city of Jerusalem. From thence we made our pilgrimage to many other Holy Places, under the protection of the great fellowship of that royal Prince who ever showed us much favor.

At last we journeyed homewards, passing by Naples and Genoa; at Damietta, in the land of Egypt, Sir Franz departed from our company to make his way to Venice. It was with care and grief that I saw him set forth on his way alone, and Herdegen was like-minded; in their misfortune he had learned to mark much that was good in him, and during our long journeying had seen that not only was he sick in body, but likewise that a shroud hung over his soul and brain. Also, if Ursula were yet free to work her will, the very worst might haply befall him in Venice, by reason that the Giustinianis were of a certainty evil-disposed towards him, and the power and dignity of that family were by no means lessened, although, as at that time Antonio Giustiniani had dishonored his name in Albania, and had been punished by the Forty with imprisonment and sundry penalties. Yet his cousin Orsato was one of the greatest and richest of the signori at Venice, and Ursula's husband would have found in him a strong upholder, as in truth we heard at Naples, where tidings reached us that the Pregadi, who had passed judgment upon him, had amerced him in a penalty of no more than two thousand ducats, which Orsato paid for him by reason that he would not suffer that his kinsman should be in prison.

At Genoa we found many letters full of good tidings of our kindred at home, all overflowing with love and the hope of speedily seeing us there. Hereupon Herdegen could not refrain himself for impatience and, if I had suffered it, he would have ridden onward by day and by night with no pause nor rest, taking fresh horses as he might need them; for my part what I chiefly cared for was to bring him home as fresh and sound as I might, and so preserve Ann from grief of heart. Herdegen had given me her letters to read, and how true and deep a love, how lofty and pure a soul spoke in those lines! Howbeit, when I heard her, as it were, cry out by those letters, how that she longed for the moment when she might again stroke his flowing locks and press his dear faithful hand to her lips as his dutiful maid, my heart beat with fresh fears. He held him more upright, to be sure, and his countenance was less pale and hollow than it had been; but nevermore might he be a strong man. His light eyes were deep in their sockets, his hair was rarer on his head, and there were threads of silver among the gold. Ah, and those luckless hands! It was by reason of his hands—albeit you will doubtless smile at the confession—that I moved him to refrain his longing, even when we were so near our journey's end as Augsburg, and to grant me another day's delay, inasmuch as that I cared most that he should at first hide them in gloves from the womankind at home. And in all the great town was there not a pair to be and that would fit him, and it would take a whole day to make him a pair to his measure. Thus were we fain to tarry, and whereas we had in Augsburg, among other good friends, a faithful ally in trading matters at the Venice Fondaco, Master Sigismund Gossenprot, we lodged in his dwelling, which was one of the finest that fine city; and, as good-hap ruled it, he had, on the very eve of that day, come home from Venice.

He and his worthy wife had known Herdegen of old, and I was cut to the heart to see how the sight of him grieved them both. Nay, and the fair young daughter of the house ne'er cast an eye on the stranger guest, whose presence had been wont to stir every maiden's heart to beat faster. Howbeit, here again I found comfort when I marked at supper that the sweet damsel no longer heeded my simple person, whereas she had at first gazed at me with favor, but hearkened with glowing cheeks to Herdegen's discourse. At first, to be sure, this was anything rather than gay, inasmuch as Master Gossenprot was full of tidings from Venice, and of Sir Franz's latter end, which, indeed, was enough to sadden the most mirthful.

When the Bohemian had come to Venice he had lodged at a tavern, by name "The Mirror," and there mine host had deemed that he was but a gloomy and silent guest. And it fell that one day the city was full of a dreadful uproar, whereas it was rumored that in the afternoon, at the hour when Dame Ursula Giustiniani was wont to fare forth in her gondola, a strange man clad in black had leaped into it from his own and, before the serving-men could lay hands on him, he had stabbed her many times to the heart with his dagger. Then, as they were about to seize him, he had turned the murderous weapon still wet with his victim's blood, on himself, and thus escaped the avenging hand of justice.

As soon as the host of The Mirror heard this tale, he minded him of that strange, dark man and, when that way-farer came not home to his inn, he made report thereof to the judges. Then, on making search in his wallet, it was discovered that he had entered there under a false name, and that it was Sir Franz von Welemisl who had taken such terrible vengeance on Ursula for her sins against himself and Herdegen.

From Augsburg we now made good speed, and when, one fine June morning, our proud old citadel greeted our eyes from afar, and I saw that Herdegen's eyes were wet as he gazed upon it, mine eyes likewise filled with tears, and as we rode we clasped hands fervently, but in silence.

I sent forward a messenger from our last halting-place to give tidings of our coming; and when, hard by Schweinau, behold a cloud of dust, our eyes met and told more than many and eloquent words.

Great and pure and thankful joy filled and bore up my soul; but presently the cloud of dust was hid by a turn in the road behind the trees, and even so, quoth my fearful heart, the shroud of the future hid what next might befall us.

The cruel blows of fate which had fallen on Herdegen had not been all in vain, and the growing weakness of his frame warned him not to spend his strength and eagerness on new and ever new things. Yet what troubled me was that he was not aware of the changes that had come upon him within and without. From all his speech with me I perceived that, even now, he might not conceive that life could be other than as he desired: notwithstanding it gave me secret joy to look upon this dear fellow, for whom life should have had no summer heats nor winter frosts, but only blossoming spring-tide and happy autumn days.

But now we had got round the wood, and we might see what the cloud of dust had concealed. Foremost there came a train of waggons loaded with merchandise and faring southwards, and the first waggon had met a piled-up load of charcoal coming forth from the forest at a place in the road where they were pent between a deep ditch on one hand and thick brushwood and undergrowth on the other; thus neither could turn aside, and their wheels were so fast locked that they barred the road as it had been a wall. Thus the second waggon likewise had come to hurt by the sudden stopping of the first, and it was but hardly saved from turning over into the ditch. There was a scene of wild turmoil. The waggons stopped the way, and neither could the rest of the train, nor their armed outriders, nor our own folks come past, by reason that the ditch was full deep and the underwood thick. We likewise were compelled to draw rein and look on while the six fine waggon horses which had but just come from the stable, their brown coats shining like mirrors, were unharnessed, and likewise the draughtoxen were taken out of the charcoal-waggon; which was done with much noise and cursing, and the brass plates that decked the leathern harness of the big horses jingling so loud and clear that we might not hear the cries of our kinsfolks. Nay, it was the plume in Gotz's hat, towering above the throng, which showed us that they were come.

Now, while Herdegen was vainly urging and spurring his unwilling horse to leap down into the ditch and get round this fortress of waggons, two of the others—and I instantly saw that they were Ann and her father, on horseback—had made their way close to the charcoal waggon; howbeit, they could get no further by reason that it had lurched half over and strewed the way with black charcoal-sacks.

My heart beat as though it would crack, and lo, as I looked round to point them out to Herdegen, he had put forth his last strength to make his horse take the leap, and could scarce hold himself in the saddle; his anguish of mind, and the foolish struggle with the wilful horse, had exhausted the strength of his sickly frame. His face was pale and his breath came hard as he sat there, on the edge of the ditch, and held his great hand to his breast as though he were in pain. Hereupon I likewise felt a deep pang of unspeakable torment, albeit I knew from experience that for such ills there was no remedy but perfect rest. I looked away from him and beheld, a little nearer now, Ann high on her saddle, diligently waving her kerchief, and at her side her father, lifting his councillor's hat.

In a few moments we were united once more. But no....

As I wrote the foregoing words with a trembling hand I vowed that I would set down nought but the truth and the whole truth. And inasmuch as I have not shrunk from making mention of certain matters which many will deem of small honor to Herdegen, who was, by the favor of Heaven, so far more highly graced in all ways than I, who have never been other than middling gifted, it would ill-become me to shrink from relating matters whereof I myself have lived to repent.

There, by the ditch, was my dear only brother, weary and pale, a man marked for an early grave; and in front of me, within a few paces, the woman to whom my heart's only and fervent love had been given even as a child. She sat like a King's daughter on a noble white horse with rich trappings. A magnificent garment of fine cloth, richly broidered with Flanders velvet, flowed about her slender body. The color thereof was white and sapphire-blue, and so likewise were the velvet cap and finely-rounded ostrich feather, which was fastened into it with a brooch of sparkling precious stones. I had always deemed her fairest in sheeny white, and she knew it, while Herdegen had taken blue for his color; and behold she wore both, for love per chance of both brothers. Never had I seen her fairer than at this minute and she had likewise waxed of a buxom comeliness, and how sweet were her red cheeks, and swan-white skin, and ebony-black hair, which flowed out from beneath her little hat in long plaits twined with white and sapphire-blue velvet ribbon.

Never did a maid seem more desirable to a man. And her father on his great brown horse—he was no more a craftsman! In his councillor's robes bordered with fur, with the golden chain round his neck, his well-favored, grave, and manly countenance, and the long, flowing hair down to his shoulders, meseemed he might have been the head of some ancient and noble family. None in Nuremberg might compare with these two for manly dignity and womanly beauty, and was that sickly, bent horseman by the ditch worthy of them? "No, no," cried a voice in my heart. "Yes, Yes!" cried another; and in the midst of this struggle I could but say to myself: "He has an old and good right to her, and as soon as he has found breath he will claim it."

But she? What will she do; how will she demean her; is she aware of his presence? Will she shrink from him as Dame Gossenprot did at Augsburg, and the inn-keeper's smart wife at Ingolstadt, who of old was so over-eager to be at his service? Would Ann, who had rejected many a lordly suitor, be as sweet as of yore to that breathless creature? And if she were to follow the example which he long since set her, if she now cut the bond which he of old had snatched asunder, or if—Merciful Virgin!—if his sickness should increase, and he himself should shrink from fettering her blooming young life to his own—then, oh, then it might be my turn, then....

And on a sudden there was a cry from the depths of my heart, but heard by none: "Look on this side. Look on me, my one and only beloved! Turn from him who once turned from thee, and hearken to Kunz who loves thee with a more faithful and fervent love than that man, who to this day knows not what thy true worth is, whose heart is as fickle as mine is honest and true. Here I stand, a strong and stalwart man, the friend of every good man, willing and able to carry you in my strong hands through a life crowned with wealth and happiness!"

And while the voice of the Evil One whispered this and much more, my gaze, meseemed, was spellbound to her countenance, and the light of her eyes from afar shone deep into mine. And on a sudden I flung up my arms and, without knowing what I did, stretched them forth, as though beside myself, towards that hotly-loved maiden. Whether she saw this or no I may never learn. And the grace of the Blessed Virgin or of my guardian Saint, preserved me from evil and disgrace, for whereas all that was in me yearned for that beloved one, a clear voice called to me by name, and when I turned, behold it was Margery, who had leaped her light palfrey into the ditch and now had sprung up the grassy bank. It was a breakneck piece of horsemanship, to which she had been driven by longing and sisterly love; and behind her came a man, my cousin Gotz, whose newly-married wife's daring leap was indeed after his own heart. One more plunge, and their horses were on the highroad, and I had lifted Margery out of her saddle and we held each other clasped, stammering out foolish disconnected words, while we first laughed and then wept.

This went on for some while till I was startled by an outcry, and behold, Eppelein, in his impatience to greet his dear master, had been fain to do as Margery and Gotz had done, but with less good fortune, inasmuch as that he had fallen under his horse, which had rolled over with him. His lamentable outcry told me that he needed help, and once more in my life I fulfilled my strange fate, which has ever been to cast to the winds that for which my soul most longed, for another to take it up. While Margery turned to greet Herdegen I hastened down the bank to rescue the faithful fellow who had endured so much in my brother's service, ere the worst should befall him.

And this, with no small pains, I was able to do; and when I was aware that he had suffered no mortal hurt, I clambered up on to the road again, and then once more my heart began to beat sadly. Ann and Herdegen had met again, and once for all. How was she able to refrain herself as she beheld the changed countenance of her lover, and to be mistress of her horror and dismay?

Now, when I had climbed the bank with some pains, in my heavy riding-boots, I saw that the waggon-men had harnessed the six brown horses to their cart once more, and behind them, on the skirt of the wood, were the pair that I sought; and as I went nearer to them Ann had drawn the glove, for which we had tarried so long in Augsburg, from off her lover's battered right hand, and was gazing at it lovingly, with no sign of horror, but with tears in her eyes; and she cried as she kissed it again and again: "Oh, that poor, dear, beloved hand, how cruelly it has suffered, how hard it must have tolled! And that? That is where the blue brand-mark was set? But it is almost gone. And it is in my color, blue, our favorite sapphire-blue!" And she pointed joyously to her goodly array, and she confessed that it was for him alone, that he might see from afar how well she loved and honored him, that she had arrayed herself in the color of fidelity in which he had ever best loved to see her. And he clasped her to him, and when she kissed his thin, streaked hair, and spoke of those dear flowing curls, to which love and care would restore their beauty, I swore a solemn vow before God that I would never look on the union of Herdegen and Ann but with thanksgiving and without envy, and ever do all that in me lay for those two and for their welfare.

Of the glad meeting with our other kith and kin I will say nought. As to Cousin Maud, she had remained at home to welcome her darling at the gate of the Schopperhof, which she had decked forth bravely. Yea, her warm heart beat more fondly for him than for us. She could not wholly conceal her dismay at seeing him so changed. She would stroke him from time to time with a cherishing hand, yet she went about him as though there were somewhat in him of which she was afeard.

Howbeit, in the evening it was with her as it had been with me in the land of Egypt, and she found him again for whom her heart yearned so faithfully. Now, that which had seemed lacking came to light once more, and from that hour she no longer grieved for what he had lost and which a true mother peradventure might never have missed; indeed as his bodily health failed, and she shared the care of tending him with Ann, none could have conceived that he was not verily and indeed her own son.

The evil monster which had crept into my brother's breast grew, thank Heaven, but slowly; and when the young pair had been wed, with a right splendid feast, and my brother had taken Ann home to the Schoppers' house as his dear wife, a glad hope rose up in me that Master Knorr had taken an over-gloomy view of the matter, and that Herdegen might blossom again into new strength and his old hearty health. Howbeit it was but his heart's gladness which lent him so brave and glad an aspect; the sickness must have its course, and it was as it were a serpent, gnawing silently at my joy in life, and its bite was all the more cruel by reason that I might tell no man what it was that hurt me save the old Waldstromers. But they likewise grew young again after their son's homecoming, and notwithstanding her feeble frame, Aunt Jacoba saw Margery's eldest son grow to be six years of age. And she sent him his packet of sweetmeats the first day he went to school; but when the little lad went to thank his grandmother, the old dame was gone to her rest; and her husband lived after her no more than a few months.

One grief only had darkened the latter days of this venerable pair, in truth it was a heavy one; it was the death of my dear brother Herdegen, which befell at the end of the fifth year after he was happily married.

At the end of the fourth year his sickness came upon him with more violence, yet he went forth and back, and ever hoped to be healed, even when he took to his bed four weeks before the end.

On the very last day, on a certain fine evening in May, it was that he said to Ann: "Hearken, my treasure, I am surely better! On the day after tomorrow we will go forth into the sweet Spring, to hear Dame Nightingale who is singing already, and to see Margery. Oh, out in the forest breezes blow to heal the sick!"

Yet they went not; two hours later he had departed this life. By ill fortune at that very time I was at Venice on a matter of business, and when the tidings came to me that my only beloved brother was dead, meseemed as though half my being were torn away, aye, and the nobler and better half; that part which was not content to grieve and care for none but earthly estate and for all that cometh up and passeth away here below, but which hath a position in the bliss of another world, where we ask not only of what use and to what end this or that may be, as I have ever done in my narrow soul.

When Herdegen's eyes closed in death, my wings were broken as it were; with him I lost the highest aim and end of all my labors. For five hard years had I toiled and struggled, often turning night into day, and not for myself, but for him and his, ever upheld and sped forward by the sight of his high soul and great happiness. Our grand-uncle Im Hoff had left me his house and the conduct of his trade, as you have learned already from Margery's little book; and during my long journeyings many matters had not been done to my contentment, and the sick old man had taken out overmuch moneys from the business. A goodly sum came to us from our parents' estate, and my brother and sister and Cousin Maud were fain to entrust me with theirs; but how much I had to do in return!

Moreover a great care came upon me from without, by reason that Sir Franz's kin and heirs refused to repay the moneys for the ransom which Master Michieli of Venice had laid down, and for which Herdegen and I had been sureties. Albeit in this matter we had applied to the law, we might not suffer Michieli to come to loss by reason of his generosity, so I took upon me the whole debt, and that was a hard matter in those times and in my case; and the fifteen thousand ducats which were repaid me by judgment of law, thirty years afterwards, made me small amends, inasmuch as by that time I had long been wont to reckon with much greater sums.

I made good my friend's payment of Herdegen's ransom to the last farthing; yet what pressed me most hardly, so long as my brother lived, was his housekeeping; few indeed in Nuremberg could have spent more.

My eldest brother was the only one of us three who might keep any remembrance of our father, whose trade with Venice and Flanders had yielded great profits, and he could yet mind him how full the house had ever been of guests, and the stables of horses. Now, therefor, he was fain to live on the same wise, and this he deemed was right and seemly, inasmuch as he took the moneys which I gave him as half the clear profits of the Im Hoff trade, which were his by right. And I was fain to suffer him to enjoy that belief, albeit at that time concerns looked but badly. It was I, not he, whose part it was to care for those concerns; and I rejoiced with all my heart when he and his lovely young wife rode forth in such bravery, when he sat as host at the head of a table well-furnished with guests, and won all hearts by his lofty and fiery spirit, which conquered even the least well-disposed. Yet was it not easy to supply that which was needed, or to refrain from speech or reproof when, for instance, my brother must need have from the land of Egypt for Ann such another noble horse as the Emirs there are wont to ride. Or could I require him to pay when, after that Heaven had blessed him with a first born child, Herdegen, radiant with pride and joy, showed me a cradle all of ivory overlaid with costly carved work which he had commanded to be wrought for his darling by the most skilled master known far and wide, for a sum which at that time would have purchased a small house? Albeit it was nigh upon quarter day, I would have taken this and much more upon me rather than have quenched his heart's great gladness; and when I saw thee, Margery the younger, who art now thyself a grandmother, sleeping like a king's daughter in that precious cradle, and perceived with how great joy it filled thy parents to have their jewel in so costly a bed, I rejoiced over my own patience.

It did my heart good, though I spoke not, to hear the Schoppers' house praised as the friendliest in all Nuremberg; yet at other times meseemed I saw shame and poverty standing at the door; and whereas, indeed, those years of magnificence, which for sure were the hardest in all my life, came to no evil issue, I owe this, next to Heaven's grace, to the trust which many folks in Nuremberg placed in my honesty and judgment, far beyond my desert. And when once, not long before my brother's over-early death, I found myself to the very brow in water, as it were, it was that faithfulest of all faithful friends, Uncle Christian Pfinzing, who read the care in my eyes and face during the very last great banquet at Herdegen's table, and led me into the oriel bay, and offered me all his substance; and this is a goodly sum indeed and saved my trade from shipwreck.

Next to him it is Cousin Maud that we three links the Schopper chain ought ever to hold dearest in memory; and it was by a strange chance that he and she died, not only on the same day, but, as it were, of the same death. Death came upon him at the Schoppers' table with the cup in his hand, after that Ann, his "watchman" had warned him to be temperate; and this was three years after her husband's death. And Cousin Maud, as she came forth from the kitchen, whither she had gone to heat her famous spiced wine for Uncle Christian, who was already gone, fell dead into Margery's arms when she heard the tidings of his sudden end.

Among the sundry matters which long dwelt in the minds both of Margery and Ann, and were handed down to their grandchildren, were the Magister's Latin verses in their praise. It is but a few years since Master Peter Piehringer departed this life at a great age, and when Gotz's boys went through their schooling so fast and so well they owed it to his care and learning. But chiefly he devoted himself to Ann's daughters, Margery and Agnes, and indeed it is ever so that our heart goeth forth with a love like to that for our own sons or daughters to the offspring of the woman we have loved, even when she has never been our own.

Eppelein Gockel, my brother's faithful serving-man, was wed to Aunt Jacoba's tiring-woman. After his master's death I made him to be host in the tavern of "The Blue Sky," and whereas his wife was an active soul, and his tales of the strange adventures he had known among the Godless heathen brought much custom to his little tavern parlor, he throve to be a man of great girth and presence.

By the seventh year after our home-coming my hardest cares for the concerns of my trade were overpast, albeit I must even yet keep my eyes open and give brain and body no rest. Half my life I spent in journeying, and whereas I perceived that it was only by opening up other branches of trade that I might fulfil the many claims which ever beset me, I set myself to consider the matter; and inasmuch as that I had seen in the house of Akusch how gladly the women of Egypt would buy hazel-nuts from our country, I began to deal in this humble merchandise in large measure; and at this day I send more than ten thousand sequins' worth of such wares, every year, by ship to the Levant. Likewise I made the furs of North Germany and the toys of Nuremberg a part of my trade, which in my uncle's life-time had been only in spices and woven goods. And so, little by little, my profits grew to a goodly sum, and by God's favor our house enjoyed higher respect than it ever had had of old.

And it is a matter of rejoicing to me that at this time there is again an Im Hoff at its head with me, so that the old name shall be handed down; Ann's oldest daughter, Margery Schopper, having married one Berthold Im Hoff, who is now my worthy partner.

The sons of the elder Margery, the young Waldstromers, had much in them of the hasty Schopper temper, and a voice for song; and all three have done well, each in his way. Herdegen is now the Hereditary Ranger, and held in no less honor than Kunz Waldstromer, my beloved godson, who is a man of law in the service of our good town. Franz, who dedicated himself to the Church at an early age, under the protection of my lord Cardinal Bernhardi, has already been named to be the next in office after our present aged and weakly Bishop.

The son of Agnes, Herdegen's younger daughter, is Martin Behaim, a high-spirited youth in whom his grandfather's fiery and restless temper lives again, albeit somewhat quelled.

And if you now enquire of me how it is that I, albeit my heart beats warmly enough for our good town and its welfare and honor, have only taken a passing part in the duties of its worshipful Council, this is my answer: Inasmuch as to provide for the increase of riches for the Schopper family took all the strength I had, I lacked time to serve the commonwealth as my heart would have desired; and by the time when my dear nephew Berthold Im Hoff came to share the conduct of the trade with me I was right willing to withdraw behind my young partner, Ann's son-in-law, and to take his place in the business, while he and Kunz Waldstromer were chosen to high dignity on the Council. Nevertheless it is well-known that I have given up to the town a larger measure of time and labor and moneys than many a town-mayor and captain of watch. Of this I make mention to the end that those who come after me shall not charge me with evil self-seeking.

Likewise some may ask me wherefor I, the last male offspring of the old Schopper race, have gone through life unwed. Yet of a certainty they may spare me the answer to whom I have honestly confessed all my heart's pangs at the meeting of Herdegen with Ann.

After the death of her best-beloved lord the young widow was overcome with brooding melancholy from which nothing could rouse her. At that time you, my Margery and Agnes, her daughters, clung to me as to your own father; and when, at the end of three years, your mother was healed of that melancholy, it had come about that you had learned to call me father while I had sported with you and loved you in "your" mother's stead, and taught you to fold your little hands in prayer and led you out for air walking by your side. Your mother had heeded it not; but then, when she bloomed forth in new and wondrous beauty, and I beheld that Hans Koler and the Knight Sir Henning von Beust, who had likewise remained unwed, were again her suitors, the old love woke up in my heart; and one fair May evening, out in the forest, the question rose to my lips whether she could not grant me the right to call you indeed my children before all the world, and her....

But to what end touch the wound which to this day is scarce healed?

In this world and the next she would never be any man's but his to whom her heart's great and only love had been given. But from that evening forth I, the rejected suitor, must suffer that you children should no longer call me father, but Uncle Kunz; and when afterwards it came to be dear little uncle you may believe that I was thankful. She no less rejected the suit of Koler and of von Beust; but the last-named gentleman made up for his dismissal by marrying a noble damsel of Brandenburg. At a later time when he came to Nuremberg he was made welcome by Margery, and then, meeting with Ann once more, he showed himself to be still so youthful and duteous in his service to her, in despite of her grey hairs, that for certain it was well for his happiness at home that he should have come without his wife.

Not long after Ann's rejection I confessed to Margery what had befallen, and when she heard it, she cast her arms about my neck and cried: "Why, ne'er content, must you crave a new home and family? Are not two warm hearths yours to sit at, and the love and care of two faithful house-wives; and are you not the father and counsellor, not alone of your nephews and nieces, but of their parents likewise?" All this she said in an overflow of sisterly love; and if it comforted me, as I here make record of it, by reason that I sorely needed such good words, if I here recall how sad life often seemed to me.

Nay, nay! It was sweet, heavenly sweet, and worthy of all thanksgiving that I, who of the three Schopper links was so far the most humbly gifted, was suffered by Fate to be of some use to the other two, and even to their children and grandchildren, and to help in adding to their well-being. In this—insomuch I may say with pride—in this I have had all good-speed; thus my life's labor has not been in vain, and I may call my lot a happy one. And thus I likewise have proved the truth of old Adam Heyden's saying, that he who does most for other folks at the same time does the best for himself.